His mouth fou
this time the kis
brand cattle.

A fiery mix of passion and lust, making her forget she didn't kiss strangers like this, on an open dance floor with half the town watching. But Brooks didn't let up and she couldn't pull back or move away, it was that good.

She played with the curling ends of his hair.

He slid his hands lower on her back.

She tucked herself into him.

He groaned and kissed her harder.

The music ended and they hardly noticed. She stared into his blue eyes.

"What now?" he rasped. "You want another dance?"

She shook her head. "I need air."

He took her hand and led her off the dance floor and out the door of the C'mon Inn. They went around back to an iron and wood bench near a walled garden. "Would you like to sit?" he asked, and before she could answer, he took a seat and reached for her, giving her the option of where on the bench she wanted to plop down.

She chose his lap.

* * *

The Texan's One-Night Standoff
is part of the Dynasties: The Newports series—
Passion and chaos consume
a Chicago real estate empire!

THE TEXAN'S ONE-NIGHT STANDOFF

BY
CHARLENE SANDS

All rights reserved including the right of reproduction in whole or in part in any form. This edition is published by arrangement with Harlequin Books S.A.

This is a work of fiction. Names, characters, places, locations and incidents are purely fictional and bear no relationship to any real life individuals, living or dead, or to any actual places, business establishments, locations, events or incidents. Any resemblance is entirely coincidental.

This book is sold subject to the condition that it shall not, by way of trade or otherwise, be lent, resold, hired out or otherwise circulated without the prior consent of the publisher in any form of binding or cover other than that in which it is published and without a similar condition including this condition being imposed on the subsequent purchaser.

® and ™ are trademarks owned and used by the trademark owner and/or its licensee. Trademarks marked with ® are registered with the United Kingdom Patent Office and/or the Office for Harmonisation in the Internal Market and in other countries.

First Published in Great Britain 2016
By Mills & Boon, an imprint of HarperCollins*Publishers*
1 London Bridge Street, London, SE1 9GF

© 2016 Harlequin Books S.A.

Special thanks and acknowledgement are given to Charlene Sands for her contribution to the Dynasties: The Newports series.

ISBN: 978-0-263-91888-5

51-1216

Our policy is to use papers that are natural, renewable and recyclable products and made from wood grown in sustainable forests. The logging and manufacturing processes conform to the legal environmental regulations of the country of origin.

Printed and bound in Spain
by CPI, Barcelona

Charlene Sands is a *USA TODAY* bestselling author of more than forty romance novels. She writes sensual contemporary romances and stories of the Old West. When not writing, Charlene enjoys sunny Pacific beaches, great coffee, reading books from her favorite authors and spending time with her family. You can find her on Facebook and Twitter, write her at PO Box 4883, West Hills, CA 91308, USA, or sign up for her newsletter for fun blogs and ongoing contests at www.charlenesands.com.

To my very talented editor, Charles Griemsman,
who is also a wonderful person and someone
I call friend. Thanks, Charles, for all you do!

One

Brooks Newport swiveled around on the bar stool at the C'mon Inn, his gaze fastening on the raven-haired Latina beauty bending over a pool table, challenging her opponent with a fiercely competitive glint in her eyes. With blue jeans hugging her hips and a cropped red plaid blouse exposing her olive skin, the lady made his mouth go dry. He wasn't alone. Every Stetson-wearing Texan in the joint seemed to be watching her, too.

His hand fisting around the bottle, Brooks took a sip of beer, gulping down hard. The woman's moves around the pool table were as smooth and as polished as his new Justin boots.

"Five ball, corner pocket," she said, her voice sultry with a side of sass, as if she knew she wasn't going to miss. Then she took her shot. The cue ball met its mark and sure enough, the five ball rolled right into the pocket.

She straightened to full height, her chest expanding

to near button-popping proportions. She couldn't have been more than five-foot-two, but what she had in that small package was enough to make him break out in a sweat. And that was saying something, since he'd come to Texas for one reason, and one reason only.

To meet his biological father for the first time in his life.

He'd spent the better part of his adulthood trying to find the man who'd abandoned him and his twin brother, Graham in Chicago. Sutton Winchester, his bitter older rival and the man Brooks thought might be his biological father turned out not to be his blood kin after all. Thank God. But Sutton had known the truth of his parenthood all along, and the ailing man, plagued by a bout of conscience—or so Brooks figured—had finally given up the information that led to the name and location of his and Graham's father.

Brooks would have been speaking with his real father at Look Away Ranch in Cool Springs right now if he hadn't gotten a bad case of nerves. So much was riding on this. The trek to get to this place in time, to solving the mystery surrounding the birth of the Newport twins, as well as his younger brother Carson, would finally come to fruition.

So, yeah, the powerful CEO of the Newport Corporation from Chicago had turned chicken. Those bawking noises played out in his head. He'd never run scared before and yet, as he was breezing through this dusty town, the Welcome sign and Christmas lights outside the doors of the C'mon Inn had called to him. He'd pulled to a stop and entered the lodge, in need of a fortifying drink and a good night's rest. He had a lot to think about, and meeting Beau Preston in the light of day seemed a better idea.

He kept his gaze trained on the prettiest thing in the joint. The woman. She wielded the pool cue like a weapon and began wiggling her perfectly trim ass in an effort to make a clean shot. He sipped beer to cool his jets, yet he couldn't tear his gaze away. He had visions of bending over the pool table with her and bringing them both to heaven.

Long strands of her hair hung down to touch her breasts, and as she leaned over even further to line up her shot, those strands caressed green felt. She announced her next shot and *bam*, the ball banked off the left side and then ricocheted straight into the center pocket.

The whiskered man she was playing against hung his head. "Man, Ruby. You don't give a guy a chance."

She chuckled. "That's the rule I live by, Stan. You know that."

"But you could miss once in a while. Make it interesting."

So her name was Ruby. Brooks liked the sound of it, all right. It fit.

He had no business lusting after her. Woman trouble was the last thing he needed. Yet his brain wasn't doing a good job of convincing his groin to back off.

The game continued until she handed the older guy his vitals on a silver platter. "Sorry, Stan."

"You'd think after all these years a man could do better against a teeny tiny woman."

She grinned, showing off a smile that lit the place on fire, then set a sympathetic hand on the man's shoulder and reached up to kiss his cheek.

The old guy's face turned beet red. "You know that's the only reason I endure this torture. For that kiss at the end."

Her deep, provocative chuckle rumbled in Brooks's

ears. "You're sweet for saying that, Stan. Now, go on home to Betsy. And kiss your sweet grandson for me."

Nodding, Stan smiled at her. "Will do. You be good now, you hear?"

"I can always try," she said, hooking her cue stick on the wall next to a holly wreath.

Stan walked off, and Ruby did this little number with her head that landed all of her thick, silky hair on one shoulder. Brooks's groin tightened some more. If *she* was any indication of what Cool Springs was like, he was quickly gaining an affinity for the place.

The woman spotted him. Her deep-set eyes, the color of dark cocoa, met his for a second, and time seemed to stop. Blood rushed through his veins. She blinked a time or two and then let him go, as if she recognized him to be an out-of-towner.

He finished off his beer and rose, tossing some bills onto the bar and giving the barkeep a nod.

"Hey, sweet doll," a man called out, coming from the darkest depths of the bar to stand in front of her. "How about giving me a go-round?"

Ruby tilted her head up. "No thanks. I'm through for the night."

"You ain't through until you've seen me wield my stick. It's impressive." The big oaf wiggled his brows and crowded her against the pool table.

She rolled her eyes. "Pleeeze."

"Yeah, babe, that's exactly what you'll be crying out once we're done *playing*."

"Sorry, but if that's your best come-on line, you're in sad shape, buster."

She inched her body away, brushing by him, trying not to make contact with the bruiser. But the jerk grabbed her arm from behind and gave a sharp tug. She struggled to wiggle free. "Let go," she said.

Brooks scanned the room. All eyes were still on Ruby, but no one was making a move. Instead they all had smug looks on their faces. Forget what he'd thought about this town; they were all jerks.

The muscles in his arms bunched and his hands tightened into fists as Brooks stepped toward the two of them. He couldn't stand by and watch this scene play out, not when the petite pool shark was in trouble. "Get your hands—"

The words weren't out of his mouth before Ruby elbowed the guy in the gut. "Oof." He doubled over, clutching his stomach, and cursed her up and down using filthy names.

Crap. Now she was in deep. The guy's head came up; the unabashed fury in his eyes was aimed her way. Brooks immediately pulled his arm back, fists at the ready, but before he could land a punch, Ruby grabbed the guy's forearm. The twist of her body came so fast, Brooks blinked, and before he knew it, she'd tossed the big oaf over her shoulder WWF-style and had him down for the count. As in, she'd laid him out flat on his back.

Someone from the bar groused, "No one messes with Ruby unless she wants to be messed with."

Apparently the oaf hadn't known that. And neither had Brooks. But hell, the rest of them had known.

She stepped over the man to face Brooks, her gaze on the right hook he'd been ready to land. "Thanks anyway," she said, out of breath. Apparently she wasn't Supergirl. The effort had taxed her, and he found himself enjoying how the ebb and flow of her labored breaths stretched the material of her blouse.

He stood there somewhat in awe, a grin spreading his mouth wide. "You didn't let me do my gladiator routine."

"Sorry. Maybe next time." Her lips quirked up.

Behind her, the bartender and another man began dragging the patron away.

"Does that happen often?" he asked her.

"Often enough," she said. "But not with guys who know me."

He rubbed at his chin. "No. I wouldn't imagine."

He kept his gaze trained on her, astonished at what he'd just witnessed. Her eyes danced in amusement, probably at his befuddled expression. And then some-one turned up the volume on the country song playing, and his thoughts ran wild. He was too intrigued to let the night end. This woman wasn't your typical Texas beauty queen. She had spunk and grit and so much more. Hell, he hadn't been this turned on in a long, long time.

A country Christmas ballad piped in through the speakers surrounding the room. "Would you like to dance?" he asked.

She smiled sweetly, the kind of smile that suggested softness. And he would've believed that if he hadn't seen her just deck a man. A big man.

Her head tilted to the left, and she gauged him thought-fully.

He was still standing, so that was a plus. She didn't find him out of line.

"Sure. I'd like that, Galahad."

"It's Brooks."

"Ruby."

She led him to the dance floor and he took over from there, placing his hand on the small of her back, enfold-ing her other hand in his. Small and delicate to big and rough. But it worked. *And how*, did it work.

He began to move, holding her at arm's length, breathing her in as they glided across the dance floor.

"I thought you were in trouble back there," he said.

"I gathered."

"Are you a black belt or something?"

"Nope, just grew up around men and learned early on how to take care of myself. What about you? Do you have a knight in shining armor complex or something?"

He laughed. "Where I come from, a man doesn't stand by and watch someone abuse a lady."

"Oh, I see."

"Apparently I was the only other guy in the place who didn't know you could handle yourself."

She was looking at him now, piercing him with those cocoa eyes and giving him that megawatt smile. "It was sorta sweet, you coming to my rescue." Was she flirting? *Man, oh man.* If she was, he wasn't going to stop her.

"I was watching you, like every other guy at the bar."

"I like to play pool. I'm good at it," she said, shrugging a shoulder. "It's a great way to blow off steam."

"That's exactly why I stopped into the bar myself. I needed to do the same."

"You get brownie points for not saying the obvious."

"Which is?"

Her lips twitched and she hesitated for a second, as if trying to decide whether to tell him or not. "That you know a better way to blow off steam."

Her raven brows rose, and he stopped dancing for a second to study her. "You must drive men wild with your mouth."

She shook her head, grinning. "You're sinking, Brooks. Going under fast."

"I was talking about your sass."

She knew. She was messing with him. "Most men hate it."

"Not me. It's refreshing."

He brought her closer, so that the tips of her breasts grazed his shirt and the scent of her hair tickled his nostrils. She didn't flip him over her shoulder with that move. She cuddled up closer. "So far, I have two brownie points," he said. "What can I do to earn another?"

Her gaze drifted to his mouth with pinpoint accuracy. Air left his chest. A deep hunger, like none he'd experienced before, gnawed into his belly.

"You'll think of something, Galahad."

The stranger's lips touched hers, a brief exploration that warmed up her insides and made her question everything she'd done since setting eyes on this guy. Usually she wasn't this brazen with men. She didn't flirt and plant ideas in their heads. But there was something about Brooks that called to her. He had manners. And he knew how to speak to a woman. He seemed familiar and safe in a way, even though they'd never met before. He wasn't hard on the eyes either, with all that blond hair, thick and wavy and catching the collar of his zillion-dollar shirt. He was as citified as they came, even if he wore slick boots and sported five-o'clock stubble. As soon as she'd spotted him at the bar, she knew he didn't belong. Not here, in a dusty small town out in the middle of nowhere. Cool Springs wasn't exactly a mecca of high society, and this guy was that and then some. His coming to her rescue, all granite muscles and fists ready to pummel, was about the nicest thing a man had done for her in a long while.

Trace came to mind, and she immediately washed his image from her head. She wasn't going to think about her breakup with him. He was six months long gone, and she'd wasted enough time on him.

Instead she wrapped her arms around Brooks's neck and clung to him, her body sizzling from the heat surrounding them. He began to move again, slower, closer, his scent something expensive and tasteful. Her nerves were raw. Something was happening to her. Something unexpected and thrilling. Her life was too predictable lately, and it was time to change that.

His mouth found hers again, and this time the kiss was hot enough to brand cattle. A fiery mix of passion and lust, making her forget she didn't kiss strangers like this, on an open dance floor with half the town watching. But Brooks didn't let up, and she couldn't pull back or move away. It was that good.

She played with the curling ends of his hair.

He slid his hands lower on her back.

She tucked herself into him.

He groaned and kissed her harder.

The music ended and she hardly noticed.

She stared into his blue eyes.

He gave her a smile.

Her body was shaking.

He was trembling, too.

"What now?" he rasped. "You want another dance?"

She shook her head. "I need air."

He took her hand and led her off the dance floor and out the door of the C'mon Inn. Clouds shadowed half the full moon, and the bite of December air should've cooled her down. But Brooks kept her close to his side, his body shielding her from the cold. Any shivering she was doing was caused by the man beside her and not the dropping winter temperature. He led her around back, where a bench made of iron and wood sat unoccupied near a walled garden. "Would you like to sit?" he asked, and before she could answer, he took a seat and reached for her, giving her the option of where on the bench she wanted to plop down. She chose his lap.

His satisfied smile was her reward, and she wrapped her arms around his neck. "You're beautiful, Ruby. You probably hear that all the time." His hand grazed her neck as he held her hair back to nibble on her throat. Then his tongue moistened her skin as he laid out a row of sensual kisses there. Her insides went a little squishy from his tender assault. Whatever this was, it was happening fast. His rock-hard erection pressing against her legs told her he was as turned on as she was.

"Not really. I tend to scare men off." By her own choosing, she warded off men's advances before giving them half a chance. She'd been waiting around for Trace, hoping he'd come back to her, but that hadn't happened. And now she found pleasure in this man's arms. She didn't know a thing about him, other than her instincts said he was a decent man.

"Little ole you," he whispered softly before claiming her lips again. The taste of alcohol combined with his confidence was a sweet elixir to her recent loneliness. His mouth pressed hers harder, and the tingles under her skin bumped up another notch. "You didn't scare me off."

"Maybe that's why I'm here with you."

"I like the sound of that." The rasp in his voice intensified.

They stopped talking long enough to work up a sweat. Sharp and quick tingles ran up and down her body, and her breaths came in short bursts. She was aware of him at every turn. His well-placed touches made her tremble. His kisses swamped her in heat. Brooks wasn't far behind. His passion swept her up, and the proof of his desire strained the material of his dark pants. She arched her body in a curving bow, craving more, wanting his hands on her everywhere. Under her cropped shirt, her nipples tightened, and an ache throbbed below her waist.

Finally Brooks touched her breasts, and the beauty of the sensation purred from her lips. "Oh, yes."

Low guttural sounds surfaced from his chest, groans of pleasure and want as his hands moved over her body, palms wide, so he could grasp every inch of her. He flattened her erect nipples, followed the curve of her torso and dipped down lower to her hips. He ran his hands along her legs, up and down her thighs, and from under her jeans she felt the burn on her skin.

Laughter coming from patrons leaving the inn rang in her ears.

Brooks stopped and listened.

The sounds became softer and eventually ceased. Thank goodness those people weren't coming back here.

"Ruby, honey. I'm not one for public groping." He hesitated a second. "I have a room."

She bit down on her lower lip, his taste lingering on her mouth. It helped her make the decision. She wasn't ready for this to end. "Take me there."

Ruby drove him wild and crazy with want. Yeah, he'd been without a woman for several months, but this woman was more than he'd ever dreamed of. This woman, he couldn't have even imagined. She was the hottest female he'd met in his life, and she was exactly what he needed to…ah, hell, *blow off steam*. Her flipping that oaf on his back had been just the beginning. From then on, every word that came out of her mouth, every tempting gesture and coy smile, had been perfect. Brooks had it bad for her. Suggesting taking her to his room had been brash. Insane, really, since he'd known her less than an hour.

No one messes with Ruby unless she wants to be messed with.

Apparently he'd made the grade. 'Cause he was messing with her, and had her full approval.

He scooped her up from the bench, and she automatically wound her arms around his neck as he climbed the outside staircase that led to his room. She was petite and lightweight, and it wasn't a struggle to carry her up the stairs in his arms. Darkness concealed them for most of the way. Once he slid the key card into the lock and shoved the door open with a hip, he moved inside and set her on her feet. She still clung to him.

Lord have mercy.

They were finally alone. Brooks's deep sense of decorum kicked in big time. He knew what he was dealing with. She wasn't some floozy who staked men out in a bar. She wasn't an easy piece who'd consider him another conquest. He could tell that from the warm glow in her eyes now, from the way all the men at the bar respected her, from the way she'd chosen *him* and not the other way around. For all those reasons, he wasn't going to take advantage of the situation.

He brushed a kiss to her lips. "Welcome."

As antiquated as the inn was, at least the place was clean. There was no flat-screen television on the wall, no wet bar or cushy king-size bed for added luxury. Nor was there a spacious wardrobe closet or a sunken bathtub or any of the things Brooks was accustomed to. Ruby strolled over to peer out the back window. From where he stood, the view was hardly noteworthy or attractive: just a vast amount of unincorporated land. The lack of illumination was actually a plus since there was nothing to see out there. "I've never been inside one of these rooms," she said.

"I figured."

She whirled around. "You think you've got my number, Galahad?"

"Maybe. I know you don't do this."

Her bright laughter ended with an unfeminine snort. "You'd like to believe that, right?"

"I do believe it. So, why me?"

She glanced out the window again, gazing into the darkness. "Maybe I like you. Maybe it's because you came to my rescue—"

"Which you didn't need."

She continued, "You came to my rescue with no thought of the danger to your own hide."

He took a step toward her. "Are you saying I couldn't take that guy?"

"Hold on to your ego. I'm only saying that you're the one I want to be with tonight. Can't we leave it at that?"

He nodded and inclined his head toward the door. "We were about to combust out there. That's never happened to me before."

"So, you're saying you don't like losing control and decided to slow down the pace?"

"What I'm saying is, you deserve better than that."

She smiled, and the natural sway of her body as she walked toward him fueled his juices. "There, you see? Things like that are exactly what a girl wants to hear. So, what did you have in mind?"

Her scent filled him up, and the shimmering sheet of dark, straight hair falling off her shoulders gave him pause—was he crazy to slow things down?

Her eyes were on him, warm and soft and patient.

"A drink, for starters?"

Another survey of the room had her gaze landing on the amber bottle of whiskey he'd brought from Chicago sitting on the bedside table. "Okay."

He grabbed two tumblers and poured the whiskey. The very best stuff. He'd figured he would need some fortification before meeting his biological father, but he'd never thought he would entertain a lady with it.

Standing before her, he offered her a glass. "Here you go."

She eyed the golden liquid. "Thanks. What should we drink to?"

"To unexpected meetings?"

She smiled. "I'm glad you didn't say 'to new beginnings.'"

He wouldn't. He wasn't in the market for a lover or a girlfriend. And apparently, Miss Ruby—he didn't know her last name—wasn't looking for a relationship, either. She'd dropped enough hints about that tonight. Somebody must've hurt her along the way, but Brooks couldn't delve too deeply into her past. He wouldn't want anyone prying into his, and tonight was all about the present, not the past or the future.

He touched his glass to hers, and a definitive clink sounded in the room. "To unexpected *pleasant* meetings."

She gave him a brief nod and then took a sip, taking time to relish the taste before swallowing. "This is pretty amazing stuff. It surely didn't come out of any minibar."

He was surprised she would notice the quality. "Are you a whiskey expert?"

"Let's just say I know good whiskey when I taste it."

She took a seat on the bed and continued to sip. He sat beside her, enjoying her quiet company. His heart was still racing, but he was glad he'd toned things down some. She wasn't a woman to be rushed. And he wanted to savor her tonight, in the same way she was savoring her whiskey.

"Tell me," she said, "aren't you afraid that I'll come to my senses and walk out on you?"

"I don't think you're a flight risk, Ruby. So, no. But if you think better of this, I would respect your decision. When I make love to you, I want you to be sure and all in."

She smiled, and her eyes drifted down to the amber liquid in her glass. "You don't mince words."

"You don't, either."

She nodded, and her soft gaze met his stare. He reached out to touch her face with a sole finger to her cheek. She gasped, and a warm light flickered in her eyes.

"What do you want, Ruby?"

"Just a night," she whispered, breathy and guileless. "With you."

He sensed she needed it as much as he did. To have one night with her before his life would change forever.

Taking the glass from her and setting both of their drinks down on the nightstand, he cupped her face with his hands and gazed into her eyes. "One night, then."

"Yes," she said. "One night."

And then he pulled her up to a standing position so they were toe-to-toe, her face lifting to his. He peered into warm, dark eyes giving him approval and then slowly lowered his head, his mouth laying claim to hers.

Their night together was just beginning.

Two

Brooks's touch was like a jolt of electricity running the course of her body. One touch, one simple finger to her cheek, one slight meshing of his whiskey-flavored lips with hers, was giving her amnesia about the other men in her life. Men who'd trampled on her heart. Men like Trace, who'd taken from her and hadn't given back. Trace, the man she'd waited for all these months. She squeezed that notion from her mind.

Her time to wait was over.

Brooks's giving and patient mouth didn't demand. Instead, he encouraged her to partake and enjoy. She liked that about this man. He wasn't a player of women. No, her gladiator and presumptive keeper of her virtue was a man of honor. He didn't take. He gave. And that's exactly why she'd decided to come to his room tonight.

She placed her trust in him.

He wasn't asking her to bare her soul. But she would bare her body. For him.

Her fingers nimbly played with the tiny white buttons on her blouse until the material slipped from her shoulders, trapping her arms. Cool night air grazed her exposed skin.

Brooks's sharp intake of breath reached her ears. "You're unbelievably beautiful."

He worked the sleeves of her blouse down her arms until they gathered at her wrists. He held her there, mercilessly tugging her closer until her bra brushed his torso. "Yeah, I like you in red." He stroked her hair and then snapped the silky strap of her bra.

"It's my color," she whispered, and he smiled.

"I won't disagree."

He nipped at her lips then, several times, until his mouth claimed hers again. The kiss swept her into another world, where the only thing that mattered, all that she felt, was the pleasure he was giving. His tongue plunged in and met hers in a sparring match that ignited a fiery inferno within her. Whimpering, she ached for his touch. Finally his fingers dipped inside her bra to caress her nipples. Everything unfolded from there—the pleasure too great, the sighs too loud, the hunger too strong.

He worked magic with his mouth while his hands found the fastener of her bra. Within seconds, and none too soon, she was free of her blouse and restraints. Her breasts spilled out into his awaiting hands, and the small ache at her core began to pulse as he touched, fondled and caressed her. She was pinned to the spot, unwilling to move, unwilling to take a step, his invisible hold on her body too strong. Her nipples stood erect and tightened to pebble hardness. Aching for more, she leaned way back and was granted the very tip of his tongue dampening her with moisture.

"Oh, so good, Brooks."

His outstretched palms bracing the small of her back, he answered only with a low guttural groan.

And once he was through ravaging her, he brought her up to eye level, drinking her in from top to bottom. Shaking his head, he fixed his gaze on the full measure of her breasts. She had a large bust for a petite woman and this time she didn't mind having a man's eyes transfixed on her. "I can't believe you," he muttered. "You're not real."

The compliment went straight to her head.

Brooks was a city dude, a man who didn't fit in her world, yet here she was, nearly naked with him and enjoying every sensual second of it.

"I'm very real," she breathed, closing the gap between them and lacing her arms around his neck. His erection stood like a stout monument, and there was no missing it. "And I want more."

"Whatever the lady wants," he said, running his hands up and down the sides of her body, his fingertips grazing the sides of her breasts. Another round of heat pinged her as anticipation grew.

He turned her around, came up behind her and slowly grazed the waistband of her jeans with his hands. His powerful arms locked her in, and his mouth was doing a number on her throat while his long fingers nudged her sweet spot. She murmured her approval, and lights flashed before her eyes. He stroked between her thighs, and a cry ripped from her throat. And then he was pulling the zipper of her jeans down, slowly, torturously, his erection behind her, a thrilling reminder of what was to come.

"Kick off your boots," he whispered in her ear.

Goose bumps erupted on her arms.

Her legs were a mass of jelly.

She kicked her boots off obediently, and then his index

fingers were inside her waistband, gently lowering the jeans down her legs. She stepped out of them easily. "Red lace panties," he murmured appreciatively. He cupped one cheek, fitting her left buttock in his palm. He stroked her, smoothing his hand up and over, up and over. "Oh, man," he muttered, the heat of his body bathing her.

From where she stood with her back against his chest, she felt his body shudder. Quickly she turned around. The room was dimly lit with a sole lamp, and they were cast in shadow, but there was enough light to see a deep, burning hunger in his eyes.

"Lie down on the bed," he told her.

Her heart was pounding like a drum, beating hard, beating fast. He was a man who took control. She wasn't one to obey so easily, but there was a look in his eyes telling her to trust him. She did as she was told and lay on the queen bed, naked but for the panties she wore.

His gaze roamed over her body, slowly, the gleam in his eyes filled with promise.

"Galahad?"

"Hmm?"

"Having second thoughts?"

He laughed at her, giving his head a shake. "Are you kidding me? You have no idea…"

"What?"

"…how turned on I am. I'm trying to keep from jumping your bones, Ruby."

She glanced at the flagpole erection bulging in his pants. "What if I want you to jump my bones? Isn't that why we're here?"

He squeezed his eyes shut. "Yeah, but… I want this night to last."

She rolled to the side and leaned on her elbow. His eyes sought the spill of her hair touching her breasts.

"Come to bed, Brooks. I'm a big girl. I can take whatever you have in mind."

"Doubtful, honey. What I'm thinking…"

She grabbed his hand and tugged. He landed on his butt in an upright position on the bed. "Do it, Brooks. But first take off your clothes."

He grinned. "How did I get so lucky?"

"Judging by the cut of your cloth, you were probably born lucky." She was guessing.

He grunted. And that was all the reply he gave her.

Sitting up on her knees, she helped him lift his shirt over his head and pull off his boots between kisses. Her hands sought his chest, all powerful and rippled with muscle, smooth and hard, like the planes of a solid board. She reveled in touching him, her fingertips toying with his flattened nipples.

That move landed her on her back, her arms locked by one strong hand above her head. "Two can tease," he said.

And then he was pulling her panties down and touching her where she'd prayed he'd touch. Her body instantly responded, and soft moans rose from her throat. She undulated with each stroke of his hand, each caress of a fingertip. He kept her pinned down, covering her with his body, the soft flesh of his palm applying pressure at the apex of her thighs.

"I'm… I'm going to lose it," she moaned, the pleasure unbearable.

"Don't fight it, honey," he rasped.

And then she shattered, and spasms wracked her lower body in beautiful jolts that electrified her body. Her hips were arched, and she didn't remember how they got that way. Slowly she lowered herself and finally opened her eyes to swim in Brooks's deep blue gaze. He watched her carefully, a satisfied smile on his lips as he unzipped his pants and removed them.

"Your turn," she said.

He shook his head. "Our turn."

And then he fitted a condom on his erection and moved back over her.

His hands molded her breasts. His kiss went deep, his tongue delicious and probing. "Tell me when you're ready, sweetheart," he murmured before kissing her again.

She ran her hands through his longish blond hair, her fingers curling around the locks at the back of his neck. Then her gaze drifted to his eyes. "I don't think I'll ever be more ready."

He made a caveman sound, raw and brash, and then braced her in a protective way to roll them over on the bed. She found herself on top of him. "Set the pace, Ruby. I don't want to hurt you."

She bit the corner of her lip. Sure, she was petite, but Galahad worried that he was too big for her small frame. She could actually fall for a guy like this. She gave him a nod and straddled his thighs. "You won't hurt me," she said, fitting herself over his shaft, tossing her head back and shuddering from the feel of him inside her.

Then she began to move.

Spooned against Brooks's large frame, with his arm resting possessively around her torso, Ruby slowly opened her eyes. It was past midnight and she'd promised Brooks she'd stay the night with him. She didn't doubt her decision but instead smiled as he snuggled her closer and brought his hand to rest just under her breast.

"Are you awake?" he whispered, his breath warm on her neck.

"Just," she answered. "I dozed."

"Me, too. I haven't been this relaxed in a long time."

"Had a lot on your mind lately?" she murmured.

"You have no idea. But I don't want to talk about that right now."

His hand made lazy circles around her breast, his fingers feathery light over her nipple. Her body heated instantly. He had the ability to make her yearn, and the longing was potent. His leg moved over both of hers, and she was locked to him now, the soft flesh of her thighs meeting with legs of steel.

"I don't want to talk at all," he said, fisting her hair and planting kisses at the back of her neck. "Do you?"

"No." Oh God, what he was doing to her? Her body flamed. She was going up in smoke. "Talking is overrated. Not when we could be doing better things."

Ruby had never given herself so freely before. She'd never really been the *bad* girl, and everyone who knew her well knew that for a fact. She'd had only three relationships in her twenty-six years, and only the last one had really meant anything to her. The *last* one had hurt her.

She'd been in love.

Or so she'd thought.

But tonight with Brooks was different. It was all about having a man appreciate her. Give to her. Excite her and make her feel like a woman.

He rolled over on top of her, careful of her small frame, his hands bracing the bed on both sides of her head. She gazed into his deep blue eyes. "I want you again, Ruby."

Ruby smiled. "I want you, too."

He nodded and let go of a deep breath. "I was praying you'd say that, honey."

He bent his head and touched his mouth to hers. Already the taste of him, the firmness of his lips, seemed familiar and welcome. She'd never see him again. She wasn't in the market for a man. But Brooks would leave her with a good memory.

And then his mouth moved from her lips down her chest toward her navel, streaming kisses along the way. Her hips lifted; she was eager and willing, waiting. She didn't have to wait long. He touched his tongue to her center and suckled her sweetest spot. She whimpered and moved wildly as his mouth performed magic. It was a torturous, beautiful few minutes of pleasure. And when she was on the brink, ready for a powerful release, he rose over her and joined their bodies. Oh…it was bliss, the best of the best as he moved inside her. And then, moments later, his eyes darkened, his body stiffened and every sensation between them intensified. He moaned her name, an utterance of pleasured pain, and then he broke apart at the seams. It was enough to turn her inside out, and she, too, shuddered with an incredible release.

"Wow," she said once her breathing returned to normal.

"Yeah, wow," he said, keeping her close. He kissed her forehead, stroked her hair and tucked her body into his.

She closed her eyes and waited for the exquisite hum of her body to ease her into sleep.

Brooks tiptoed back into the room, holding two cups of coffee and a white paper bag filled with muffins and buttered biscuits from the café at the inn. There wasn't a croissant to be had in this hokey Texas town, and he liked that about this place. Clean, simple and… He glanced at Ruby asleep in the bed, her hair smooth black granite against the pillow. Beautiful. Yep, Cool Springs left him with a good impression.

The mattress groaned as he sat down.

"Is that coffee I smell?" a soft, sultry voice whispered from the other end of the bed.

"Can't fool you," he said, turning to find Ruby coming to a sitting position. "Leaded and dark as mud." Apparently that's how they made coffee in Texas. He showed her the two cups.

"I think I love you," she said, reaching for one. She'd worn one of his shirts to bed. The thing hung down to her knees and covered most of her up, but she still looked sexy as sin.

Her lips pursed as she blew on the rising steam.

He shook his head and talked down his lust. "Got biscuits, too, all buttered up, with honey."

"I adore you even more," she said. He handed her one and she wasted no time. She took a big bite, chewed with gusto and then took another bite.

"You've got an appetite."

"I had a busy day and *night*."

He joined in, sipping coffee and digging into the biscuits. "Maybe I should've taken you out for a nice big breakfast."

She shook her head. "This is perfect," she said, reaching for the bag from his hand. "What kind of muffins did you get?"

"Banana and blueberry. So, you wouldn't want to go out for breakfast with me?"

She chose blueberry. "It's nothing personal, but showing up somewhere public at this hour will cause talk. You know what they say about small towns. All of it is true. And you don't owe me anything, but I appreciate your gallantry."

"Just call me Galahad."

"I do." She laughed before putting her teeth into the muffin.

He laughed, too, and was sorry he had to leave Ruby behind. She wasn't like most females he'd met, and he had a feeling she wasn't going to put up a fuss about saying goodbye.

He wasn't entirely sure he liked that idea, but he had a new life waiting for him. His emotions were keyed up, and he was too damn confused to add a woman to the mix.

They drank coffee and chatted quietly about nothing in particular. And after they'd taken their last sips, Brooks rose from the bed and began packing his belongings. "Sorry, but I have to hit the road soon. I have an important meeting."

Ruby rose from the bed and padded over to him. "Brooks," she said.

"Hmm?"

She stood before him, her expression unreadable. "Don't forget your shirt."

Slowly she began undoing the buttons, her nimble fingers working one after another. Once done, she shrugged out of the shirt, and it fell easily to her feet. His gaze fastened on a beautiful body in red lace. "Ruby," he said, sucking in oxygen and pulling her into his arms, her skin smooth and her muscles toned under his fingertips. "I wish I could postpone my meeting."

"No problem." Her eyes were soft and warm. He was never going to forget that particular deep cocoa color. Who was he kidding? He was never going to forget *her*. That was for damn sure. "I've got a busy day myself. I'll take a shower. You'll probably be gone by the time I get out."

Like a fool, he nodded. That was the plan. He had to leave. Now.

He claimed her lips one last time, putting all of himself

into that kiss. Then, mustering every ounce of his will-power, he turned away from her. But a thought struck, and he reached into his pocket to pull out a business card. "In case," he said with a lift of his shoulder, "I don't know, if you want to talk. Or need me or something." He set the card on the bedside table.

By the time he turned back around, she had disappeared into the bathroom.

"Goodbye, Brooks," she said just as the door was closing.

The lock clicked.

He closed his eyes. It was time to get on with the rest of his life.

Three

Brooks pulled into the gates of Look Away Ranch, his gaze drawn to the size and scope of Beau Preston's horse farm. The animals grazing freely in white-fenced meadowlands had a majestic presence. They were tall, their coats gleaming in browns and blacks and golds. Brooks didn't know much about horses, but even an amateur could tell by looking at them that these stallions, mares and geldings were top-notch.

He smiled at the notion that the apple didn't fall far from the tree. If what he'd been told by Roman Slater, the PI he'd hired to find his biological father, was true, then Brooks's drive to succeed above all else must've been in his blood. Because Look Away Ranch had all the makings of hard-earned success, much like his very own Newport Corporation.

He, Graham and Carson had worked their asses off for years in order to create one of the leading real estate and land development companies in the country. He was proud of what they'd accomplished, coming up the real estate ranks in Chicago and becoming genuine competitors of Sutton Winchester's Elite Industries. Winchester was their biggest rival both professionally and privately. And Brooks had done his very best to take the ruthless older man down, more for personal reasons than professional.

For a time, Brooks had believed that the now ailing Sutton fathered him and his twin brother Graham. The knowledge only fueled his desire to destroy the man he believed abandoned his mother in her time of need, when she was pregnant. It turned out none of that was true. But paternity tests had revealed that his baby brother, Carson, was indeed Sutton Winchester's biological child. Sutton and his late mother, Cynthia, had history together. She'd been his secretary once, and they'd had a love affair.

He hoped his true father, Beau, would fill in the rest of the blanks. After years of wondering and months now of tracking the man down, Brooks was ready to meet the man who'd fathered him.

He pulled up into the portico-covered drive that circled the stately ranch house and killed the engine. A man was waiting on the steps. Brooks's first glimpse was of a tall rancher, his hair once blond and now dusted with silver, dressed in crisp jeans and a snap-down Western shirt. He immediately approached, marching down the steps, his gait extremely similar to his twin brother's and probably Brooks's as well. Warmth swamped his chest.

He was out of the car quickly, walking toward the man whose blood flowed through his veins. They came face-to-face, and Brooks took in the blue eyes, the firm jaw and the hint of a wicked smile bracing the man's mouth. "Beau?"

Tears welled in the man's eyes. His lips quivered and he nodded. "Yes, son. I'm Beau Preston. I'm your father."

His father's legs wobbled, and Brooks grabbed his shoulders to steady him. As emotion rocked him, Brooks's own legs went numb, too. Then his father broke down, sobbing quietly and taking Brooks into his big, sturdy arms as he would a little boy. "Welcome, son. Welcome. I've been searching for you for a long time."

A few seconds later, Beau backed away, wiping at his tears. "I'm sorry. I'm just so happy, boy. Come inside. We have a lot to talk about."

"Yes, I'd like that," Brooks said.

They walked shoulder to shoulder into the house.

"Forgive me for not showing you around just yet," Beau said.

"I understand. We have a lot of catching up to do."

But Brooks noticed things about the rooms he walked through, the sturdy, steady surroundings, dark wood floors polished to a mirror shine, bulky wood beams above and wide-paned windows letting the outside in. The wood tones were brightened by the red blooms of poinsettia plants placed in several of the rooms, and his nostrils filled with the holiday scent of pine.

His father led him into the great room, which contained a giant flat-screen television, a corner wet bar, and tan and black leather couches. He got the feeling this was his father's comfort zone, the room he relaxed in after a long, grueling day. "Have a seat," the older man said. "Can I offer you coffee or iced tea? Orange juice?"

Brooks had had morning coffee with Ruby. A slice of regret barreled through him that he'd never see her again. He sat down on a tan sofa. "No thanks. I'm fine."

"You found the place okay?" His father took a seat facing him, his gaze latching onto Brooks and gleaming as bright as morning sunshine. All of Brooks's apprehension over this meeting vanished. Beau was as glad they'd found each other as he was.

"Yep, didn't have any trouble finding Look Away Ranch. It's pretty amazing, I have to say."

"What's amazing is that you're finally here. And look at you, boy. You're the spitting image of me when I was your age."

"There are two of us, you know. But Graham wanted to lay back and let me make the first contact with you. We didn't want to overwhelm you and, well…we have questions. He thought it'd be easier for you and me to speak privately before he joins us, since I was the one hell-bent on finding you."

His father rubbed at the back of his neck, a pained look entering his eyes. "I have to explain. I didn't know about you boys in the beginning. I didn't know your mama, Mary Jo, was carrying my babies when she ran away from Cool Springs. And once I started receiving anonymous notes and photos, I wasn't sure any of it was true, but as the photos kept coming, I saw the resemblance. It was unmistakable, and I moved heaven and earth to find Mary Jo. To find you boys."

"It's weird to hear you call my mother Mary Jo. As far as we knew, Mom's name was Cynthia Newport."

He shrugged a shoulder and got a faraway look in his eyes. "Mary Jo and I were desperately in love. She must've been scared out of her mind to run from me the way she did. That son of a bitch father of hers…" He paused to gauge Brooks's reaction. "Sorry, I forget he's your grandfather. But he was mean to the bone. Mary Jo was convinced if he found out she was seeing me, he'd kill both of us. I tried like the dickens to calm her down and tell her I'd protect her, but she must've panicked when she found out she was pregnant. God, I keep thinking how desperate she must've been back then. Alone in the world and carrying twins, no less. She wouldn't have run off if she wasn't terribly frightened of the consequences. That's all I can figure. She must've thought her daddy would beat the stuffing out of her, and harm her babies, if he ever found out the truth.

"I didn't know she'd changed her name and started a new life. I surely didn't know she was with child. But I want you to know, to be clear, I searched high and low for her in those early days. Trouble was, I was searching for Mary Jo Turner, not this…this Cynthia Newport person."

"I understand. I don't fault you for any of this. I've, uh, well, I'm just now coming to terms with all of this myself. I must admit, I was a bit obsessed with finding you."

"I'm glad you never let up, son."

Brooks gave him a nod. "Mom, she was a survivor. She did whatever it took to keep me and my brothers safe and cared for. She hid so many things from us during our lives. But Graham and I and our younger brother, Carson, who has a different father, don't blame her for any of it. We had a good life, living on the outskirts of Chicago with our Grandma Gerty. That woman befriended Mom when she was at a low point, and she took all of us in. She let us live with her in a modest home in a nice neighborhood, and she helped get us through school. We were a family in all respects. My brothers and I always looked upon her and loved her as if she was our real grandmother. I have a sneaking suspicion she was the one sending those updates and photos to you."

"Sounds like a wonderful woman." Beau sighed as he leaned farther back in his seat. "If she was the one, then I owe her a great debt. I'd long believed that your mother was gone to me forever, but just knowing you boys were out there somewhere gave me hope. I wish like hell Gerty would've just told me where to find you, but your mama probably held her to a promise to keep the secret."

"Grandma Gerty died about ten years ago."

"That's about when the updates stopped coming. It makes sense," his father said, "as much as any of this makes sense." He laughed with no real amusement.

"Grandma Gerty had a keen sense of duty. She must've believed in her heart she was doing the right thing. She only wanted what was best for my mom."

"I'm sorry Mary Jo isn't with us anymore. We were so young when we were in love, and…well, I have fond memories of her. Such a tragedy, the way she died."

"The aneurism took us all by shock. Mom was pretty healthy all of her life, and to lose her that way, after all she'd been through…well, it wasn't fair." Brooks took a second to breathe in and out slowly. After composing himself he added, "I miss her like crazy."

"I bet you do. The Mary Jo I remember was worthy of your love. I have no doubt she was a wonderful mother."

"Do you know what ever happened to my grandfather?"

"Still kicking. The mean ones don't die young. He's in a nursing home for dementia patients and being cared for by the state of Texas. I'm sorry, son. I know he's your relation, but if you knew how he treated your mama, you wouldn't give him a second of thought."

Brooks closed his eyes. This part was hardest to hear. His mother had never mentioned her abuse to him or any of her children. She'd shielded them all from hurt and negativity and made their lives as pleasant and as full of love as she possibly could. She'd come to Chicago hell-bent on changing her circumstances, but those memories of her broken youth must've haunted her. To think of her as that young girl who'd been treated so poorly by the one person who should've been loving and protecting her burned Brooks like a hot brand. "I suppose I should visit him."

"You can see him, son. But I'm told he's lost his mind. Doesn't recognize anyone anymore."

Brooks nodded. Another piece of his family lost to him. But perhaps in this case it was for the best that his grandfather wouldn't know him. "I'll deal with him in my own way at some point."

"I'm glad you agreed to stay on at the ranch awhile. You're welcome at the house. It's big enough and always open to you. But when we spoke on the phone, you seemed to like the idea of staying at the cabin right on our property and…well, I think it's a good choice. You can take things at your own pace without getting overwhelmed." His father grinned and gave his head a prideful tilt. "Course, here I am talking about you getting overwhelmed when you're the owner of a big corporation and all."

Brooks grinned. That apple not falling far from the tree again. "And here you are with this very prosperous horse farm in Texas. You have a great reputation for honesty and quality. Look Away Ranch is top-notch." Aside from having Beau Preston investigated by Slater, Brooks had Googled him and found nothing lacking.

"It's good to hear you say that. Look Away has been a joy in my life. I lost my wife some years ago, and this place along with my sons helped me get through it. You'll meet your half brothers soon."

"I'll look forward to that. And I'm sorry to hear about you losing your wife."

"Yeah, it was a tough one. I think you would've liked her. I know Mary Jo would've approved. My Tanya was a good woman. She filled the hole inside me after losing your mama."

"I wish I could've known her, Beau."

His eyes snapped up. "Son, I'd appreciate it if you called me Dad."

Dad? A swell of warmth lodged deep in his heart. He'd never had the privilege of calling any man that. While growing up, he, Carson and Graham had always been the boys without a father. Grandma Gerty had made up for it in many ways, her brightness and light shining over them, but deep down Brooks had wanted better answers from his mother about his father's absence in their lives. "You're better off not knowing," she'd say, cutting off his further questions.

Brooks gave Beau a smile. "All right, *Dad*. I'm happy to call you that after all these years."

His father's eyes lit up. "And I'm happy to hear it, son. Would you like to get settled in? I can drive you to the cabin. It's barely more than a stone's throw from here, only a quarter mile into the property."

"Yeah, that's sounds good."

"Fine, and before we do, I'll give you the grand tour of the house. Tanya did all the decorating and she loved the holidays, so we've kept up the tradition of putting out all her favorite things. We start early in December, and it takes us a while to bring the trees in and get the house fully decorated in time for our annual Look Away Ranch Christmas shindig. C'mon, I'll show you around now."

"Thanks. I've got no doubt I'm going to like your place."

"I hope so, son."

After his father left him at the cabin, a rustic, wood-beamed, fully state-of-the-art three-bedroom dwelling that would sell for a million bucks in the suburbs of Chicago, Brooks walked his luggage into the master suite and began putting away his belongings in a dark oak dresser. Lifting out the shirt Ruby had worn just this morning, Brooks brought the collar to his nose and breathed in. The shirt smelled of her still, a wildly exotic scent that had lured him into his best fantasy to date.

He'd hold on to that memory for a long time, but now he was about to make new ones with his father and his family. Brooks walked the rooms, getting familiar with his new home—for the next few weeks, anyway—and found he was antsy to learn more, to see more.

He grabbed a bottle of water from the fridge, noting that Beau Preston didn't do things halfway. The fridge was filled with everything Brooks might possibly need during his stay here. If Beau wanted him to feel welcome, he'd succeeded.

Locking the cabin door with the key his dad had given him, he headed toward the stables to explore. What he knew about horses and ranching could fit in his right hand, and it was about time to change that. Brooks didn't want to admit to his father he'd seen the saddle side of a horse only once or twice. What did a city kid from Chicago know about riding?

Not much.

Huddled in a windbreaker jacket fit for a crisp December day in Texas, his boots kicking up dust, he came upon a set of corrals first. Beautiful animals frolicked, their groomed manes gently bouncing off their shoulders as they played a game of equine tag. They nipped at each other, teased and snorted and then stormed off, only to return to play again. They were beauties. *His father's horses.*

The land behind the corrals was rich with tall grazing

grass, strong oaks and mesquite trees dotting the squat hills. It was unfamiliar territory and remote, uniquely different from what Brooks had ever known.

He ducked into one of the stables. Shadows split the sunshine inside, and a long row of stalls on either side led to a tack room. The stable was empty but for a dozen or so horses. Beau had told him to check out Misty, an eight-year-old mare with a sweet nature. He spotted her quickly, a golden palomino with blond locks, not too different in color from his own.

"Hey, girl, are you and I going to get along?" The horse's ears perked up, and she sauntered over to hang her head over the split door. "That's a girl." He stroked the horse's nose and looked into her big brown eyes. "Hang on a sec," he said and walked over to the tack area. The place smelled of leather and dust, but it was about as clean and tidy as a five-star hotel.

That told him something about his father.

"Can I help you?" A man walked out of the tack room and eyed him cautiously. "I'm Sam Braddox, the foreman."

Brooks put out his hand. "I'm Brooks Newport. Nice to meet you."

The man's expression changed to a quick smile. "You're one of Beau's boys."

"Yes, I am. I just got here a little while ago."

"Well, welcome. I see the resemblance. You have your daddy's eyes. And Beau only just this morning filled the crew in on the news you'd be arriving."

"Thanks. I'm… I'm just trying to get acquainted with the place. Learn a little about horses." He scratched his head and then shrugged. "I'm no horseman, but Beau wants to take me out riding one day."

Sam studied him. "How about a quick lesson?"

"Sure."

"C'mon. I'll show you how to saddle up." He led Misty out of her stall and into an open area.

"Misty's a fine girl. She's sweet, but she can get testy if you don't show her who's boss from the get-go."

"Okay."

The foreman grabbed a worked-in saddle and horse blanket and walked over to Brooks. "Here we go."

Sam tossed the blanket over the horse just as one of the crew dashed in. "Hey, Boss. Looks like Candy is ready to foal. She's having a struggle. Brian sent me to get you."

"Okay." Sam sighed. "I'll be right there." He gave Brooks a glance and set the saddle on the ground. "Sorry about this. Candy has had a hard pregnancy. I'd better get right to it."

"No problem at all. I'll see you later, Sam."

"You okay here?"

"I'm gonna try my hand at it. I'll Google how to saddle a horse."

Sam gave him a queer look. "All right." Then he strode out like his pants were on fire.

"How hard can this be?" Brooks said to himself.

He fixed the blanket over the horse's shoulders, sheepskin side down, and then lifted the saddle. The darn thing weighed at least fifty pounds. He set it onto the horse and grabbed the cinch from underneath the horse's belly.

"You're doing it all wrong." The female voice stopped him short. What in hell? He whipped around, uneasy about where his thoughts were heading. Sure enough, there was Ruby of his fantasies coming forward. His mouth could've dropped open, but he kept his teeth clamped as he tried to make sense of it. He'd just left Ruby a few hours ago, and now here she was in the flesh, appearing unfazed at seeing him again. He, for sure, wasn't unaffected.

"Ruby?"

"Hello, Brooks."

She practically ignored him as she went about removing the saddle like a pro—a saddle that weighed probably half her body weight—and shoving it into his arms. "The blanket has to be even on both sides. You put it on closer to Misty's shoulders and then slide it into the natural channel of her body. Make sure it's not too far down on her hips, either. It's the best protection the horse has for—"

"Ruby?" He took hold of her arm gently.

She didn't budge, didn't face him. "I work here. I'm Look Away Ranch's head wrangler and horse trainer."

As if that explained it all. "Did you know who I was last night?"

Her eyes snapped up. "God, no." She shook her head, and the sheet of beautiful raven hair shimmered. "Beau told us about you only this morning. He wanted to make sure you were really coming before he shared his news. Welcome to the family, Brooks."

His heart just about stopped. "The family?"

She nodded. "Beau's like a father to me."

Brooks released the breath he'd been holding. She'd had him scared for a second that they could be related in some way. "Like a father? What does that mean?"

"My father worked for Beau all of his life, until he died ten years ago. I was sixteen at the time. It was hard on me. I, uh…it almost broke me. My dad was special to me. We both loved horses, the land and everything about Look Away, so when he passed, I couldn't imagine my life without him. But Beau and his boys were right by my side the entire time. Beau never let a day go by without letting me know I was welcome and wanted here. He took me in and I worked at Look Away, making my way up to head wrangler."

"You live here?"

"I have an apartment in town, but often I stay in the old groundskeeper's cottage, especially during the holidays. It's where my dad lived out the last years of his life. It's home to me, too, and Beau's family is now my family."

Brooks nodded at this new wrinkle in his life. "What about your mother?"

"Mom died when I was very young. I don't remember too much about her."

"I'm sorry." He put his hands on his hips. "So, what do we do now?"

"Now?" Her brows knit together. "What do you mean?"

"About us?"

Her olive skin turned bright pink, and her embarrassment surprised him. The Ruby he'd met yesterday had been fearless and uninhibited. "Oh, that. Well, it'd be best if we didn't discuss what happened between us last night. Beau wouldn't approve. It was really nice, Brooks. But not to be repeated."

"I see."

"Glad you do," she said, dismissing the subject with a flip of her hair. "You want to learn how to saddle this horse correctly?"

Dumbfounded, he began nodding, not so much because he gave a damn about saddling, but because Ruby living on his father's ranch blew his mind. "Uh, sure."

"Okay, so the blanket has to be even and protecting the horse from the saddle." Next this petite five-foot-something of a woman positioned the heavy saddle on her knee. "Put the stirrups and straps over the saddle seat so you don't hit the horse or yourself by accident when you're saddling up. Now use your leg for support and then knee it up in a whipping motion like this." With the grace of a ballerina, she heaved the weighty saddle onto the horse's back. "You want the saddle up a little high on the shoulders first, then slowly go with the grain of the horse's hair to slide it into place. This way you won't cause any ruffle to the hair that might irritate the horse later on. Proper saddling should cause your mount no harm at all. Doing it wrong can cause all kinds of sores and injuries."

"Got it."

Ruby gave Misty several loving pats on the shoulder. She spoke kindly to the animal, as one would to a friend, and the horse stood stock-still while she continued with a ritual she probably did every day.

Ruby adjusted the front cinch strap. "Make sure it's not too loose or too tight. Just keep tucking until you run out of latigo. Take a look at how I did this one and you do the back one."

"Okay, will do." He made a good attempt at fastening the cinch, Ruby standing next to him. His concentration scattered as she brushed up against him to fix the cinch and buckle it.

"Not bad, Brooks. For your first try."

Her praise flattered him. And her sweet scent filtering up to his nose blocked out the stable smells.

"Now that Misty is saddled, you want to make sure all buckles are locked in and all your gear is in good shape. Here's a trick. Slide your hand under the saddle up front." She placed her small hand under the blanket and saddle. "If your hand goes under with no forcing, you're good to go and you know your horse isn't being pinched tight. Isn't that right, Misty?"

As she stroked Misty's nose, the horse responded with a turn of her head. The two were old pals, it seemed. Ruby's big brown eyes lifted to him. "If you want some pointers on riding, I've got some time."

Mentally he winced. He had trouble focusing. He kept thinking about Ruby in his bed. Ruby naked. Ruby making love to him. Feisty, fierce Ruby. He should back away and make an excuse. Gain some perspective. But she was offering him something he needed.

Just like last night.

"Yeah, show me what you've got."

She stared at him for a beat of a second, her face coloring again. They were locked into the memory of last night, when she'd shown him what she had. And it was not to be equaled. "Stop saying stuff like that, Brooks. And we'll do just fine."

It was good to know that she wasn't as unaffected as she wanted him to believe.

"Right. All I can promise is I'll try."

Once Brooks was away from the stable and on horseback, Ruby could breathe again. She'd never expected her one-time, one-night fling to end up being Beau Preston's long-lost son. The irony in that was killing her.

"You're not a bad rider, Brooks," she said to him.

"I'll take that as a compliment." He tipped the hat she'd given him to wear. He didn't look half bad in a Stetson.

"Actually, you learn fast. You saddled up my horse pretty darn well."

"If you're trying to butter me up, it's working, honey."

"Just speaking the truth. And can you quit the endearments?"

He smiled. "You don't like me calling you honey?"

"I'm not your honey, Brooks. Ruby Lopez never has

been anyone's honey." Except for Trace's at one time, but the sweetness of the term had soured along with the relationship.

They rode side by side along a path that wound around the property. She wanted out of this conversation. Brooks didn't need to know about her lack of a love life. But for some reason, when he was around, she did and said things she normally wouldn't.

"Ruby?"

"Hmm."

"I find that hard to believe. There's been no one in your life?"

"No one I care to talk about."

"Ah, I thought so. You've been burned before. The guy must be a loser."

"He isn't." Why on earth was she defending Trace?

"Must be, if he hurt you."

"Remember what I told you? When you want the horse to stop, pull back on one rein. Not two. Two can toss you forward, and that's a fight you can't win."

"Yeah, I remember, but why—"

"See you later, Brooks!" Ruby gave Storm Cloud a nudge, and the horse fell into a gallop. The ground rumbled underneath her stallion's hooves, and she leaned back and enjoyed the ride, grinning.

She thought she'd left Misty and her rider in the dust, but one quick look back showed her she was wrong. Brooks wasn't far behind, encouraging Misty to catch up. Ruby had five lengths on them, at best. But it wasn't a race. She couldn't put Brooks in danger. For all his courage and eagerness to learn, he was still a novice. "Whoa, slow up, Cloud." A slight tug on the rein was all that was needed. Cloud was a gem at voice commands. Beau had given her Storm Cloud on her eighteenth birthday, and she'd trained him herself. They were simpatico.

Brooks caught up to her by a copse of trees and came to a halt. "Is that your way of changing the subject?" His mouth was in a twist.

She shrugged a shoulder. "I don't know what you mean."

"Cute, Ruby."

"Hey, I'm impressed you caught up."

"Because you let me."

"Okay, I let you. But I couldn't endanger Beau's long-lost son."

"*One* of his sons. I've got a twin brother."

"Oh, no. There are two of you?" She smiled at him. This morning Beau had briefed her on all the sad events of his early life. He'd lost the woman he loved and his twins when she ran away from her abusive father. It was something Ruby had heard rumored, but it was never really spoken about in the Preston household.

"Yeah, I'm afraid so."

She tilted her head. "Can the world handle it?"

"The world likes the Newport brothers for the most part. But the question is, can you handle it?"

"I already told you, I'm good with you being here."

"I might be staying quite a while."

It was time to set him straight, and she hoped to heaven she could heed her own warning. "You're a city guy who's out of place in the country. You run a big company, and I'm at home in a barn. You're also the son of my best friend and mentor. The man is almost a father to me. You'd better believe I can handle it. There's no other option, Brooks."

He gave her a nod, his mouth turning down. "You're right. But when I look at you and remember…"

"Don't look at me."

"You're hard to miss, honey."

Honey again? "It's time to head back." She didn't wait for his reply. She turned Storm Cloud around. "Let's go, Cloud." With a slight nudge of the stirrup, the horse took off in a canter.

"I didn't peg you for a runner," Brooks called out.

But that's exactly what she was.

This time.

With this man.

She wasn't lying. She had no other choice.

Four

"You're cooking?" Brooks asked Ruby as he walked into his father's kitchen later that day.

Ruby glanced at him from her spot at the stove. She wore a black dress that landed just above her knees, fitting every curve on her body like a glove. A pink polka-dotted apron tied at the neck and waist didn't detract from the look. Brooks was beginning to think Ruby looked sexy in everything she wore.

"I'm cooking. Beau wanted me to make you a special dinner for your first night here."

"Do you cook every night?"

"No, that's Lupe's job. She's the best cook in the county, but this recipe comes from my father's family, and it's something Beau likes me to cook on occasion."

Brooks walked over to the stove. "I'm the occasion?"

She smiled. "You're the occasion."

He lifted the top off the enamel pot. Steam drifted up, and the scents of Mexico filled the room.

"Be careful. It's hot," she said, shoving a pot holder into his hand.

"What is it?"

"It's called *receta de costillas de res en salsa verde*. It's braised short ribs in tomatillo sauce."

"Smells delicious."

"It's not too spicy for a gringo." Her mouth twisted.

"You're all the spice I can manage in his house."

Ruby whipped her head around to the kitchen door. "*Dios!* Don't say things like that," she whispered. "I don't like lying to Beau."

"How did you lie?"

"It was a lie of omission. I didn't tell him I've already met you."

She'd met him and slept with him. And Brooks was having a hard time forgetting it. "He won't hear it from me, Ruby." He wasn't a kiss-and-tell kind of man. "I'm starving. Can I have a taste?" he asked.

"I suppose."

She grabbed a fork and dipped it into the stew. The meat she pierced fell easily away, and she lifted the steamy forkful up to his mouth. "Here. Tell me if it needs anything."

Brooks looked into her dark brown eyes as she fed him a morsel. The heat on the stove didn't compare to how he was heating up just being close to Ruby again. And then he began to chew. The seasoned meat blasted his palate with savory goodness. "Mmm. The lady can toss a man over her shoulder, ride a horse like nobody's business *and* cook."

"So, you like it?"

He nodded and stepped inches closer to her. "Is there anything you don't do well?" She didn't back away, and he didn't bother pretending he wasn't talking about her prowess in the bedroom.

She nibbled on her lower lip. "Brooks."

He ignored her warning tone, sensing she was as caught up as he was. He leaned forward and focused on her tempting mouth.

"Well, I see you've met Ruby already, Brooks."

The booming voice startled him, and he quickly stepped away. Ruby turned back to the stove, and Brooks answered his father. "Yes, I've met Ruby. She was kind enough to give me a taste of her stew."

Beau nodded. "It's a favorite of mine. I figured you might like it, too."

He bypassed Brooks to give Ruby a gentle kiss on the cheek. "Ruby's like a daughter to me." He gazed warmly into her eyes, and Ruby gave him a sweet, affectionate smile. "She's been with us since she was a tot. Her daddy was foreman around here, and Ruby grew up at the Look Away for all intents and purposes. I don't think there's a better horse wrangler in all of Texas, and everybody knows it."

"Thank you," she said.

"Actually, Ruby and I went for a ride this afternoon," Brooks said, to add something to the conversation.

"Good, good." Beau beamed with pride. "I want you to feel comfortable on Look Away. Did Ruby teach you a few things?"

Brooks met her eyes. "More than a few things."

The feisty Latina with the killer body blushed and put her head down to stir the stew, avoiding eye contact with him altogether now. It was clear this meal was going to be awkward, to say the least.

"My boys—your half brothers—will join us another night," Beau commented. "They're giving us time to get better acquainted. I hope you don't mind it'll just be you and me. And Ruby, of course."

"I can give you two time alone, too, Beau," Ruby jumped in, obviously trying to remove herself from the situation.

"I won't hear of it," Beau said. "Not after you cooked all afternoon for us. You're gonna sit right down and enjoy the meal along with us, Ruby. You work too hard as it is. Tonight we're gonna relax and get to know Brooks."

Ruby's gaze dimmed, and Brooks hid his amusement, but somehow Ruby knew he was laughing at her. From behind Beau's back, she gave him the stink eye.

Now that she was at the ranch, he couldn't imagine keeping away from her. Not touching her again was messing with his mind. He had bigger problems, but the idea of delicate, petite Ruby Lopez sitting by his side at dinner had him tied up in knots.

She was about as off-limits as a woman could get.

Brooks had never run from a challenge in his life, as old man Sutton Winchester could testify.

But Brooks was used to getting what he wanted in life.

And he was beginning to think Ruby was all that and more.

Once they were seated at the table and diving into the food, Beau asked, "So, what do you think about the ranch so far? Seeing it on horseback is a good way to gain perspective on the property, son."

Son? Would there ever come a day when Brooks would tire of hearing his father call him that? For so many years, Brooks had wondered what it would be like to know his true father, to sit down with him and have a meal. Now he was living the reality, and it all seemed surreal. "It's… it's a great spread, pretty impressive."

"And I bet Ruby picked out a good horse for you to ride."

"He rode Misty," she said.

"Ah, good," Beau said, nodding. It was the horse Beau had suggested.

"You know, Brooks, Ruby learned from the best. Her daddy, Joaquin, was my foreman and head wrangler for many years." Beau's eyes once again touched on Ruby with affection. "It'd make me real proud and happy if you'd think of Ruby as family, son. I mean, once you two get better acquainted."

Ruby's olive skin flushed with color. She immediately scraped her chair back, rose from her seat and went over to open the refrigerator. "I forgot the iced tea," she mumbled.

Beau ran a hand down his face and gave his head a shake. "Uh, sorry, honey. I forget how independent you are. I didn't mean to make you uncomfortable."

"You didn't," she said, pouring tea into three glasses, her back to them. "I'm fine, Beau."

Brooks's gaze dipped to her rear end in that tight-fitting dress, her long hair falling down her back like a sheet of black silk. He wasn't about to touch upon this subject, so he stayed silent. His father's request only cemented his need to keep far away from Ruby, which wasn't going to be easy since they'd be living on the ranch together now. Every time he laid eyes on the woman, something clicked inside his head. And way farther south.

Shelve those thoughts, man.

She came back to the table, delivered the drinks and scooted back into her chair.

"Thanks," Brooks said.

"You're welcome," she said, giving him a quick smile.

"Yeah, thanks honey. Meal's real delicious."

"Yes," Brooks added. "You're a talented cook, Ruby."
Among other things.

Ruby escaped the dinner early, claiming a case of fatigue and a desire for Beau to get to know Brooks on a one-on-one basis. Beau was ecstatic to have his son finally home. She saw it in his eyes, heard it in his tone. And she was truly happy for him. He'd told her he'd been haunted for years, had searched for and lamented the loss of the children he knew were out there somewhere. Now he'd been given a second chance to father them and bring them into the family.

Twins, no less.

Dios, it was weird having Brooks here. He made her nervous, and she couldn't say that about too many things. She was a woman who usually didn't go in for one-night flings, yet the one time she'd indulged, fate pulled a fast one on her by bringing Brooks right to her doorstep. Weren't one-night stands supposed to be just that—secret liaisons that both parties could walk away from?

She needed to purge thoughts of Brooks Newport Preston. He'd taken up too much space in her mind today. She made a detour and walked the path to the stables. Checking in on her horses always made her feel better.

One peek inside the dimly lit stable told her all was right in the horse world at Look Away. Beau bred dozens of horses to sell, and it was her job to make sure they were healthy and happy and well-trained. She knew enough not to form an emotional attachment to most of them. She knew not to love them, because that bond was sure to be broken as soon as the sale became final. Her papa had warned her enough times when she was a young girl, and after a few pretty brutal heartbreaks, she'd learned that lesson the hard way. Now Ruby knew when to love and when not to love.

Unfortunately she hadn't been that astute when it came to men.

But the horses in this stable weren't in danger of being sold off. They all belonged to the Preston family, except for Storm Cloud. He was all hers.

"Hey, Cloud," she whispered, tiptoeing to his stall. "You still up?"

Cloud wandered over to her, his head coming over the split door to say hello with a gentle nudge. "Yes, you are." Ruby stroked the side of his face, pressing a kiss above his nose. The horse gave a little snort, and Ruby chuckled. "You want a treat, don't you?"

She grabbed her secret stash from a bag hooked on the wall and came up with a handful of sugar cubes. "Only a few," she said. "And let's be quiet about it. Or the others will wake up."

Cloud gobbled them within seconds, and Ruby spent a few more minutes with him before she said good-night. Feeling better, she walked toward the cottage she called home while she was staying on the Look Away. Carrie Underwood's "Before He Cheats" banged out of her phone, and she glanced at the screen.

Trace?

Her heart sped up. Why was he calling now, of all times? He hadn't had the balls to call her for six months. She'd invested almost two years in him, mainly during the off-season of the rodeo. They'd dated and had an amazing time together. But it wasn't all fun and games on her part. She'd fallen hard for the bull rider, giving him something she'd always protected and kept safe— her heart. Yet when the rodeo started up again this year, he'd left her high and dry. He hadn't called. He hadn't written. A few texts in the beginning, and that had been it, for heaven's sake. She'd spent the first months making excuses for him because the rodeo was an important part of his life. He was busy. He was focused on making a name for himself. But in the end, Ruby came to the conclusion that Trace had not only tried to make a name for himself but also made a damn fool out of her.

Carrie Underwood was about to carve her name in her guy's leather seats, and Ruby had a mind to do that very thing to Trace's truck if she ever saw him again. But her curiosity got the better of her. Before her cell went to voice mail, she answered the call.

"Hello."

"Ruby? Baby, is that you? It's Trace."

"I know who it is, Trace. Are you bleeding or on your last breath or something?"

Silence for a few seconds, and then, "No, baby. I'm not. What I *am* is missing you."

"You're not dying and trying to ease your conscience?"

"Ruby, listen to me. I know it's been a while."

"A while? Is that what you call six months of deafening silence? Why are you calling me now, Trace?"

"I told you, babe. I miss you like crazy. It's been hell on the circuit and I couldn't think straight, so I had to close off my mind to everything but what I was trying to accomplish. I needed the space to keep my head in the game. You can ask anybody around here. They all know about you, baby. They're sick of me pining for you. They all know I'm crazy about you."

Ruby's heart dipped a little. Trace was saying all the right things. He had charm and dark dastardly good looks. His voice, that deep Southern drawl, could melt an iceberg. But her wounds were deep, and she wasn't through being mad at him. "Not good enough, Trace. I'm sorry. I've got to go."

"Ruby, baby…wait."

"I have, Trace. For too long. Good night."

She pushed End and then squeezed her eyes shut. Pain burned through her belly, and those old feelings she'd managed to bury threatened to bust their way back up and slash her again and again.

He's like the horse I wasn't supposed to love.

Dios, why did he have to call her tonight?

She didn't want to think about him anymore.

Carrie's voice carried the same tune again, Ruby's cell phone drowning out the night sounds and coyote calls. No, damn it. She wasn't going to answer her phone again. No matter how many times Trace called. Her finger was ready to push the end button again. Until she saw the name flashing on the screen.

Serena.

Oh, thank goodness. She picked up quickly.

"Serena, hi," Ruby said anxiously. "I'm glad you called. You must've been reading my mind."

"Ruby, wow. Is everything all right? You sound stressed."

"I just got a call from Trace. And yeah, I'm a little stressed. I need to talk to you."

"Tell me. I'm listening."

"Oh boy, it's almost too much to explain over the phone. Can we meet for lunch tomorrow?"

"Of course, sure. That's the reason I was calling anyway. I wanted to catch up with you. It's been weeks since I've seen you. I miss my friend."

"I miss you, too. And there's a *whole lot* to catch up on. I'm buying. Root beer floats and sliders at the diner sound okay?"

"I won't pass up that offer. I'll see you there at noon."

Ruby sighed. Her bestie from high school was the only one she could confide in. "Thank you. I don't know what I'd do without you." Ruby didn't have a mom or an aunt or anyone female in her family she could talk to. Without Serena, she'd have been lost. Ever since they were kids, they'd shared their secrets with each other. Ruby ended the call, feeling a little better about things. Just knowing Serena would listen and not judge her made all the difference in the world. Though they didn't share bloodlines, they were sisters in all other respects. She'd relied on Serena's friendship to see her through some of the really tough times in her life.

"I'm eager to show you around Look Away, Brooks. Mind if we saddle up after breakfast and take us a ride?" Beau asked on Brooks's second morning on the ranch. "I'd love for you to see our operation."

"Uh, sure. I'd like that," he said, setting aside his coffee cup and patting his belly. "If I won't break poor Misty's back after the giant meal I just consumed. It was delicious, Lupe. I ate up everything in sight." Breakfast had included maple-smoked bacon, ham, eggs, chile-fried potatoes and homemade biscuits with gravy. "If I keep eating like this, I'll be as big as this house, but smiling all the way."

Lupe gave him a nod. "*Gracias*, Brooks. I'm happy to cook for Beau's son."

"Lupe is a triple threat to all of us. Breakfast, lunch and dinner. We have to work out hard around here to avoid putting the pounds on."

Beau's eyes were on him—the blue in them the exact same hue as his own—and he was beaming. Having his father look at him that way humbled him and made him feel as if he belonged. Even though ranch living was foreign to Brooks, it felt damn good knowing he was welcomed and—yes—loved by this obviously decent, successful and well-respected man.

A sudden case of guilt spilled into his good mood. Would Beau approve of the tactics he'd used to bring Sutton Winchester down? Brooks hadn't taken any prisoners on that score, too eager to exact his revenge on the man he believed had immeasurably hurt his mother and his family. Brooks had looked upon Sutton as his enemy and hadn't held back, using all the tools at his disposal to get back at the dying man.

But was Sutton the monster he'd made him out to be? Or had he simply protected his mother's secrets at her urging, thus refusing to reveal who Cynthia really was? Had Sutton truly loved his mother enough to withstand all the media and personal attacks Brooks had thrown his way? It was hard thinking of Sutton in softer terms, as a man who'd go the distance for a woman to protect her. Everything else about Winchester pointed to him being a ruthless bastard.

Brooks was still sorting this all out in his mind.

"Son?"

Beau was on his feet, waiting for him.

"Yep, I'm ready, Dad." His lips twitched, and suddenly he felt like a child being given an unexpected gift. He had a sense that Beau was feeling that way, too, as they walked out of the kitchen, ready to take a ride together as father and son.

Minutes later, Brooks had saddled up and mounted Misty. Beau was atop a stunning black gelding named Alamo. "I figured you'd be a fast learner. You saddled up that mare almost perfectly."

Brooks lowered the brim of his hat and nodded at his

father's praise. "Thanks. The truth is, I don't know much about horses. I don't get out of the city much. My friend Josh Calhoun owns a dairy farm in Iowa, and that's about the only time I've seen the backside of a horse. Let me tell you, it wasn't pretty."

Beau chuckled. "I think I learned to ride before I could walk, son. You'll get the hang of it, and if you need any help, just ask me or Ruby. She's actually the expert. She's got the touch, you know."

He knew.

"That girl can tame the most stubborn of animals."

Beau went on to explain that in the summer months, Ruby gave lessons to children three mornings a week, teaching them how to respect and care for the animals. "It's a sight to see. All those kids swarming around her, asking her questions. Anyone who knows Ruby knows she's not the most patient kind. She likes things to get done, the faster the better, as long as they're done right. But Ruby, with those kids…well, it's my favorite time of year, watching her school those young kids."

Ruby with kids? Now that was an image that entered Brooks's head and lingered.

They rode out a ways, Beau showing him all the stables and corrals and training areas. There were outbuildings and supply sheds and feed shacks on the property. They rode along the bank of a small lake and then over flatlands that bordered the property. Beau's voice filled with pride when he spoke of his land and the improvements he'd made on the horse farm through the years.

"Enough about me, son. I want to hear all about you and your brothers. And your life in Chicago."

"Where do I start?"

"From the beginning…as you remember it."

"Well, let's see. Going back to my earliest years, Mom

was always there for us. We lived with Mom's best friend, an older widow named Gerty, as you know. She was Grandma Gerty to us, and there wasn't a day that went by that my brothers and I didn't feel loved. As adults, we found out what a truly generous woman she was. She put a roof over our heads, raised us while Mom was working and helped all three of us get through college."

Brooks sighed, relieved. "That's good to hear, son."

"We had a good life, but all throughout growing up, Mom always told us we were better off that our father wasn't in our lives. I guess that was Mom's way of protecting us. And you, as well. I'm guessing she feared her fake identity would be discovered. Gosh, her father must've really done a number on her."

Beau's brows pushed together, and his scowl said it all. "You don't want to know."

Brooks nodded. Maybe he didn't.

He went on. "While she was pregnant, she worked for Sutton Winchester as his personal secretary. They fell in love, and she must've shared her secret with him about her life and the true father of her twins. I think he protected her secret all those years, and then things went bad between them. His ex was making all kinds of trouble, and Mom walked away, but by then, she was pregnant with Carson."

"It's quite a story."

"I know, but all through it, Mom was our constant. I miss her so much. But I will admit to being angry with her, with you, with Winchester. I became obsessed with learning the truth."

"Good thing, or we would've never found each other, son."

"That much is true. But I'm pretty relentless when I go after something."

"You saying you have regrets?"

He shrugged. "Maybe. But not about coming here and being with you, Dad."

Sitting tall in the saddle, riding the range with his father and learning about Look Away all seemed sort of right to him. Though he had a full life in Chicago, a successful business to run and family he could count on, being in Texas right now gave him a sense of belonging that he'd not had for a long time.

"I think we all have regrets," Beau said. "I shouldn't have stopped until I found Mary Jo. Gosh, son, you have to know how much losing her ate me up inside. After a time, I really thought she was dead. And I blamed her old man for it. He's a shell of what he once was, but I never knew a meaner man."

"He must've been for my mom to run from you and her hometown, the only place she'd ever lived. Only goes to show how strong my mother was."

"And brave, Brooks. I don't know too many women who would be able to assume a new identity, get a job, raise her boys and give them a life filled with love. Mary Jo was something."

"Yeah, Mom was that."

As they continued their ride, Brooks scanned the grounds, looking for signs of Ruby. She hadn't joined them for breakfast, which was a disappointment. He'd been looking forward to seeing those big brown eyes and the pretty smile this morning. He knew enough to stay away from her, but he had an uncanny, unholy need to see her again.

Now, as they headed back to the stables, he kept his eyes peeled.

"Ruby's got a date this afternoon," his dad said, practically reading his mind. Was Brooks that obvious about what he'd been searching for? He had no right to feel any emotion, yet the one barreling through his belly at hearing Ruby was on a date was undeniable jealousy. "Or she'd be on the ranch today. I've asked her to show you a little about her horse training program. Looks like it's gonna have to wait until tomorrow, if that's okay with you, son?"

"Of course. I'm on Ruby's schedule. She's not on mine. If she's seeing someone, that takes precedence." Damn, if those words weren't hard to force out.

His dad chuckled. "No, it's not like that. Gosh, I'm sure glad that ship has sailed."

"What do you mean?"

"Oh, the man she was seeing a while back didn't sit straight with me. I'm glad he's out of the picture now."

"Didn't like him much, huh?" Brooks shouldn't have been prying, but he couldn't help but want to know more. Ruby fascinated him in every way.

"No. Trace Evans wasn't the man for her. Hurt her real bad, too, and she's moved on. She's having lunch with a girlfriend, and you know how that goes. She could be gone for hours. I told her not to worry and to take all the time she needs. Man, it sure is different raising a girl, that's for sure."

Too much relief to be healthy settled in his gut. "I wouldn't know, having two brothers."

"Yeah, I hear ya. When Ruby came into the family, my boys had to clean up their act. Not a one of them ever disrespected her, and that's what I want for her. Whoever takes her heart better damn well treat it with tender care. I owe it to her and her daddy."

The more he was around Beau, the more respect Brooks had for him. He liked that Beau was watching out for Ruby, and again it underscored his need to keep their relationship platonic. If only he could think of Ruby as a half sister.

Instead of the sexy, hot woman who'd heated up his sheets two nights ago.

Five

Ruby bit into a pulled pork slider, and barbeque sauce dripped down her chin. She dabbed at it with her napkin. "Yum, I feel better already."

Serena Bartolomo chuckled as she lifted her slider to her mouth and took a big bite, too. When it came to settling nerves, there wasn't anything better than the Cool Springs Café's food, and the combination of being with Serena and downing pulled pork made Ruby's hysteria from yesterday seem like a thing of the past.

"So, let me get this straight, Rube. You've got two hot guys in your life right now, and that's what's making you crazy? I should be so lucky."

Serena had her own set of issues with the opposite sex; namely, she was looking for the perfect man. Someone kind, strong, honest and funny, *just like her daddy*, and all others need not apply. It was a tall order, and so far, Serena hadn't found the man of her dreams.

"Luck has everything to do with it," Ruby said. "Bad luck. I thought I had it clear in my mind what I wanted. If the right guy comes along, fine. That would make me happy, I guess. But if he doesn't, and I'm certainly not looking, then I'm good with my horses and family. I'm in no hurry to get hurt again."

"Yeah, Trace did a number on you. I can see you not wanting to jump back into that arena."

"But you should've heard him on the phone, Serena. He was really sweet, and he said everything I wanted to hear. How he missed me. How he's been thinking about me night and day."

"Are you buying it?"

"I shouldn't. But he sounded sincere."

"The rodeo season is over. What will you do if he comes knocking on your door?"

Ruby shrugged. It wasn't as if she hadn't asked herself that question a dozen times already. "I don't know. Wait and see. I'm not rushing into anything."

"That's good, hon."

She released a sigh that emptied her lungs. "And then there's Brooks."

"Yeah, tell me about him."

"Smart, confident, handsome. We had that one night together. A crazy impetuous fling, and afterward we parted ways amicably, only the next day he shows up at Look Away as Beau's long lost son. I never thought I'd see him again, and now he's a fixture at the ranch and I've got to pretend nothing's happened between us."

"Is that hard?"

She sipped from her float, the icy soda sliding down her throat as she contemplated her answer. "Well, it's not easy. Especially with the way he looks at me with those dreamy blue eyes. And he's funny, too. We laugh a lot."

"Uh-oh, that's dangerous. A man who can make you laugh—that's the kiss of death." Serena began shaking her head. "Do you think of Trace at all when you're with him?"

"*Dios*, no. I don't think of any other man when I'm with Brooks. He may not know it yet, but he's so much like his father."

"Being like Beau Preston is a good, good thing."

"So true. But Brooks has a sharper edge, I think. He's pulled himself up from humble beginnings, and this whole situation with not knowing who his real father was has hurt him and maybe made him bitter."

"Wow, that's heavy. Did he tell you that?"

Ruby dipped her head sheepishly, hating to admit the truth. "No, I Googled him. I wanted to find out more about him. He's entering the Preston family, and they've had enough heartache in their lives. Is that horrible? I feel like I'm spying on him."

"It's the way of the world, hon. Don't beat yourself up. You were concerned about Beau, right?"

"Yes, that's part of it. Anyway, now you know my dilemma. Brooks is off-limits to me. He's part of Beau's family now, which means he's my family, too. And then there's Trace. I have to admit, hearing from him last night really threw me off balance."

"Ruby, we've been friends a long time. I know how strong you are. You can handle this. You're Ruby Lopez. Anybody who messes with you lives to regret it."

Ruby laughed. "That's my persona, anyway."

"Hey, you're forgetting I've seen you in action. You've got self-defense skills any woman would love to have."

"Yeah, I can toss a man over my shoulder, no problem. But can I evict him from my heart? That's a totally different matter."

* * *

Texas breezes ruffled Brooks's shirt on this warmer than usual December day and brought freshness to the morning as he strode down the path toward the lake. He didn't mind the walk; it helped clear his head. Beau, so proud of his operation here, had recommended that Brooks check out Ruby in action. Hell, he'd already seen her in action. She'd downed a big oaf of a man in that saloon. And then he'd been private witness to her other skills in the bedroom. But of course, Beau had meant something entirely different.

"You want to get a better sense of what we do on Look Away, then go see Ruby down at the lake this morning," his father had said. "She's working with a one-year-old named Cider. Beautiful filly."

The truth was, Brooks hadn't laid eyes on Ruby yesterday, and he'd missed her like crazy. It baffled him just how much. Now, with his boots pounding the earth as he headed her way, his hands locked in his pockets Texas-style, a happy tune was playing in his head. He liked it here. He liked the sun and sky and vastness. He liked the howl of a coyote, the smell of hay and earth and, yes, horse dung. It all seemed so natural and beautiful. But mostly, it was Ruby in this setting that he liked the most.

And there she was, about twenty yards up ahead, near a nameless body of water his father simply called the lake, holding a lead rope in one hand and a long leather stick in the other. She wore a tan hat, her long raven locks gathered in a ponytail that spilled down the back of her red blouse. Skin-tight jeans curved around her ass in a way that made him gulp air.

He lodged himself up against a tree, his arms folded, to take in the scene for a few seconds before he made his presence known. How long had it been since he could simply enjoy watching a woman do her job? Probably never.

Ruby was sweet to the horse, though she wasn't a pushover. She spoke in a friendly voice, using the rope and the stick as tools to train the filly. She was patient, a trait he hadn't associated with Ruby, but then, he really didn't know her all that well. The time she took with the horse notched up his respect for her even more.

"Why don't you come away from the tree, Brooks," she called, catching him off guard. He hadn't seen her look his way; he thought her focus was mainly on the horse she was training. "Cider knows you're here, too."

Brooks marched over to her. "I didn't want to disturb you."

"Too late for that," she said quickly, with a blink of her eyes, maybe surprising herself. He got the feeling she wasn't speaking about the training session. "Actually, I'm glad you're here. Beau wants you to see how we train the horses. And I'm just beginning with Cider."

With gloved hands, she gathered the rope into a circle, her tone businesslike and stiff. It had to be this way, but Brooks didn't like it one bit. He knew she was untouchable, but of course the notion made him want her all the more.

"For the record, you disturb me too, Ruby." He didn't give her a wink or a smile. He wasn't flirting or teasing. He meant it.

"Brooks." She sighed, giving him an eyeful of her innermost thoughts by the sag of her shoulders and the look of hopelessness on her face. Then she turned her full attention to the horse, patting Cider's nose and stroking her long golden mane. "We need to be just friends."

She was stating the obvious.

"I can try," he said.

"For Beau."

"Yeah, for Beau."

Because they both knew if they got together and it
didn't work out, Beau would be hurt, as well. Brooks
didn't want friction in the Preston family. He was the
newcomer. He was trying to fit in and become a part of
this family. It would do no good to have a repeat of what
happened at the C'mon Inn. His father and this family
deserved more than that from him.

Brooks's brain was on board. Now if the rest of him
would join in, it wouldn't be an issue at all.

That settled, he gave the horse's nose a stroke. Under
his palm, the coarse hair tickled a bit, yet it was also
smooth as he slid his hand down. "So, what are you doing
with her today?"

"Today, we're working on gullies and water." Ruby
jumped right in, eager to share her knowledge. "People
sometimes think horses know what's expected of them
from birth, but nothing is further from the truth. This girl
is water-shy, and she doesn't know how to jump over a
gully. Both frighten her. So I'm working with her today
to make her more comfortable with both of those situ-
ations. Here, let me show you." She walked Cider over
to a dip in the property, the gully no more than a yard
across. "First I'll let her get familiar with the terrain."

Ruby released the lead rope and, using her stick,
tapped the horse on the shoulder. "Don't worry, I'm not
hurting her. The stick on the withers or neck lets her
know she's crowding my space. When she gets scared,
she closes in on me. I'm trying to get her into her own
space."

Ruby worked the horse up and down the area. The
horse avoided the gulley altogether. Ruby gave the horse
room to investigate, leading her with the rope. "See

that, Brooks? She's stopped to sniff and get her bearings. That's good. Now I'm going to bring her in a little closer. She won't like it much—she doesn't know what to do about the gully—but she'll figure it out. I keep sending her closer and closer to the gap and tapping, like this." She tapped Cider again and then gave the horse time to overcome her fear. Back and forth, back and forth. Then Cider stopped again, put her head down and sniffed around. The next time Ruby led her close to the gulley, she jumped. "There! Good girl. That's wonderful, Cider." She stroked the horse again, giving praise. "Good girl. Want to try it one more time?

"I'll keep this going," Ruby explained to him. "Leading her back and forth near the gully. And soon she'll be a pro at jumping over it. It's a start."

"It's amazing how she responds to you, Ruby. I saw a change in her in just a few minutes. Will she go in the water?"

"She'll go near it and take a drink. But she won't go into the water. That takes a bit more time. She's thirsty now, which will work in my favor. But I won't push her right now. She can have a peaceful drink."

Ruby let the rope hang very loose, taking off any pressure, and approached the water. Cider resisted for a few seconds. Then, without being prompted by the stick or the rope, she walked over to the bank and dipped her head to lap up water. "See how wary she is? She won't put her feet in. But she will, very soon."

"I never thought about horses not feeling inherently comfortable with their surroundings. I don't know a whole lot about horses, that's for damn sure. I guess I figured they were naturally at ease with jumping and going in the water."

"Yeah, I know that's the perception. But horses, like

children, need to be trained to do the things we know they are capable of doing. They certainly don't understand what it means when we put saddles on them or bits in their mouths. The truth is, when I train the horses, they tell me what they need help with. And I listen and watch. The reason this method works so well is that I give the horse a purpose. I kept sending Cider across that gully and let her figure out how to solve the problem. It's a matter of knowing what they need and providing it."

Brooks spent the remainder of the morning watching Ruby work miracles with this horse, completely impressed with her knowledge and the ease with which she worked. When his stomach grumbled, he grinned. "Are you going back to the house for lunch?"

"No. I'm not done with Cider yet. I brought my lunch out here."

"You're eating here?"

"Yep, under that tree you were holding up earlier."

He laughed. "Sounds peaceful."

She stared into his eyes. "It is."

"Okay, then, I should get going. Let you have your lunch."

He turned and began walking.

"There's enough for two," she said, a hitch in her throat, as if she couldn't believe she'd just said that. Hell, if she was inviting, he wouldn't be refusing.

He turned and smiled. "If it's Lupe's leftover fried chicken, I'm taking you up on it."

"And what if it isn't?" she asked.

"I'm still staying."

Ruby's mouth pulled into a frown as if she was having second thoughts.

"As your friend," he added.

Her tight expression relaxed, and a glint gleamed in

her pretty brown eyes. "I lied. It is chicken, and Lupe packed me way too much."

"So then, I'd be doing you a favor by staying and eating with you. Wouldn't want all that food to go to waste."

She rolled her eyes adorably, and Brooks was glad to see the Ruby of old come back.

She grabbed her backpack, and together they walked over to the tree where swaying branches provided shade on the packed-dirt ground. Ruby tossed her stuff down, but before she sat, he put up his hand. "Wait a sec."

She stood still, her eyes sharp as he pulled his shirt out of his jeans and began unbuttoning until his white T-shirt was exposed. "Never did like this shirt anyway." He took off his shirt and made a bit of a production laying it on the ground. Then he gestured to Ruby. "Now you can sit."

Her expression warmed considerably. "Galahad. You're too much."

"That's what they tell me."

She plopped herself comfortably down on his shirt so that her perfect behind wouldn't be ground into the dirt. "Thank you. You know, that's about the sweetest thing a man's done for me in a long while."

"Well then, you're meeting the wrong kind of men. Present company excluded. And boy, am I glad you're not into all that feminism stuff, or I'd be dead meat right now."

She smiled. "Who says I'm not? I believe in the power of women."

"So do I."

"But I can also recognize a gentleman when I see one, and I don't feel like it's diminishing my role in the world."

"And this is Texas, after all," he said.

"Right."

"And I have developed Southern charm."

"Don't press your luck, Preston."

Brooks blinked. And then he looked straight into Ruby's spirited chocolate eyes. "Thanks. It feels good to be called by my father's name."

"You're welcome. You've earned it."

He stared at her and nodded, holding back a brand-new emotion welling behind his eyes.

Brooks headed to the main house that evening, thoughts of Ruby never far from his mind. The more time he spent with her... Okay, forget it. He couldn't go down that road, especially when the main reason his thoughts had splintered was standing not ten feet away on the sweeping porch of the residence.

As soon as Beau spotted Brooks, he called him over with a wave of the hand. "Come here, son. Meet the rest of the family."

The three men—all wearing Stetsons in varying colors and appearing younger than Brooks by several years—stood at attention next to Beau. Brooks's half brothers.

He walked up, and Beau gave his shoulder a squeeze. "Brooks, I'm proud to introduce you to Toby, Clay and Malcolm. They're your brothers."

He shook each one of their hands and greeted them kindly. It was strange and awkward at first, but Beau's boys made him feel welcome.

"We're surely glad to meet you," Toby said. He was the oldest and tallest of the three. "I'm sorry we missed out on knowing you all those years."

"Yeah, I'm sorry, too. Life took me down a different path," he said.

Malcolm stood against the post, his boots crossed, his gaze narrowing in on Brooks's face. "But you're here now, and we're glad of it. You look more like Dad than any of us."

Beau chuckled. "Poor guy."

"Mom wouldn't agree," Clay said, chiming in. "She was always telling us how handsome you were."

"Yeah," Malcolm said. "Damn near gave us a complex."

Beau shook his head. "Your mama thought the sun rose and set on you boys, and you know it."

"Seems like your mom was a pretty great lady from what I'm told," Brooks said. He'd heard from Beau, but just about everyone else on the ranch had nice things to say about Tanya, too.

"That she was," Beau said, the pride in his voice unequalled.

"My brothers and I, well, we're sorry to hear news of your mother's passing, Brooks," Malcolm said. The others nodded in agreement.

"Thank you. Mom was also quite a woman. And she died unexpectedly. My brothers and I miss her terribly."

"It's not easy," Beau said, the brightness in his eyes dimming. "But we have each other now, and that's something to celebrate. Shall we go in to dinner? Lupe promised us a feast, and we're opening a few special bottles of wine to toast the occasion."

"I'm nearly starved," Toby said, patting his stomach.

"Yeah, me, too," Clay said. "Oh, and new brother?"

Brooks gave him a glance. "Yeah?"

"I'm apologizing in advance for the interrogation. We're all so dang curious about your life, I'm afraid we're gonna grill you. We want to hear about Graham, too. Dad says he's the spitting image of you."

"Yep, there are two of us. We're identical twins."

"You boys will meet him soon," Beau said as he ushered them all into the house. "I'm hoping Graham will be here by next week in time for our Christmas party."

"I don't mind your questions," Brooks added. "I've got quite a few for you. We all have some catching up to do."

In the formal dining room, on Beau's cue, Clay, Malcolm and Toby spent the next few minutes asking about Brooks's early life, his college days and how he came to build such a successful real estate development business. "Lots of hard work, long hours and a driving need to make my way in the world," he answered. "Mom was a survivor, and she raised her children to be independent thinkers."

Beau smiled, getting a faraway look in his eyes. Was he thinking about the young woman he'd loved and lost? Then, with a shake of the head, he shifted and turned his attention back to the conversation.

Lupe came in, carrying plates filled with twelve-ounce rib eye steaks, potatoes, creamed corn and Texas-sized biscuits. "Looks delicious, Lupe. Thank you," Beau said.

Toby and Malcolm immediately rose to help her bring the rest of the food in from the kitchen. And just as they were sitting down, ready to take their first bite, Ruby walked in.

She didn't immediately make eye contact with Brooks, so he looked his fill. Her jeans and blousy top were white, but her ankle boots were as black as the mass of long raven hair falling down her back. The contrast of black to white was striking, and he took a swallow of water to keep his mouth from going dry. "Hey, everyone," she said.

"Better late than never, Rube," Clay said, teasing. "Had another hot date with a horse?"

Toby and Malcolm chuckled.

"Wouldn't you like to know," she said, smiling and

scooting her fine little ass into her seat. "At least horses can take direction. Unlike most men I know."

Beau choked out a laugh.

Ruby arched a brow and shot daggers at Clay. Apparently she wasn't through with him yet. "And tell me again, who are you dating at the moment?"

"Oh, you've dug yourself a hole now, Clay," Malcolm said. "You know better than to get into it with Ruby. You're not gonna win."

"You see," she said, "Malcolm understands. At least he has a girlfriend."

"This is a picture of what it was like when the kids were growing up," Beau explained, grinning. "I gotta say, it's still amusing."

Ruby glanced at Brooks then, giving him a nod of acknowledgment. He smiled, acknowledging how Ruby held her own with Beau's boys. She was a handful, a woman with spunk who took no prisoners and didn't apologize for it. If only he could stop noticing all her admirable traits. As it was now, she was off the charts.

Wine was poured and Beau lifted his glass. Everyone at the table took his cue, and the deep red wine in the raised glasses glistened under chandelier light. "To my family," he said. "I couldn't be happier to have Brooks here. And soon Graham will join us. I love you all," he said, his voice tight, "and look forward to the day we can all be together."

Glasses clinked and Brooks was touched at the welcome he'd received by his new family at Look Away Ranch.

They settled into the meal. The steak was the most tender he'd ever had. Texans knew a thing or two about raising prime cattle and delivering a delicious meal. His brothers surely looked the picture of health—all three were sturdy men—and a sense of pride in his newfound family washed over him. He doubted he'd ever feel as close to these young men as he did Graham—he and Graham had shared too much together—but he hoped they'd all become the family Beau had longed for.

"Dad says our little sis taught you a thing or two about horse training," Toby remarked. "What'd you think?"

Brooks hesitated a second, finishing a sip of wine while contemplating how to answer the innocent question. He couldn't give too much away. He couldn't say that Ruby was the most amazing woman he'd ever met, or that her talent and skill and patience had inspired him. That would be too telling, wouldn't it? "What I know about horses, I'm afraid to say, can fit in this wineglass. But watching Ruby at work and hearing her thoughts on training gave me a whole new perspective. It's eye-opening. It seems Ruby has just the right touch."

Toby nodded. "She does. We've all had a hand in horse training growing up, and all of our techniques are different, but the honest truth is, when we'd come up against a stubborn one that gave us trouble, we turned to Ruby and she'd find a way. Now she pretty much runs the show."

Brooks looked at Ruby, giving her a smile. "I see that she pretty much runs the show around here, too."

Beau chuckled. "Didn't take you long to figure that out."

"There's an advantage to being the only female in the family," Malcolm said.

"I can speak for myself, Mal," she chimed in. "There's an advantage to being the only female in the family."

Everyone laughed.

Ruby's eyes twinkled, and in that moment, Brooks felt like one of them. A Preston, through and through.

* * *

The next morning, Beau suggested that they spend the day with Ruby. There was more she could teach Brooks, and if he really wanted to get a sense of how the operation was run, he needed to get his hands dirty.

"Ruby will put you in touch with your inner wrangler," Beau joked.

Well, she'd already put him in touch with *something*: namely, rock-solid lust. The woman turned him inside out, and there was no help for it.

Before Brooks had even met Ruby, he'd asked for this training, and Beau was more than happy to accommodate his request. But now it meant that Brooks and Ruby would get to spend more time together at the Look Away. Yet Brooks wanted to learn. He needed to catch up on the history of the ranch and the day-to-day operation of running it. It would give him a chance to meet Beau and his half brothers on equal ground. He'd have more in common with each one of them if he could grasp at least a basic knowledge of horses, training and all that went with them.

So they'd walked over to one of the corrals and stood by the fence, watching Ruby securing a saddle on an unruly stallion.

The air was brisk this morning, the sun shadowed by gray clouds. He huddled up in his own wool-lined jacket and noted that Ruby, too, was dressed in a dark quilted vest over a flannel shirt. Only Ruby Lopez could make regular cowgirl gear look sexy. "Morning," she said, greeting both of them.

"Morning," he replied. But she had already turned away, busy with the horse, restraining his jerky movements with a firm hand on his bridle.

"This is Spirit," Beau said. "He's got a lot to learn, doesn't he, Ruby?"

"He sure does. He's not taken kindly to wearing a saddle. He's going to hate it even more once I ride him. But that's not happening today."

The horse snorted and shuffled his feet, pulling back and away from her. "Hold steady, boy," Ruby said, her voice smooth as fine silk. "You're not gonna like any of this, are you now?"

The horse bucked, and Brooks made a move to lunge over the fence to help Ruby. Beau restrained him with a hand to the chest. "Hang on. Ruby's a pro. She won't put herself in danger."

Brooks wasn't too sure about that. The tall stallion dwarfed Ruby in size and weight. Watching her outmaneuver the animal made Brooks's heart stop for a moment. Hell, she could be crushed. She slid him a sideways glance, her beautiful eyes telling him she'd just seen what he'd done. What was it she called him? Galahad. Hell, he was no knight in shining armor. To most of the people who knew him in Chicago, that label would be laughable. But today, right in this moment, he didn't give a crap about what anyone called him. But he did care about Ruby, and it surprised him how much. He didn't want to see her get trampled. "Are you sure? That horse looks dangerous."

"He could be, but Ruby knows her limitations. She's got a way about her that outranks his stature. She's gaining his trust right now. Though it doesn't look like it, she's giving him some leeway to put up a fuss. This is his second day wearing a saddle. He's got to get used to it, is all."

"It takes a lot of patience, I see."

"Yep," Beau said. "For the trainer and the animal."

For the next hour, Brooks watched Ruby put the horse

through his paces. Every now and then, she'd inform him what she was doing and how the horse should respond. Nine times out of ten, the horse didn't make a liar out of her.

Beau had excused himself a short time ago. He had a meeting with his accountant, and though he invited Brooks to join in, he'd also warned that it would bore him out of his wits. Brooks had opted to stay and watch Ruby work with the stallion. He could watch that woman for hours without being bored, but he didn't tell his father that.

When Ruby was done, she unsaddled Spirit carefully, speaking to the horse lovingly and stroking him softly on the withers. Then she set him free, and he took off running along the perimeter of the large oval corral, his charcoal mane flying in the breeze.

Ruby closed the gate behind her and walked over to Brooks, removing her leather gloves and pocketing them.

"Impressive," he said.

"Thanks. Spirit will come around. He's a Thoroughbred, and they tend to be high-strung."

"Is that so?" Brooks met her gaze. "Sort of reminds me of someone I know."

Her index finger pressed into her chest. "Me?"

"Yeah, you." Her finger rested in the hollow between her breasts. If only he didn't remember how damn intoxicating it'd been when he'd touched her there. How soft she'd felt, how incredibly beautiful and full her breasts were. The thought of never touching Ruby like that again grated on him.

"Well, you're half-right," she said. "Both my parents were Mexican, so I'm a purebred."

"What about the other half?"

"I'm not high-strung or high-maintenance. I'm strong-willed, determined. Some have called me feisty."

"And they lived to tell about it?"

She snapped her head up and saw his grin. "You're teasing me, Galahad."

What he was doing was flirting. He couldn't help it. Ruby, being Ruby, was an aphrodisiac he couldn't combat. And he was beginning to like her nickname for him. "Yeah, I am."

She smiled back for a second, her eyes latching onto his. Then his gaze dropped to her perfectly sweet mouth. Suddenly all the things he'd done to that mouth came crashing into his mind. And all the things she'd done to him with that mouth...

"Spirit," she said, "uh, he'll bring in a good sum." She began walking. And now she was back to business and a much safer subject. It was necessary, but Brooks had to say he was disappointed. He walked beside her as they headed into the stable.

"He will?"

"Absolutely, once we find the right buyer."

He squinted to adjust to the darkness inside the furthest reaches of the barn. It was even colder in here than outside.

Ruby grabbed a bucket, a brush and a shoe pick. "Beau's been great about giving me input on who our horses end up with. Especially the stallions. They're in demand, but not everyone is cut out to own one."

"You mean you can tell when someone is all wrong for the horse?"

She handed him the brush and a bucket.

"Pretty much."

"That's a talent I never knew existed."

"It's no different than anything else. You wouldn't buy

a car you didn't feel was the right fit. A mom of three wouldn't do too well in a sports car. The same holds true for a single guy on the dating scene. He isn't going to buy a dependable sedan to impress a girl, now is he?"

Brooks smiled. "I never thought of it that way."

"The horses I train need to go to good homes. They need to fit. Spirit wouldn't do well with a young boy, for instance. He's not going to be someone's first horse. But a seasoned rider, someone who knows animals, will be able to handle him, no problem. Beau has built his business on putting his horses with the right owners. It's a partnership."

Ruby removed her hat and stuck it on a knob on the wall. With a flick of the wrist, she unleashed her mane of dark hair, and it tumbled down her back. It was the little uncensored, unknowing moves that made Ruby so damn appealing. She was pretty without trying and as free a spirit as the horse she'd just trained.

"What?" she asked, catching Brooks staring.

"Nothing." He stepped closer. "No, that's not true," he said. "I'm standing here, looking at you and wondering how the hell I'm going to keep from touching you again."

She got a look in her eyes, one he couldn't read, and bit down on her lip. "We, uh, w-we can't."

But it was what she said with her eyes, and her stutter when she denied him, that gave him hope. "It's hard for you, too. You like me."

"I like a lot of things. But I love Beau. And I don't want to—"

"Ruby." The bucket and brush fell from Brooks's hands and thumped to the ground. She gasped as he approached. He took hold of her arms gently, and her chin tipped up. He gazed into defiant eyes. Was she telling him to back off or daring him to kiss her? There was only one way to find out. "Ruby," he rasped and walked her backward against the wall. There was no way anyone could glimpse them from outside. They were alone but for dozens of horses. "You want this, too," he whispered, and then his mouth touched hers, and the sweetest purr escaped her throat. He deepened the kiss, tasting her again, her warmth, the softness of her lips burning through him.

She threaded her arms around his neck, tugging him forward, making him hot all over. She was a dynamo, a fiery woman who kissed him back with enough passion to set the darn barn on fire. Their bodies melded together, a perfect fit of small to large. They'd made it work one time before, and it had been heaven on earth. He wanted that again. He wanted to touch her and make her cry out. He wanted to strip her naked and watch her body move under his.

One kiss from Ruby had him forgetting all else. It was crazy. It was the middle of the day and they were in his father's stable. But none of that mattered right now. Brooks couldn't stop. He couldn't walk away from Ruby. He grabbed thick locks of her hair, the shiny mass silky in his hands. He gave a tug and gazed down at her, so beautiful, so full of passion. "Is there somewhere we can go?" His voice was rough, needy.

Her eyes closed for a second as she decided, the pause making his heart stop. But then she whispered, "My office behind the tack room. There's a lock."

Relieved, he gave a slight nod of his head and then gripping her bottom, lifted her. Her legs wrapped around his waist, and he carried her to the office. He maneuvered them inside, turned the lock and then lowered her down. As soon as her feet hit the ground, she moved to the window and twisted the lever to close the blinds.

It gave him a second to do a cursory survey of her office. Warm tones, a wood floor, a cluttered desk and a dark leather sofa were all he needed to know about the decor before he turned to Ruby again, taking her back into his arms and claiming her mouth.

It wasn't long before their desperate whimpers and growls filled the room. He stripped Ruby of her vest pretty quickly and then worked the buttons of her blouse. She helped, and then he pushed the layers off her shoulders and undid her lacy black bra. Her breasts spilled out, and he simply looked at her in awe for a few seconds before filling his hands. He flicked his thumbs over both nipples. She sucked in oxygen and squeezed her eyes closed, the pleasure on her face adding fuel to his fire.

As he bent his head and drew her nipple into his mouth, she moaned low and painfully deep. Her hands were in his hair, holding him there, as if he needed the extra encouragement.

"Galahad," she whispered softly.

"Hmm?"

"Get naked."

She was impatient, and maybe he was, too, because if he stopped to analyze this, to really think about what was happening and *where*, rational thoughts would intrude and possibly kill the moment. He couldn't have that. He was too far gone, and so was Ruby. He could tell by the sounds she was making and the desperate look in her eyes.

This was dangerous in so many ways, and yet neither of them could put a halt to what they were doing, so he quickly unfastened all the buttons on his shirt.

And then Ruby's hands were on him, pulling his shirt off and tossing it aside. Her fingertips began grazing his skin, probing his chest as she planted kisses here and there. She reached for the waistband of his jeans and pulled his zipper down. "You're right," he murmured. "You are feisty."

"Determined," she corrected him, and he actually chuckled through the flames burning him to the quick.

"Your turn," he said, dipping into the waistband of her jeans. Within seconds, he had her naked and trembling. He couldn't blame her; he was equally turned on. All the secrecy and danger might have added to it, but it could simply have been Ruby. She was a man's dream. Maybe she could've been *his* dream in a different life.

She was feathery light in his arms as he lifted her and carried her to the sofa. He laid her down and gazed at her for a moment. Her hair, her skin, her body, everything that was Ruby made him shiver and want to please her. He came down next to her, squeezing in beside her on the sofa. He kissed her hard then, crushing his mouth to hers while moving his hand to her sweet spot. She bucked as he began to caress her. "Enjoy this, Ruby. Don't hold back. You understand?"

She nodded eagerly.

And he worked up a sweat pleasing her, using his kisses to muffle her whimpers and moans. And when her final jolt released her ultimate pleasure, he was there with her to press his mouth to hers and swallow her soft cries.

It was a heady thing, satisfying Ruby, but they weren't through yet. He rose up immediately, and she helped him take off the rest of his clothes. He grabbed for the packet he carried in his pocket and sheathed himself before coming up over Ruby. She stretched her arms up, reaching around his neck to pull him down and kiss him again. He was ready, so ready, and when Ruby invited him into her warmth, he joined them together in one breathtaking plunge.

Aw, hell. It was better than he remembered. He stilled, absorbing the feel of her, loving the body that so readily welcomed him.

"Don't hold back, Galahad. You understand?"

Good God, Ruby was something. He kissed her again and again, and as he moved deeper, filling her body, she moved with him, keeping pace, rising and lifting and enjoying.

It happened swiftly, neither one wanting to wait, both desperate to find that place that would unite them on the highest ground. She called out his name, and quickly he muted her with a powerful kiss. Then her hips bowed up, and he propelled her even higher with one final all-consuming push. The rush made her convulse around him, and he couldn't hold back any longer. He came as close to heaven as any mortal man could.

Afterward he lay holding Ruby in his arms. "You all right?"

She nodded, unable to speak.

He kissed her forehead, stroking her arm and grazing his fingers over the peaks of her lush breasts. Then he slid his hand down to her legs. He caressed her there, taking in the smooth, soft skin under his palms, not knowing when he'd have the privilege of doing this again.

He heard the thud of footsteps coming toward the office. Voices filtered in.

Ruby's eyes rounded, and she gasped. "It's Sam and one of the boys," she whispered. "He may be looking for me. I left Spirit in the corral, and the grooming equipment is all over the ground. Damn it."

"Shh. Don't panic. I locked the door."

"But Sam knows I never lock the door when I'm working. If he knocks on the door, I won't be able to look him in the eye. Not with you in here. I've got to go."

She rose and donned her clothes hastily, then wove her fingers through her hair to tame the messy locks. "Get dressed, Brooks. And don't come out of the office until I get them out of here."

"Ruby, it wouldn't be the end of the world if they saw me in your office."

"Are you insane? I'd never be able to pull that off. Sam will know something's up and it's the last thing either of us need right now. Stay until it's safe for you to leave."

She opened the door and was gone.

Leaving him locked in the office, buck naked.

What the hell?

Six

Ruby sat down in front of her flat-screen TV and began eating cold chicken salad. She'd deliberately not gone to dinner at the main house tonight. How could she possibly have faced Brooks across the table, eaten a meal with her family and pretended there was nothing between her and Brooks? She was still at odds with herself for what had happened in her office this afternoon. They'd come very close to being discovered. Sneaking around wasn't in her DNA. She didn't like subterfuge.

But wow. And double wow. When it came to Brooks, she didn't seem to have much resistance. Just a look, a word from him, tied her into knots. She had trouble fending him off and found that most times, she didn't want to. She enjoyed his company a little too much.

A nighttime soap opera played on the screen, a story about oil and country music and cowboys who were too much trouble. She stared at the TV as she forked lettuce into her mouth, trying to concentrate on the story and not the city dude with the deep sky-blue eyes who had turned her simple ranch life upside down lately.

A familiar voice sounded and she blinked. Trace Evans walked into the picture and her spine straightened as she sat up and took notice. Trace was on television?

He had a bit part; he spoke a few words before he disappeared again.

Now, this was news. Trace hadn't told her anything about it. But then, she hadn't spoken with him in ages, except for that one phone call a few days ago. Funny that he didn't mention anything about being on *Homestead Hills*, even if it was only a small role. She continued to watch, finishing her salad and waiting for him to appear again.

He didn't.

A knock at her door made her jump. She clicked off the TV and rose from the sofa. Her mind still on Trace, she walked to the door and looked through the peephole. It was Brooks. Seeing him on her doorstep caused her belly to stir immediately. He always made her forget all about Trace and the heartache he'd put her through.

She opened the door and stared into smiling, deep blue eyes. He held a bunch of flowers in one hand and a lavender box from Cool Springs Confections in the other. "Hello, Ruby."

"Brooks, come inside." She ushered him in before someone spotted him with date night goodies in his arms. She scanned her yard before closing the door, thankful that no one was in sight. She had no business being alone with Brooks, but she wasn't about to throw him out, either.

He stood just inside her cottage and grinned. "You look uptight, Ruby."

If it wasn't for the light in his eyes, she might have

been offended. "Thanks to you. You really shouldn't be here."

"I do a lot of things I shouldn't do. These are for you." He handed her a dozen beautiful white roses and the box of chocolates. "Listen, I'm not courting you. Well, not in the usual sense."

"Not in any sense," she pointed out.

"Still, we've been thrown together and it's been... amazing." He pushed his hand through his blond hair as he struggled for words. "I don't know. I had to come. To give you something nice, something you deserve. The way you had to run out from the office after we made love didn't sit well with me."

"Thank you, Brooks. But you don't owe me anything. As you said, we're not dating. We never could be, and I did what was necessary."

"I've learned never to say never, Ruby." He glanced at her arms loaded with his gifts. "You want to put those flowers in water?"

"Uh, sure. Follow me," she said, leading him into the kitchen. She set the box of candy on the table and then opened a cupboard door. "They really are gorgeous."

"I'm glad you like them."

"I don't remember seeing such perfect white roses this time of year in Cool Springs."

"They're not from Cool Springs. I had them flown in from Chicago."

She craned her head around. "You didn't."

He shrugged and gave her a simple nod. Her heart beat a little bit harder.

"My florist is known for his perfect roses. Cool Springs didn't have anything that comes close."

She kept forgetting he was a zillionaire. He probably did this kind of thing all the time for the women in his

life. Though that might be true, the sweet gesture and
the trouble he'd gone through weren't lost on her. "It's
nice of you, Brooks."

She found a crystal vase, an heirloom from her grandmother, and filled it with water. Arranging the flowers,
she placed the vase in the center of her glass-top kitchen
table. "Here we go."

"It's a nice place you have here," Brooks said.

"It was my father's house, and I've sort of made it
my own."

Once Ruby was old enough to make changes, she had
redecorated the place, adding modern furniture and window treatments that aligned more with who she was.
The cottage wasn't rustic anymore but had a bit of style
and flair. She enjoyed living here when she wasn't at her
apartment in town.

"I can see your personality here," Brooks said.

Why did he always know the right thing to say?

"Then I've succeeded. It was a labor of love decorating the cottage."

Brooks looked down at the box of candy on the table.
"I hear Cool Springs Confections makes a pretty good
chocolate buttercream candy."

"That's what they're known for. Want to try one? I
can make coffee, or—"

"Sure, I'll try one. And coffee would be great."

"Have a seat. I'll get the coffee going."

"Can I do anything?"

"Grab two mugs from the cupboard above the stove."

"Sure thing."

A few minutes later, she poured two cups of coffee
and sat down with Brooks at her kitchen table, realizing
this could be dangerous. Spending time with Brooks always seemed to be, yet he was easy company and some-

one she truly liked. She opened the box and glanced at a dozen luscious candies. "It's going to be hard to choose. Here's a buttercream for you." She pointed it out and he grabbed it.

"I think I'll try the raspberry chocolate," she said.

"Is that your favorite?" he asked.

"It is." She didn't wait for Brooks. She took a big bite and let the soft, creamy raspberry center ooze down her throat. "Oh, yum."

Brooks grinned and then downed his candy in one giant swallow. "Wow, that was good."

"Have another," she said. "I'm going to."

They sipped coffee between bites and managed to polish off half the box of chocolates. Brooks took a last swallow of coffee and then set down his mug. "We're not going to talk about what happened in the stable?"

She replaced the lid on the box, stalling for time, and then finally replied, "No. I don't think so."

"So we just pretend there isn't this *thing* between us."

"We don't have to pretend anything."

"All right," he said, rising and reaching for her hand. "No more pretending we're not hot for each other, Ruby. The truth is, I can't stop thinking about you." He gave her hand a tug, lifting her from her seat. He was deadly handsome, but more than that, he wasn't playing games with her the way Trace had. With Brooks she felt special and cared for, and maybe he was what she needed to get over Trace. She'd protected her heart and would continue to do so, but she had Brooks on the brain lately. She knew he would eventually go back to Chicago. He belonged in the city, and her place was here. Maybe they could keep things light. "I came here only to give you the flowers, Ruby," he said. "I had no ulterior motive."

"Really? I thought you needed a good reason to down half a box of candy."

"That, too." But the truth was in his eyes, and her heart did that thing it did when she was with him. It spun out of control.

She lifted herself on tiptoe and placed a soft kiss on his lips. "You're sweet."

He growled from deep in his throat, a desperate sound that resembled exactly how she was feeling right now, and then his gaze fell to her mouth. His eyes darkening, he backed up a step and put some distance between them. "It really was about the flowers, Ruby. I'd better go." He turned and headed toward the door.

Seeing him retreat put thoughts of the lonely night ahead in her mind. "You don't have to go," she blurted the second he reached for the doorknob. "I mean…you don't have to rush off. I was just going to pop a movie in and kick back. If you care to join me, I have popcorn."

"That was the deal breaker," he said, his lips twitching. "'Cause if you didn't have popcorn, I was out the door."

"Go sit in the living room, Galahad. I'll be right in."

"Thanks—and oh, I like lots of butter."

She rolled her eyes, and he laughed. "Anything else?"

"No, just you and the popcorn make it a perfect night."

Ruby hummed her way into the kitchen and grinned the whole time the kernels were popping.

Ruby sat cross-legged on the sofa next to Brooks, the fireplace giving heat and a warm glow to the room. They'd emptied the popcorn bowl a long while ago, and the movie was ending, but she wasn't ready for him to leave. She was nestled comfortably in the crook of his shoulder, and neither one of them made a move to sepa-

rate when the credits rolled. There was a sense of right-
ness when they were together, which should have scared
her off. She wasn't looking to get her heart broken again.
But it was harder to see him leave than it was to have him
here. She didn't know what to make of that.

"That was good," she said of the classic Western they'd
just watched. "I've seen it half a dozen times, and it never
disappoints." What wasn't to like about horses and range
wars and white hats against black hats? It was clear who
to cheer for, who were the good guys. If only life was
that easy to figure out.

Her body had been in a constant state of high alert
since Brooks entered the house. She'd tried hard to tamp
down her feelings, to treat him as a guest and not the
man who'd turned her inside out. A part of her wanted
him to go, so that they could end whatever they had before he tore her life up in shreds. And another part of her
wanted him to stay. To keep her company throughout the
cold winter night.

She lifted away from Brooks and unfolded her pretzel
position to stretch out her legs.

He planted his feet on the floor, bracing his elbows
on his knees, and turned to her. "Thanks for the movie.
I really liked it. But I think a lot of that had to do with
the company."

She smiled. "Thank you."

"Welcome. Popcorn was good, too. I can't remember
enjoying an evening like this back home."

"You don't go to movies in Chicago?"

He shook his head. "No, not really. I'm usually too
busy. It's not high on my list of priorities."

"I guess Cool Springs is a totally different experience
from what you're used to."

"It is, but not in a bad way. Back home, my phone is

ringing constantly. My life is full of dinner meetings and weekends of work. I don't get to play very often."

"Is that what you're doing here? Playing?"

"If you knew how hard I tried to find Beau, you wouldn't even have to ask. I went to great lengths and sometimes, now that I think back, didn't employ the most honorable means to locate my father. My coming to Look Away is very serious. But I am finding some peace here, and it's quite surprising."

"I meant with me, Brooks."

He reached out to grab her hand, then turned it over in his palm as he contemplated her question. "Not with you, either, Ruby. I don't make a habit of playing games, period."

"You probably don't have to."

"Meaning?"

"Meaning, you're handsome and wealthy and I bet—"

"You'd bet wrong. I'd be the first one to tell you I've been obsessed lately with finding the truth of my parentage. I haven't had a moment for anything else. I haven't dated in months, and I—"

She pressed her fingers against his lips. "Okay, I believe you."

He kissed her fingertips. "Good." He rose then and lifted her to her feet on his way up. "I really should go."

She waited a beat, debating over whether to have him in her bed tonight, to wake with him in the morning. Picturing it was like a dream, but she couldn't do it. She couldn't invite him to stay. The long list of reasons why not infiltrated her mind, making it all very clear.

"I'll walk you out." She tugged on his hand and headed to the door, ignoring the regret in his eyes and willing away her own doubts about letting him go. "Thanks for the candy and flowers, Brooks."

He bent his head and kissed her lightly on the lips. The kiss was over before she knew what was happening. "You're welcome. I had a nice time tonight," he said and walked out the door.

He had had no ulterior motive for showing up here tonight.

Her heart warmed at the thought.

Galahad had been true to his word.

The next morning, Ruby entered the shed attached to the main house. It was nearly as big as the Preston five-car garage. Back in the day, the Preston boys would play in here, pretending to camp out in the dark walled recesses and holding secret meetings. Ruby was never a part of that all-boy thing, but she had her own secrets in this place. The shed was where twelve-year-old Rusty Jenkins had given her her first kiss. It had been an amateur attempt, she realized years later, as the boy's lips were as soft as a baby's and he'd kinda slobbered. But it had thrilled her since Rusty was a boy she'd really liked. And every time she walked in here, those old, very sweet memories flooded her mind.

She lifted the first box she found marked Christmas in red lettering and loaded it into her arms. Ever since Tanya had passed on, Beau enlisted Ruby's help in decorating the entire house, claiming the place needed a woman's touch. And she was happy to do it. It was serious business getting the house ready for the holidays.

When the shed door opened, letting in cool Texas air, she called, "Beau, I'm back here."

"We're coming," Beau said in a nasal voice.

She turned to find not one but two Prestons approach-

ing. She should've known Brooks would be with him.
There was no help for it; Beau was anxious to spend as
much time as he could with his son.

Immediately Beau took the box out of her arms.
"Morning, Ruby."

"Good morning," she said to both of them. But her
gaze lingered on Brooks, dressed in faded blue jeans
and a white T-shirt that hugged his biceps. She looked
away instantly—she couldn't let Beau catch her drool-
ing over his son. Brooks had *hunk* written all over him,
and how well she knew. Every time he entered a room,
her blood pulsed wildly. It usually took a few moments
to calm down. "Brooks is going to help us decorate the
tree, if that's okay with you." Beau barely got the words
out before he began coughing, and his face turned candy
apple red.

"Are you sick, Beau?" she asked.

"Trying to catch a cold is all, Rube."

But he coughed again and again. Brooks grabbed the
box out of his arms.

"Not trying," she said. "You sound terrible. You're
congested, Beau."

"I think so, too, but he insisted on helping decorate
the tree today," Brooks said.

Beau pursed his lips. It was the closest the man came
to pouting. "Is it so wrong to want to put up a tree with
my son for the first time?"

Ruby glanced at Brooks and then gave Beau a sweet
smile. "Not at all, but if you're not feeling well, you
should rest. The Look Away Christmas party is happening this weekend, and Graham and his fiancée will
be here by then. You want to be healthy for that, Beau.
A little rest will do you a world of good. I can manage
the tree."

"I'll help, Ruby," Brooks added, nodding. "Why not take a rest and come down later for dinner?"

Beau turned his head away and coughed a blue streak. "Okay," he managed on a nod. He couldn't argue after that coughing spell. "I guess you two are right. I can't be sick when Graham and Eve get here. Not with her being pregnant and all. That's my first grandbaby." Pride filled his voice.

"Yeah, and I'm gonna be an uncle." Brooks's eyes gleamed, showing Ruby just how much Beau and Brooks looked alike.

"That you are." Then Beau drew out a sigh as if he wanted to do anything but rest on his laurels this morning. "I'll go now. See you both later on."

He walked away, and the sound of his coughing followed him out the door.

Now Ruby was alone in the shed with deadly handsome Brooks. He stared at her, a smile on his face.

"What?" she asked.

"You're a bossy mother hen."

She shook her head. "I already lost one father. Don't want to lose another."

Brooks flinched, and she wished she could take her words back. Brooks hadn't meant anything by his comment. He was teasing; it was what he did, and she shouldn't have lashed out. But the man made her a little jumpy and whole lot of crazy.

"I'm sorry. It's just that my father worked himself into the ground, and I was too young to know enough to stop him. Losing him as a teen was hard. I had no other family, and when Beau took me in and treated me as his own, well…it meant a lot to me. So I'm protective."

Brooks moved a stray hair from her cheek and tucked it back behind her ear. "I get that. I was only teasing."

"I know." She lifted her chin and cracked a small smile.

"Ruby," he said quietly. His eyes softened to a blue glow, his hand moving to the back of her neck to hold her head in place.

There was silent communication between them. She sensed that he understood, and in the silence of the shed, her heart pounded as she stared at him, wishing that he was someone else. Not Beau's son. Not a man who would eventually leave Cool Springs. And her.

"I'm not going to hurt you," he said as if reading her mind. As if he realized the pain she'd experienced losing her mother, her father and a lover who had abandoned her. Her heart was guarded. She'd built up an impenetrable wall of defense against further hurt and pain.

"I can't let you, Brooks."

"I won't. I promise," he said, his gaze dipping to her mouth. She parted her lips and he took her then, in a kiss that was simple and brief and sweet. Moments ticked by as she stared at him, sad regret pulling at her heart. And their fate was sealed. They had come to terms with their attraction and would put a halt to anything leading them astray.

It was quiet in the shed, and cool and dark. Ruby trembled, and that brought her out of her haze. "We should get these boxes into the house. We've got a full day of decorating ahead. Have you seen the tree yet?"

"No, not yet. We should get to it, then."

Brooks got right on it, pulling down two big boxes and loading up his arms while she grabbed one, too. "You know, I haven't decorated for Christmas since I was a kid," he said as they made their way toward the house. "My mom would get this small three-foot tree and put it up on Grandma Gerty's round coffee table. That made it look just as big and tall as the ones we'd see around town. Then Graham and I would put the ornaments on the taller branches, and my little brother, Carson, would decorate the bottom half."

"Did you use tinsel?" she asked, her mood lighter now as she pictured Brooks as a boy.

"My mom always made a popcorn garland. And my grandmother would give us candy canes to stick on the tree."

"My dad and I always used silver tinsel," Ruby said. "It wasn't Christmas until we had the tree covered in it."

"Sounds nice," Brooks said. "I'm sorry Beau isn't going to be decorating with us today. Seems silly now that I'm a grown man, doesn't it?"

"Not at all. You missed out on a lot with Beau. But you know what? I bet before we finish the tree, Beau will come down."

As they entered the massive living room, Brooks took one look at the tree and the ladder beside it and halted his steps, inclining his head. "Wow. Now, that's a tree. Must be a fifteen-footer."

"At least. Every year Beau has the biggest and best Douglas fir delivered to the house. Tanya loved filling up the entire corner of the room with the tree."

They set their boxes down. Brooks scanned the room again and sighed. "It's weird, you know. Having a family here I didn't know about. I'm not complaining. I had a good life. My mother made sure of it. But to think while I was decorating our Christmas tree at home, my father and his family were setting their own Christmas traditions."

"Just think, Brooks. Now you'll have both—a Chicago and a Cool Springs Christmas."

He chuckled. "You're right, Ruby. I guess that's not half-bad."

"No, it's not. Now, here," she said, digging into a box and coming up with a string of large, colorful lights. "Before we can hang any ornaments, we need to make this tree shine. Start at the top and work your way down, Mr. Six-Foot-Two. You've got a lot of catching up to do."

Hours later, Brooks put his arm around Ruby's shoulders as they stepped back from the tree to admire their handiwork. The tree was stunning, the lights in holiday hues casting a soft glimmer over the large formal living room. "It's beautiful," Ruby said quietly.

"It is. We went through six boxes on the tree alone."

"It looks almost perfect," Ruby said, noticing a flaw.

"Almost?"

"Yeah, I see a spot we missed."

"Where?"

She pointed to a bare space toward the top of the tree that had been neglected. "Right there. I'll get it," she said, breaking away from Brooks to grab a beautiful horse ornament, a palomino with a golden mane. "We'll just get this guy up on that branch."

She hugged the side rails of the ladder and began climbing. Making it to the highest rung, she thought was safe and reached out to a branch just as the ladder wobbled beneath her. "Oh!"

"I've got you," Brooks said, steadying the ladder first and then fitting her butt cheeks into his hands from his stance on the floor.

"Brooks." She swatted at his hands. "Stop that."

"What?" He put innocence in his voice. "I'm only keeping you from falling."

"Shh," she said, her entire body reacting to the grip he had on her. They'd worked together all day long in close quarters, and it was hard enough to keep from touching him, from brushing her body against his, from breathing in his intoxicating scent while trying to focus on the task. "Lupe might hear you. Or Beau might come down."

"Lupe went shopping for groceries, remember? And I heard Beau snoring just a second ago. Doesn't seem like he's going to come down anytime soon."

"Smart aleck. You're got it all figured out, don't you?"

"Hell, I wish I did, Ruby."

She ignored the earnest regret she heard in his voice. "I'm coming down. That means you can take your hands off my ass now."

He grinned and then released her. "I'll be right here, waiting."

"Why does that worry me?" she said as she lowered herself slowly down.

He stood at the base of the ladder, and when she turned around, he was there, crowding her with his body, his scent, his blue beautiful eyes. "I think I have a shelf life around you, Ruby," he said in explanation. "A few hours without touching you is all I can manage."

The compliment seared through her system and warmed all the cold spots. "I know what you mean," she said softly. She felt the same way, and it was useless to deny the attraction.

He gave her a bone-melting smile. "Now, that's honest."

"I'm always honest. Or at least, I try to be."

He held her trapped against the ladder, his arms roped around the sides, blocking her in. When he lowered his head, her eyes closed naturally, and she welcomed his kiss.

"Mmm," she hummed against lips that fit perfectly with hers. Lips that gave so much and demanded even more. The connection she had with Brooks was sharp and swift and powerful. They were like twin magnets that clicked together the minute they got close.

He took her head in his hands and dipped her back, deepening the kiss, probing her with his tongue. He swept inside so quickly she gasped, the pleasure startling her and making her pulse race out of control.

He whispered, "Come to my cabin tonight, Ruby."

"I, uh…" A dozen reasons she shouldn't swarmed into her mind. The same reasons she'd tried to heed before, the same reasons that had kept her up nights.

He kissed her again, meshing their bodies hip to hip, groin to groin. There was no mistaking his erection and the blatant desire pulsing between them. She had to come to terms with wanting Brooks. Not for the future, not because of the past, but for now. In the present. Could she live with that?

"Yes," she said, agreeing to another night with him. "I'll come to you," she promised. And once she said it, her shoulders relaxed and her entire body gave way to relief. She'd put up a good fight, but it was time to realize she couldn't fight what was happening between them. She could only go along for the ride and see where it would take her.

"Ruby, you sure you don't want to watch the end of the game with me and Brooks?" Beau asked from his seat at the head of the dinner table. "We can catch the last half. Looks like the Texans might make the playoffs if they win tonight."

His boys had invited them all to catch the game at the C'mon Inn as they usually did once a week, drinking beer and talking smack, but mother hen that she was, Ruby delicately squashed that idea. Beau needed his rest and some alone time with Brooks, since he'd missed out on being with him today.

"No thanks, Beau. I'll just help Lupe straighten up in the kitchen and then head home. You boys enjoy the game. And remember, don't stay up too late. You may be feeling better, but you still need to turn in early."

"Yes, ma'am, I promise," Beau said, giving her a wink.

He seemed much better than he had this morning. He'd coughed only once during dinner, and his voice had lost that nasal tone. She congratulated herself on getting him to rest today. It had done him a world of good.

"Thanks again to both of you for fixing up the house. Looks real pretty."

"You're welcome." Brooks looked as innocent as a schoolboy as he nodded at his father, but his innocence ended there. He'd been eyeballing Ruby all during dinner, making it hard for her to swallow her food. She was eager to be with him again, to have him nestle her close and make her body come apart.

"It was a lot of fun, Dad. Ruby taught me the finer points of decorating a tree."

Ruby wanted to roll her eyes. Everything Brooks said lately seemed to have a double meaning. Or was she just imagining it?

"She's had enough experience," Beau went on. "She took over from Tanya, you know. And I know my wife would approve of the way you both made the house look so festive. The party's on Saturday night, and son, I can't wait to introduce you to my friends."

"I'll look forward to that."

Beau smiled and then was hit by a sudden fit of coughing. Concerned, Ruby put a hand on his shoulder until he simmered down. "S-sorry," he said.

"Don't apologize, Dad. Maybe I should go so you can turn in early."

"Nah, don't go yet. It's just a tickle. I'm fine."

Beau seemed to recover quickly. He didn't want to miss out on watching football with his son. It was sweet of him, and Brooks seemed to understand.

"All right, then," Brooks said.

"I'm making you a cup of tea, Beau," Ruby said. "No arguments. Go have a seat in the great room and finish the game. I'll bring it in to you. Brooks, would you like some tea?"

"I'll just get myself another beer, if you don't mind. I'll meet you in the other room, Dad."

"Okay, sure," Beau said, heading out.

Brooks cocked his mouth in a smile and followed behind Ruby. When she was almost through the kitchen doorway, his hand snaked out and tugged on her forearm. He spun her around to face him squarely. "What?" she asked, her brows gathering.

"Look up."

She didn't have to. The scent of fresh mistletoe filled her nostrils from above, and before she could comment, Brooks was swooping down, giving her a kiss. It was short-lived, but filled with passion—a kiss that had staying power. "Shelf life," he whispered, searching her face with sea-blue eyes.

"You set me up." He'd put up mistletoe in half a dozen rooms in the house.

"Guilty as charged."

She shoved at his chest, but he didn't budge. "Go," she pleaded. "Watch football with your father." Lupe was clearing the dinner dishes from the dining room table and would be back in the kitchen any second.

"Bossy. I love that about you," he whispered over her lips.

Her skin heated at his seductive words. She pointed toward the great room. "Go. Pleeeze."

He saluted her. "Yes, ma'am. See you soon." Then he turned and walked away.

If he wanted to give her a preview of what was in store for her later that evening, he'd succeeded. The kiss had staying power; it had her nerves jumping and her body primed for his touch.

After delivering a steaming mug of chamomile tea to Beau, she bundled up in a warm wool jacket and exited the house. She was halfway home when her phone rang out—Carrie Underwood again, keying her ex-boyfriend's car.

The screen displayed the caller. "Trace," Ruby muttered.

She couldn't talk to him tonight. She let the call go to voice mail.

But curiosity had her putting the phone to her ear to listen to his message. "Hey, baby. It's Trace. I'm missing you like crazy. I'm coming home tomorrow. I need to see you, babe. We need to talk."

He sounded serious. Trace wanted to talk to her? The entire time they'd dated, he'd put her off about matters of the heart. He'd always said he would rather show her how he felt than ramble off meaningless words. And she'd bought that, hook, line and sinker. For a time, his actions had spoken louder than words. He'd been an attentive boyfriend, showing up with thoughtful gifts, taking her to country music concerts, letting her drive his most prized possession, his fully restored 1964 Ford truck. For a while Ruby had felt like the queen of the world. And she'd fallen hard for him, thinking him the perfect man for her—a man born and raised in Texas, a man who understood her love of horses, a man of the earth.

Together they could enjoy life here in Cool Springs.

But then something had happened. It had started out gradually. Trace had become restless. His attention had drifted. He seemed unsatisfied, as if he needed and wanted more out of life. He was systematically yet subtly pushing her away, and it had taken his being gone for months on the rodeo circuit without calling her for her to realize she'd been dumped. She'd spent many nights crying over him. Wondering what had gone wrong. She'd been in love with him. She'd banked her future on him, and she'd been sucker-punched in the gut when she realized they were truly over.

She'd asked herself if he'd been tired of *her*, or if it was his life that needed a big change. She didn't know, but what she did know was that he didn't want her anymore. Maybe he'd never really loved her. She'd wasted a great deal of time on a man who, in the end, didn't want a future with her.

She wouldn't be that gullible again.

So as she entered her cottage, she showered and changed her clothes and set her mind on keeping her feelings for Brooks neutral. He was a city guy, Beau's long-lost son and a man who'd be leaving town after the holidays. She couldn't give herself fully to Brooks, but she could enjoy spending time with him and look forward to the pleasures they could give each other. Once again she asked herself if her attraction to Brooks was real or simply a way to redeem her blistered and battered soul.

Brooks made her feel feminine and special and beautiful.

That was enough for now.

* * *

Shortly after, Ruby parked her car so it was completely hidden from sight behind a feed shed and walked up to Brooks's cabin. She knocked briskly. Her heart was pounding, her mind made up. When Brooks opened the door, she studied the handsome face, the beautiful blue eyes gazing back at her. "My shelf life for you has just expired."

Brooks's eyes flickered, and a growl emanated from his throat.

He took her hand and tugged her inside.

Then slammed the door shut behind them.

Brooks seemed to know. He really seemed to know she didn't need mindless words as he peeled her dress down her arms and over her hips until she was clad only in a pink bra and panties. His groan of approval gave way to him ripping at the buttons of his shirt and yanking it off. Then he lifted her silently, his strong arms under her legs and his mouth covering hers as he moved down the hall. He didn't let up on her lips until they reached the bedroom. His room was bathed in candlelight—a nice touch—and the soft beams delicately caressed the bedsheets.

Instead of lowering her onto the bed, Brooks guided her down his body until her feet met with cool wood floor planks. He reached around and unhooked her bra, then slipped his fingers under the straps, pulling them away and freeing her breasts. He gazed at them for several heartbeats before he hooked her panties with a finger and slid them all the way down her legs. With the slightest move of her feet, she stepped out of them.

It amazed her how much she trusted him. How she allowed him to bear witness to her naked body without worry or shyness. Maybe it was the glow of admiration in his eyes, the way they seemed to touch and warm her at the same time. Her nipples tightened under his scrutiny, and he noticed. "You're cold."

She shook her head no.

She wasn't cold. She was turned on. Ready for whatever Brooks wanted to do.

He walked around her and pressed his body to hers. The length of his manhood rubbed against her backside, and her eyelids lowered ever so slowly. He reached around and cupped her heavy breasts in his hands much like he had her rear end earlier in the day, and then nibbled lustily on the back of her neck. If he was trying to drive her crazy, he was doing a good job. Her body was throbbing now, hot and eager for more.

He wasn't through tormenting her. Next he used his palms to mold her skin from her shoulders down along the very edge of her breasts. He smoothed his hands to the hollow curves of her waist and lower still until his fingertips touched the apex of her thighs, teasing and tempting, bringing her immense pleasure. Instincts had her spreading her legs, welcoming the onslaught, and her breathing escalated. She couldn't think of anything but what he was doing to her. What she wanted him to do to her.

He rubbed against her as he brought her closer still, pressed so tight there was no doubt about his own thick arousal. And then his hand moved to her core, making her gasp and silently plead for more. His fingertips worked the folds of her skin and drew her out with tender but targeted strokes that jolted her body. "Easy now," Brooks whispered as he wrapped his free arm around her waist to steady her while he continued his torment. She was so ready, so primed that it took only a few more infinitely refined strokes to send her sailing over the edge.

She rocked back and shuddered long and hard, the

spasms ridiculously powerful. When they were over, Brooks braced her in his arms, bestowing kisses on her shoulders, her back, and then spun her around and looked deep into her eyes.

Ruby was in too much awe to say a word.

Brooks wasn't much in the mood for talking, either. He whipped off his belt and then removed the rest of his clothes. Her eyes dipped to his beautifully ripped and aroused body, and she fell to her knees before him and gave him the same pleasure he'd given her. He groaned from deep in his chest with utter approval, and it wasn't long before he was reaching for her, lifting her up.

"I need to be inside you," he rasped.

"Lie down, Galahad."

And once he was in position, taking up the length of the bed and wearing protection, she threw her leg over his hips and straddled him. "Ah man, Ruby," he said. "You have no idea how you look right now."

"Like I'm about to ride?"

Even through his heated expression, he chuckled. "You comparing me to a horse?"

"Take it as a compliment," she said as she pressed herself down onto him. A low, guttural sigh emerged from his throat as her body took all of him inside. Then she began a slow, steady climb. Brooks's hands were on her hips, holding on or guiding her—she couldn't tell—and then the pace changed, surging and building to a crescendo that had her crying out.

Brooks, too, was there, grunting and sighing in a mix of pain and pleasure.

The climax hit them hard together, and their cries echoed from the cabin walls.

Ruby fell atop him and he gathered her in, holding her tight, cradling her in his arms.

She was spent, her limbs like jelly.

It was a good thing she had Brooks on the brain tonight.

Tomorrow she would have to deal with Trace.

Seven

Ruby stood at the gates of the Cool Springs Christmas Carnival on the outskirts of town. She used to barrel race at these fairgrounds as a young girl. Ruby smiled at the memories. Oh, how she'd always loved it when the carnival came to town. With her father looking on, she'd put her horse through the paces, leaning and reining and guiding those sharp turns, feeling at one with the animal. She'd brought home a few trophies in her day, but once her papa had passed on, Ruby turned to something she loved even more: training horses. It was his legacy that she now carried on at Look Away.

Strings of twinkling lights crisscrossed the carnival grounds. There were giant holly wreaths as well as red-and-green banners announcing the holiday. The chatter of fun-seeking crowds, children's laughter and shouts from hawkers selling cotton candy and funnel cakes brought it all home. Ruby smiled.

It was here that Trace Evans first kissed her, back behind the shack that now sold hot chocolate and coffee. Her heart warmed despite the brisk December night as she stood there taking it all in.

And then she saw him.

Trace.

Approaching from inside the gates, his smile was as broad and sure as she remembered. His polished snakeskin boots leaving dust behind, the six-foot-tall hunk of man worked his way through the crowd as if all the others surrounding him didn't exist, his deep, dark eyes set only on her.

Just like it used to be.

All the worries she'd been plagued with in coming here vanished the instant she laid eyes on him. Seeing Trace, tall in his Stetson, broad in a black-and-white snap-down plaid shirt and giving her a megawatt smile, flooded her senses, and a shiver of warmth ran down her body. Crap. She was here only to put him off. To tell him they were officially over, so that they could both move on with their lives.

She needed to do this face-to-face.

But his *face* was filled with genuine joy. "Ruby," he said, his voice husky and laced with that down-home drawl. "It's good to see you."

She stood there immobilized as he paid for her ticket and tugged her through the gate. She realized he held her hand, and when she tried to pull away, he drew her up close, bent his head and gave her a quick kiss. "Sorry," he said, dipping his head in that charming way he had. "I've been dreamin' about doing that ever since you agreed to meet me here. Gawd, you look good, Ruby. I've missed you, honey."

"Trace." She put force in her words, ignoring the crazy, mixed-up stirrings in her heart. "I'm here only to—"

"I know, I know. You're not happy with me right now. I get that. How about we enjoy the evening a little before we get all serious? Look over there. Funnel cakes. I'm dying for one. I bet you are, too."

"I, uh…"

"Don't you remember how much we used to crave those things? With all the fixin's, too. Strawberries and whipped cream, the more powdered sugar the better. You game? Come on," he said, taking her hand again. "I'm about to die of starvation."

She rolled her eyes, but a big smile emerged regardless of the company she was in. She was craving a funnel cake, too. They were available only once a year, at this carnival. This was her chance to indulge in a gooey, deep-fried concoction with all the heart-stopping extras. "Okay, sounds good."

"*Delicious* is a better word, sweetheart."

She wasn't his sweetheart and she was ready to tell him, but a few young women and two school-age boys butted into the line, asking Trace for his autograph. He seemed genuinely delighted, giving them each individual attention as he took their names and signed their tickets, flyers, whatever paper article they could produce. Trace had made a name for himself in the field of bull riding. As far as rodeo champions went, he was equivalent to a soap opera star rather than an Academy Award winner, but to the folks around these parts, he was a local hero. Trace ate up all the attention.

"Sorry about that, Ruby," he said, guiding her toward a two-seater café table.

"Do you get that a lot?" she asked, curious now.

"Some," he said, trying for humble, though his grin gave him away. "More and more."

Then his grin faded as his gaze roamed her face, and he sighed from deep in his chest. "I'm sure glad to see you. I've been lonely for you, honey."

"Last I checked, you broke up with me, Trace."

"I never did. Not officially. I, uh, like I told you on the phone, I had to focus on my career, and that meant blocking out everything else."

"That's not exactly comforting, Trace."

She'd felt fully and totally dumped, and there was no way he could salvage what happened between them by using phony excuses.

"Only because being with you was so damn distracting. When we were together, you were all I could ever think about."

He was talking like a man still in love, and if Ruby was that same gullible girl he'd left behind, she might have swallowed that line again. "When you care for someone, you call. You want to know how they're doing. You—"

"I made mistakes. I'm not denying it." He played with his fork but didn't dig into the funnel cake he craved. "But I'm home now, for good."

"What does that mean, for good?"

"It means I'm gonna stay on in Cool Springs."

"You quit the rodeo?"

He smiled sadly. "I think it quit me, Rube. I'm not cut out for the life. I'm never gonna make it big. Not like I wanted. I gave eight years of my life to the rodeo."

"But you love bull riding." He'd been nineteen when he won his first local rodeo, and the entire town had gotten behind him. Some small businesses in the area sponsored him so he could pursue his dream. It seemed strange to her that he would give it up now. Yes, it was a young man's sport, but he still had years left in him.

"I did. I loved it, but it didn't love me back, Ruby. I gave it my all, and I hope I didn't lose you as a result of my pursuit. I just never got where I wanted to go, and I'm done with all of it. So I'll be home now, just like we'd planned. If I'm lucky enough to win you back, I'm staying put right here."

For her equilibrium's sake, she had to ignore the winning-you-back part. This was all too much to take in. She straightened in her seat to keep from showing her total surprise. "So, what will you do?"

He shrugged. "Dad's getting on in years. He wants me to take over the ranch full-time."

It didn't sound like Trace. He'd always had big plans, and none of them included becoming a local rancher. He was Texan through and through, but Ruby had begun to believe his true heart was elsewhere.

"I saw you on television the other night. *Homestead Hills?*"

"Oh, that. Yeah, I did that on a whim. Met some casting guy at the rodeo who said I'd be perfect in the role. I gave it a try, is all."

"A try?" From what she'd heard, people busted their butts and did all sorts of crazy things to win a role in a hit TV series.

"Nothing much came of it," he said dismissively.

"You haven't touched your funnel cake," she said, finally raising her fork and digging in. The airy pastry, all sugared up, got her taste buds going. When she finally swallowed, a burst of deliciousness slid down her throat. "Mmm, it's good. I shouldn't, but I think I'm going to eat every last bite."

Trace smiled, his gaze focused on her mouth for several beats, and suddenly her insides quaked and her belly quivered. Those familiar yearnings returned. She couldn't believe that one year ago, they'd been doing this very thing: eating funnel cakes and talking about their future.

"Soon as I start," he said, lifting his fork and gazing into her eyes, "this here dessert is gonna be history."

True to his word, Trace demolished his funnel cake.

Ruby wound up leaving half of hers behind. Her stomach was tied in knots once everything Trace had said to her finally sank in. She'd been raised to forgive with an open heart. But would she be a fool to do so?

As they rode the Ferris wheel, circling to the highest point, sitting hip to hip, their legs brushing, they took in the nighttime view of all of Cool Springs, the moon and stars appearing close enough to touch. Trace took her hand, entwining their fingers, and gave her a slight squeeze. In that moment, she saw a glimpse of what life with Trace could be like again.

And a few moments later, Trace set his money down at a gaming booth and wasn't satisfied until he hit the bull's-eye target with a dart gun to win her an adorable stuffed reindeer. "Here you go, miss," he said, bowing and presenting her with the toy.

He used to be her hero.

Could he be again?

She was as confused as ever, with the Trace she remembered returning to her and saying all the right things, making her feel like she mattered to him. She was a long way from forgiving him…and then there was Brooks.

A sigh blew from her lips, and Trace turned to her. "What?"

She shook her head. "Nothing. I should go."

"You sure? We haven't gone into Santa's Village yet."

"I'm sure."

Disappointment dimmed the gleam in his eyes. "Okay, I'll walk you to your car."

He took hold of her hand again. She didn't want to make a fuss by pulling free of him, so they walked hand in hand into the parking lot.

Now's your chance. Tell him you're not taking him back. Tell him he hurt you and...

The words didn't come. She couldn't yank them out of her throat. Not when he was being so dang sweet and trying so hard to impress her.

When they reached her car, she hoped to make a quick getaway. Launching into her handbag for her key fob, she moved away from him, breaking their connection. "Good night, Trace. Thanks for the funnel cake," she said, opening the car door.

He glanced at her hand on the door handle and knew enough not to press her tonight. "I'll call you tomorrow."

She should tell him no. There was no point. "Okay."

Before he could say anything more, she slid into the seat and pressed the ignition button.

The car didn't rev right up. In fact, nothing happened. She pressed the button again, giving the engine gas.

Again nothing.

Shoot. Trace walked over. He had a keen sense of cars, and judging by the expression on his face, this couldn't be good. After fiddling with the ignition button, he spent a few minutes under the hood and came up looking bleak. "You want the good news or the bad news?"

"Bad."

"The car's not going anywhere tonight. Not without a tow."

Ruby silently cursed under her breath.

"The good news is, I can give you a lift home."

* * *

Parked in front of her cottage now, Ruby slid across the pristine leather seat, angling for the truck's door handle. "Thanks for the ride, Trace." Her head was spinning from spending time with him tonight. It was almost too much to take in. What they had once was pretty darn remarkable. Being with him tonight at the carnival had brought back memories of the good times they'd shared when Trace had loved her.

Before he'd had second thoughts.

Before he'd turned into a jerk.

"Hold up a sec, Ruby." The urgency in his voice stilled her. He climbed out of his truck and spun around the hood to open the door for her. He offered his hand, and she fitted her palm inside his as she stepped out. Now that they were alone under beautiful moonlight, she waited for the butterflies to attack her stomach, but nothing seemed to happen. No flip-flops. No queasy feeling. No little bursts of excitement.

That was a good thing, right?

As soon as her boots landed on Preston soil, she pulled her hand free, grabbing for her purse, ready to end this night. Earlier, rather than have her wait for a tow, Trace had insisted on taking her home. His good buddy Randy over at Cool Springs Auto promised to tow her car to the shop and take a look at it first thing in the morning. Ruby couldn't argue with that logic. She would've had to do the same thing, and Trace had effortlessly taken care of everything for her.

Ruby had always thought of herself as an independent woman. She could fend for herself, but having Trace take over the reins tonight and deal with her car issues was nice for a change.

"I'll walk you to your door," he said.

She didn't like the prospect of Trace giving her a good-night kiss, one more potent than the one he'd given her at the festival. He'd been her first love, and the splinters of his betrayal were still stabbing her. The pain wasn't as strong as it had once been, but it left behind scars that had yet to heal. She couldn't be a fool twice. "There's no need, Trace." Her door was ten feet away, and having him walk her there implied much more than she was willing to concede right now.

"Okay. But before you go, Ruby, I, uh…"

Brisk night breezes put a chill in her bones as she faced him, her back against the bed of the truck. He stepped closer and removed his hat, hesitating as if searching for the right words. Whatever he had to say had to be important for him to stumble this way. Usually confident, he rubbed at the back of his neck and inhaled from deep in his chest. She'd never seen him quite like this, and she almost wanted to put a hand on his arm to steady him. Almost.

"I wanted to say I'm sorry…deeply sorry for the way I treated you. I should've realized what we had was special, and now that I'm home to stay, I want to make it up to you. I want to start fresh. You and me, we were good together. I want that—"

The sound of footsteps crunching gravel came from the road behind them. She swiveled her head as a figure came out of the shadows and into the ring of moonlight surrounding them.

Trace saw him, too. "Who in hell is that?" he asked none too quietly.

Ruby tried not to react. "Beau's son."

Now that Brooks was upon them, his brows arched as his inquisitive glance went from her to Trace and back again. "Evenin'," he said. He was picking up a Texas drawl, probably from spending time with Beau. She almost chuckled, except seeing her ex-boyfriend meet up with her current lover wasn't a laughing matter.

"Hi, Brooks." There was cheery lightness in her voice worthy of a big Hollywood award.

"Ruby."

"Oh, um, Brooks, I'd like you to meet Trace Evans. Trace, this is one of Beau's twin sons, Brooks. He's visiting here from Chicago, getting to know the family."

Trace sized Brooks up as he put out his hand. "Nice meetin' ya."

"Same here," Brooks said without much enthusiasm as the two pumped hands.

"So, you're one of the lost boys Beau's been searching for. I heard about you. Not from Ruby, though. She didn't say a word about you all night, but word spreads quickly when someone new shows up in Cool Springs."

"I met Trace at the Christmas carnival in town," she was quick to explain. "My car broke down and Trace offered me a lift home."

Trace took a place beside Ruby against the truck. "Yeah, just like old times. Ruby and I go back a ways. Don't know if she told you about us, but I'm back in town now." He gave Brooks a smile. Was he warning Brooks off or simply making conversation? Trace had no reason to suspect anything, not that it mattered anyway. He didn't have a claim on her anymore. "So, how are you liking Cool Springs so far?" he asked.

"I'm liking it just fine." Brooks said the words slowly, giving nothing away by his tone. Yet his gaze shifted to her every so often as if puzzling out what was happening. "I'm beginning to feel right at home here at Look Away."

Ruby edged away from Trace. If he put his arm around her to haul her closer, she'd cringe.

"Must be, if you're out taking a walk this time of night in the cool air."

"I'm used to cold weather. Chicago winters can be brutal. Actually, I wasn't out walking for the sake of walking. I came to ask Ruby a favor. Is all," he added.

Ruby kept her lips buttoned. Brooks playing the country bumpkin was enough to make her laugh. But she didn't dare.

"That so?" Trace asked.

"Yeah."

"Ruby and I were in the middle of a conversation," Trace announced, as if that wasn't obvious.

"Was I interrupting?" A choir boy couldn't have appeared more innocent.

"You were, actually," Trace replied, his chest expanding as he stood a bit taller.

This was not going well, and it was clear Brooks wasn't going to back down.

"Don't let me stop you," Trace said, gesturing with a royal sweep of his arm. "Go ahead and ask Ruby your favor."

"Actually Trace, I'm not up for this conversation tonight," Ruby said. "It's been a long day, and I'm tired. Brooks, can your question wait until tomorrow?"

He glanced at Trace, eyeing him for a second before nodding. "Sure thing. It can wait."

"Okay, then. We'll talk tomorrow. And Trace, thanks again for the lift."

"You're welcome. I enjoyed our date, honey."

It wouldn't do any good denying it was date. Trace had it in his head it was.

Both men stood like statues, refusing to move.

"Well, good night, then." She made her way past Trace and rolled her eyes at Brooks as she brushed by him. His lips twitched in amusement, and for that split second, devilish images of tossing him over her shoulder played out in her head.

She left them both standing there and walked to her door. Curiosity had her turning around briefly to see Trace waiting until Brooks was well on his way before getting into his truck and starting the engine.

Men.

"So what's with your ex showing up?" Brooks wasted no time with pleasantries, yet his tone coming through her cell phone was more curious than accusatory.

"Where are you?" It hadn't been but ten minutes since he'd left her. Cozy in her pajamas and tucked into bed already, she really was unusually tired tonight and…confused. She hadn't expected the man she'd banked all her dreams on once to show up with apologies and promises.

Promises that she'd waited so long to hear.

"I'm at my place. Sitting here wondering what's going on with you. Are you okay?"

"I'm okay. It wasn't really a date, Brooks. Trace wanted to talk to me and apologize, I guess. I agreed to meet him at the Christmas carnival."

"So, are you forgiving him?"

"I don't know what I am at the moment, Brooks."

The line went silent. A moment ticked by, and then a sigh came through. "Is it none of my business?"

Now, that also was unexpected. Brooks had a way of getting to the heart of the matter. "It may be your business, a little, since we've been seeing each other."

She hadn't had to deal with the reality of their relationship until now. But it was evident Brooks had made her no promises and he was bound to leave for Chicago after the holidays, while Trace was offering her something that she'd always wanted. "I want to continue seeing you, Ruby."

"I, uh, I just don't know, Brooks." Could she be blunt and tell him she couldn't afford to get her heart broken again if she gave in to her feelings for him and he left town? Could she tell him that he hadn't offered her the sun, the moon and the stars the way Trace once had? It was silly to think Brooks would. They'd known each other only a couple of weeks. Though things had been humming along very smoothly until Trace showed up. "I can't be pressured right now."

"I don't want to pressure you, Ruby. But this guy's hurt you once, and I wouldn't want to see that happen again. I care about you."

"I care about you, too, Brooks. But we both know…" She hesitated, biting her lip, searching for a way to put it that wouldn't seem callous or crude. The truth was, they were hot for each other. They'd had a chance meeting in a bar—the cliché hook-up—and it would've ended there if Brooks hadn't turned out to be a Preston. Now they couldn't seem to keep their hands off each other.

"What do we know?" he asked.

"We've been thrown together under strange circumstances, wouldn't you say?"

"I suppose. When I first met you, I never once thought you'd be a part of the Preston family. Shoot, it blew my mind when you walked into the barn that day. But I'm not sorry you did. Are you?"

The truth was, no. She wasn't sorry she'd met Brooks. She liked him, and maybe her feelings went much deeper than that, but she wouldn't face them. She couldn't. It wasn't just because he was Beau's son. Or because of all of the secrecy and guilt involved in seeing Brooks. No, she couldn't face deeper feelings because her heart wasn't healed enough to let another man inside. So even though she'd slept with Brooks, readily giving him her body, she'd held a small part of herself back. She couldn't give herself wholly to him, and at this point, he hadn't asked that of her, either. "No, I'm not sorry." Enough said for now on the subject. And because her curiosity was tapped, she asked, "Did you really come by to ask me a favor, or was that a little fib?"

"No fib. Although I'll admit, I wanted to see you tonight." His voice turned husky, and whenever it deepened like that, she melted a little inside.

"Did you want to go out for another ride tomorrow or something?"

"I'd love to. But that's not the favor. The truth is, I've been thinking about my grandfather. I need to make my peace about him, and I've been putting off a visit to his nursing home. I'm not sure I'm ready to go it alone and face him. That man caused my family a lot of grief, and I don't know how I'm going to react. But I need to put it behind me so I can move on."

"Would you like me to go with you, Brooks?"

His relief came in the way of a quick sigh. "Would you?"

"Yes, of course. I'll go with you whenever you want."

"Really? That's great. I'm… I'm thinking I'll arrange an appointment sometime before the holiday party this weekend. I want to—"

"I'll clear my calendar whenever you can arrange it."

"Okay," he said, his voice cracking a little. As if he was barely holding it together, as if this visit to his grandfather had been festering in his mind. "It means a lot." Breath whooshed out of his lungs. "Thank you, Ruby."

"Of course."

Sadness swept through her when she heard the pain

in Brooks's voice. It only served to prove how much she cared about him. If she could do anything to bring him some peace and sense of closure, she was right on it. But it was more than that. She wanted to be by Brooks's side, to give him the support and encouragement he might need to make that visit easier for him.

He was her friend, at the very least.

Eight

Brooks stood shoulder to shoulder with Beau on the steps of the ranch house as a black limo pulled up and parked. His father took a deep breath in anticipation of seeing his other son for the first time. "I'm the better-looking twin," Brooks said, smiling.

Beau's chuckle caught in his throat as Graham stepped out of the car. "My God."

"Yeah, I know." It was the typical reaction people had when they met the Newport twins for the first time. One face on two very different men. "Graham cut his hair a bit shorter than usual just so you could tell us apart."

"That's…smart," Beau said with a catch in his throat. Then he took off straight toward the limo, and Brooks followed.

Graham was reaching inside the limo to help his fiancée out of the car. It had been a while since Brooks had seen Eve Winchester. Because she was Sutton Winchester's daughter, she'd been an immediate adversary, and he hadn't liked her for a time, but Graham was head over heels in love with Eve, and Brooks had finally made his peace with her.

"Welcome, son," Beau said, trying his best to keep his composure. As Brooks sidled up next to him, he spotted tears glistening in his father's eyes. "I've waited a long time to meet you."

"So have I."

The two men embraced, and Brooks gave Eve a smile and a peck on the cheek.

Graham broke away first from the bear hug, taking Eve's hand and gently tugging her forward.

"Beau, I'd like you to meet Eve. My fiancée," Graham said.

Beau embraced Eve carefully. Despite the beige leather jacket and blouse underneath, Eve's baby bump couldn't be missed on her slender, athletic body. "Pleased you meet you, Eve. Welcome to my home, and congratulations on the little one. I couldn't be happier about all of this. My two sons, a new soon-to-be daughter and a grandbaby on the way."

"We're excited about it, too," Graham said, and there were smiles all around.

"I'd appreciate it if both of you called me Dad."

Graham shot Brooks a quick glance as if to say, *Finally. We have a dad.* "I think we'd both like to do that, right Eve?"

Her green eyes glittered. "Yes, of course."

Beau's lips curved up in a wide smile. Then he scratched his head, shifting his gaze from Graham to Brooks. "You two boys are certainly identical. That much can't be denied."

"No, but I've wanted to deny this guy was my brother

a time or two," Graham said, eyes twinkling. It was meant as a joke, but there was some truth there, too. They'd had their differences, especially lately. Graham hadn't exactly approved of the tactics Brooks had used to go after Sutton Winchester.

"Is that so?" Beau asked, puzzled.

"But it's all good now, right Graham?" Brooks was quick to point out.

"Right." His brother had the good grace to nod and agree. Brooks didn't want to dredge up the past, not now, when they'd finally found their family. It was all about the future now.

"Graham, I've gotten a chance to get to know Brooks, and he's told me some about the two of you growing up. I can't wait to get to know more about you and get acquainted with Eve. I have to admit…there was a time when I didn't t-think this day…would e-ever come." Beau choked up.

Graham's eyes watered a little, too. "Well, we're here now for a few days and we'll have lots of time to catch up."

"You'll stay for the holiday?"

"Of course."

"I'm happy to have you here for as long as you want. Let's get out of the weather. Come on inside. I'll show you to your room."

The chauffeur brought the bags in behind his family as they entered the house, but Brooks held back. There was something missing, or rather, *someone*.

He did a quick scan of the grounds, looking for signs of Ruby. Since their conversation two days ago, he hadn't stopped thinking about her or his reaction to seeing her with Trace Evans. Jealousy had surged as strong as he'd ever felt it, making him stop and assess exactly what was going on between him and Ruby. He'd never met a woman quite like her, and the thought of her going back to her ex put an ache in his gut.

His hands were tied right now. Ruby didn't want anyone to find out about their affair, and he couldn't openly date her. But he wanted to. And that surprised him. He'd never let a woman get close to him. He'd dated, but only halfheartedly and without any notion of commitment. He'd been married to his work and, more recently, too obsessed with finding his true parentage to pursue anyone seriously.

In the back of his mind, he'd always thought that if he met the right woman, all things would fall into place. That had never happened.

With Ruby, it wasn't just about sex. He'd figured that out straightaway. It wasn't even that she was forbidden in every sense of the word. Although that had been dangerously exciting. Everything about her seemed to turn him on. Her independence. Her spunk. The way she never gave in or gave up.

But love and romance had taken a backseat in his life lately, and he couldn't trust what he was feeling. He was out of his element here on Look Away and more vulnerable than he'd ever been before. Yet the more comfortable he was becoming on the ranch, the more he could begin to see himself with Ruby Lopez.

That's why he'd picked up the phone yesterday and placed a call to Roman Slater to find out more about Trace Evans. A secret little investigation from his friend, a top-notch PI, seemed in order. Brooks had a feeling Trace wasn't what he seemed. Beau didn't have a good opinion of the guy, either, and the last thing Brooks wanted was for Ruby to get hurt again.

Then his gaze hit upon the beautiful raven-haired Latina approaching the barn some distance away, and just seeing her again sent his pulse racing. Dressed in a black quilted vest, skin-tight jeans and tall riding boots, she was a vision in her work clothes. He couldn't believe how badly he wanted to be there when she met his brother. He wanted to be the one to introduce them.

"Ruby," he called out as he began to take long strides in her direction.

She'd finally spotted him and stopped in her tracks, staring at him from just outside the barn.

"Ruby," he said again, more softly this time, as he finally came face-to-face with her.

"Hi, Brooks." Her almond-shaped eyes widened in a curious stare, waiting for him to speak.

"Hi." He smiled like an idiot. He couldn't even pretend to be cool around her anymore. "Good seeing you."

She nodded but said nothing more. Yet the question in her eyes gave him pause.

"Are you working this afternoon?" he asked.

"Yeah, I was planning on taking Spirit out. Why?"

"My brother's here with his fiancée. They just arrived. I wanted to introduce you."

"Right now?"

He shrugged. He felt like an ass. And Ruby was trying not to look at him as if he'd lost his mind. Beau had invited everyone for dinner tonight to meet Eve and Graham, and as far as Brooks knew, all of the half brothers and Ruby were coming. "Well, yeah. I want you to meet Graham and Eve right now."

Ruby's brows drew together. "It's important to you?"

"It'll take only a minute or two, and yeah, it's important to me." Ruby was becoming *important* to him, more and more. It had taken seeing her with her ex to make him realize it. He was having some heavy-duty trepidation about his relationship with her and where it was going. Or not going. He'd grown up in a small family, without a father figure to look up to and sharing this part of himself with her meant a great deal to him.

Ruby eyed him for a short while, making up her mind, and then nodded. "I can do that."

"Okay, great." He wanted to wrap her up in his arms and kiss her senseless right there on the spot. He wanted to tell her she was more than a fling to him, more than a secret affair. She was beginning to fill up the voids inside him that he hadn't even known were there. But now was not the time to tell her.

"I'll just go to my place and change."

"Change? Good God, Ruby." He took in that shining sheet of black hair, those incredible cocoa eyes, the way her clothes hugged her body. "You don't need to change a thing. You're perfect just the way you are." He put out his hand. "Come with me?"

She flushed pink at his compliment. "Galahad. You do have a way about you."

And when Ruby put her hand in his, a sense of peace settled over him.

The introductions had gone well yesterday and Brooks was glad of it. Who knew Eve and Ruby would hit it off so well? The pretty green-eyed president of Elite Industries, soon to be his new sister-in-law, and Ruby, horse trainer extraordinaire, had talked fashion, country rock music, Cool Springs versus Chicago, and football, of all things. And because Graham and his fiancée were anxious to see some local Texas color, he and Ruby had brought them to the C'mon Inn for drinks tonight.

Now, as the Newport brothers nursed their whiskeys at the very place Brooks first set eyes on Ruby, the girls chatted and filled the corner booth with bright laughter. Both women were beyond pretty. Both were strong-willed and determined and accomplished.

Sitting beside his fiancée, Graham reached for Eve's hand, claiming the woman as his, while Brooks looked on, wishing he could do the same with Ruby. His brother kept his eyes on Ruby and him, and that twin thing happened. Graham had figured out something was up. Brooks would be hearing about it later. Graham wasn't one to keep his thoughts to himself.

The conversation turned to the feud between the Winchesters and the Newports, and Eve was trying to put things as delicately as she could. "So, you see, Brooks had this vendetta against my father and dug up some dirt—that proved not to be true, by the way—and went to the media to reveal the whole sordid scandal."

Ruby's gaze fell solidly on him. "That doesn't sound like Brooks."

"How well do you know my brother?" Graham was teasing, but the comment fell flat.

"I thought I knew him well enough," she answered.

"It's a long story and the bottom line is, we've resolved those differences," Brooks said in his own defense. "Haven't we, Eve?"

The uncertain look in Ruby's eyes was knifing through his gut. What she thought of him mattered, and he didn't want to lose his Galahad status with her. At the time, he'd had good reason to go after Winchester, but that was over and done with, and he'd made his peace with his brother's fiancée.

Eve was cordial enough to agree. "Yes. Thanks to Graham. He took back all the allegations and, well, stole my heart in the process. But I will confess that Brooks thought he was justified in going after my father. For a time, it was thought that my dad, Sutton, could've fathered the twins, since he and their mother had been in love. And Brooks thought Sutton was hiding something."

"As it turned out, Sutton is our younger brother's father," Graham said. "But our mom hid that pregnancy from Sutton and moved on with her life. He only recently found out Carson was his son."

Brooks sipped whiskey. The entire mess that was his life these past few years was coming to light. He wasn't ashamed of his actions—he'd thought he had good reason—but if he had to do it over again, he might've done some things differently.

His obsession with Sutton Winchester was coming to a close. The man was dying, and there'd been enough grief and heartache already over the mistakes and actions of the many people involved. It wasn't just Sutton. Brooks's mother wasn't entirely faultless. Nor was his Grandma Gerty. There was enough blame to go around.

"Well," Graham said. "It all turned out okay since I now have Eve and a baby on the way. So something wonderful came of all of it."

Brooks raised his glass. "I'll drink to that."

Graham brought his tumbler up, and the women raised their iced tea glasses.

"To family," Brooks said, staring into Ruby's eyes.

"To family," they all parroted, and then clinked glasses and sipped their drinks.

"Ruby, would you like something stronger?" Brooks asked.

"No thanks. I think I'll lay off tonight. I ate too much of Lupe's tamale pie at dinner."

"Gosh, me, too. It was delicious," Graham said, patting his stomach. "I hear you're a pretty good pool player, Ruby."

"She's a hustler," Brooks said, grinning.

"Is that right? Eve's pretty good, too."

The women exchanged glances.

"Want to?" Ruby asked.

"Sounds like fun," Eve replied.

"This I gotta see." Graham rose from his seat to let Eve scoot out.

Brooks did the same, and Ruby's exotic flowery scent wafted to his nose as she brushed by him. His lust had to give way to decorum. He and Ruby were in a stand-off right now, and he doubted she'd be inviting him into her bed anytime soon.

The women headed to the pool table at the back of the room, secured pool sticks and cued up as Brooks and his brother leaned against the far wall. "Go easy on her, Ruby," Brooks called. "She's a guest in Cool Springs."

"Go easy, nothing," Eve countered, the fierceness in her eyes indicating she was ready for battle. "Don't hold back, Ruby. I can handle it."

Graham chuckled and said quietly, "She can. She's pretty amazing."

"It's good to see you happy, bro."

"Yeah, I am. I managed not to blow it with Eve. Thank God for that. And meeting Beau was pretty great, too. I wasn't sure about any of this, coming here to Texas and being brought into a whole new family. But Beau's made it real easy. He's a good man, and there was no awkward-ness between us."

"Because I paved the way," Brooks said, giving his brother grief. "As usual."

"Smart-ass. So what's with you and Ruby? And don't tell me nothing's going on. I can practically see the steam rising between the two of you from across the booth. Have you fallen for her?"

Brooks drew oxygen into his lungs and kept his voice low. The women were preoccupied; Eve was about to make the first shot. "I'm in the process, I think." What the hell kind of answer was that? He was in the process of falling for her? While trying to keep things light with Ruby, it had gotten hot and heavy real fast. "It's complicated."

"I hear you. Couldn't be more complicated than me falling for Winchester's daughter, now, could it?"

"I don't know about that. Ruby's like a daughter to Beau, and if I hurt her, there'll be hell to pay. Not exactly the impression I want to make on our father."

"Hell, man. Make it a priority not to hurt her, then."

Brooks stared at his brother, letting his words sink in. Was it that easy? Did he want Ruby? He darted a glance at her. She was taking aim, her hot body stretched across the pool table, her eyes laser-focused, her kissable mouth pursed tight as she drew back the stick and *clack*, the cue ball sailed across the table and hit its mark. The striped ball dropped into the side pocket.

Hell yeah, he wanted Ruby. From the moment he'd first laid eyes on her right here at the C'mon Inn, he'd been drawn to her. She had substance and class and a sassy mouth that made him smile, even when that sass was aimed at him. He admired her passion and knowledge of horses and her open method of teaching that came straight from the heart. He couldn't imagine not seeing her day in and day out. Not speaking to her and not laughing with her. Up until this moment, he hadn't thought about the time when he'd have to go back to Chicago for good.

He'd never been really serious about a woman before. For one, he'd been preoccupied with work, striving for and finally attaining the financial independence he'd craved ever since the more humble days of his youth. He'd worked hard building the Newport Corporation and didn't have time to play much. As a result, women had come and gone in his life. Rightfully so. He hadn't been ready for a strong commitment. He had only so much to give, and getting serious with the opposite sex had taken a backseat to all else. More recently, he'd been too caught up in meeting his father after years of searching to let his mind go anywhere else. But now that he was faced with the possibility of losing Ruby to her ex-boyfriend, he had to make a stand.

Sooner rather than later.

But first, there was something he had to do.

And he wanted Ruby by his side.

Hutchinson's Nursing Home, twenty miles outside Cool Springs, sat nestled inside brick walls and a set of wrought iron gates. The grounds were groomed carefully. Right now, the cold Texas weather prevented any flowers from blooming in the beds next to the long, sweeping veranda, but Ruby could picture them thriving there in the spring, their color cheering up the dementia patients who would sit in patio chairs outside to get a little air.

Brooks rested his arms on the steering wheel, staring at the large mansion-like brick home with its pretty white shutters. He sighed. "This is it."

It wasn't going to be a loving homecoming, this much Ruby knew. But she understood his need to come here for closure, while his brother Graham had no desire to meet his grandfather. The twins may have looked exactly alike, but they were two very different men in the way they dealt with life.

Ruby reached for Brooks's hand and squeezed. "We

can make this quick," she said. "And I'll be with you every step of the way."

"Thanks." Brooks rubbed the back of his neck and gave her a solemn look. "I don't think I could do this without you." His blue eyes melted her heart. She felt honored and a little awed that Brooks had counted on her so much. That he needed her.

It was one thing to be wanted.

But to be needed by such a strong man was something else entirely.

"I'm here, Brooks. Let's go meet your grandfather."

Once they were inside a few minutes later, a nurse escorted them to the visitors' room, where they were told to stand just inside the doorway. The woman walked over to a man with a shock of pearl-gray hair seated by a window and spoke a few words to him. He barely acknowledged her, but he turned his head slightly to the door, his expression blank but for a sliver of light entering his eyes.

Ruby felt Brooks freeze up, his body stiffening. He closed his eyes, and she tightened her hold on his hand. "It's going to be okay," she whispered.

"Yeah," he said quietly, but he hesitated.

The nurse waved them over and placed two chairs by the window to face the old man, who was slumped over in his seat.

"Ready?" Ruby asked.

Brooks nodded. She was by his side as they walked over and sat down.

"Hello," Ruby said first. "I'm Ruby."

"You're a pretty thing," the old man said in a childlike voice. "I don't know you, do I?"

Ruby shook her head. "No."

He blinked and seemed to stare straight through her.

The nurse put her hand on Bill Turner's shoulder. "Mr. Turner, this is your grandson, Brooks."

"My grandson?" Bill stared blankly at Brooks. "I don't have a grandson."

"You have two grandsons," Brooks said. "Twins. I have a brother named Graham."

As the nurse walked off, the man began shaking his head.

"They are your daughter Mary Jo's children," Ruby offered.

At the mention of Mary Jo, Bill Turner's eyes switched on. "My daughter? She sits by the fireplace and reads. She likes to read. Quiet little girl. Where is Mary Jo? Is she coming?"

"No, she's not coming today," Brooks said, moisture pooling in his eyes.

Ruby ached inside as she watched Brooks swipe at his tears.

"Maybe she'll come another day," the old man said. "I would like to see her."

"Maybe she will," Ruby said. "How do you like it here, Mr. Turner?"

He shrugged. "I guess I like it fine."

"The people seem nice."

"Where's Mary Jo?" He looked toward the doorway. "She likes to read. Her nose is always in a book. She's a smart girl."

"She is a smart girl," Brooks managed to answer. "And s-she loves to read."

"Do I know you?" Bill Turner's brows gathered. The wrinkles and blankness on his face hid the handsome man he'd once been. "I don't think I know you."

"No," Brooks said, his gaze turning Ruby's way, hopelessness in his expression. He tried again. "You don't know me. But I'm your grandson. Mary Jo was my mother. You are my grandfather."

He shot Brooks another blank stare. "I'm your grandfather?"

Brooks nodded. "Yes."

Bill Turner looked out the window, focusing on a bird hopping on the ground beside a mesquite tree just a few yards away.

"Mr. Turner?" Ruby put her hand on his arm.

He swiveled his head slowly back to them. "I used to build things, you know. I built my own house. This is not my house. I didn't build this."

"No, but it's your home now, Mr. Turner," Ruby said quietly.

"Yes. It's my home now." The light in his eyes dimmed. Then he popped his head up, in search of the nurse. "I think it's time for lunch."

Brooks stared at him for several heartbeats, then sighed and rose from the chair. Ruby witnessed a depth of sadness and pain in his eyes she'd never seen before. "We have to go now, Mr. Turner," he said, taking Ruby's hand again. "Have a good lunch."

They exited without saying another word, and Brooks stopped as they reached his parked car. "It's so damn unfair."

"What?" Her stomach churned. She could guess what Brooks was about to say.

"He's like a child. He doesn't remember his abuse. He doesn't remember hurting his family. He's blacked out the bad times."

"You're angry," Ruby said.

"I'm…yeah, I guess I'm pretty pissed. I wanted to meet the son of a bitch and lay into him about my mother. Someone needed to defend her and look out for her.

Someone had to stand up to him. Even though I'm years late, I had it in my head I'd come here and tell the old guy off." He fisted his hands. "But he's in a world of his own. Nothing I'd say to him would sink in."

"Probably not, Brooks. That's the sad thing about dementia. He's trapped in his own head," Ruby said.

Brooks dropped his gaze to the ground, shaking his head.

Ruby stepped closer and stared into his handsome face, which was tightly lined in raw pain. He was fighting to keep the tears away. "It's okay to feel all the things you're feeling. Coming here will give you closure, trust me. It will. When you get back home and think about this, you'll feel better. You'll begin to feel whole again."

Brooks slowly wrapped his arms around her waist and drew her closer. She laid her head on his chest. His heart was beating so fast she placed her hand there to calm him, to give him the balm he needed right now. Nestled in his embrace, she waited for the beats to slow to a normal pace.

"How come you know me so well, Ruby?" He brushed the top of her head with a kiss.

"I just do, I guess."

He tightened his hold, locking her against his body as they swayed ever so slightly together to the music. Electricity sizzled. It always did when they were this close. "You feel so damn good in my arms."

"Humph."

"I didn't mean it that way."

"I know how you meant it, Brooks." He welcomed her comfort. He needed her here, and she wouldn't want it any other way. "I'm just giving you jazz."

"Because that's what you do."

"Yeah, that's what I do."

"Don't ever stop doing that," he whispered into her ear.

Something fierce and protective crackled and snapped inside her. And in that moment, Ruby knew she never wanted to stop giving him *anything*. She'd fallen in love with him. She loved him so much, she wanted to take away his pain, absorb it and tuck it away in some deep, dark place, never to return. She loved Brooks Newport.

But did she still love Trace, too?

Right now, in Brooks's arms, she was giving him all he needed. She wouldn't think about the future and the fact that Brooks would be leaving after the holidays.

He had a home in Chicago.

A thriving business there.

And none of it included her.

The next day, Ruby licked around her cone of dark chocolate fudge ice cream, enjoying every second of her indulgence. Sitting beside her at the Fudge You Ice Cream Factory, Eve was doing the same, digging into her chocolate cone, and Serena, who was happy to join them today, sat across the booth, devouring a dish of French vanilla scoops topped with caramel sauce.

"Yum," Eve said, crunching down on the sugar cone. "I can't remember the last time I had ice cream."

"You don't crave ice cream?" Serena asked. "Isn't that the go-to craving when you're pregnant?"

"That's what I hear. But for me it's more potato chips and dip. Give me salt and I'm happy. But I'd never turn down good ice cream. If I don't watch it, I'll be floating away like a balloon soon."

"Eve, you look fantastic. You don't have to watch anything," Ruby said, hiding the fact that it was her craving for ice cream and not Eve's that had brought them here today.

Eve chuckled. "Thanks for that. The ice cream is amazing. And so is the company." Eve smiled at both of them.

"It's your reward for beating me at pool," Ruby added. "I told you if you won, I'd have something fun in store for you." Fun and indulgent. Ruby needed that, too, now more than ever. Coming here with Eve and Serena was much better than suffering alone at her cottage and digging into a pint or two of decadent ice cream in front of the television set, pining over the state of her love life.

How could one man make her so happy and so sad at the same time?

Brooks had been hurting yesterday and it was only natural for her to comfort him, to allow him time to grieve over his grandfather…because that's exactly what he had done. He'd met Bill Turner for the first time and said farewell to the old man, probably never to see him again, all in one afternoon. The ordeal had shaken Brooks, and seeing him that way had sent her own wobbly emotions out of whack.

"Actually, it's really sweet of you to entertain me today while Graham and Brooks are out riding with Beau," Eve said. "Graham couldn't wait to ride on one of his dad's Thoroughbreds."

Ruby turned her attention back to the girls. "Are you kidding? My stomach is doing somersaults right now. It's been too long since I've had Fudge You ice cream. I'm happy to do it."

"This does beat eating lunch," Serena said. "I'm glad I'm on winter break right now so I could join you."

"Serena is the new principal of Cool Springs High School," Ruby explained to Eve. "The kids love her over there. She's made going to the principal's office a cool thing."

"Oh, really? How so?" Eve asked, her brows lifting as she turned to Serena.

"Well, there are still times it sucks getting summoned to the principal's office," Serena said, "but now, if students do something remarkable like helping a fellow student out of a jam or achieving higher grades than expected because of hard work, I reward them."

"She takes them to lunch," Ruby said, "or lets them skip gym for a week, or gives them a season pass to the football games."

"Among other things," Serena said. "It gives the kids an incentive to do well. They seem to like it."

"They sure do," Ruby said, praising her friend. "And they like Serena a whole helluva lot more than we cared for Mr. Hale, our principal back in the day. That man never cracked a smile."

"I like your creative approach," Eve said. "I can see why the kids adore you."

Ruby gobbled up her cone before the girls were halfway through theirs. She gazed longingly at the mounds of ice cream under the glass case, wishing she could have another cone or maybe a sundae with whipped cream and cherries on top. What was wrong with her? Even with the Trace-and-Brooks-induced stomachache she'd had lately, her appetite was voracious.

Too soon, all the cones were history, and Serena was rising from her seat. "Sorry to dash out, but I've got an errand list a mile long for this afternoon. It was nice meeting you, Eve. I hope to see you again."

"Same here, Serena," Eve said. "I'm glad you joined us."

"Serena's coming to Look Away for our Christmas party, so you'll see her again," Ruby said.

"That's great," Eve said. "Well then, I'll see you in a few days."

"I'm looking forward to it. Bye girls." Serena exited the shop.

"She's nice," Eve said. "You've been friends a long time?"

"We have. Serena's like a sister to me."

"And Beau's like a father."

"He is. He's a good man. I'm fortunate to have the Prestons. We're pretty tight."

Eve sipped water and smiled. "I can see that. It's really refreshing. My family…well, we've had our differences. But my sisters and I are close. You know, in a sense, you and I will be sisters, too. In-laws, but sisters."

"Yeah, I'm happy about that."

"So am I," Eve said. And then, suddenly she gripped her belly, and the blood drained from her face. "Oh."

"What's wrong?" Ruby rose halfway out of her seat.

Eve waved her off. "Nothing. Just a bout of queasiness. I get that sometimes. But I'm… I'm okay."

Ruby sat down, relieved.

Seconds ticked by before the color returned to Eve's face. "Pregnancy sometimes knocks you for a loop, you know."

Ruby didn't know. None of her friends had children yet, so she didn't have any firsthand knowledge of the subject. She knew how mares gave birth and had pulled foals on the ranch under the supervision of her father, but the whole human pregnancy thing was new to her. "How do you mean?"

"Well, first off, you get all these weird sensations. In the beginning, you're hungry all the time and feel like you can't get enough food in you. One day, and I'm ashamed to admit this, I consumed two omelets for breakfast and a thick foot-long sandwich for lunch, and I still had room for a barbeque chicken dinner with chocolate cake for dessert. I inhaled food in those early weeks. I couldn't believe it."

"Eating for two?"

"More like an army," Eve said, her eyes twinkling. "But that's passed. Now I'm sensitive all over." She pointed to her chest. "I'm full and tender here all the time."

Ruby froze up, holding her breath tight in her throat. The only thing moving were her eyes. And they were blinking rapidly. She'd been feeling those very sensations lately, too. If she put her bra on too hastily, her nipples would tingle and actually hurt. The pain was foreign to her, and it would take a while before it disappeared. She hadn't thought much of it, but now, as she took another glance at the mountain of ice cream sitting in the refrigerator case, her stomach grumbled. She was still hungry. She could do major damage to those big cartons. Chocolate. Strawberry. Vanilla. And every other flavor.

Good God. Had she missed her period this month?

"Ruby?"

She tried to calculate back in her mind.

"Ruby, you're turning green right before my eyes. Are you okay?"

Ruby stopped blinking and focused on what Eve was saying. She forced herself to recover from the shock and shoved her doubts to the back of her mind. "I'm fine. Um, are you ready to see the best Cool Springs has to offer by way of shopping? It's no Rodeo Drive, but there's a shopping district that has some pretty neat boutiques."

Eve's brows knit together as she subtly scrutinized her, making Ruby wonder if she'd actually fooled her. "Sure, I'd love to. We can walk off the ice cream calories." Eve reached across the table to touch her hand. "Thanks for making me feel welcome in Cool Springs. I think of us as friends already." There was a flicker in Eve's eyes that said she was willing to listen if Ruby needed to talk.

"I feel the same way," she replied genuinely.

Astute as Eve was, Ruby suspected she had already guessed about her involvement with Brooks. But admitting it would make it all too real, and there would be questions she couldn't answer. And feelings she'd have to face. About Trace. About Brooks. And the wrinkle that she might be carrying a child even though she'd been very careful, was all too much for her right now.

It was better to put her head in the sand and let the world keep on turning for a while.

Nine

Brooks gave the living area of his cabin a final once-over. Dozens of roses he'd had flown in from his hometown were arranged in vases and glass bowls all around the room. Their unequalled beauty and sweet scent reminded him of the woman who had stolen his heart. He had pillar candles ready to flicker at the strike of a match. Ideally tonight, after the Christmas party, he would finally show Ruby how much he cared about her.

It had been days since he'd touched her, days since he'd held her in his arms and kissed the daylights out of her. He totally understood that Ruby was torn in two by the return of her ex. She'd banked her future on Trace Evans and had envisioned a life with him. And Trace had failed her. The guy wasn't good enough to shine Ruby's boots, and tonight was Brooks's chance to win her over. To show her that they needed more time together, that what they'd started at the C'mon Inn was worth pursuing.

In just a few hours, he'd be face-to-face with her, and he wouldn't let up until Ruby was his.

A knock at his door shook him out of his own head. It was his brother Graham.

"Hey."

"Hey. Thanks for showing up on time."

"My brother calls and I come."

Graham stepped inside the cabin, immediately took in the romantic setting, lifted his nose in the air and grinned. "Smells like a funeral home in here."

Oh man, Graham was such a pain sometimes. "Don't make me sorry I let you in here."

"You're doing this for Ruby?" Graham walked farther into the room.

"Yep. You know I don't like to lose. And Ruby is worth winning."

Graham eyed him carefully. "Just don't blow it, Brooks. Seems weird saying this, but she's family now. And you'd have the entire Preston house come down on you if Ruby gets hurt."

"I don't intend to hurt her," Brooks said, hearing the commitment in his voice.

"Man, you're really hooked, aren't you? I mean, you two are polar opposites."

"Let me worry about that. And we're not that different when it comes right down to it."

"Hey, I have my hands full with wedding plans and the baby coming. I'm not going to say another word, except you deserve to be happy." He looked over the place again. "Nice touch with the candles. Ruby will love what you've done. I hope it works out."

The sincerity in Graham's voice made up for his crap from earlier. "I appreciate that."

"So, what's up?"

"I've been thinking."

"About Bill Turner? I do plan to see him one day, but after what you told me, apparently there's no rush. He won't know who I am, right?"

"Probably not, but if you need to see him, to meet with him, I wouldn't stop you. Ruby said..." Brooks paused. Everything Ruby had told him was true. She'd gotten him through a tough day, and that was only one of the reasons he was crazy about her.

"What did Ruby say?" Graham asked.

"A lot, and I'll tell you later, but first I want to run something by you. I think I'm ready."

"Ready?" His brother gestured to the decked-out room. "Obviously, if you've gone to so much trouble for Ruby—"

"I'm talking about my vendetta against Winchester. I think I'm through, Graham. Once and for all. I wanted to get your opinion. I want to make peace."

His brother's brows shot up. "Really?"

"Yeah. It's time. Being here at Look Away has cleared my head some. I'm not the same man I once was. Vengeance can be taken only so far before it destroys you. Coming here made me see that I want to look to the future and not bury myself in the past. What's done is done."

"I like what I'm hearing, Brooks. And Eve will be grateful if you could put the past behind you. She's come here to support me in meeting my father while her own father is very ill. Sutton isn't long for this earth. Eve, Nora and Grace are struggling with all of it. I mean, say what you might about the man, but he is their father, and he's dying."

Brooks drew breath in his lungs. He'd had a long-running feud with Sutton Winchester and had come to learn the man hadn't been guilty of many of the things Brooks had once believed. Winchester's biggest crime had been to love his mother, Cynthia, so much that he hadn't revealed her secrets. In a way, that had been honorable. Though it had caused the Newport sisters a lot of grief, Brooks's anger had softened recently. "Yeah, I know."

"I've already put the past behind me, for Eve's sake and for the sake of our baby. It's no good clinging to a grudge. I'm a happier man for it and I think you would be, too." Graham slapped him on the back. "You've got my full support."

"Wonderful. I'll make that happen soon. Now get out of here. I've got to get ready to sweep Ruby off her feet tonight."

Shortly after his conversation with his brother, Brooks got dressed in a Western tux, a bolo tie and a black Stetson. He took a final look at himself in the mirror. This was it. He would make his stand for Ruby's affection tonight and, he hoped, make this Christmas holiday one of the best ever for both of them.

Any doubts warring in his head were quickly replaced with positive thoughts as he exited his cabin and approached the Preston home. Surrounding oak, cottonwood and white birch trees glimmered with thousands of lights. The path leading up to the house sparkled from the ground up, and an array of colorful twinkling lights outlined the beautiful home's architecture.

Peace settled in his heart.

A part of him had always known there was something more for him than city life. A part of him had always known something was missing. Now, as he gazed at this home in all its magnificent yet simple splendor, a sense of true belonging nestled deep down in his bones.

Beau greeted him at the door with a big papa bear

hug. The man was not ashamed of wearing his emotions on his sleeve, and Brooks hugged him back with the same enthusiasm. "Welcome, son. The party's just getting started." Beau smiled wide, his eyes bright. "My dream of having my whole family under one roof is the best gift I could ever receive."

Brooks got that all too well. Except for Carson, everyone who mattered most to him now was right here at Look Away.

"Let me introduce you and Graham to some of my closest friends."

Brooks followed his father into the house. But as he began shaking many hands and making small talk with Beau's neighbors and friends, he kept one eye on the front door.

And then she walked in.

Ruby.

He swallowed a quick breath. And then excused himself from a conversation that couldn't compete with the stunning creature removing her coat at the front door. She wore her hair partly up in a sweep secured with rhinestones, the rest of her raven tresses flowing down her back. The dress she wore was ruby red, the color perfect for the holidays and perfect on her. The dress exposed her olive skin, dipping into a heart shape in the front that cradled her full breasts.

His heart beat wildly at the vision she made. And suddenly, his legs were moving and his focus was solely on her. He couldn't seem to get to her fast enough as he strode the distance to put him face-to-face with the Ruby of his fantasies.

"Ruby, you look incredible." He hadn't seen her since he'd visited his grandfather. "That dress on you...is a knockout."

"Thank you." She gave him a smile. "You do a pretty good version of a cowboy for a city dude."

"I tried."

"I love the tie on you." She gave it a sharp tug. "And the hat."

He removed it immediately. "Uh, sorry. I, uh…" Why was he tongue-tied?

"It's cool, Brooks." She took the hat from his hand and set it back on his head. "I like the look. Don't take it off on my account."

He ran his hands down his face. Tonight any guests with eyes in their heads would figure out that Brooks had it bad for Ruby, and he wasn't about to hold back. No more pretending. No more hiding out. He was ready to make his claim on her. "Come with me for a second?"

"Sure, but where are we going?"

"You'll see." He took her hand and tugged her through the festively decorated rooms until they reached the kitchen doorway, out of sight to all but a half-dozen caterers. Her knowing eyes glittered. "Look up."

Mistletoe again, and this time she understood exactly where she was and what he was about to do.

He brought his mouth to hers. From the moment their lips met he was a goner, lost in the taste and pleasure and sweetness of her. It was too hot, too amazing to let up. He'd waited for her, craved her and now she was in his arms and he didn't give a good goddamn who saw them or what they thought about it. He was consumed by Ruby. She was his anchor. He'd never had feelings this strong or powerful. The little throaty sounds she was making turned him inside out. She wasn't immune to him. They worked. And he had to make her see that.

"Ruby," he murmured near her ear, the desperation coming through clearly in his voice. "I miss you like hell."

She lifted up on tiptoe and whispered, "If you're talking about making love, I miss you, too."

"Oh, yeah, I am," he said, but he was talking about much more. And he had to bide his time until the end of the evening to show her just how he felt about her. "For starters."

"Starters? Sounds promising, Galahad." Her breath fanned over the side of his face, making his nerves go raw. This woman was a tease, but he didn't mind as long as her teasing was aimed his way. At least she wasn't refusing him. Had she made up her mind about Trace?

"Come back to the cabin with me. We can leave the party right now."

Ruby set a hand on his chest and tilted her head to look into his eyes. "No, we can't. Beau has waited too long to have you here with him."

She had a penchant for being rational and right, and if Brooks wasn't so damn head over heels for her, that would have annoyed the life out of him.

"Just enjoy the party, Brooks."

"As long as you're by my side, I can do that." God, the truth in that was powerful.

"That's where I want to be, too," she whispered.

Brooks breathed a sigh of relief. He had to be respectful of his father and his new family. Wisely, Ruby had put him in his place. He was glad of it, but it was torture just the same.

Christmas music with a country twang streamed into the house, and it seemed everyone was beginning to make their way to the backyard to listen.

"It's a local country band," Ruby offered. "They're pretty good. Beau's hired them for the night."

"Yeah, he told me about them. TLC or something?"

"It stands for Tender Loving Country," she said.

"There's a dance floor set up. Will you dance with me?" He offered her his hand.

"Of course."

And they walked outside hand in hand and danced under the electric warmth of strategically placed heaters. The night was cool, but thankfully devoid of Texas breezes that could make your hair stand on end. Brooks didn't need the artificial heat blasting from the heaters, though; he was already revved up enough inside just holding Ruby in his arms.

"They *are* pretty good," he whispered, nuzzling her hair. She smelled of something tropical and exotic. He brought her as close as he possibly dared. He didn't want to make her uncomfortable—he'd gotten her message loud and clear—so he'd bide his time until he could get her alone in his cabin.

Where he would lay his heart on the line.

They danced every dance until the band took a break, and then Brooks led her off the dance floor. She began fanning herself. "That was fun, but I'm afraid I've got to go...*powder my nose*."

Brooks chuckled. Ruby was something. He was about to suggest escorting her, but she was snatched away immediately by Eve and Serena. What was it about women going to the john in groups? He'd never understand that.

Toby walked up and caught him red-handed staring at Ruby's shapely ass. "So, you've got the hots for Ruby, huh?"

Brooks gave his half brother a sideways glance, unsure how to answer that.

"It's okay. We get it."

"We?" Brooks turned to face him.

"My brothers and me. We've all had a crush on her at one point or another in our lives, but Dad put a halt to any of that. Let's just say he didn't nip it in the bud—he slashed it to the ground until it was crushed to a pulp. But that was years ago, when we were teens."

Brooks swallowed hard. "That so?"

"Yeah, she's just our little sis now."

"Beau's plenty protective," Brooks said, his voice trailing off as he stated the obvious. He felt an ache in the pit of his stomach.

Toby noticed his change in demeanor and must've taken pity on him. "Actually, when Dad was out here watching the two of you dancing, he was smiling. Maybe he doesn't think it's so bad, you and Ruby. I'd say go for it."

Clay walked up, looking distracted as his gaze scoured the guests milling about. "Have you guys seen Ruby?"

"Who wants to know?" Toby asked.

"Trace Evans is outside the house. He's pretty liquored up, and he's asking to see her."

Brooks blinked. "He's crashing the party?"

Clay shrugged. "I suppose. He wasn't invited."

Now the back of Brooks's hair really did stand on end. He didn't want the guy within fifty feet of Ruby, much less snatching her away from the Christmas party in a drunken state. "I'll take care of it."

Toby gave Clay a crooked smile. "He's a Preston, all right."

It was a compliment Brooks appreciated. "Tell Ruby I'll be back soon." And then he stalked off, ready to face his rival head-on.

Brooks found Trace leaning against his pickup truck, taking a chug from a bottle of whiskey. Wearing jeans and a chambray shirt, his hat tipped back off his forehead, he wasn't exactly dressed for the occasion.

"What do you want, Evans?"

Trace shot back a hard glare. "Ruby. I want Ruby."

Brooks ground his teeth at Trace's possessive tone. "She's not coming out here to see you."

"She'll see me. I have things to say to her."

Brooks held his temper in check. "Now's not the time. She's enjoying the party."

Trace's lips pulled into a twist, and he pointed his index finger straight at Brooks. "You don't speak for her, Newport."

"Why don't you get the hell out of here and sober up. Better yet, I'll get someone to take you home. You're in no shape to drive."

Trace threw his head back in a hearty laugh and gestured with the bottle. The amber liquid inside sloshed back and forth. "What? You mean this? You're obviously not a Texan. This is nothing. Trust me, greenhorn, I'm not blistered. And I need to see Ruby."

"Why, so you can lie to her and hurt her again?"

"You don't know squat about me and Ruby. We had something real special and I made a mistake, is all."

"You made *a lot* of mistakes. Like screwing a married woman. Yeah, I know about your mistakes, Evans. You owe thousands from gambling, and you got kicked off the rodeo circuit for banging the rodeo boss's wife. Now you need Ruby to bail you out."

Evans came toward Brooks with venom in his eyes. "What are you doing snooping into my private life?"

Brooks stood firm. He could take Trace if it came to a fistfight. "Ruby deserves much better. So yeah, I hired an investigator and found out all your dirty little secrets."

"You son of a bitch. I was going to tell her all about it. That's why I needed to see her."

"It's too late to confess your sins, Evans. Just give up."

"I have no plans of doing that. Ruby loves me."

"Yeah, well, she's been loving me lately."

Evans's free hand fisted, and his eyes hardened to stones. "I should knock you to hell and back."

"I'm shaking in my boots." Brooks shouldn't have let the guy get to him. He would've never betrayed Ruby's trust like that otherwise. He wasn't a kiss-and-tell kind of guy. But hearing Evans say Ruby loved him was like a knife twisting in his gut.

"How much cash would it take for you to leave Ruby alone?" Brooks asked. "I want you out of her life, *for good*. Twenty-five thousand? It's enough to cover your gambling debts. I'll write you a check right now."

"Asshole. You think everything can be settled with money."

"*Fifty* grand?"

Evans's brows rose in interest. "You bartering for Ruby?"

"I'm trying to protect her." The man's pride was keeping him from grabbing the brass ring. Brooks had to press him. "I'll make it a *hundred* grand. You want the deal or not?"

A loud gasp came from behind them, and his stomach clenched in dread as he pivoted around. Ruby stood just five feet away, her arms tight around her middle and her eyes spitting red-hot fire. The burn seared through him like a scorching poker. "Ruby, how long have you been out here?"

"Long enough to hear you both acting like jerks."

"Hey, he was the one trying to buy me off," Evans shouted.

"And you were about to accept my offer."

"Don't listen to him, Ruby." Evans took a step toward her.

She put up a halting hand that said, *Don't you dare come close.* Unfortunately, the gesture was meant for Brooks, too. "I. Am. Not. Going. To. Listen. To. This. I'm done with both of you. You can go straight to hell." With that, she spun on her heel and marched away, her shoulders ramrod stiff but the rest of her body trembling.

Brooks watched helplessly as she walked away. Her words cut deep, but nothing hurt as much as seeing the disappointment and accusation on her face.

"Looks like you blew it, Newport."

"Screw you, Evans."

Brooks took off after her, following her to the steps of the house. "Ruby, wait!"

She spun around instantly. The big, fat tears welling in her eyes stopped him in his tracks. "Leave me alone, Brooks."

Serena and Eve stepped out of the house just then and, noting Ruby's upset state, immediately ushered her into the house, flanking her like a human fortress. With a turn of their heads, the two women shot him glares that could have downed an F-16.

He ran his hands over his face, pulling the skin taut. Then he punched the air out of frustration. He should've known Ruby was enough of her own woman not to need his interference. Had he learned nothing from the past?

Now she was hurt and furious.

It was the last thing he wanted.

And yet somehow, he ended up being the bad guy in all of this.

In black spandex and her comfy Horses Are a Woman's Best Friend sweatshirt, Ruby sat on her sofa, going over the events from last night in her head. Her emotions had been on a high after spending the better part of the evening with Brooks, but when she walked out-side and found him in a bidding war *over her* with Trace, she couldn't believe her ears. Brooks had been trying to pay her ex off to stop pursuing her, as if Ruby couldn't make that decision on her own. As if he had the right to decide for her. The worst of it was facing the fact that she really didn't know Brooks Newport at all. Was he the ruthless manipulator that she'd read and heard about? Was he trying to control her? Or had he really believed he was protecting her?

Her phone buzzed and she glanced at the text. It was Brooks again. He'd called and texted her last night until after midnight, apologizing in every way imaginable. She'd refused to answer any of his messages, but in each he'd called himself an imbecile, a jerk or a fool for hurt-ing her, and that had put a smile on her face. The lofty, self-confident man was trying. She had to give him that.

But today's text was different. Today he wrote,

I'm going to Chicago today to make all things right in my life. And then I'm coming back...for you.

A warm shiver ran up and down her body. "Oh, Gala-had."

Her doorbell chimed and she rose, checking the peep-hole before opening the door. Eve had called earlier to check up on her and invited herself over. Ruby was grate-ful she had. She needed a good friend today, and Eve was quickly becoming that. "Good morning."

Eve's warm smile immediately faded. "Oh, Ruby. You look exhausted. I bet you didn't get a wink of sleep."

"Maybe an hour or two. Come in."

"Are you sure? I can come back later if you want to rest."

"Heavens, no. Moping around isn't my thing. I could use the company."

Eve entered and wrapped her arms around Ruby, pulling her in tight. The hug was exactly what she needed at the moment. "I'm sorry you're upset."

"I'm…yeah. I guess *upset* is the right word. My emotions are all over the place."

"I'm here if you want to talk," Eve said.

Spilling her heart out wasn't easy, but Eve was a thoughtful listener and someone Ruby knew she could trust. They entered the living room and took seats on the sofa next to each other.

Ruby faced Eve and didn't hold back. She told Eve everything about Trace, how she'd fallen for him and waited for him like a fool all those months. She explained how he'd returned to Cool Springs and laid his heart on the line, trying his best to make up with her, offering her everything she'd wanted from him, a life…a future. None of the things Brooks had ever hinted at. She explained about meeting Brooks for the first time at the C'mon Inn and how they'd hit it off from the start. How surprised she'd been the next day to find out that he was one of Beau's long lost sons.

Last night, after dancing with Brooks, she'd finally come to realize she wasn't in love with Trace anymore. And that was before she'd heard about his indiscretions. That was before she'd learned he was trying to use her to bail him out of a financial jam.

"As painful as it is, Ruby, at least you know the truth about Trace Evans," Eve said. "You can cross him off your list. I'm sorry he hurt you, but you dodged a bullet. And don't be mad at me for saying this—Brooks did you a service by exposing him."

Ruby lowered her head and rubbed at her temples.

"My brain knows you're right, Eve. But my heart…isn't so sure."

"According to Graham, Brooks is crazy about you. Believe me when I say this. He wouldn't have gone to this extreme with Trace unless he was all in with you. Brooks has his flaws when it comes to confronting adversaries, but he's passionate in what he believes and a really good guy."

"Do good guys take off at the first sign of trouble?" She searched Eve's earnest face, hoping to gain better perspective.

Eve took hold of her hand, and her warmth seeped into all of Ruby's cold places. "He went to Chicago for all the right reasons, Ruby. He's making his peace with the past. Graham and I believe it's so he can come to you with an open heart, as cliché as that sounds."

"No, that sounds…pretty good. If I can believe it. He hasn't stopped messaging me."

"Maybe you can cut the guy some slack?"

Ruby smiled. "Maybe."

Eve took both of her hands now, holding her gently at the wrists, and adjusted her position on the sofa to face her full-on. "I have something for you, Ruby. I hope I haven't overstepped a line here, but…" She released her wrists to dig into her handbag and came up holding a pink rectangular box. "Being in your shoes a few months ago, I kind of recognize the signs," she said, softening her voice.

Ruby's eyes widened. She wasn't ready for this. But maybe it was time to stop procrastinating. It wasn't like Ruby Lopez not to face life head-on. She took the box from Eve and, seeing the concern on her face, gave her a smile. "Do you always walk around with an extra pregnancy test in your purse?"

Eve chuckled. "Oh, Ruby, I was worried how you

would take it. You might think us city people are too pushy."

Ruby shook her head. "Yeah, well, city folk are more upfront, I will say that. Country folk tend to gossip behind your back. It all washes out the same."

"It's okay, then?"

"Of course. I should've done this myself. I think I needed the nudge."

"You think you might be?" Eve's voice escalated to a squeak, and a twinkle of hope sparkled in her eyes.

Ruby shrugged. "I don't know. I'm eating like the world is ending tomorrow, and lately I get supertired. Emotionally, I'm a wreck. But that just might be Brooks's doing. I guess... I'll find out soon. Thank you, Eve."

"You're welcome. I'll get going now and let you rest." Eve stood up and Ruby didn't try to stop her, although resting was the last thing on her mind. Her grip on the pregnancy test tightened. She had some major thinking to do, no matter what she found out.

She walked Eve to the front door, and they hugged. "Call me if you need to talk again," Eve whispered.

"I will. And thanks again." Ruby closed the door behind her and leaned against it. Sighing, she glanced at the pink box with light purple lettering in her hand. To think, peeing on a stick could change her life forever. Ruby placed her hand on her belly, and tears misted her eyes as she made a heartfelt wish.

Something she hadn't done since before her daddy passed away.

Ten

Brooks stood on the threshold of Sutton Winchester's master bedroom as one of his nurses laid a plaid wool blanket on his lap and turned his wheelchair around. Brooks came face-to-face with his adversary. With a man he'd hated so powerfully, he'd wanted to destroy him. Now, his emotions raw, he hoped to God that Winchester would hear him out, because he was also the man who had loved his mother dearly and had fathered his younger brother, Carson.

"He's having a good day today, Mr. Newport," the nurse said.

"I'm glad to hear it," Brooks responded as he and Winchester exchanged glances. "Good afternoon, Mr. Winchester."

Cancer seemed to have sucked Winchester's one-time bluster and hard-nosed demeanor right out of his frail body. Hunched over, he appeared a shell of the man Brooks had opposed so vehemently in the past. Warm-colored walls, floral bouquets and December sunshine streaming in the windows contrasted sharply with the sterile environment of medical equipment, drips and tubes, and the constant *blip, blip, blip* of a monitor over the soft music piping in from hidden speakers.

With a feeble wave of his hand at the nurse, Winchester stopped the music. "You know me well enough to call me Sutton, boy."

"Okay, thanks. I will."

"Did you come here to gloat?" He lifted his head to look into Brooks's eyes.

"No, sir, I would never do that."

"Have a seat," the older man ordered in a voice that had long lost its depth.

Brooks sat in a chair three feet from Sutton's wheelchair. "Thank you."

"How is my Eve?" he asked.

"She's doing well. Graham brought her down to Texas, as you know. She's looking wonderful, excited about the baby."

Sutton turned his head to gaze out the window. "That's good. I want my children to be happy."

"Sutton, I know how much you loved my mother."

Slowly Winchester turned his head back and raised his brows, looking him square in the eyes. "Cynthia was a special woman. I wished she would've told me about Carson, though. She left me without telling me she was pregnant. I missed out on my son's life."

"Mom had a lot of pride."

"She was a stubborn one." His eyes twinkled as if he admired that trait. As if he'd loved every single thing about Cynthia Newport. He and Brooks had that in common.

"I'm glad you loved her, Sutton. I'm glad because if

you didn't, she wouldn't have had Carson. So I guess I have you to thank for my brother. And I'm doing that now. Thank you."

Sutton stared at him and then acknowledged him with a nod. "I have no intention of cutting Carson out of my will, by the way. As you can see, I'm not long for this earth. Carson is my son and an heir. He will get what is rightfully his."

It had been a bone of contention these past months, something that had grated on Brooks. That his younger brother wouldn't be acknowledged by his father. That he would lose what was due him, being an heir to the Winchester fortune. Carson had already been robbed of a father growing up—they all had—but this was one thing that could make things right in principle. "Carson knows that now. It wasn't ever about the money."

"We have agreed that when the time comes," Sutton said, speaking slowly, "his inheritance will go to charity. That's fine by me. Whatever the boy wants. He deserves it." His voice crumbled a little. "I have many regrets when it comes to Cynthia. Things I should've done differently with her. I lived my life a little recklessly, but I never betrayed her trust. I never told her secret. Seeing how it hurt you and Graham, maybe that wasn't the smartest thing to do."

"We've all made mistakes. I'm here to make peace between our families. I'm here to tell you that I was wrong for pursuing vengeance against you. I was wrong to try to destroy Elite Industries. I understand why you kept my mother's secret all those years. I've only just recently come to understand the crazy things one will do out of love. I, uh, I get it now. So I'm throwing in the towel. I've ordered my attorneys to back off. There'll be no more legal battles. No more disparaging comments to the press.

No more trying to undermine you or your company. I've already spoken to Eve, Nora and Grace about this. I've made my peace with them. But I wanted to face you in person. To say it's over."

Sutton nodded, the movement slight, all he could manage. "It's over."

All those months of personal attacks and secrets and truths coming to the surface were finally coming to an end. There would be no more harsh statements, conniving or retribution. The Winchester-Newport feud was done. Finished.

Brooks had one more thing to accomplish to unite the families. "That being said, I'm also here to invite you and your family to Cool Springs for Christmas. On behalf of my father, Beau, and his family. We'd all like the Winchesters to share the holiday with us. Carson and Georgia will be coming. And your daughters are onboard if you think you can make the trip. I'll send a private jet, and you'll have expert nursing care while you are there. I promise you'll be as comfortable as possible. It'll be a time of healing for all of us."

Sutton inhaled slowly, closed his eyes and seemed to give it some good thought. "I'd like to be with my family for Christmas. One last time. Yes, I'll make the trip."

Brooks put out his hand, holding his breath. There'd been a lot of bad blood between them, but he hoped they could put it all behind them. Sutton glanced at Brooks, then slowly offered his frail hand. It was putty soft, devoid of any strength, but he shook with Brooks and then smiled. Something Sutton Winchester rarely did. "It's a deal."

"Deal," Brooks said. "I'll work with your staff to make the arrangements."

"Thank you."

Brooks sighed in relief. He was making strides, and it felt like a heavy weight had been lifted from his shoulders. He was free now to head back to Texas and make things right with one hot gorgeous woman. He only hoped Ruby would agree to see him. She was a stubborn one, too. She hadn't answered any of his messages. Which worried him. But once he returned to Look Away, he vowed not to take no for an answer.

Brooks stood on the veranda with Beau, looking out at the cloudless night. There were hundreds of stars decorating the Texas sky, twinkling brighter than he'd ever seen before. He hugged his wool coat around his middle against the chilly winds. The Douglas fir tree decorating the veranda released the fresh scent of evergreen. It was Christmas Eve, and to spend it with his father for the first time locked up his fate good and tight. Brooks knew what he wanted to do with his life.

"Well, Dad. Here I go. Wish me luck."

"You won't need luck, son. Just tell the truth. There's power in that, and you'd be surprised how much it's appreciated." Beau faced him. "I certainly appreciated hearing it from you tonight."

Beau wrapped his arms around him good and tight, drawing him close. Beau was a hugger, and Brooks loved that about him. When they broke apart, his father said, "I'm behind you one hundred percent."

He had his father's love and support and, like a young boy would, he beamed inside. "Thanks, Dad."

"All right now, go. I've got a houseful of guests I don't want to neglect."

The Winchesters had arrived this morning, and Beau had been a cordial host. Any awkwardness that might have occurred had been wiped clean straightaway by his father's warm hospitality.

"I'm going. I'm going."

Beau grinned and pivoted around to enter the house, leaving Brooks alone to make his move. He took a deep breath and sighed, a smile spreading across his face. What the hell was he waiting for?

Holding Ruby's image in his mind, he climbed down the steps and walked the distance to her cottage. A light was on in her living room, which was encouraging. He took a moment to gather himself and then knocked. When nothing happened, he knocked again, harder this time. "Ruby, it's Brooks."

Silence.

He reached for his cell phone and called her number. When no one answered, he sent her a text.

Still no reply.

He closed his eyes and sent up a prayer. He hoped he wasn't too late. He hoped Ruby hadn't gone back to Trace Evans. Though he couldn't imagine it, Brooks knew she had a soft spot for the guy. Who knew what lies Evans might have told her to claim his innocence? Had Brooks waited too long? Had his lack of commitment sent Ruby back into Trace's arms?

Brooks's shoulders sagged. He'd stand out here all night waiting for her, but catching pneumonia out in the cold would be a fool thing to do. He had no other option but to go home and try to speak with Ruby tomorrow. She'd be at the house bright and early for Christmas breakfast.

His hopes plummeting, he began the trek to his cabin, wishing now he'd thought to drive. The wind kicked up, lifting his hat from his head. He caught hold of it right before the darn thing sailed away and kept it flattened to his head as he walked on.

Oh man, his bones were chilled, and he had no doubt it was going to be a long, cold, sleepless night for him. Once he reached his cabin door, a wreath of pine and holly berries greeted him, something that hadn't been there when he'd left for Chicago three days ago. The staff or maybe Beau himself must've put it up as a way of welcoming him back. Or maybe it was simply a Preston tradition to decorate every door on the ranch. Christmas cheer seemed especially important on Look Away.

Brooks entered the cabin, and as soon as his boots hit the wood planks, warmth rose up and smacked him in the face. It went a long way in taking the chill off from his cold trek. The fireplace crackled, and his gaze traveled to the tangerine flames partially lighting the room. He stepped farther inside, removing his coat and hat, rubbing at the back of his neck and wondering about the fire.

"Brooks?" Ruby's soft voice had him turning toward the bedroom doorway.

As soon as he spotted her, his breath caught tight in his throat. She stood at the threshold clad in one of his white dress shirts, the sleeves pushed up and the tail reaching to midthigh on her gorgeous legs. Firelight christened her face and was reflected in her dark chocolate eyes. The lovely vision she made heated his blood, and hope sprang to life inside his body. Good God, she was beautiful.

And *here*.

"I hope it's okay. Beau gave me the key to the cabin."

Tongue-tied, Brooks barely got the words out. "No, uh, it's fine."

"I did some decorating."

He tore his gaze from her to scan the room. A tree sat on a corner table. This one would make Charlie Brown proud. The awkward branches were filled with tiny ornaments and multicolored lights. It was a clear winner and perhaps his favorite Christmas tree ever.

Centered in the middle of the dining room table, a big glass bowl of shiny red and green Christmas balls caught his attention. Atop the mantel, a family of snowmen and Santa trinkets along with cinnamon-scented pillar candles added to the holiday warmth.

"I like it." He was a little dumbfounded, standing there, drinking in the sight of Ruby in his cabin after days and days of no communication. "So, does this mean you're talking to me again?"

"If you want an answer to that, you'll have to come here."

"Baby, you don't have to ask twice." Her subtle, familiar scent, sheet of glossy hair raining down her back and mysteriously sexy voice lured him in. He took the steps necessary to come face-to-face with the woman of his fantasies, giving him the little boost he needed to lay his heart on the line. He'd been a fool not to claim her before this. Not to tell her what she meant to him.

"I like your shirt," he said, tracing a finger on her rosy lips, then skimming it along her sweet chin to her neckline and down to the hollow where the shirt dipped into her mind-numbing cleavage.

"Ask me why I'm here."

"With you dressed like that, I'm supposed to think straight?"

She chuckled, the deep sound coming up from her throat catching him off guard. "Try."

"You picked me?"

"Galahad, it was never really a contest. Trace isn't the man for me."

"You ditched him?"

"I told him I didn't love him anymore. That we weren't meant to be. I'm not happy about you bribing him, but afterward I had a heart-to-heart talk with him, and he was honest with me about everything. He's messed up his life and swore up and down that he never meant to hurt me."

"And you forgave him?" *The cheater, the creep*, Brooks wanted to add, but he was in too hopeful a mood to press his luck.

She nodded. "It's easier when you're no longer emotionally invested. He'll get on the right track again. He got an offer to do a reality show on a country cable television station, and he jumped at the chance. He'll be moving to Nashville soon."

"That's good to hear, because I wouldn't have let you go. I wouldn't have given up on you."

"Because that's what white knights do?"

"Because I'm crazy about you, Ruby. I'm out of my mind in love with you."

Ruby's face brightened, and she smiled. "I love you too, Brooks. This isn't a passing thing for me. This is the real deal."

Thank God.

He didn't need the mistletoe above their heads for permission to kiss her. He circled his arms around her waist and brought her up against him. Her chin tilted, and he gazed into the most stunning pair of dark eyes he'd ever seen. The glow in them promised more than he could ever hope for. Ruby was going to be his. And then his mouth came down on hers, meeting her flesh to flesh. Her soft lips slid over him exquisitely. Her petite body, all five-foot-two of her, crushed against him and put his brain in jeopardy of shutting completely down.

He broke the kiss to her defiant whimper and then dipped down to lift her. Her brows arched in question, but she didn't stir otherwise. Her arms automatically roped around his neck, and he carried her to a chair beside the sizzling fire. A log broke apart, and golden flames climbed the height of the fireplace, bringing intense heat. He sat down in the warmth, and Ruby wiggled in his lap. But Brooks had to contain his lust for just a few more seconds. "Ruby, I thought I'd blown it with you. Foolishly I left town without telling you how I felt about you. Maybe I shouldn't have had Trace investigated…"

"You think?"

"Okay, I get it. It wasn't my business to interfere, but I was trying my best to protect you from getting hurt again. Ever since the night we met at the C'mon Inn, when that guy was pestering you, I've had this need to protect you."

"Are you apologizing?"

"For not trusting in you? Yes. You're more than capable of making up your own mind about things."

She gently took his hand in hers and stroked his fingers, sending tingles up and down his arm. "I didn't mind the first time, Brooks. I thought it was really kinda sweet of you, coming to my rescue. You didn't know me, and still you were willing to help me. But with Trace, it was different. I really don't want to talk about him anymore tonight. It's over and done with. I know in my heart you had good intentions."

"I did and I still do, sweetheart. Actually, you call me Galahad, but in truth, you're the rescuer in this duo. You've saved me, Ruby. From the very moment I met you, my life changed. I've become a better person, a more tolerant man, because of you. I came here looking for my true father and found a new way of life, as well. I've discovered something within me that I wouldn't have realized if not for you. You taught me about the ranch and how things work in the country, but you also helped ease the pain of my past. Coming with me to meet my grandfather for the first time meant a lot. That was a hard reunion, but having you there comforting me and showing me how to let go worked miracles for me. You helped me turn away from the past and look forward. To the future. You gave me something special that day. You made me see what my life could be."

He lifted her fingertips and kissed each one. Just looking at her filled his heart with so much joy, he could hardly think straight. "I've always felt something was missing in my life. I thought it was because of my childhood. I thought it was because I never knew my father. In a sense, that's true. I missed knowing Beau as a boy, having his guidance and love, but I've come to realize I've also missed this place. Look Away and Texas. It feels right being here, with you. I've known only city life, but now that I'm here, I don't want to leave. I'm going to work it out so that I can stay closer to my family. The company is in good hands. I can run it long-distance."

"You're staying?" The hope in Ruby's voice swelled his heart.

"I want to, yes. I hear there are some pretty nice ranches for sale close by." Brooks rose with Ruby still in his arms. Her warmth mingled with his, and as soon as he lowered her down and her feet touched the floor, he felt the loss. "I went to your place looking for you. And nearly died when I couldn't find you."

"I had a surprise for you, Brooks."

"Having you here was the best surprise I could ever hope for," he said. And then he dropped to one knee and gazed into a pair of astonished eyes as firelight caressed her beautiful face. "Ruby Lopez, I promise to love and cherish and yeah, probably protect you for the rest of my life. I can't help it. I'll always be your Galahad." He fished inside his pocket for the wedding ring he'd brought with him from Chicago, a diamond ring that had once been his Grandma Gerty's. It was all he had left of the woman who'd taken his family in during a precarious time in their lives.

Brooks held up the ring, and it glistened under the firelight. Clearing his throat, he presented it to her and said, "Ruby, this ring was given to me by my grandmother. She told me one day I'd give it to a special woman. That day has come, sweetheart. I want to give you this ring and along with it, my heart and soul. I ask that you do me the honor of marrying me. Ruby, will you be my wife?"

Tears spilled from Ruby's eyes, raining down her face without warning. Brooks held his breath, hoping they were happy tears. "I went to Beau and asked for his blessing, Ruby. I asked him for your hand in marriage, and he was touched and happy for us."

"Oh, Brooks," she said, grasping his wrists as he rose. "That's the sweetest thing…"

Facing her now, he stared into her eyes, waiting patiently for her answer. "Ruby?"

She began nodding quickly, the tears still trekking down her cheeks. "Yes, Brooks. I'll marry you. I'll be your wife."

He laughed, and the sound of his relief and joy filled the room. "You had me worried there, sweetheart."

"No, no. It's just that I didn't expect this."

Using the pads of his thumbs, he wiped at her tears, carefully drying her eyes. Cupping her face, he said softly, "I didn't expect it, either. It happened so darn fast, but it's the right thing. For both of us. I promise you, Ruby, we'll have a great life."

"I know we will." And then she took his hand and walked him over to the scraggly Christmas tree. Turning to face him, she smiled sweetly. "You've given me this beautiful ring and a promise of your love. It's a wonderful gift, and now I have a gift for you, my sweet love." She handed him a small box decorated with snowmen and reindeer wrapping paper. "Merry Christmas."

He lifted the lightweight box in his hands and jiggled it. Nothing moved. He shot her a glance. She gave nothing away, and he had no idea what she was up to, but her expression was hopeful, and her eyes positively beamed. "Let's see," he said, ripping away the wrapping and opening the small box. After separating the tissue paper, he lifted out a small white garment.

"It's called a onesie," Ruby said softly.

Puzzled, Brooks read the printed saying on the front. "Future Look Away Ranch Wrangler."

He blinked. And blinked again. Normally he wasn't slow on the uptake, but this…this was like a lightning bolt striking his heart. Something else lay at the bottom of the box. Cute, small, adorable tan leather baby boots.

He stared at them for a second. "A *baby*? Ruby," he said, tears burning the backs of his eyes so hard he could barely get the words out, "are we having a baby?"

She began nodding her head. "Yes. We're going to have a baby, Brooks."

Joy burst inside him, and his face stretched wide as he grinned. Thankfully he didn't shed tears, but his emotions were off the charts. "A baby…" he said, awed, as he pulled Ruby back into his arms and kissed her cheek, her chin and finally her lips. "It's the best Christmas gift in the world."

"Yes," she whispered. "I think so, too. But I wasn't sure how you'd feel…"

"I love you, Ruby." He set his hand very gently on her belly. "And I love our baby already. I couldn't be happier. To have you and our child in my life, it's a dream come true."

"I love you, too. You'll be a great father, Brooks." Ruby covered his hand with hers and positioned it where new life was growing inside her. Then she leaned in to kiss him. The kiss bonded them together forever, and Brooks had never been happier in his life. He was complete. His life held new meaning and purpose.

Here on Look Away Ranch, he had finally found home.

Epilogue

Christmas morning on Look Away was usually a chaotic affair of eating, joking, opening gifts and spreading the love, and today was no different, except that the family had expanded to include the Winchesters. Ruby had coordinated with the household staff to make sure they were as comfortable as possible.

Sutton Winchester had his own set of nurses, and the older man who'd played a role in Brooks's, Graham's and particularly Carson's lives was holding his own this morning. His wheelchair was right next to the warm flames of the fireplace, and he seemed to be in good spirits. Occasionally Ruby would see him smile at his daughters, Nora, Grace and Eve. For a powerful man who wasn't long for this earth, his eyes still held a bit of mischief, and though he spoke seldom, what did come out of his mouth was witty and charming.

Ruby knew the history he had with Brooks's mother.

Last night, while in bed with her new fiancé and father of her unborn child, Brooks had recounted to her all he'd known of their relationship. Sutton was Carson's father, and it was sad that Carson had come to know him only in the last months of his life.

"Gather around the tree, everyone," Beau said after they'd eaten a Christmas morning meal that would probably stay with them throughout the entire day. Except for her. She was still ravenous. And now Brooks was watching her like a hawk, eyeing her with love in his eyes, but also concern over every little move she made. It was sweet, for now, as they were both getting used to the idea of her pregnancy and overjoyed at the little one who'd be making an appearance in eight months.

Married now, Nora and Reid Chamberlain took their places along with newly engaged Grace and Roman Slater. Carson stood with his fiancée, Georgia, next to Sutton's wheelchair, and his allegiance to his ailing father was inspiring. Toby, Malcolm and Clay were to Beau's right, and next to him on the other side were Graham and Eve.

Brooks grabbed Ruby's hand and angled them beside Graham.

"Want to sit down?" he asked her.

"No, I'm fine," she told him quietly. Ruby's heart was thumping wildly in her chest. No one knew their news yet, and she was enjoying this special secretive time with her new fiancé, but a part of her just wanted to scream it from the rooftops. The ring, which she'd hated taking off, was in Brooks's pocket.

Lupe came around with a tray of mimosas and sparkling cider. Brooks snapped up two ciders and handed Ruby one, giving her a quick, adorable smile.

"Thank you all for making the trip to Look Away for

the holiday," Beau began, holding up his glass. "I'm not one for making speeches, but it seems lately there's a need. So I'll make this toast short. The past has been hard on many of us. But looking around this room, I have renewed faith in the future. I see love here in many forms, and it's heartwarming."

Beau's gaze found hers, and his smile made Ruby blush down to her toes.

"I, for one, am grateful that Graham and Brooks are here with me this holiday. They have met their three half brothers and our Ruby, and it's been all that I had hoped. And I'm so happy having Carson here, along with all you wonderful Winchester girls and your father. It's all a blessing.

"I cannot hold a grudge about the past. It serves no purpose and so, with that in mind, I hope that this coming together of the Prestons, Newports and Winchesters brings with it peace to all families. Let's set aside our differences, put salve on our wounds and try to move forward. Especially at this time of year, when goodwill abounds, let's have ourselves a very Merry Christmas." Glasses clinked and good-natured chatter began. The families were united and, at least for this holiday, all was well.

"Dad, if you don't mind, I'd like to say something." Brooks's tone was reverent, and everyone stopped talking to listen.

"Of course, son."

Brooks's arm came around Ruby's shoulder, tugging her in even closer, and many sets of eyes rounded in surprise. "I didn't know what to expect when I came to Look Away. I'd been hell-bent on finding my father, as everyone here knows. And when I finally met him…well, when I met you, Beau…" Brooks said, speaking directly to his father now and choking up a bit. Ruby put her arm around his waist, supporting him. She'd always be there for him when he needed her. "When I met you, Beau, saw you for the decent, kind man you are, I was floored, inspired and thrilled to know you. To be your son. But I also felt one with this land. It was like a part of me became suddenly alive again. And I knew I belonged here. I knew that Texas and Look Away was my real home. Ruby played a role in that."

He spoke to her now, and she lifted her chin to look into his eyes. "Ruby and I have fallen deeply in love. With Beau's blessing, I've asked her to marry me, and she said yes. We are officially engaged as of last night." Brooks dug into his pocket and formally put the ring on her finger.

Applause and congratulations broke out. Brooks bent his head and brought his lips to hers, giving her a taste of the passion that would always consume their lives. She had no doubt.

"There's one more thing," Ruby said, raising her voice above the din. Everyone grew silent again. "It seems that Graham and Eve aren't the only ones who will be making Beau a grandfather."

Gasps broke out, and Ruby thought she heard Eve chant, "All right!"

"Brooks and I are going to have a baby."

Tears poured down Ruby's cheeks again. Even though she tried her best to maintain decorum, she couldn't help it, and Brooks did his best to wipe them away.

Beau was the first to come over, wrapping his arms around both of them and hugging tight. "Congratulations, you two. I couldn't be happier." His voice broke, and Ruby knew he was crying, too. "You've got yourself a wonderful girl, son."

"I couldn't agree more," Brooks said, brushing a kiss across her cheek.

After everyone congratulated them and the Christmas festivities moved on, Brooks took her by the hand and led her outside to the front veranda. Wrapping his arms around her from behind, he bestowed kisses on the back of her neck as they swayed back and forth in full harmony, gazing out on the land, the pasture, the horses, all that was Look Away. "We're going shopping tomorrow," he announced quietly.

"For baby things?"

He chuckled. "First I need to put a roof over our heads, sweetheart. We're buying our own ranch, one we can call home. And even though I'm in real estate—"

"You're not *in* real estate. You're the king of real estate."

"But you're the expert in ranching. I value your opinion in all things, but I especially defer to you when it comes to Texas and ranches."

"You're letting me choose?"

"I want you to have your heart's desire, Ruby. The house, the ranch. I'll build it for you if you can't find something you absolutely love."

"I already have."

Brooks's brows arched. "You found a place?"

"I found something I absolutely love."

And then she roped her arms around his neck and kissed her handsome fiancé something fierce with all the love she had in her heart, thanking her lucky stars she'd met her very own knight in shining armor that night at the C'mon Inn.

"You, Galahad. I found you."

* * * * *

***

She hardly noticed when Sam carried her through the main room and dropped her onto her bed.

In a few short seconds, they were both naked. The quilt felt cool beneath her, but he was there, sliding on top of her, to bring the heat.

"Been wanting to peel you out of those sweaters for days now," he murmured, trailing kisses from her belly to her breasts.

"Been wanting you to do it," Joy assured him, and ran the flat of her hands over his shoulders.

She hadn't felt this way in… ever. He shifted, kissing her mouth, tangling his tongue with hers. She lifted her hips into his touch and held his head to hers as they kissed, as they took and gave and then did it all again. Their breath mingled, their hearts pounded in a wild tandem that raced faster and faster as they tasted, explored, discovered.

It was like being caught in a hurricane.

There was no safe place to hide, even if she wanted to. And she didn't. She wanted the storm, more than she'd ever wanted anything in her life.

MAID UNDER
THE MISTLETOE

BY
MAUREEN CHILD

All rights reserved including the right of reproduction in whole or in part in any form. This edition is published by arrangement with Harlequin Books S.A.

This is a work of fiction. Names, characters, places, locations and incidents are purely fictional and bear no relationship to any real life individuals, living or dead, or to any actual places, business establishments, locations, events or incidents. Any resemblance is entirely coincidental.

This book is sold subject to the condition that it shall not, by way of trade or otherwise, be lent, resold, hired out or otherwise circulated without the prior consent of the publisher in any form of binding or cover other than that in which it is published and without a similar condition including this condition being imposed on the subsequent purchaser.

® and ™ are trademarks owned and used by the trademark owner and/or its licensee. Trademarks marked with ® are registered with the United Kingdom Patent Office and/or the Office for Harmonisation in the Internal Market and in other countries.

First Published in Great Britain 2016
By Mills & Boon, an imprint of HarperCollins*Publishers*
1 London Bridge Street, London, SE1 9GF

© 2016 Maureen Child

ISBN: 978-0-263-91888-5

51-1216

Our policy is to use papers that are natural, renewable and recyclable products and made from wood grown in sustainable forests. The logging and manufacturing processes conform to the legal environmental regulations of the country of origin.

Printed and bound in Spain
by CPI, Barcelona

Maureen Child writes for the Mills & Boon Desire line and can't imagine a better job. A seven-time finalist for a prestigious Romance Writers of America RITA® Award, Maureen is an author of more than one hundred romance novels. Her books regularly appear on bestseller lists and have won several awards, including a Prism Award, a National Readers' Choice Award, a Colorado Romance Writers Award of Excellence and a Golden Quill Award. She is a native Californian but has recently moved to the mountains of Utah.

To all the moms who are out there right now,
making magic

One

Sam Henry hated December.

The days were too short, making the nights seem an eternity. It was cold and dark—and then there was the incessant Christmas badgering. Lights, trees, carols and an ever-increasing barrage of commercials urging you to shop, spend, buy. And every reminder of the holiday season ate at the edges of his soul and heart like drops of acid.

He scowled at the roaring fire in the hearth, slapped one hand on the mantel and rubbed his fingers over the polished edge of the wood. With his gaze locked on the flames, he told himself that if he could, he'd wipe the month of December from the calendar.

"You can't stick your head in the snow and pretend Christmas isn't happening."

Sam flicked a glance at the woman in the open doorway. His housekeeper/cook/nag, Kaye Porter, stood there glaring at him through narrowed blue eyes. Hands at her wide hips, her gray-streaked black hair pulled back into a single thick braid that hung down over one shoulder, she shook her head. "There's not enough snow to do it anyway, and whether you like it or not, Christmas is coming."

"I don't and it's only coming if I acknowledge it," Sam told her.

"Well, you're going to have to pay attention because I'm out of here tomorrow."

"I'll give you a raise if you cancel your trip," he said, willing to bargain to avoid the hassle of losing the woman who ran his house so he didn't have to.

A short bark of laughter shot from her throat. "Not a chance. My friend Ruthie and I do this every year, as you well know. We've got our rooms booked and there's no way we're canceling."

He'd known that—he just hadn't wanted to think about it. Another reason to hate December. Every year, Kaye and Ruthie took a month-long vacation. A cruise to the Bahamas, then a stay at a splashy beachside hotel, followed by another cruise home. Kaye liked to say it was her therapy to get her through the rest of the year living with a crank like himself.

"If you love Christmas so much, why do you run to a beach every year?"

She sighed heavily. "Christmas is everywhere, you know. Even in hot, sandy places! We buy little trees, decorate them for our rooms. And the hotel lights up all the palm trees…" She sighed again, but this time, it was with delight. "It's gorgeous."

"Fine." He pushed away from the hearth, tucked both

hands into the pockets of his jeans and stared at her. Every year he tried to talk her out of leaving and every year he lost. Surrendering to the inevitable, he asked, "You need a ride to the airport?"

A small smile curved her mouth at the offer. "No, but thanks. Ruthie's going to pick me up at the crack of dawn tomorrow. She'll leave her car there so when we come back we don't have to worry about taking one of those damn shuttles."

"Okay then." He took a breath and muttered, "Have a great time."

"The enthusiasm in that suggestion is just one of the reasons I need this trip." One dark eyebrow lifted. "You worry me, Sam. All locked away on this mountain hardly talking to anyone but me—"

She kept going, but Sam tuned out. He'd heard it all before. Kaye was determined to see him "start living" again. Didn't seem to matter that he had no interest in that. While she talked, he glanced around the main room of what Kaye liked to call his personal prison.

It was a log home, the wood the color of warm honey, with lots of glass to spotlight the view that was breathtaking from every room. Pine forest surrounded the house, and a wide, private lake stretched out beyond a narrow slice of beach. He had a huge garage and several outbuildings, including a custom-designed workshop where Sam wished he was right at that moment.

This house, this *sanctuary*, was just what he'd been looking for when he'd come to Idaho five years ago. It was isolated, with a small town—Franklin—just fifteen minutes away when he needed supplies. A big city, with the airport and all manner of other distractions, was just an hour from there, not that he ever went. What he needed, he had Kaye pick up in Franklin and only rarely went to town himself.

The whole point of moving here had been to find quiet. Peace. *Solitude*. Hell, he could go weeks and never talk to anyone but Kaye. Thoughts of her brought him back to the conversation at hand.

"...Anyway," she was saying, "my friend Joy will be here about ten tomorrow morning to fill in for me while I'm gone."

He nodded. At least Kaye had done what she always did, arranged for one of her friends to come and stay for the month she'd be gone. Sam wouldn't have to worry about cooking, cleaning or pretty much anything but keeping his distance from whatever busybody she'd found this year.

He folded his arms over his chest. "I'm not going to catch this one rifling through my desk, right?"

Kaye winced. "I will admit that having Betty come last year was a bad idea..."

"Yeah," he agreed. She'd seemed nice enough, but the woman had poked her head into everything she could find. Within a week, Sam had sent her home and had spent the following three weeks eating grilled cheese sandwiches, canned soup and frozen pizza. "I'd say so."

"She's the curious sort."

"She's nosy."

"Yes, well." Kaye cleared her throat. "That was my mistake, I know. But my friend Joy isn't a snoop. I think you'll like her."

"Not necessary," he assured her. He didn't want to like Joy. Hell, he didn't want to *talk* to her if he could avoid it.

"Of course not." Kaye shook her head again and gave him the kind of look teachers used to reserve for the kid acting up in class. "Wouldn't want to be human or anything. Might set a nasty precedent."

"Kaye…"

The woman had worked for him since he'd moved to Idaho five years ago. And since then, she'd muscled her way much deeper into his life than he'd planned on allowing. Not only did she take care of the house, but she looked after *him* despite the fact that he didn't want her to. But Kaye was a force of nature, and it seemed her friends were a lot like her.

"Never mind. Anyway, to what I was saying, Joy already knows that you're cranky and want to be left alone—"

He frowned at her. "Thanks."

"Am I wrong?" When he didn't answer, she nodded. "She's a good cook and runs her own business on the internet."

"You told me all of this already," he pointed out. Though she hadn't said what *kind* of business the amazing Joy ran. Still, how many different things could a woman in her fifties or sixties do online? Give knitting lessons? Run a babysitting service? Dog sitting? Hell, his own mother sold handmade dresses online, so there was just no telling.

"I know, I know." Kaye waved away his interruption. "She'll stay out of your way because she needs this time here. The contractor says they won't have the fire damage at her house repaired until January, so being able to stay and work here was a godsend."

"You told me this, too," he reminded her. In fact, he'd heard more than enough about Joy the Wonder Friend. According to Kaye, she was smart, clever, a hard worker, had a wonderful sense of humor and did apparently everything just short of walking on water. "But how did the fire in her house start again? Is she a closet arsonist? A terrible cook who set fire to the stove?"

"Of course not!" Kaye sniffed audibly and stiffened as if someone had shoved a pole down the back of her sweatshirt. "I told you, there was a short in the wiring. The house she's renting is just ancient and something was bound to go at some point. The owner of the house is having all the wiring redone, though, so it should be safe now."

"I'm relieved to hear it," he said. And relieved he didn't have to worry that Kaye's friend was so old she'd forgotten to turn off an oven or something.

"I'm only trying to tell you—" she broke off to give him a small smile of understanding "—like I do every year, that you'll survive the month of December just like you do every year."

He ground his teeth together at the flash of sympathy that stirred and then vanished from her eyes. This was the problem with people getting to know too much about him. They felt as if they had the right to offer comfort where none was wanted—or needed. Sam liked Kaye fine, but there were parts of his life that were closed off. For a reason.

He'd get through the holidays his way. Which meant ignoring the forced cheer and the never-ending lineup of "feel good" holiday-themed movies where the hard-hearted hero does a turnaround and opens himself to love and the spirit of Christmas.

Hearts should never be open. Left them too vulnerable to being shattered.

And he'd never set himself up for that kind of pain again.

* * *

Early the following day Kaye was off on her vacation, and a few hours later Sam was swamped by the empty silence. He reminded himself that it was how he liked his life best. No one bothering him. No one talking at him. One of the reasons he and Kaye got along so well was that she respected his need to be left the hell alone. So now that he was by himself in the big house, why did he feel an itch along his spine?

"It's December," he muttered aloud. That was enough to explain the sense of discomfort that clung to him.

Hell, every year, this one damn month made life damn near unlivable. He pushed a hand through his hair, then scraped that hand across the stubble on his jaw. He couldn't settle. Hadn't even spent any time out in his workshop, and usually being out there eased his mind and kept him too busy to think about—

He put the brakes on that thought fast because he couldn't risk opening doors that were better off sealed shut.

Scowling, he stared out the front window at the cold, dark day. The steel-gray clouds hung low enough that it looked as though they were actually skimming across the tops of the pines. The lake, in summer a brilliant sapphire blue, stretched out in front of him like a sheet of frozen pewter. The whole damn world seemed bleak and bitter, which only fed into what he felt every damn minute.

Memories rose up in the back of his mind, but he squelched them flat, as he always did. He'd worked too hard for too damn long to get beyond his past, to live and breathe—and hell, *survive*—to lose it all now. He'd beaten back his demons, and damned if he'd release them long enough to take a bite out of him now.

Resolve set firmly, Sam frowned again when an old blue four-door sedan barreled along his drive, kicking up gravel as it came to a stop in front of the house. For a second, he thought it must be Kaye's friend Joy arriving. Then the driver stepped out of the car and that thought went out the window.

The driver was too young, for one thing. Every other friend Kaye had enlisted to help out had been her age or older. This woman was in her late twenties, he figured, gaze locked on her as she turned her face to stare up at the house. One look at her and Sam felt a punch of lust that stole his breath. Everything in him fisted tightly as he continued to watch her. He couldn't take his eyes off her as she stood on the drive studying his house. Hell, she was like a ray of sunlight in the gray.

Her short curly hair was bright blond and flew about her face in the sharp wind that slapped rosy color into her cheeks. Her blue eyes swept the exterior of the house even as she moved around the car to the rear passenger side. Her black jeans hugged long legs, and her hiking boots looked scarred and well-worn. The cardinal-red parka she wore over a cream-colored sweater was a burst of color in a black-and-white world.

She was beautiful and moved with a kind of easy grace that made a man's gaze follow her every movement. And even while he admitted that silently, Sam resented it. He wasn't interested in women. Didn't want to feel what she was making him feel. What he had to do was find out why the hell she was there and get her gone as fast as possible.

She had to be lost. His drive wasn't that easy to find—purposely. He rarely got visitors, and those were mainly his family when he couldn't stave off his parents or sister any longer.

Well, if she'd lost her way, he'd go out and give her directions to town, and then she'd be gone and he could get back to—whatever.

"Damn." The single word slipped from his throat as she opened the car's back door and a little girl jumped out. The eager anticipation stamped on the child's face was like a dagger to the heart for Sam. He took a breath that fought its way into his chest and forced himself to look away from the kid. He didn't do kids. Not for a long time now. Their voices. Their laughter. They were too small. Too vulnerable.

Too breakable.

What felt like darkness opened up in the center of his chest. Turning his back on the window, he left the room and headed for the front door. The faster he got rid of the gorgeous woman and her child, the better.

"It's a fairy castle, Mommy!"

Joy Curran glanced at the rearview mirror and smiled at the excitement shining on her daughter's face. At five years old, Holly was crazy about princesses, fairies and everyday magic she seemed to find wherever she looked.

Still smiling, Joy shifted her gaze from her daughter to the big house in front of her. Through the windshield, she scanned the front of the place and had to agree with Holly on this one. It did look like a castle.

Two stories, it spread across the land, pine trees spearing up all around it like sentries prepared to stand in defense. The smooth, glassy logs were the color of warm honey, and the wide, tall windows gave glimpses of the interior. A wraparound porch held chairs and gliders that invited visitors to sit and get comfortable. The house faced a private lake where a long dock jutted out into the water that was frozen over for winter. There was a wide deck studded with furniture draped in tarps for winter and a brick fire pit.

It would probably take her a half hour to look at everything, and it was way too cold to simply sit in her car and take it all in. So instead, she turned the engine off, then walked around to get Holly out of her car seat. While the little girl jumped up and down in excitement, pigtails flying, Joy grabbed her purse and headed for the front door. The cold wrapped itself around them and Joy shivered. There hadn't been much snow so far this winter, but the cold sliced right down to the bone. All around her, the pines were green but the grass was brown, dotted with shrinking patches of snow. Holly kept hoping to make snow angels and snowmen, but so far, Mother Nature wasn't cooperating.

The palatial house looked as if it had grown right out of the woods surrounding it. The place was gorgeous, but a little intimidating. And from everything she'd heard, so was the man who lived here. Oh, Kaye was crazy about him, but then Kaye took in stray dogs, cats, wounded birds and any lonely soul she happened across. But there was plenty of speculation about Sam Henry in town.

Joy knew he used to be a painter, and she'd actually seen a few of his paintings online. Judging by the art he created, she would have guessed him to be warm, optimistic and, well, *nice*. According to Kaye, though, the man was quiet, reclusive to the point of being a hermit, and she thought he was lonely at the bottom of it. But to

Joy's way of thinking, if you didn't want to be lonely, you got out and met people. Heck, it was so rare to see Sam Henry in town, spotting him was the equivalent of a Bigfoot sighting. She'd caught only the occasional rare glimpse of the man herself.

But none of that mattered at the moment, Joy told herself. She and Holly needed a place to stay for the month, and this housesitting/cooking/cleaning job had turned up at just the right time. Taking Holly's hand, she headed for the front door, the little girl skipping alongside her, chattering about princesses and castles the whole way.

For just a second, Joy envied her little girl's simpler outlook on life. For Holly, this was an adventure in a magical castle. For Joy, it was moving into a big, se-cluded house with a secretive and, according to Kaye, cranky man. Okay, now she was making it sound like she was living in a Gothic novel. Kaye lived here year-round, right? And had for years. Surely Joy could sur-vive a month. Determined now to get off on the right foot, she plastered a smile on her face, climbed up to the wide front porch and knocked on the double doors.

She was still smiling a moment later when the door was thrown open and she looked up into a pair of suspi-cious brown eyes. An instant snap of attraction slapped at Joy, surprising her with its force. His black hair was long, hitting past the collar of his dark red shirt, and the thick mass lifted slightly as another cold wind trick-led past. His jaws were shadowed by whiskers and his mouth was a grim straight line. He was tall, with broad shoulders, narrow hips and long legs currently encased in worn, faded denim that stacked on the tops of a pair of weathered brown cowboy boots.

If it wasn't for the narrowed eyes and the grim expression on his face, he would have been the star of any number of Joy's personal fantasies. Then he spoke and the already tattered remnants of said fantasy drifted away.

"This is private property," he said in a voice that was more of a growl. "If you're looking for town, go back to the main road and turn left. Stay on the road and you'll get there in about twenty minutes."

Well, this was starting off well.

"Thanks," she said, desperately trying to hang on to the smile curving her mouth as well as her optimistic attitude. "But I'm not lost. I've just come from town."

If anything, his frown deepened. "Then why're you here?"

"Nice to meet you, too," Joy said, half tugging Holly behind her. Not that she was afraid of him—but why subject her little girl to a man who looked like he'd rather slam the door in their faces than let them in?

"I repeat," he said, "who are you?"

"I'm Joy. Kaye's friend?" It came out as a question though she hadn't meant it as one.

"You're kidding." His eyes went wide as his gaze swept her up and down in a fast yet thorough examination.

She didn't know whether to be flattered or insulted. But when his features remained stiff and cold, she went for insulted.

"Is there a problem?" she asked. "Kaye told me you'd be expecting me and—"

"You're not old."

She blinked at him. "Thank you for noticing, though I've got to say, if Kaye ever hears you call her 'old,' it won't be pretty."

"That's not—" He stopped and started again. "I was expecting a woman Kaye's age," he continued. "Not someone like you. Or," he added with a brief glance at Holly, "a child."

Why hadn't Kaye told him about Holly? For a split second, Joy worried over that and wondered if he'd try to back out of their deal now. But an instant later she assured herself that no matter what happened, she was going to hold him to his word. She needed to be here and she wasn't about to leave.

She took a breath and ignored the cool chill in his eyes. "Well, that's a lovely welcome, thanks. Look, it's cold out here. If you don't mind, I'd like to come in and get settled."

He shook his head, opened his mouth to speak, but Holly cut him off.

"Are you the prince?" She stepped out from behind her mother, tipped her head back and studied him.

"The what?"

Joy tensed. She didn't want to stop Holly from talking—wasn't entirely sure she *could*—but she was more than willing to intervene if the quietly hostile man said something she didn't like.

"The prince," Holly repeated, the tiny lisp that defined her voice tugging at Joy's heart. "Princes live in castles."

Joy caught the barest glimmer of a smile brush across his face before it was gone again. Somehow, though, that ghost of real emotion made her feel better.

"No," he said and his voice was softer than it had been. "I'm not a prince."

Joy could have said something to that, and judging by the glance he shot her, he half expected her to. But irritating him further wasn't going to get her and Holly into the house and out of the cold.

"But he looks like a prince, doesn't he, Mommy?"

A prince with a lousy attitude. A dark prince, maybe.

"Sure, honey," she said with a smile for the little girl shifting from foot to foot in her eagerness to get inside the "castle."

Turning back to the man who still stood like an immovable object in the doorway, Joy said reasonably, "Look, I'm sorry we aren't what you were expecting. But here we are. Kaye told you about the fire at our house, right?"

"The firemen came and let me sit in the big truck with the lights going and it was really bright and blinking."

"Is that right?" That vanishing smile of his came and went again in a blink.

"And it smelled really bad," Holly put in, tugging her hand free so she could pinch her own nose.

"It did," Joy agreed, running one hand over the back of Holly's head. "And," she continued, "it did enough damage that we can't stay there while they're fixing it—" She broke off and said, "Can we finish this inside? It's cold out here."

For a second, she wasn't sure he'd agree, but then he nodded, moved back and opened the wide, heavy door. Heat rushed forward to greet them, and Joy nearly sighed in pleasure. She gave a quick look around at the entry hall. The gleaming, honey-colored logs shone in the overhead light. The entry floor was made up of huge square tiles in mottled earth tones. Probably way easier to clean up melting snow from tile floors instead of wood, she told herself and let her gaze quickly move over what she could see of the rest of the house.

It seemed even bigger on the inside, which was hard to believe, and with the lights on against the dark of winter, the whole place practically glowed. A long hallway led off to the back of the house, and on the right was a stairway leading to the second floor. Near the front door, there was a handmade coat tree boasting a half-dozen brass hooks and a padded bench attached.

Shrugging out of her parka, Joy hung it on one of the hooks, then turned and pulled Holly's jacket off as well, hanging it alongside hers. The warmth of the house surrounded her and all Joy could think was, she really wanted to stay. She and Holly needed a place and this house with its soft glow was…welcoming, in spite of its owner.

She glanced at the man watching her, and one look told her that he really wanted her gone. But she wasn't going to allow that.

The house was gigantic, plenty of room for her and Holly to live and still stay out of Sam Henry's way. There was enough land around the house so that her little girl could play. One man to cook and clean for, which would leave her plenty of time to work on her laptop. And oh, if he made them leave, she and her daughter would end up staying in a hotel in town for a month. Just the thought of trying to keep a five-year-old happy when she was trapped in a small, single room for weeks made Joy tired.

"Okay, we're inside," he said. "Let's talk."

"Right. It's a beautiful house." She walked past him, forcing the man to follow her as she walked to the first doorway and peeked in. A great room—that really lived up to the name.

Floor-to-ceiling windows provided a sweeping view

of the frozen lake, a wide lawn and a battalion of pines that looked to be scraping the underside of the low-hanging gray clouds. There was a massive hearth on one wall, where a wood fire burned merrily. A big-screen TV took up most of another wall, and there were brown leather couches and chairs sprinkled around the room, sitting on brightly colored area rugs. Handcrafted wood tables held lamps and books, with more books tucked onto shelves lining yet another wall.

"I love reading, too, and what a terrific spot for it," Joy said, watching Holly as the girl wandered the room, then headed straight to the windows where she peered out, both hands flat against the glass.

"Yeah, it works for me." He came up beside her, crossed his arms over his chest and said, "Anyway…"

"You won't even know we're here," Joy spoke up quickly. "And it'll be a pleasure to take care of this place. Kaye loves working here, so I'm sure Holly and I will be just as happy."

"Yeah, but—"

She ignored his frown and the interruption. On a roll, she had no intention of stopping. "I'm going to take a look around. You don't have to worry about giving me a tour. I'll find my own way—"

"About that—"

Irritation flashed across his features and Joy almost felt sorry for him. Not sorry enough to stop, though. "What time do you want dinner tonight?"

Before he could answer, she said, "How about six? If that works for you, we'll keep it that way for the month. Otherwise, we can change it."

"I didn't agree—"

"Kaye said Holly and I should use her suite of rooms

off the kitchen, so we'll just go get settled in and you can get back to what you were doing when we got here." A bright smile on her face, she called, "Holly, come with me now." She looked at him. "Once I've got our things put away, I'll look through your supplies and get dinner started, if it's all right with you." *And even if it isn't*, she added silently.

"Talking too fast to be interrupted doesn't mean this is settled," he told her flatly.

The grim slash of his mouth matched the iciness in his tone. But Joy wasn't going to give up easily. "There's nothing to settle. We agreed to be here for the month and that's what we're going to do."

He shook his head. "I don't think this is going to work out."

"You can't know that, and I think you're wrong," she said, stiffening her spine as she faced him down. She needed this job. This place. For one month. And she wouldn't let him take it from her. Keeping her voice low so Holly wouldn't overhear, she said, "I'm holding you to the deal we made."

"*We* didn't make a deal."

"You did with Kaye."

"Kaye's not here."

"Which is why we are." *One point to me.* Joy grinned and met his gaze, deliberately glaring right into those shuttered brown eyes of his.

"Are there fairies in the woods?" Holly wondered aloud.

"I don't know, honey," Joy said.

"No," Sam told her.

Holly's face fell and Joy gave him a stony glare. He could be as nasty and unfriendly with her as he wanted to be. But he wouldn't be mean to her daughter. "He means he's never seen any fairies, sweetie."

"Oh." The little girl's smile lit up her face. "Me either. But maybe I can sometime, Mommy says."

With a single look, Joy silently dared the man to pop her daughter's balloon again. But he didn't.

"Then you'll have to look harder, won't you?" he said instead, then lifted his gaze to Joy's. With what looked like regret glittering in his eyes, he added, "You'll have a whole month to look for them."

Two

A few hours in the workshop didn't improve Sam's mood. Not a big surprise. How the hell could he clear his mind when it was full of images of Joy Curran and her daughter?

As her name floated through his mind *again*, Sam deliberately pushed it away, though he knew damn well she'd be sliding back in. Slowly, methodically, he ran the hand sander across the top of the table he was currently building. The satin feel of the wood beneath his hands fed the artist inside him as nothing else could.

It had been six years since he'd picked up a paintbrush, faced a blank canvas and brought the images in his mind to life. And even now, that loss tore at him and his fingers wanted to curl around a slim wand of walnut and surround himself with the familiar scents of turpentine and linseed oil. He wouldn't—but the desire was always there, humming through his blood, through his dreams.

But though he couldn't paint, he also couldn't simply sit in the big house staring out windows, either.

So he'd turned his need for creativity, for creation, toward the woodworking that had always been a hobby. In this workshop, he built tables, chairs, small whimsical backyard lawn ornaments, and lost himself in the doing. He didn't have to think. Didn't have to remember.

Yet, today, his mind continuously drifted from the project at hand to the main house, where the woman was. It had been a long time since he'd had an attractive woman around for longer than an evening. And the prospect of Joy being in his house for the next month didn't make Sam happy. But damned if he could think of a way out of it. Sure, he could toss her and the girl out, but then what?

Memories of last December when he'd been on his own and damn near starved to death rushed into his brain. He didn't want to repeat that, but could he stand having a kid around all the time?

That thought brought him up short. He dropped the block sander onto the table, turned and looked out the nearest window to the house. The lights in the kitchen were on and he caught a quick glimpse of Joy moving through the room. Joy. Even her name went against everything he'd become. She was too much, he thought. Too beautiful. Too cheerful. Too tempting.

Well, hell. Recognizing the temptation she represented was only half the issue. Resisting her and what she made him want was the other half. She'd be right there, in his house, for a month. And he was still feeling that buzz of desire that had pumped into him from the moment he first saw her getting out of her car. He didn't want that buzz but couldn't ignore it, either.

When his cell phone rang, he dug it out of his pocket and looked at the screen. His mother. "Perfect. This day just keeps getting better."

Sam thought about not answering it, but he knew that Catherine Henry wouldn't be put off for long. She'd simply keep calling until he answered. Might as well get it over with.

"Hi, Mom."

"There's my favorite son," she said.

"Your *only* son," he pointed out.

"Hence the favorite," his mother countered. "You didn't want to answer, did you?"

He smiled to himself. The woman was practically psychic. Leaning one hip against the workbench, he said, "I did, though, didn't I?"

"Only because you knew I'd harangue you."

He rolled his eyes and started sanding again, slowly, carefully moving along the grain. "What's up, Mom?"

"Kaye texted me to say she was off on her trip," his mother said. "And I wanted to see if Joy and Holly arrived all right."

He stopped, dropped the sander and stared out at the house where the woman and her daughter were busily taking over. "You knew?"

"Well, of course I knew," Catherine said with a laugh. "Kaye keeps me up to date on what's happening there since my favorite son tends to be a hermit and uncommunicative."

He took a deep breath and told himself that temper would be wasted on his mother. It would roll right on by, so there was no point in it. "You should have warned me."

"About what? Joy? Kaye tells me she's wonderful."

"About her daughter," he ground out, reminding himself to keep it calm and cool. He felt a sting of betrayal because his mother should have understood how having a child around would affect him.

There was a long pause before his mother said, "Honey, you can't avoid all children for the rest of your life."

He flinched at the direct hit. "I didn't say I was."

"Sweetie, you didn't have to. I know it's hard, but Holly isn't Eli."

He winced at the sound of the name he never allowed himself to so much as think. His hand tightened around the phone as if it were a lifeline. "I know that."

"Good." Her voice was brisk again, with that clipped tone that told him she was arranging everything in her mind. "Now that that's settled, you be nice. Kaye and I think you and Joy will get along very well."

He went completely still. "Is that right?"

"Joy's very independent and according to Kaye, she's friendly, outgoing—just what you need, sweetie. Someone to wake you up again."

Sam smelled a setup. Every instinct he possessed jumped up and shouted a warning even though it was too late to avoid what was already happening. Scraping one hand down his face, he shook his head and told himself he should have been expecting this. For years now, his mother had been nagging at him to move on. To accept the pain and to pick up the threads of his life.

She wanted him happy, and he understood that. What

she didn't understand was that he'd already lost his shot at happiness. "I'm not interested, Mom."

"Sure you are, you just don't know it," his mother said in her crisp, no-nonsense tone. "And it's not like I've booked a church or expect you to sweep Joy off her feet, for heaven's sake. But would it kill you to be nice? Honestly, sweetie, you've become a hermit, and that's just not healthy."

Sam sighed heavily as his anger drained away. He didn't like knowing that his family was worried about him. The last few years had been hard. On everyone. And he knew they'd all feel better about him if he could just pick up the threads of his life and get back to some sort of "normal." But a magical wave of his hands wasn't going to accomplish that.

The best he could do was try to convince his mother to leave him be. To let him deal with his own past in his own way. The chances of that, though, were slim. That was the burden of family. When you tried to keep them at bay for their own sake, they simply refused to go. Evidence: she and Kaye trying to play matchmaker.

But just because they thought they were setting him up with Joy didn't mean he had to go along. Which he wouldn't. Sure, he remembered that instant attraction he'd felt for Joy. That slam of heat, lust, that let him know he was alive even when he hated to acknowledge it. But it didn't change anything. He didn't want another woman in his life. Not even one with hair like sunlight and eyes the color of a summer sky.

And he for damn sure didn't want another child in his life.

What he had to do, then, was to make it through December, then let his world settle back into place. When nothing happened between him and Joy, his mother and Kaye would have to give up on the whole Cupid thing. A relief for all of them.

"Sam?" His mother's voice prompted a reaction from him. "Have you slipped into a coma? Do I need to call someone?"

He laughed in spite of everything then told himself to focus. When dealing with Catherine Henry, a smart man paid attention. "No. I'm here."

"Well, good. I wondered." Another long pause before she said, "Just do me a favor, honey, and don't scare Joy off. If she's willing to put up with you for a month, she must really need the job."

Insulting, but true. Wryly, he said, "Thanks, Mom."

"You know what I mean." Laughing a little, she added, "That didn't come out right, but still. Hermits are *not* attractive, Sam. They grow their beards and stop taking showers and mutter under their breath all the time."

"Unbelievable," he muttered, then caught himself and sighed.

"It's already started," his mother said. "But seriously. People in those mountains are going to start telling their kids scary stories about the weird man who never leaves his house."

"I'm not weird," he argued. And he didn't have a beard. Just whiskers he hadn't felt like shaving in a few days. As far as muttering went, that usually happened only when his mother called.

"Not yet, but if things don't change, it's coming."

Scowling now, he turned away from the view of the house and stared unseeing at the wall opposite him. "Mom, you mean well. I know that."

"I do, sweetie, and you've got to—"

He cut her off, because really, it was the only way. "I'm already doing what I have to do, Mom. I've had enough change in my life already, thanks."

Then she was quiet for a few seconds as if she was remembering the pain of that major change. "I know. Sweetie, I know. I just don't want you to lose the rest of your life, okay?"

Sam wondered if it was all mothers or just his who refused to see the truth when it was right in front of them. He had nothing left to lose. How the hell could he have a life when he'd already lost everything that mattered? Was he supposed to forget? To pretend none of it had happened? How could he when every empty day reminded him of what was missing?

But saying any of that to his mother was a waste of time. She wouldn't get it. Couldn't possibly understand what it cost him every morning just to open his eyes and move through the day. They tried, he told himself. His whole family tried to be there for him, but the bottom line was, he was alone in this. Always would be.

And that thought told Sam he'd reached the end of his patience. "Okay, look, Mom, good talking to you, but I've got a project to finish."

"All right then. Just, think about what I said, okay?"

Hard not to when she said it every time she talked to him.

"Sure." A moment later he hung up and stuffed the phone back into his pocket. He shouldn't have answered it. Should have turned the damn thing off and forced her to leave a message. Then he wouldn't feel twisted up inside over things that could never be put right. It was better his way. Better to bury those memories, that pain, so deeply that they couldn't nibble away at him every waking moment.

A glance at the clock on the wall told him it was six and time for the dinner Joy had promised. Well, he was in no mood for company. He came and went when he liked and just because his temporary housekeeper made dinner didn't mean he had to show up. He scowled, then deliberately, he picked up the sander again and turned his focus to the wood. Sanding over the last coat of stain and varnish was meticulous work. He could laser in on the task at hand and hope it would be enough to ease the tension rippling through him.

It was late by the time he finally forced himself to stop working for the day. Darkness was absolute as he closed up the shop and headed for the house. He paused in the cold to glance up at the cloud-covered sky and wondered when the snow would start. Then he shifted his gaze to the house where a single light burned softly against the dark. He'd avoided the house until he was sure the woman and her daughter would be locked away in Kaye's rooms. For a second, he felt a sting of guilt for blowing off whatever dinner it was she'd made. Then again, he hadn't asked her to cook, had he? Hell, he hadn't even wanted her to stay. Yet somehow, she was.

Tomorrow, he told himself, he'd deal with her and lay out a few rules. If she was going to stay then she had to understand that it was the *house* she was supposed to take care of. Not him. Except for cooking—which he would eat whenever he damn well pleased—he didn't want to see her. For now, he wanted a shower and a sandwich. He was prepared for a can of soup and some grilled cheese.

Later, Sam told himself he should have known better.

He opened the kitchen door and stopped in the door-way. Joy was sitting at the table with a glass of wine in front of her and turned her head to look at him when he walked in. "You're late."

That niggle of guilt popped up again and was just as quickly squashed. He closed and locked the door behind him. "I don't punch a clock."

"I don't expect you to. But when we say dinner's at six, it'd be nice if you showed up." She shrugged. "Maybe it's just me, but most people would call that 'polite.'"

The light over the stove was the only illumination and in the dimness, he saw her eyes, locked on him, the soft blond curls falling about her face. Most women he knew would have been furious with him for missing a dinner after he'd agreed to be there. But she wasn't angry, and that made him feel the twinge of guilt even deeper than he might have otherwise. But at the bottom of it, he didn't answer to her and it was just as well she learned that early on.

"Yeah," he said, "I got involved with a project and forgot the time." A polite lie that would go down better than admitting *I was avoiding you.* "Don't worry about it. I'll fix myself something."

"No you won't." She got up and walked to the oven. "I've kept it on warm. Why don't you wash up and have dinner?"

He wanted to say no. But damned if whatever she'd made didn't smell amazing. His stomach overruled his head and Sam surrendered. He washed his hands at the sink then sat down opposite her spot at the table.

"Did you want a glass of your wine?" she asked. "It's really good."

One eyebrow lifted. Wryly, he said, "Glad you approve."

"Oh, I like wine," she said, disregarding his tone. "Nothing better than ending your day with a glass and just relaxing before bed."

Bed. Not a word he should be thinking about when she was so close and looking so…edible. "Yeah. I'll get a beer."

"I'll get it," she said, as she set a plate of pasta in a thick red meat sauce in front of him.

The scent of it wafted to him and Sam nearly groaned. "What is that?"

"Baked mostaccioli with mozzarella and parmesan in my grandmother's meat sauce." She opened the fridge, grabbed a beer then walked back to the table. Handing it to him, she sat down, picked up her wineglass and had a sip.

"It smells great," he said grudgingly.

"Tastes even better," she assured him. Drawing one knee up, she propped her foot on her chair and looked at him. "Just so you know, I won't be waiting on you every night. I mean getting you a beer and stuff."

He snorted. "I'll make a note."

Then Sam took a bite and sighed. Whatever else Joy Curran was, the woman could *cook*. Whatever they had to talk about could wait, he thought, while he concentrated on the unexpected prize of a really great meal. So he said nothing else for a few bites, but finally sat back, took a drink of his beer and looked at her.

"Good?"

"Oh, yeah," he said. "Great."

She smiled and her face just—lit up. Sam's breath caught in his chest as he looked at her. That flash of something hot, something staggering, hit him again and he desperately tried to fight it off. Even while that strong buzz swept through him, remnants of the phone call with his mother rose up in his mind and he wondered if Joy had been in on whatever his mother and Kaye had cooking between them.

Made sense, didn't it? Young, pretty woman. Single mother. Why not try to find a rich husband?

Speculatively, he looked at her and saw sharp blue eyes without the slightest hint of guile. So maybe she wasn't in on it. He'd reserve judgment. For now. But whether she was or not, he had to set down some rules. If they were going to be living together for the next month, better that they both knew where they stood.

And, as he took another bite of her spectacular pasta, he admitted that he was going to let her stay—if only for the sake of his stomach.

"Okay," he said in between bites, "you can stay for the month."

She grinned at him and took another sip of her wine to celebrate. "That's great, thanks. Although, I wasn't really going to leave."

Amused, he picked up his beer. "Is that right?"

"It is." She nodded sharply. "You should know that I'm pretty stubborn when I want something, and I really wanted to stay here for the month."

He leaned back in his chair. The pale wash of the stove light reached across the room to spill across her, making that blond hair shine and her eyes gleam with amusement and determination. The house was quiet, and the darkness crouched just outside the window made the light and warmth inside seem almost intimate. Not a word he wanted to think about at the moment.

"Can you imagine trying to keep a five-year-old entertained in a tiny hotel room for a month?" She shivered and shook her head. "Besides being a living nightmare for me, it wouldn't be fair to Holly. Kids need room to run. Play."

He remembered. A succession of images flashed across his mind before he could stop them. As if the memories had been crouched in a corner, just waiting for the chance to escape, he saw pictures of another child. Running. Laughing. Brown eyes shining as he looked over his shoulder and—

Sam's grip on the beer bottle tightened until a part of him wondered why it didn't simply shatter in his hand. The images in his mind blurred, as if fingers of fog were reaching for them, dragging them back into the past where they belonged. Taking a slow, deep breath, he lifted the beer for a sip and swallowed the pain with it.

"Besides," she continued while he was still being dogged by memories, "this kitchen is amazing." Shaking her head, she looked around the massive room, and he knew what she was seeing. Pale oak cabinets, dark blue granite counters with flecks of what looked like abalone shells in them. Stainless steel appliances and sink and an island big enough to float to Ireland on. And the only things Sam ever really used on his own were the double-wide fridge and the microwave.

"Cooking in here was a treat. There's so much space." Joy took another sip of wine. "Our house is so tiny, the kitchen just a smudge on the floor plan. Holly and I can't be in there together without knocking each other down. Plus there's the ancient plumbing and the cabinet doors that don't close all the way...but it's just a rental. One of these days, we'll get our own house.

Nothing like this one of course, but a little bigger with a terrific kitchen and a table like this one where Holly can sit and do her homework while I make dinner—"

Briskly, he got back to business. It was either that or let her go far enough to sketch out her dream kitchen. "Okay, I get it. You need to be here, and for food like this, I'm willing to go along."

She laughed shortly.

He paid zero attention to the musical sound of that laugh or how it made her eyes sparkle in the low light. "So here's the deal. You can stay the month like we agreed."

"But?" she asked. "I hear a *but* in there."

"But." He nodded at her. "We steer clear of each other and you keep your daughter out of my way."

Her eyebrows arched. "Not a fan of kids, are you?"

"Not for a long time."

"Holly won't bother you," she said, lifting her wine-glass for another sip.

"All right. Good. Then we'll get along fine." He finished off the pasta, savoring that last bite before taking one more pull on his beer. "You cook and clean. I spend most of my days out in the workshop, so we probably won't see much of each other anyway."

She studied him for several long seconds before a small smile curved her mouth and a tiny dimple appeared in her right cheek. "You're sort of mysterious, aren't you?"

Once again, she'd caught him off guard. And why did she look so pleased when he'd basically told her he didn't want her kid around and didn't particularly want to spend any time with *her*, either?

"No mystery. I just like my privacy is all."

"Privacy's one thing," she mused, tipping her head to one side to study him. "Hiding out's another."

"Who says I'm hiding?"

"Kaye."

He rolled his eyes. Kaye talked to his mother. To Joy. Who the hell *wasn't* she talking to? "Kaye doesn't know everything."

"She comes close, though," Joy said. "She worries about you. For the record, she says you're lonely, but private. Nice, but shut down."

He shifted in the chair, suddenly uncomfortable with the way she was watching him. As if she could look inside him and dig out all of his secrets.

"She wouldn't tell me why you've locked yourself away up here on the mountain—"

"That's something," he muttered, then remembered his mother's warning about hermits and muttering. Scowling, he took another drink of his beer.

"People do wonder, though," she mused. "Why you keep to yourself so much. Why you almost never go into town. I mean, it's beautiful here, but don't you miss talking to people?"

"Not a bit," he told her, hoping that statement would get her to back off.

"I really would."

"Big surprise," he muttered and then inwardly winced. Hell, he'd talked more in the last ten minutes than he had in the last year. Still, for some reason, he felt the need to defend himself and the way he lived. "I have Kaye to talk to if I desperately need conversation—which I don't. And I do get into town now and then." Practically never, though, he thought.

Hell, why should he go into Franklin and put up

with being stared at and whispered over when he could order whatever he wanted online and have it shipped overnight? If nothing else, the twenty-first century was perfect for a man who wanted to be left the hell alone.

"Yeah, that doesn't happen often," she was saying. "There was actually a pool in town last summer—people were taking bets on if you'd come in at all before fall."

Stunned, he stared at her. "They were betting on me?"

"You're surprised?" Joy laughed and the sound of it filled the kitchen. "It's a tiny mountain town with not a lot going on, except for the flood of tourists. Of course they're going to place bets on the local hermit."

"I'm starting to resent that word." Sam hadn't really considered that he might be the subject of so much speculation, and he didn't much care for it. What was he supposed to do now? Go into town more often? Or less?

"Oh," she said, waving one hand at him, "don't look so grumpy about it. If it makes you feel better, when you came into Franklin and picked up those new tools at the hardware store, at the end of August, Jim Bowers won nearly two hundred dollars."

"Good for him," Sam muttered, not sure how he felt about all of this. He'd moved to this small mountain town for the solitude. For the fact that no one would give a damn about him. And after five years here, he found out the town was paying close enough attention to him to actually lay money on his comings and goings. Shaking his head, he asked only, "Who's Jim Bowers?"

"He and his wife own the bakery."

"There's a bakery in Franklin?"

She sighed, shaking her head slowly. "It's so sad that you didn't know that."

A short laugh shot from his throat, surprising them both.

"You should do that more often," she said quietly.

"What?"

"Smile. Laugh. Lose the etched-in-stone-grumble expression."

"Do you have an opinion on everything?" he asked.

"Don't you?" she countered.

Yeah, he did. And his considered opinion on this particular situation was that he might have made a mistake in letting Joy and her daughter stay here for the next month.

But damned if he could regret it at the moment.

Three

By the following morning, Joy had decided the man needed to be pushed into getting outside himself. Sitting in the kitchen with him the night before had been interesting and more revealing than he would have liked, she was sure. Though he had a gruff, cold exterior, Joy had seen enough in his eyes to convince her that the real man was hidden somewhere beneath that hard shell he carried around with him.

She had known he'd been trying to avoid seeing her again by staying late in his workshop. Which was why she'd been waiting for him in the kitchen. Joy had always believed that it was better to face a problem head-on rather than dance around it and hope it would get better. So she'd been prepared to argue and bargain with him to make sure she and Holly could stay for the month.

And she'd known the moment he tasted her baked

mostaccioli that arguments would not be necessary. He might not want her there, but her cooking had won him over. Clearly, he didn't like it, but he'd put up with her for a month if it meant he wouldn't starve. Joy could live with that.

What she might not be able to live with was her body's response to being near him. She hadn't expected that. Hadn't felt anything remotely like awareness since splitting with Holly's father before the little girl was born. And she wasn't looking for it now. She had a good life, a growing business and a daughter who made her heart sing. Who could ask for more than that?

But the man…intrigued her. She could admit, at least to herself, that sitting with him in the shadow-filled night had made her feel things she'd be better off forgetting. It wasn't her fault, of course. Just look at the man. Tall, dark and crabby. What woman wouldn't have a few fantasies about a man who looked like he did? Okay, normally she wouldn't enjoy the surly attitude— God knew she'd had enough "bad boys" in her life. But the shadows of old pain in his eyes told Joy that Sam hadn't always been so closed off.

So there was interest even when she knew there shouldn't be. His cold detachment was annoying, but the haunted look in his eyes drew her in. Made her want to comfort. Care. Dangerous feelings to have.

"Mommy, is it gonna snow today?"

Grateful for that sweet voice pulling her out of her circling thoughts, Joy walked to the kitchen table, bent down and kissed the top of her daughter's head.

"I don't think so, baby. Eat your pancakes now. And then we'll take a walk down to the lake."

"And skate?" Holly's eyes went bright with excitement at the idea. She forked up a bite of pancake and chewed quickly, eager now to get outside.

"We'll see if the lake's frozen enough, all right?" She'd brought their ice skates along since she'd known about the lake. And though she was no future competitor, Holly loved skating almost as much as she loved fairy princesses.

Humming, Holly nodded to herself and kept eating, pausing now and then for a sip of her milk. Her heels thumped against the chair rungs and sounded like a steady heartbeat in the quiet morning. Her little girl couldn't have been contained in a hotel room for a month. She had enough energy for three healthy kids and needed the room to run and play.

This house, this place, with its wide yard and homey warmth, was just what she needed. Simple as that. As for what Sam Henry made Joy feel? That would remain her own little secret.

"Hi, Sam!" Holly called out. "Mommy made pancakes. We're cellbrating."

"Celebrating," Joy corrected automatically, before she turned to look at the man standing in the open doorway. And darn it, she felt that buzz of awareness again the minute her gaze hit his. So tall, she thought with approval. He wore faded jeans and the scarred boots again, but today he wore a long-sleeved green thermal shirt with a gray flannel shirt over it. His too-long hair framed his face, and his eyes still carried the secrets that she'd seen in them the night before. They stared at each other as the seconds ticked past, and Joy wondered what he was thinking.

Probably trying to figure out the best way to get her and Holly to leave, she thought.

Well, that wasn't going to happen. She turned to the coffeemaker and poured him a cup. "Black?"

He accepted it. "How'd you guess?"

She smiled. "You look like the no-frills kind of man to me. Just can't imagine you ordering a half-caf, vanilla bean cappuccino."

He snorted, but took a long drink and sighed at the rush of caffeine in his system. Joy could appreciate that, since she usually got up a half hour before Holly just so she could have the time to enjoy that first, blissful cup of coffee.

"What're you celebrating?" he asked.

Joy flushed a little. "Staying here in the 'castle.'"

Holly's heels continued to thump as she hummed her way through breakfast. "We're having pancakes and then we're going skating on the lake and—"

"I said we'll see," Joy reminded her.

"Stay away from the lake."

Joy looked at him. His voice was low, brusque, and his tone brooked no argument. All trace of amusement was gone from eyes that looked as deep and dark as the night itself. "What?"

"The lake," he said, making an obvious effort to soften the hard note in his voice. "It's not solid enough. Too dangerous for either of you to be on it."

"Are you sure?" Joy asked, glancing out the kitchen window at the frigid world beyond the glass. Sure, it hadn't snowed much so far, but it had been below freezing every night for the last couple of weeks, so the lake should be frozen over completely by now.

"No point in taking the chance, is there? If it stays this cold, maybe you could try it in a week or two…"

Well, she thought, at least he'd accepted that she and

Holly would still be there in two weeks. That was a step in the right direction, anyway. His gaze fixed on hers, deliberately avoiding looking at Holly, though the little girl was practically vibrating with barely concealed excitement. In his eyes, Joy saw real worry and a shadow of something darker, something older.

"Okay," she said, going with her instinct to ease whatever it was that was driving him. Reaching out, she laid one hand on his forearm and felt the tension gripping him before he slowly, deliberately pulled away. "Okay. No skating today."

"Moooommmmmyyyyy…"

How her daughter managed to put ten or more syllables into a single word was beyond her.

"We'll skate another day, okay, sweetie? How about today we take a walk in the forest and look for pinecones?" She kept her gaze locked on Sam's, so she actually saw relief flash across his eyes. What was it in his past that had him still tied into knots?

"Can we paint 'em for Christmas?"

"Sure we can, baby. We'll go after we clean the kitchen, so eat up." Then to Sam, she said, "How about some pancakes?"

"No, thanks." He turned to go.

"One cup of coffee and that's it?"

He looked back at her. "You're here to take care of the house. Not me."

"Not true. I'm also here to cook. For you." She smiled a little. "You should try the pancakes. They're really good, even if I do say so myself."

"Mommy makes the *best* pancakes," Holly tossed in.

"I'm sure she does," he said, still not looking at the girl.

Joy frowned and wondered why he disliked kids so much, but she didn't ask.

"Look, while you're here, don't worry about breakfast for me. I don't usually bother and if I change my mind I can take care of it myself."

"You're a very stubborn man, aren't you?"

He took another sip of coffee. "I've got a project to finish and I'm going out to get started on it."

"Well, you can at least take a muffin." Joy walked to the counter and picked a muffin—one of the batch she'd made just an hour ago—out of a ceramic blue bowl.

He sighed. "If I do, will you let me go?"

"If I do, will you come back?"

"I live here."

Joy smiled again and handed it over to him. "Then you are released. Go. Fly free."

His mouth twitched and he shook his head. "People think I'm weird."

"I don't." She said it quickly and wasn't sure why she had until she saw a quick gleam of pleasure in his eyes.

"Be sure to tell Kaye," he said, and left, still shaking his head.

"'Bye, Sam!" Holly's voice followed him and Joy was pretty sure he quickened his steps as if trying to outrun it.

Three hours later, Sam was still wishing he'd eaten those damn pancakes. He remembered the scent of them in the air, and his stomach rumbled in complaint. Pouring another cup of coffee from his workshop pot, he stared down at the small pile of blueberry muffin crumbs and wished he had another one. Damn it.

Wasn't it enough that Joy's face kept surfacing in

his mind? Did she have to be such a good cook, too? And who asked her to make him breakfast? Kaye never did. Usually he made do with coffee and a power bar of some kind, and that was fine. Always had been anyway. But now he still had the lingering taste of that muffin in his mouth, and his stomach was still whining over missing out on pancakes.

But to eat them, he'd have had to take a seat at the table beside a chattering little girl. And all that sunshine and sweet innocence was just too much for Sam to take. He took a gulp of hot coffee and let the blistering liquid burn its way to the pit of his sadly empty stomach. And as hungry as he was, at least he'd completed his project. He leaned back against the workbench, crossed his feet at the ankles, stared at the finished table and gave himself a silent pat on the back.

In the overhead shop light, the wood gleamed and shone like a mirror in the sun. Every slender grain of the wood was displayed beautifully under the fresh coat of varnish, and the finish was smooth as glass. The thick pedestal was gnarled and twisted, yet it, too, had been methodically sanded until all the rough edges were gone as if they'd never been.

Taking a deadfall tree limb and turning it into the graceful pedestal of a table had taken some time, but it had been worth it. The piece was truly one of a kind, and he knew the people he'd made it for would approve. It was satisfying, seeing something in your head and creating it in the physical world. He used to do that with paint and canvas, bringing imaginary places to life, making them real.

Sam frowned at the memories, because remembering the passion he'd had for painting, the rush of starting something new and pushing himself to make it all perfect, was something he couldn't know now. Maybe he never would again. And that thought opened up a black pit at the bottom of his soul. But there was nothing he could do about it. Nothing that could ease that need, that bone-deep craving.

At least he had this, he told himself. Woodworking had given him, if not completion, then satisfaction. It filled his days and helped to ease the pain of missing the passion that had once driven his life. But then, he thought, once upon a time, his entire world had been different. The shame was, he hadn't really appreciated what he'd had while he had it. At least, he told himself, not enough to keep it.

He was still leaning against the workbench, studying the table, when a soft voice with a slight lisp asked, "Is it a fairy table?"

He swiveled his head to the child in the doorway. Her blond hair was in pigtails, she wore blue jeans, tiny pink-and-white sneakers with princesses stamped all over them and a pink parka that made her look impossibly small.

He went completely still even while his heart raced, and his mind searched for a way out of there. Her appearance, on top of old memories that continued to dog him, hit him so hard he could barely take a breath. Sam looked into blue eyes the exact shade of her mother's and told himself that it was damned cowardly to be spooked by a kid. He had his reasons, but it was lowering to admit, even to himself, that his first instinct when faced with a child was to bolt.

Since she was still watching him, waiting for an answer, Sam took another sip of coffee in the hopes of steadying himself. "No. It's just a table."

"It looks like a tree." Moving warily, she edged a little farther into the workshop and let the door close behind her, shutting out the cold.

"It used to be," he said shortly.

"Did you make it?"

"Yes." She was looking up at him with those big blue eyes, and Sam was still trying to breathe. But his "issues" weren't her fault. He was being an ass, and even he could tell. He had no reason to be so short with the girl. How was she supposed to know that he didn't do kids anymore?

"Can I touch it?" she asked, giving him a winsome smile that made Sam wonder if females were *born* knowing how to do it.

"No," he said again and once more, he heard the sharp brusqueness in his tone and winced.

"Are you crabby?" She tilted her head to one side and looked up at him in all seriousness.

"What?"

Gloomy sunlight spilled through the windows that allowed views of the pines, the lake and the leaden sky that loomed threateningly over it all. The little girl, much like her mother, looked like a ray of sunlight in the gray, and he suddenly wished that she were anywhere but there. Her innocence, her easy smile and curiosity were too hard to take. Yet, her fearlessness at facing down an irritable man made her, to Sam's mind, braver than him.

"Mommy says when I'm crabby I need a nap." She nodded solemnly. "Maybe you need a nap, too."

Sam sighed. Also, like her mother, a bad mood wasn't

going to chase her off. Accepting the inevitable, that he wouldn't be able to get rid of her by giving her one-word, bit-off answers, he said, "I don't need a nap, I'm just busy."

She walked into the workshop, less tentative now. Clearly oblivious to the fact that he didn't want her there, she wandered the shop, looking over the benches with tools, the stacks of reclaimed wood and the three tree trunks he had lined up along a wall. He should tell her to go back to the house. Wasn't it part of their bargain that the girl wouldn't bother him?

Hell.

"You don't look busy."

"Well, I am."

"Doing what?"

Sam sighed. Irritating, but that was a good question. Now that he'd finished the table, he needed to start something else. It wasn't only his hands he needed to keep busy. It was his mind. If he wasn't focusing on *something*, his thoughts would invariably track over to memories. Of another child who'd also had unending questions and bright, curious eyes. Sam cut that thought off and turned his attention to the tiny girl still exploring his workshop. Why hadn't he told her to leave? Why hadn't he taken her back to the house and told Joy to keep her away from him? Hell, why was he just standing there like a glowering statue?

"What's this do?"

The slight lisp brought a reluctant smile even as he moved toward her. She'd stopped in front of a vise that probably looked both interesting and scary to a kid.

"It's a wood vise," he said. "It holds a piece of wood steady so I can work on it."

She chewed her bottom lip and thought about it for a minute. "Like if I put my doll between my knees so I can brush her hair."

"Yeah," he said grudgingly. Smart kid. "It's sort of like that. Shouldn't you be with your mom?"

"She's cleaning and she said I could play in the yard if I stayed in the yard so I am but I wish it would snow and we could make angels and snowballs and a big snowman and—"

Amazed, Sam could only stare in awe as the little girl talked without seeming to breathe. Thoughts and words tumbled out of her in a rush that tangled together and yet somehow made sense.

Desperate now to stop the flood of high-pitched sounds, he asked, "Shouldn't you be in school?"

She laughed and shook her head so hard her pigtails flew back and forth across her eyes. "I go to pre-K cuz I'm too little for Big-K cuz my birthday comes too late cuz it's the day after Christmas and I can probably get a puppy if I ask Santa and Mommy's gonna get me a fairy doll for my birthday cuz Christmas is for the puppy and he'll be all white like a snowball and he'll play with me and lick me like Lizzie's puppy does when I get to play there and—"

So…instead of halting the rush of words and noise, he'd simply given her more to talk about. Sam took another long gulp of his coffee and hoped the caffeine would give him enough clarity to follow the kid's twisty thought patterns.

She picked up a scrap piece of wood and turned it over in her tiny hands.

"What can we make out of this?" she asked, holding it up to him, an interested gleam in her eye and an eager smile on her face.

Well, hell. He had nothing else to work on. It wasn't as though he was being drawn to the kid or anything. All he was doing was killing time. Keeping busy. Frowning to himself, Sam took the piece of wood from her and said, "If you're staying, take your jacket off and put it over there."

Her smile widened, her eyes sparkled and she hurried to do just what he told her. Shaking his head, Sam asked himself what he was doing. He should be dragging her back to the house. Telling her mother to keep the kid away from him. Instead, he was getting deeper.

"I wanna make a fairy house!"

He winced a little at the high pitch of that tiny voice and told himself that this didn't matter. He could back off again later.

Joy looked through the window of Sam's workshop and watched her daughter work alongside the man who had insisted he wanted nothing to do with her. Her heart filled when Holly turned a wide, delighted smile on the man. Then a twinge of guilt pinged inside her. Her little girl was happy and well-adjusted, but she was lacking a male role model in her life. God knew her father hadn't been interested in the job.

She'd told herself at the time that Holly would be better off without him than with a man who clearly didn't want to be a father. Yet here was another man who had claimed to want nothing to do with kids—her daughter in particular—and instead of complaining about her presence, he was working with her. Showing the little girl how to build...*something*. And Holly was loving it.

The little girl knelt on a stool at the workbench, following Sam's orders, and though she couldn't see what they were working on from her vantage point, Joy didn't think it mattered. Her daughter's happiness was evident, and whether he knew it or not, after only one day around Holly, Sam was opening up. She wondered what kind of man that opening would release.

The wind whipped past her, bringing the scent of snow, and Joy shivered deeper into her parka before walking into the warmth of the shop. With the blast of cold air announcing her presence, both Sam and Holly turned to look at her. One of them grinned. One of them scowled.

Of course.

"Mommy! Come and see, come and see!"

There was no invitation in Sam's eyes, but Joy ignored that and went to them anyway.

"It's a fairy house!" Holly squealed it, and Joy couldn't help but laugh. Everything these days was fairy. Fairy princesses. Fairy houses.

"We're gonna put it outside and the fairies can come and live in it and I can watch from the windows."

"That's a great idea."

"Sam says if I get too close to the fairies I'll scare 'em away," Holly continued, with an earnest look on her face. "But I wouldn't. I would be really quiet and they wouldn't see me or anything…"

"Sam says?" she repeated to the man standing there pretending he was somewhere else.

"Yeah," he muttered, rubbing the back of his neck. "If she watches through the window, she won't be out in the forest or—I don't know."

He was embarrassed. She could see it. And for some

reason, knowing that touched her heart. The man who didn't want a child anywhere near him just spent two hours helping a little girl build a house for fairies. There was so much more to him than the face he showed to the world. And the more Joy discovered, the more she wanted to know.

Oh, boy.

"It's beautiful, baby." And it was. Small, but sturdy, it was made from mismatched pieces of wood and the roof was scalloped by layering what looked like Popsicle sticks.

"I glued it and everything, but Sam helped and he says I can put stuff in it for the fairies like cookies and stuff that they'll like and I can watch them…"

He shrugged. "She wanted to make something. I had some scrap wood. That's all."

"Thank you."

Impatience flashed across his face. "Not a big deal. And not going to be happening all the time, either," he added as a warning.

"Got it," Joy said, nodding. If he wanted to cling to that grumpy, don't-like-people attitude, she wouldn't fight him on it. Especially since she now knew it was all a front.

Joy took a moment to look around the big room. Plenty of windows would let in sunlight should the clouds ever drift away. A wide, concrete floor, scrupulously swept clean. Every kind of tool imaginable hung on the pegboards that covered most of two walls. There were stacks of lumber, most of it looking ragged and old—reclaimed wood—and there were deadfall tree trunks waiting for who knew what to be done to them.

Then she spotted the table and was amazed she

hadn't noticed it immediately. Walking toward it, she sighed with pleasure as she examined it carefully, from the shining surface to the twisted tree limb base. "This is gorgeous," she whispered and whipped her head around to look at him. "You made this?"

He scowled again. Seemed to be his go-to expression. "Yeah."

"It's amazing, really."

"It's also still wet, so be careful. The varnish has to cure for a couple of days yet."

"I'm not touching."

"I didn't either, Mommy, did I, Sam?"

"Almost but not quite," he said.

Joy's fingers itched to stroke that smooth, sleek tabletop, so she curled her hands into fists to resist the urge. "I've seen some of your things in the gallery in town, and I loved them, too, by the way. But this." She shook her head and felt a real tug of possessiveness. "This I love."

"Thanks."

She thought the shadows in his eyes lightened a bit, but a second later, they were back so she couldn't be sure. "What are you working on next?"

"Like mother like daughter," he muttered.

"Curious?" she asked. "You bet. What are you going to do with those tree trunks?" The smallest of them was three feet around and two feet high.

"Work on them when I get a minute to myself." That leave-me-alone tone was back, and Joy decided not to push her luck any further. She'd gotten more than a few words out of him today and maybe they'd reached his limit.

"He's not mad, Mommy, he's just crabby."

Joy laughed.

Holly patted Sam's arm. "You could sing to him like you sing to me when I'm crabby and need a nap."

The look on Sam's face was priceless. Like he was torn between laughter and shouting and couldn't decide which way to go.

"What's that old saying?" Joy asked. "Out of the mouths of babes…"

Sam rolled his eyes and frowned. "That's it. Everybody out."

Still laughing, Joy said, "Come on, Holly, let's have some lunch. I made soup. Seemed like a good, cold day for it."

"You *made* soup?" he asked.

"Uh-huh. Beef and barley." She helped Holly get her jacket on, then zipped it closed against the cold wind. "Oh, and I made some beer bread, too."

"You made bread." He said it with a tinge of disbelief, and Joy couldn't blame him. Kaye didn't really believe in baking from scratch. Said it seemed like a waste when someone went to all the trouble to bake for her and package the bread in those nice plastic bags.

"Just beer bread. It's quick. Anyway," she said with a grin, "if you want lunch after your nap, I'll leave it on the stove for you."

"Funny."

Still smiling to herself, Joy took Holly's hand and led her out of the shop. She felt him watching her as they left and told herself that the heat swamping her was caused by her parka. And even she didn't believe it.

Four

Late at night, the big house was quiet, but not scary at all.

That thought made Joy smile to herself. She had assumed that a place this huge, with so many windows opening out onto darkness, would feel sort of like a horror movie. *Intrepid heroine wandering the halls of spooky house, alone, with nothing but a flashlight—until the battery dies.*

She shook her head and laughed at her own imagination. Instead of scary, the house felt like a safe haven against the night outside. Maybe it was the warmth of the honey-toned logs or maybe it was something else entirely. But one thing she was sure of was that she already loved it. Big, but not imposing, it was a happy house. Or would be if its owner wasn't frowning constantly.

But he'd smiled with Holly, Joy reminded herself as she headed down the long hallway toward the great room. He might have wished to be anywhere else, but he had been patient and kind to her little girl, and for Joy, nothing could have touched her more.

Her steps were quiet, her thoughts less so. She hadn't seen much of Sam since leaving him in the workshop. He'd deliberately kept his distance and Joy hadn't pushed. He'd had dinner, alone, in the dining room, then he'd disappeared again, barricading himself in the great room. She hadn't bothered him, had given him his space, and even now wouldn't be sneaking around his house if she didn't need something to read.

Holly was long since tucked in and Joy simply couldn't concentrate on the television, so she wanted to lose herself in a book. Keep her brain too busy to think about Sam. Wondering what his secrets were. Wondering what it would be like to kiss him. Wondering what the heck she was doing.

She threw a glance at the staircase and the upper floor, where the bedrooms were—where *Sam* was—and told herself to not think about it. Joy had spent the day cleaning the upstairs, though she had to admit that the man was so tidy, there wasn't much to straighten up.

But vacuuming and dusting gave her the chance to see where he slept, how he lived. His bedroom was huge, offering a wide view of the lake and the army of pine trees that surrounded it. His bed was big enough for a family of four to sleep comfortably, and the room was decorated in soothing shades of slate blue and forest green. The attached bath had had her sighing in imagined pleasure.

A sea of pale green marble, from the floors to the counters, to the gigantic shower and the soaker whirlpool tub that sat in front of a bay window with a view of the treetops. He lived well, but so solitarily it broke her heart. There were no pieces of *him* in the room. No photos, no art on the wall, nothing to point to this being his *home*. As beautiful as it all was, it was still impersonal, as if even after living there for five years he hadn't left his own impression on the place.

He made her curious. Gorgeous recluse with a sexuality that made her want to drool whenever he was nearby. Of course, the logical explanation for her zip of reaction every time she saw the man was her self-imposed Man Fast. It had been so long since she'd been on a date, been kissed…heck, been *touched*, that her body was clearly having a breakdown. A shame that she seemed to be enjoying it so much.

Sighing a little, she turned, slipped into the great room, then came to a dead stop. Sam sat in one of the leather chairs in front of the stone fireplace, where flames danced across wood and tossed flickering shadows around the room.

Joy thought about leaving before he saw her. Yes, cowardly, but understandable, considering where her imaginings had been only a second or two ago. But even as she considered sneaking out, Sam turned his head and pinned her with a long, steady look.

"What do you need?"

Not exactly friendly, but not a snarl, either. Progress? She'd take it.

"A book." With little choice, Joy walked into the room and took a quick look around. This room was gorgeous during the day, but at night, with flickering shadows floating around…amazing. Really, was there anything prettier than firelight? When she shifted her gaze back to him, she realized the glow from the fire shining in his dark brown eyes was nearly hypnotic. Which was a silly thought to have, so she pushed it away fast. "Would you mind if I borrow a book? TV is just so boring and—"

He held up one hand to cut her off. "Help yourself."

"Ever gracious," she said with a quick grin. When he didn't return it, she said, "Okay, thanks."

She walked closer, surreptitiously sliding her gaze over him. His booted feet were crossed at the ankle, propped on the stone edge of the hearth. He was staring into the fire as if looking for something. The flickering light danced across his features, and she recognized the scowl that she was beginning to think was etched into his bones. "Everything okay?"

"Fine." He didn't look at her. Never took his gaze from the wavering flames.

"Okay. You've got a lot of books." She looked through a short stack of hardbacks on the table closest to him. A mix of mysteries, sci-fi and thrillers, mostly. Her favorites, too.

"Yeah. Pick one."

"I'm looking," she assured him, but didn't hurry as he clearly wanted her to. Funny, but the gruffer and shorter he became, the more intrigued she was.

Joy had seen him with Holly. She knew there were smiles inside him and a softness under the cold, hard facade. Yet he seemed determined to shut everyone out.

"Ew," she said as she quickly set one book aside. "Don't like horror. Too scary. I can't even watch scary movies. I get too involved."

"Yeah."

She smiled to herself at the one-word answer. He hadn't told her to get out, so she'd just keep talking and see what happened. "I tried, once. Went to the movies with a friend and got so scared and so tense I had to go sit in the lobby for a half hour."

She caught him give her a quick look. Interest. It was a start.

"I didn't go back into the theater until I convinced an usher to tell me who else died so I could relax."

He snorted.

Joy smiled, but didn't let him see it. "So I finally went back in to sit with my friend, and even though I knew how it would end, I still kept my hands over my eyes through the rest of the movie."

"Uh-huh."

"But," she said, moving over to the next stack of books, "that doesn't mean I'm just a romantic comedy kind of girl. I like adventure movies, too. Where lots of things blow up."

"Is that right?"

Just a murmur, but he wasn't ignoring her.

"And the Avengers movies? Love those. But maybe it's just Robert Downey Jr. I like." She paused. "What about you? Do you like those movies?"

"Haven't seen them."

"Seriously?" She picked up a mystery she'd never read but instead of leaving with the book, she sat down in the chair beside his. "I think you're the first person I've ever met who hasn't seen those movies."

He spared her one long look. "I don't get out much."

"And isn't that a shame?"

"If I thought so," he told her, "I'd go out more."

Joy laughed at the logic. "Okay, you're right. Still. Heard of DVDs? Netflix?"

"You're just going to keep talking, aren't you?"

"Probably." She settled into her chair as if getting comfy for a long visit.

He shook his head and shifted his gaze back to the fire as if that little discouragement would send her on her way.

"But back to movies," she said, leaning toward him over the arm of her chair. "This time of year I like all the Christmas ones. The gushier the better."

"Gushy."

It wasn't a question, but she answered anyway. "You know, the happy cry ones. Heck, I even tear up when the Grinch's heart grows at the end of that little cartoon." She sighed. "But to be fair, I've been known to get teary at a heart-tugging commercial at Christmastime."

"Yeah, I don't do Christmas."

"I noticed," she said, tipping her head to one side to study him. If anything, his features had tightened, his eyes had grown darker. Just the mention of the holiday had been enough to close him up tight. And still, she couldn't resist trying to reach him.

"When we're at home," she said, "Holly and I put up the Christmas decorations the day after Thanksgiving. You have to have a little restraint, don't you think? I mean this year, I actually saw Christmas wreaths for sale in *September*. That's going a little far for me and I love Christmas."

He swiveled a look at her. "If you don't mind, I don't really feel like talking."

"Oh, you don't have to. I like talking."

"No kidding."

She smiled and thought she saw a flicker of a response in his eyes, but if she had, it wasn't much of one because it faded away fast. "You can't get to know people unless you talk to them."

He scraped one hand across his face. "Yeah, maybe I don't want to get to know people."

"I think you do, you just don't want to want it."

"What?"

"I saw you today with Holly."

He shifted in his chair and frowned into the fire. "A one-time thing."

"So you said," Joy agreed, getting more comfortable in the chair, letting him know she wasn't going anywhere. "But I have to tell you how excited Holly was. She couldn't stop talking about the fairy house she built with you." A smile curved Joy's mouth. "She fell asleep in the middle of telling me about the fairy family that will move into it."

Surprisingly, the frown on his face deepened, as if hearing that he'd given a child happiness made him angry.

"It was a small thing, but it meant a lot to her. And to me. I wanted you to know that."

"Fine. You told me."

Outside, the wind kicked up, sliding beneath the eaves of the house with a sighing moan that sounded otherworldly. She glanced toward the front window at the night beyond, then turned back to the man with darkness in his eyes. She wondered what he was thinking, what he was seeing as he stared into the flames. Leaning toward him, she locked her hands around her up-drawn knees and said, "That wide front window is a perfect place for a Christmas tree, you know. The glass would reflect all the lights…"

His gaze shot to hers. "I already told you, I don't do Christmas."

"Sure, I get it," she said, though she really didn't. "But if you don't want to, Holly and I will take care of decorating and—"

He stood up, grabbed a fireplace poker and determinedly stabbed at the logs, causing sparks to fly and sizzle on their wild flight up the chimney. When he was finished, he turned a cold look on her and said, "No tree. No decorations. No Christmas."

"Wow. Speak of the Grinch."

He blew out a breath and glared at her, but it just didn't work. It was too late for him to try to convince her that he was an ogre or something. Joy had seen him with Holly. His patience. His kindness. Even though he hadn't wanted to be around the girl, he'd given her the gift of his time. Joy'd had a glimpse of the man behind the mask now and wouldn't be fooled again. Crabby? Yes. Mean? No.

"You're not here to celebrate the holidays," he reminded her in a voice just short of a growl. "You're here to take care of the house."

"I know. But, if you change your mind, I'm an excellent multitasker." She got to her feet and held on to the book she'd chosen from the stack. Staring up into his eyes, she said, "I'll do my job, but just so you know? You don't scare me, Sam, so you might as well quit trying so hard."

Every night, she came to the great room. Every night, Sam told himself not to be there. And every night, he was sitting by the fire, waiting for her.

Not like he was talking to her. But apparently *noth-*

ing stopped *her* from talking. Not even his seeming disinterest in her presence. He'd heard about her business, about the house fire that had brought her to his place and about every moment of Holly's life up until this point. Her voice in the dark was both frustrating and seductive. Firelight created a cocoon of shadows and light, making it seem as if the two of them were alone in the world. Sam's days stretched out interminably, but the nights with Joy flew past, ending long before he wanted them to.

And that was an irritation, as well. Sam had been here for five years and in that time he hadn't wanted company. Hadn't wanted anyone around. Hell, he put up with Kaye because the woman kept his house running and meals on the table—but she also kept her distance. Usually. Now, here he was, sitting in the dark, waiting, *hoping* Joy would show up in the great room and shatter the solitude he'd fought so hard for.

But the days were different. During the day, Joy stayed out of his way and made sure her daughter did the same. They were like ghosts in the house. Once in a while, he would catch a little girl's laughter, quickly silenced. Everything was clean, sheets on his bed changed, meals appeared in the dining room, but Joy herself was not to be seen. How she managed it, he wasn't sure.

Why it bothered him was even more of a mystery.

Hell, he hadn't wanted them to stay in the first place. Yet now that he wasn't being bothered, wasn't seeing either of them, he found himself always on guard. Expecting one or both of them to jump out from behind a door every time he walked through a room. Which was stupid, but kept him on edge. Something he didn't like.

Hell, he hadn't even managed to get started on his next project yet because thoughts of Joy and Holly kept him from concentrating on anything else. Today, he had the place to himself because Joy and Holly had gone into Franklin. He knew that because there'd been a sticky note on the table beside his blueberry muffin and travel mug of coffee that Joy routinely left out in the dining room every morning.

Strange. The first morning they were here, it was *him* avoiding having breakfast with them. Now, it seemed that Joy was perfectly happy shuffling him off without even seeing him. Why that bothered him, Sam didn't even ask himself. There was no damn answer anyway.

So now, instead of working, he found himself glancing out the window repeatedly, watching for Joy's beat-up car to pull into the drive. All right, fine, it wasn't a broken-down heap, but her car was too old and, he thought, too unreliable for driving in the kind of snow they could get this high up the mountain. Frowning, he noted the fitful flurries of snowflakes drifting from the sky. Hardly a storm, more like the skies were teasing them with just enough snow to make things cold and slick.

So naturally, Sam's mind went to the road into town and the possible ice patches that dotted it. If Joy hit one of them, lost control of the car…his hands fisted. He should have driven them. But he hadn't really known they were going anywhere until it was too late. And that was because he wasn't spending any time with her except for those late-night sessions in the library.

Maybe if he'd opened his mouth the night before, she might have told him about this trip into town and he could have offered to drive them. Or at the very least, she could have driven his truck. Then he wouldn't be standing here wondering if her damn car had spun out.

Why the hell was he watching? Why did he care if she was safe or not? Why did he even bother to ask himself why? He knew damn well that his own past was feeding the sense of disquiet that clung to him. So despite resenting his own need to do it, he stayed where he was, watching. Waiting.

Which was why he was in place to see Ken Taylor when he arrived. Taylor and his wife, Emma, ran the gallery/gift shop in Franklin that mostly catered to tourists who came up the mountain for snow skiing in winter and boating on the lake in summer. Their shop, Crafty, sold local artisans' work—everything from paintings to jewelry to candles to the hand-made furniture and decor that Sam made.

Grateful for the distraction, Sam shrugged into his black leather jacket and headed out of the workshop into the cold bite of the wind and swirl of snowflakes. Tugging the collar up around his neck, Sam squinted into the wind and walked over to meet the man as he climbed out of his truck.

"Hey, Sam." Ken held out one hand and Sam shook it.

"Thanks for coming out to get the table," Sam said. "Appreciate it."

"Hey, you keep building them, I'll drive up the mountain to pick them up." Ken grinned. About forty, he had pulled his black hair into a ponytail at the base of his neck. He wore a heavy brown coat over a flannel shirt, blue jeans and black work boots. He opened the gate at the back of his truck, then grinned at Sam. "One of these times, though, you should come into town yourself so you can see the reactions of the people who buy your stuff." Shaking his head, he mused, "I mean, they all but applaud when we bring in new stock."

"Good to know," Sam said. It was odd, he thought, that he'd taken what had once been a hobby—wood-working—and turned it into an outlet for the creativity that had been choked off years ago. He liked knowing that his work was appreciated.

Once upon a time, he'd been lauded in magazines and newspapers. Reporters had badgered him for interviews, and one or two of his paintings actually hung in European palaces. He'd been the darling of the art world, and he'd enjoyed it all. He'd poured his heart and soul into his work and drank in the adulation as his due. Sam had so loved his work, he'd buried himself in it to the detriment of everything else. His life outside the art world had drifted past without him even realizing it.

Sam hadn't paid attention to what should have been most important, and before he could learn his lesson and make changes, he'd lost it and all he had left was the art. The paintings. The name he'd carved for himself. Left alone, it was only when he had been broken that he realized how empty it all was. How much he'd sacrificed for the glory.

So he wasn't interested in applause. Not anymore.

"No thanks," he said, forcing a smile in spite of his dark thoughts. He couldn't explain why he didn't want to meet prospective customers, why he didn't care about hearing praise, so he said, "I figure being the hermit on the mountain probably adds to the mystique. Why ruin that by showing up in town?"

Ken looked at him, as if he were trying to figure him out, but a second later, shook his head. "Up to you, man. But anytime you change your mind, Emma would love to have you as the star of our next Meet the Artist night."

Sam laughed shortly. "Well, that sounds hideous."

Ken laughed, too. "I'll admit that it really is. Emma drives me nuts planning the snacks to get from Nibbles, putting out press releases, and the last time, she even bought some radio ads in Boise…" He trailed off and sighed. "And the artist managed to insult almost everyone in town. Don't understand these artsy types, but I'm happy enough to sell their stuff." He stopped, winced. "No offense."

"None taken," Sam assured him. "Believe me." He'd known plenty of the kind of artists Ken was describing. Those who so believed in their own press no one could stand to be around them.

"But, Emma loves doing it, of course, and I have to give it to her, we do big business on those nights."

Imagining being in the center of a crowd hungering to be close to an artist, to ask him questions, hang on everything he said, talk about the "art"… It all gave Sam cold chills and he realized just how far he'd come from the man he'd once been. "Yeah, like I said, awful."

"I even have to wear a suit. What's up with that?" Ken shook his head glumly and followed after Sam when he headed for the workshop door. "The only thing I like about it is the food, really. Nibbles has so many great things. My favorite's those tiny grilled cheese sandwiches. I can eat a dozen of 'em and still come back for more…"

Sam was hardly listening. He'd done so many of those "artist meets the public" nights years ago that he had zero interest in hearing about them now. His life, his *world*, had changed so much since then, he couldn't even imagine being a part of that scene anymore.

Ken was still talking. "Speaking of food, I saw Joy and Holly at the restaurant as I was leaving town."

Sam turned to look at him.

Ken shrugged. "Deb Casey and her husband, Sean, own Nibbles, and Deb and Joy are tight. She was probably in there visiting since they haven't seen each other in a while. How's it going with the two of them living here?"

"It's fine." What the hell else could he say? That Joy was driving him crazy? That he missed Holly coming into the workshop? That as much as he didn't want them there, he didn't want them gone even more? Made him sound like a lunatic. Hell, maybe he was.

Sam walked up to the table and drew off the heavy tarp he'd had protecting the finished table. Watery gray light washed through the windows and seemed to make the tabletop shine.

"Whoa." Ken's voice went soft and awe-filled. "Man, you've got some kind of talent. This piece is amazing. We're going to have customers outbidding each other trying to get it." He bent down, examined the twisted, gnarled branch pedestal, then stood again to admire the flash of the wood grain beneath the layers of varnish. "Dude, you could be in an art gallery with this kind of work."

Sam stiffened. He'd been in enough art galleries for a lifetime, he thought, and had no desire to do it again. That life had ultimately brought him nothing but pain, and it was best left buried in the past.

"Your shop works for me," he finally said.

Ken glanced at him. The steady look in his eyes told Sam that he was wondering about him. But that was nothing new. Everyone in the town of Franklin had no doubt been wondering about him since he first arrived and holed up in this house on the mountain. He had no answers to give any of them, because the man he used to be was a man even Sam didn't know anymore. And that's just the way he liked it.

"Well, maybe one day you'll explain to me what's behind you hiding out up here." Ken gave him a slap on the back. "Until then, though, I'd be a fool to complain when you're creating things like this for me to sell—and I'm no fool."

Sam liked Ken. The man was the closest thing to a friend Sam had had in years. And still, he couldn't bring himself to tell Ken about the past. About the mess he'd made of his life before finding this house on the mountain. So Sam concentrated instead on securing a tarp over the table and making sure it was tied down against the wind and dampness of the snow and rain. Ken helped him cover that with another tarp, wrapping this one all the way down and under the foot of the pedestal. Double protection since Sam really hated the idea of having the finish on the table ruined before it even made it into the shop. It took both of them to carry the table to the truck and secure it with bungee cords in the bed. Once it was done, Sam stuffed his hands into the pockets of his jacket and nodded to Ken as the man climbed behind the wheel.

"Y'know, I'm going to say this—just like I do every time I come out here—even knowing you'll say 'no, thanks.'"

Sam gave him a half smile, because he was ready for what was coming next. How could he not be? As Ken said, he made the suggestion every time he was here.

"Why don't you come into town some night?" the other man asked, forearm braced on the car door. "We'll get a couple beers, tell some lies…"

"No, thanks," Sam said and almost laughed at the knowing smile creasing Ken's face. If, for the first time, he was almost tempted to take the man up on it, he'd keep that to himself.

"Yeah, that's what I thought." Ken nodded and gave him a rueful smile. "But if you change your mind…"

"I'll let you know. Thanks for coming out to pick up the table."

"I'll let you know as soon as we sell it."

"I trust you," Sam said.

"Yeah, I wish that was true," Ken told him with another long, thoughtful look.

"It is."

"About the work, sure, I get that," Ken said. "But I want you to know, you can trust me beyond that, too. Whether you actually do or not."

Sam had known Ken and Emma for four years, and if he was looking for friendships, he couldn't do any better and he knew it. But getting close to people—be it Ken or Joy—meant allowing them close enough to know about his past. And the fewer people who knew, the less pity he had to deal with. So he'd be alone.

"Appreciate it." He slapped the side of the truck and took a step back.

"I'll see you, then."

Ken drove off and when the roar of his engine died away, Sam was left in the cold with only the sigh of the wind through the trees for company. Just the way he liked it.

Right?

Five

"Oh, God, look at her with that puppy," Joy said on a sigh.

Her heart filled and ached as she watched Holly laughing at the black Lab puppy jumping at her legs. How could one little girl mean so much? Joy wondered.

When she'd first found herself pregnant, Joy remembered the rush of pleasure, excitement that she'd felt. It hadn't mattered to her that she was single and not exactly financially stable. All she'd been able to think was, she would finally have her own family. Her child.

Joy had been living in Boise back then, starting up her virtual assistant business and working with several of the small businesses in town. One of those was Mike's Bikes, a custom motorcycle shop owned by Mike Davis.

Mike was charming, handsome and had the whole

bad-boy thing going for him, and Joy fell hard and fast. Swept off her feet, she gave herself up to her first real love affair and thought it would be forever. It lasted until the day she told Mike she was pregnant, expecting to see the same happiness in him that she was feeling. Mike, though, had no interest in being anyone's father—or husband, if it came to that. He told her they were through. She was a good time for a while, but the good time was over. He signed a paper relinquishing all future rights to the child he'd created and Joy walked away.

When she was a kid, she'd come to Franklin with a foster family for a long weekend in the woods and she'd never forgotten it. So when she needed a fresh start for her and her baby, Joy had come here, to this tiny mountain town. And here is where she'd made friends, built her family and, at long last, had finally felt as though she belonged.

And of all the things she'd been gifted with since moving here, Deb Casey, her best friend, was at the top of the list.

Deb Casey walked to Joy and looked out the window at the two little girls rolling around on the winter brown grass with a fat black puppy. Their laughter and the puppy's yips of excitement brought a quick smile. "She's as crazy about that puppy as my Lizzie."

"I know." Joy sighed a little and leaned on her friend's kitchen counter. "Holly's telling everyone she's getting a puppy of her own for Christmas."

"A white one," Deb supplied.

Rolling her eyes, Joy shook her head. "I've even been into Boise looking for a white puppy, and no one has any. I guess I'm going to have to start preparing her for the fact that Santa can't always bring you what you want."

"Oh, I hate that." Deb turned back to the wide kitchen island and the tray of tiny brownies she was finishing off with swirls of white chocolate icing. "You've still got a few weeks till Christmas. You might find one."

"I'll keep looking, sure. But," Joy said, resigned, "she might have to wait."

"Because kids wait so well," Deb said with a snort of laughter.

"You're not helping."

"Have a brownie. That's the kind of help you need."

"Sold." Joy leaned in and grabbed one of the tiny brownies that was no more than two bites of chocolate heaven.

The brownies, along with miniature lemon meringue pies, tiny chocolate chip cookies and miniscule Napoleons, would be filling the glass cases at Nibbles by this afternoon. The restaurant had been open for only a couple of years, but it had been a hit from the first day. Who wouldn't love going for lunch where you could try four or five different types of sandwiches—none of them bigger than a bite or two? Gourmet flavors, a fun atmosphere and desserts that could bring a grown woman to tears of joy, Nibbles had it all.

"Oh, God, this should be illegal," Joy said around a mouthful of amazing brownie.

"Ah, then I couldn't sell them." Deb swirled white chocolate on a few more of the brownies. "So, how's it going up there with the Old Man of the Mountain?"

"He's not old."

"No kidding." Deb grinned. "I saw him sneaking into the gallery last summer, and I couldn't believe it.

It was like catching a glimpse of a unicorn. A gorgeous unicorn, I've got to say."

Joy took another brownie and bit into it. *Gorgeous* covered it. Of course, there was also *intriguing*, *desirable*, *fascinating*, and as yummy as this brownie. "Yeah, he is."

"Still." Deb looked up at Joy. "Could he be more antisocial? I mean, I get why and all, but aren't you going nuts up there with no one to talk to?"

"I talk to him," Joy argued.

"Yes, but does he talk back?"

"Not really, though in his defense, I do talk a lot." Joy shrugged. "Maybe it's hard for him to get a word in."

"Not that hard for me."

"We're women. Nothing's that hard for us."

"Okay, granted." Deb smiled, put the frosting back down and planted both hands on the counter. "But what's really going on with you? I notice you're awful quick to defend him. Your protective streak is coming out."

That was the only problem with a best friend, Joy thought. Sometimes they saw too much. Deb knew that Joy hadn't dated anyone in years. That she hadn't had any interest in sparking a relationship—since her last one had ended so memorably. So of course she would pick up on the fact that Joy was suddenly very interested in one particular man.

"It's nothing."

"Sure," Deb said with a snort of derision. "I believe that."

"Fine, it's *something*," Joy admitted. "I'm not sure what, though."

"But he's so not the kind of guy I would expect you to be interested in. He's so—cold."

Oh, there was plenty of heat inside Sam Henry. He just kept it all tamped down. Maybe that's what drew her to him, Joy thought. The mystery of him. Most men were fairly transparent, but Sam had hidden depths that practically demanded she unearth them. She couldn't get the image of the shadows in his eyes out of her mind. She wanted to know why he was so shut down. Wanted to know how to open him up.

Smiling now, she said, "Holly keeps telling me he's not mean, he's just crabby."

Deb laughed. "Is he?"

"Oh, definitely. But I don't know why."

"I might."

"What?"

Deb sighed heavily. "Okay, I admit that when you went to stay up there, I was a little worried that maybe he was some crazed weirdo with a closet full of women's bones or something."

"I keep telling you, stop watching those horror movies."

Deb grinned. "Can't. Love 'em." She picked up the frosting bag as if she needed to be doing something while she told the story. "Anyway, I spent a lot of time online, researching the local hermit and—"

"What?" And why hadn't Joy done the same thing? Well, she knew why. It had felt like a major intrusion on his privacy. She'd wanted to get him to actually *tell* her about himself. Yet here she was now, ready to pump Deb for the information she herself hadn't wanted to look for.

"You know he used to be a painter."

"Yes, that much I knew." Joy took a seat at one of the counter stools and kept her gaze fixed on Deb's blue eyes.

"He was famous. I mean *famous*." She paused for emphasis. "Then about five years ago, he just stopped painting entirely. Walked away from his career and the fame and fortune and moved to the mountains to hide out."

"You're not telling me anything I didn't know so far."

"I'm getting there." Sighing, Deb said softly, "His wife and three-year-old son died in a car wreck five years ago."

Joy felt as though she'd been punched in the stomach. The air left her lungs as sympathetic pain tore at her. Tears welled in her eyes as she tried to imagine that kind of hell. That kind of devastation. "Oh, my God."

"Yeah, I know," Deb said with a wince. Laying down the pastry bag, she added, "When I found out, I felt so bad for him."

Joy did, too. She couldn't even conceive the level of pain Sam had experienced. Even the thought of such a loss was shattering. Remembering the darkness in his eyes, Joy's heart hurt for him and ached to somehow ease the grief that even five years later still held him in a tight fist. Now at least she could understand a little better why he'd closed himself off from the world.

He'd hidden himself away on a mountaintop to escape the pain that was stalking him. She saw it in his eyes every time she looked at him. Those shadows that were a part of him were really just reflections of the pain that was in his heart. Of *course* he was still feeling the soul-crushing pain of losing his family. God, just the thought of losing Holly was enough to bring her to her knees.

Instinctively, she moved to Deb's kitchen window and looked out at two little girls playing with a puppy.

Her gaze locked on her daughter, Joy had to blink a sheen of tears from her eyes. So small. So innocent. To have that…*magic* winked out like a blown-out match? She couldn't imagine it. Didn't want to try.

"God, this explains so much," she whispered.

Deb walked to her side. "It does. But Joy, before you start riding to the rescue, think about it. It's been five years since he lost his family, and as far as I know, he's never talked about it. I don't think anyone in town even knows about his past."

"Probably not," she said, "unless they took the time to do an internet search on him."

Deb winced again. "Maybe I shouldn't have. Sort of feels like intruding on his privacy, now that I know."

"No, I'm glad you did. Glad you told me," Joy said, with a firm shake of her head. "I just wish I'd thought of doing it myself. Heck, I'm on the internet all the time, just working."

"That's why it didn't occur to you," Deb told her. "The internet is work for you. For the rest of us, it's a vast pool of unsubstantiated information."

She had a point. "Well, then I'm glad I came by today to get your updates for your website."

As a virtual assistant, Joy designed and managed websites for most of the shops in town, plus the medical clinic, plus she worked for a few mystery authors who lived all over the country. It was the perfect job for her, since she was very good at computer programming and it allowed her to work at home and be with Holly instead of sending the little girl out to day care.

But, because she spent so much time online for her job, she rarely took the time to browse sites for fun.

Which was why it hadn't even occurred to her to look up Sam Henry.

Heart heavy, Joy looked through the window and watched as Holly fell back onto the dry grass, laughing as the puppy lunged up to lavish kisses on her face. Holly. God, Joy thought, now she knew why Sam had demanded she keep her daughter away from him. Seeing another child so close to the age of his lost son must be like a knife to the heart.

And yet…she remembered how kind he'd been with Holly in the workshop that first day. How he'd helped her, how Holly had helped *him*.

Sam hadn't thrown Holly out. He'd spent time with her. Made her feel important and gave her the satisfaction of building something. He had closed himself off, true, but there was clearly a part of him looking for a way out.

She just had to help him find it.

Except for her nightly monologues in the great room, Joy had been giving him the space he claimed to want. But now she thought maybe it wasn't space he needed… but less of it. He'd been alone too long, she thought. He'd wrapped himself up in his pain and had been that way so long now, it probably felt normal to him. So, Joy told herself, if he wouldn't go into the world, then the world would just have to go to him.

"You're a born nurturer," Deb whispered, shaking her head.

Joy looked at her.

"I can see it on your face. You're going to try to 'save' him."

"I didn't say that."

"Oh, honey," Deb said, "you didn't have to."

"It's annoying to be read so easily."

"Only because I love you." Deb smiled. "But Joy, before you jump feetfirst into this, maybe you should consider that Sam might not *want* to be saved."

She was sure Deb was right. He didn't want to come out of the darkness. It had become his world. His, in a weird way, comfort zone. That didn't make it right.

"Even if he doesn't want it," Joy murmured, "he needs it."

"What *exactly* are you thinking?" Deb asked.

Too many things, Joy realized. Protecting Holly, reaching Sam, preparing for Christmas, keeping up with all of the holiday work she had to do for her clients... Oh, whom was she kidding? At the moment, Sam was uppermost in her mind. She was going to drag him back into the land of the living, and she had the distinct feeling he was going to put up a fight.

"I'm thinking that maybe I'm in way over my head."

Deb sighed a little. "How deep is the pool?"

"Pretty deep," Joy mused, thinking about her reaction to him, the late-night talks in the great room where it was just the two of them and the haunted look in his eyes that pulled at her.

Deb bumped her hip against Joy's. "I see that look in your eyes. You're already attached."

She was. Pointless to deny it, especially to Deb of all people, since she could read Joy so easily.

"Yes," she said and heard the worry in her own voice, "but like I said, it's pretty deep waters."

"I'm not worried," Deb told her with a grin. "You're a good swimmer."

That night, things were different.

When Sam came to dinner in the dining room, Joy

and Holly were already seated, waiting for him. Since every other night, the two of them were in the kitchen, he looked thrown for a second. She gave him a smile even as Holly called out, "Hi, Sam!"

If anything, he looked warier than just a moment before. "What's this?"

"It's called a communal meal," Joy told him, serving up a bowl of stew with dumplings. She set the bowl down at his usual seat, poured them both a glass of wine, then checked to make sure Holly was settled beside her.

"Mommy made dumplings. They're really good," the little girl said.

"I'm sure." Reluctantly, he took a seat then looked at Joy. "This is not part of our agreement."

He looked, she thought, as if he were cornered. Well, good, because he was. Dragging him out of the darkness was going to be a step-by-step journey—and it started now.

"Actually…" she told him, spooning up a bite of her own stew, then sighing dramatically at the taste. Okay, yes she was a good cook, but she was putting it on for his benefit. And it was working. She saw him glance at the steaming bowl in front of his chair, even though he hadn't taken a bite yet. "…our agreement was that I clean and cook. We never agreed to not eat together."

"It was implied," he said tightly.

"Huh." She tipped her head to one side and studied the ceiling briefly as if looking for an answer there. "I didn't get that implication at all. But why don't you eat your dinner and we can talk about it."

"It's good, Sam," Holly said again, reaching for her glass of milk.

He took a breath and exhaled on a sigh. "Fine. But this doesn't mean anything."

"Of course not," Joy said, hiding the smile blossoming inside her. "You're still the crabby man we all know. No worries about your reputation."

His lips twitched as he tasted the stew. She waited for his reaction and didn't have to wait long. "It's good."

"Told ya!" Holly's voice was a crow of pleasure.

"Yeah," he said, flicking the girl an amused glance. "You did."

Joy saw that quick look and smiled inside at the warmth of it.

"When we went to town today I played with Lizzie's puppy," Holly said, taking another bite and wolfing it down so she could keep talking. "He licked me in the face again and I laughed and Lizzie and me ran and he chased us and he made Lizzie fall but she didn't cry…"

Joy smiled at her daughter, loving how the girl could launch into a conversation that didn't need a partner, commas or periods. She was so thrilled by life, so eager to experience everything, just watching her made Joy's life better in every possible way. From the corner of her eye, she stole a look at Sam and saw the flicker of pain in his eyes. It had to be hard for him to listen to a child's laughter and have to grieve for the loss of his own child. But he couldn't avoid children forever. He'd end up a miserable old man, and that would be a waste, she told herself.

"And when I get my puppy, Lizzie can come and play with it, too, and it will chase us and mine will be white cuz Lizzie's is black and it would be fun to have puppies like that…"

"She's really counting on that puppy," Joy murmured.

"So?" Sam dipped into his stew steadily as if he was hurrying to finish so he could escape the dining room—and their company.

Deliberately, Joy refilled his bowl over his complaints.

"So, there aren't any white puppies to be had," she whispered, her own voice covered by the rattle of Holly's excited chatter.

"Santa's going to bring him, remember, Mommy?" Holly asked, proving that her hearing was not affected by the rush of words tumbling from her own mouth.

"That's right, baby," Joy said with a wince at Sam's smirk. "But you know, sometimes Santa can't bring everything you want—"

"If you're not a good girl," Holly said, nodding sharply. "But I am a good girl, right, Mommy?"

"Right, baby." She was really stuck now. Joy was going to have to go into Boise and look for a puppy or she was going to have a heartbroken daughter on Christmas morning, and that she couldn't allow.

Too many of Joy's childhood Christmases had been empty, lonely. She never wanted Holly to feel the kind of disappointment Joy had known all too often.

"I told Lizzie about the fairy house we made, Sam, and she said she has fairies at her house, but I don't think so cuz you need lots of trees for fairies and there's not any at Lizzie's…"

"The kid never shuts up," Sam said, awe in his voice.

"She's excited." Joy shrugged. "Christmas is coming."

His features froze over and Joy could have kicked herself. Sure, she planned on waking him up to life, but she couldn't just toss him into the middle of a fire,

could she? She had to ease him closer to the warmth a
little at a time.

"Yeah."

"I know you said no decorations or—"

His gaze snapped to hers, cold. Hard. "That's right."

"In the great room," she continued as if he hadn't said
a word, as if she hadn't gotten a quick chill from the
ice in his eyes, "but Holly and I are here for the whole
month and a little girl needs Christmas. So we'll keep
the decorations to a minimum."

His mouth worked as if he wanted to argue and
couldn't find a way to do it without being a complete
jerk. "Fine."

She reached out and gave his forearm a quick pat.
Even with removing her hand almost instantly, that
swift buzz of something amazing tingled her fingers.
Joy took a breath, smiled and said, "Don't worry, we
won't be too happy around you, either. Wouldn't want
you upset by the holiday spirit."

He shot her a wry look. "Thanks."

"No problem." Joy grinned at him. "You have to be
careful or you could catch some stray laugh and maybe
even try to join in only to have your face break."

Holly laughed. "Mommy, that's silly. Faces can't
break, can they, Sam?"

His brown eyes were lit with suppressed laughter,
and Joy considered that a win for her. "You're right,
Holly. Faces can't break."

"Just freeze?" Joy asked, her lips curving.

"Yeah. I'm good at freezing," he said, gaze meeting
hers in a steady stare.

"That's cuz it's cold," Holly said, then added, "Can
I be done now, Mommy?"

Joy tore her gaze from his long enough to check that her daughter had eaten most of her dinner. "Yes, sweetie. Why don't you go get the pinecones we found today and put them on the kitchen counter? We'll paint them after I clean up."

"Okay!" The little girl scooted off the chair, ran around the table and stopped beside Sam. "You wanna paint with me? We got glitter, too, to put on the pine-cones and we get to use glue to stick it."

Joy watched him, saw his eyes soften, then saw him take a deliberate, emotional step back. Her heart hurt, remembering what she now knew about his past. And with the sound of her daughter's high-pitched, excited voice ringing in the room, Joy wondered again how he'd survived such a tremendous loss. But even as she thought it, Joy realized that he was like a survivor of a disaster.

He'd lived through it but he wasn't *living*. He was still existing in that half world of shock and pain, and it looked to her as though he'd been there so long he didn't have a clue how to get out. And that's where Joy came in. She wouldn't leave him in the dark. Couldn't watch him let his life slide past.

"No, thanks." Sam gave the little girl a tight smile. "You go ahead. I've got some things I've got to do."

Well, at least he didn't say anything about hating Christmas. "Go ahead, sweetie. I'll be there in a few minutes."

"Okay, Mommy. 'Bye, Sam!" Holly waved, turned and raced toward the kitchen, eager to get started on those pinecones.

When they were alone again, Joy looked at the man opposite her and smiled. "Thanks for not popping her Christmas balloon."

He scowled at her and pushed his empty bowl to one side. "I'm not a monster."

"No," she said, thoughtfully. "You're not."

He ignored that. "Look, I agreed to you and Holly doing Christmas stuff in your part of the house. Just don't try to drag me into it. Deal?"

She held out one hand and left it there until he took it in his and gave it a firm shake. Of course, she had no intention of keeping to that "deal." Instead, she was going to wake him up whether he liked it or not. By the time she was finished, Joy assured herself, he'd be roasting chestnuts in the fireplace and stringing lights on a Christmas tree.

His eyes met hers and in those dark depths she saw... everything. A tingling buzz shot up her arm and ricocheted around in the center of her chest like a Ping-Pong ball in a box. Her heartbeat quickened and her mouth went dry. Those eyes of his gazed into hers, and Joy took a breath and held it. Finally, he let go of her hand and took a single step back as if to keep a measure of safe distance between them.

"Well," she said when she was sure her voice would work again, "I'm going to straighten out the kitchen then paint pinecones with my daughter."

"Right." He scrubbed one hand across his face. "I'll be in the great room."

She stood up, gathered the bowls together and said, "Earlier today, Holly and I made some Christmas cookies. I'll bring you a few with your coffee."

"Not necessary—"

She held up one hand. "You can call them winter cookies if it makes you feel better."

He choked off a laugh, shook his head and started

out of the room. Before he left, he turned to look back at her. "You don't stop, do you?"

"Nope." He took another step and paused when she asked, "The real question is, do you want me to?"

He didn't speak, just gave her a long look out of thoughtful, chocolate-brown eyes, then left the room. Joy smiled to herself, because that nonanswer told her everything she wanted to know.

Six

Sam used to hate the night.

The quiet. The feeling of being alone in the world. The seemingly endless hours of darkness. It had given him too much time to think. To remember. To torture himself with what-might-have-beens. He couldn't sleep because memories became dreams that jolted him awake—or worse, lulled him into believing the last several years had never really happened. Then waking up became the misery, and so the cycle went.

Until nearly a week ago. Until Joy.

He had a fire blazing in the hearth as he waited for her. Night was now something he looked forward to. Being with her, hearing her voice, her laughter, had become the best part of his days. He enjoyed her quick mind, and her sense of humor—even when it was directed at him. He liked hearing her talk about what was happening in town, even though he didn't know any of the people she told him about. He liked seeing her with her daughter, watching the love between them, even though it was like a knife to his heart.

Sam hadn't expected this, hadn't thought he wanted it. He rubbed his palms together, remembering the flash of heat that enveloped him when he'd taken her hand to seal their latest deal. He could see the flash in her eyes that told him she'd felt the same damn thing. And with the desire gripping him, guilt speared through Sam, as well. Everything he'd lost swam in his mind, reminding him that *feeling*, *wanting*, was a steep and slippery road to loss.

He stared into the fire, listened to the hiss and snap of flame on wood, and for the first time in years, he *tried* to bring those long-abandoned memories to the surface. Watching the play of light and shadow, the dance of flames, Sam fought to draw his dead wife's face into his mind. But the memory was indistinct, as if a fog had settled between them, making it almost impossible for him to remember just the exact shade of her brown eyes. The way her mouth curved in a smile. The fall of her hair and the set of her jaw when she was angry.

It was all…hazy, and as he battled to remember Dani, it was Joy's face that swam to the surface of his mind. The sound of *her* laughter. The scent of her. And he wanted to know the taste of her. What the hell was happening to him and why was he allowing it? Sam told himself to leave. To not be there when Joy came into the room. But as much as he knew he should, he also knew he wouldn't.

"I brought more cookies."

He turned in his chair to look at her, and even from across the room, he felt that now-familiar punch of awareness. Of heat. And he knew it was too late to leave.

At her smile, one eyebrow lifted and he asked, "More reindeer and Santas?"

That smile widened until it sparkled in her eyes. She walked toward him, carrying a tray that held the plate of cookies and two glasses of golden wine.

"This time we have snowmen and wreaths and—" she paused "—*winter* trees."

He shook his head and sighed. It seemed she was determined to shove Christmas down his throat whether he liked it or not. "You're relentless."

Why did he like that about her?

"That's been said before," she told him and took her usual seat in the chair beside his. Setting the tray down on the table between them, she took a cookie then lifted her glass for a sip of wine.

"Really. Cookies and wine."

"Separately, they're both good," she said, waving her cookie at the plate, challenging him to join her. "Together, they're amazing."

The cookies were good, Sam thought, reaching out to pick one up and bite in. All he'd had to do was close his eyes so he wasn't faced with iced, sprinkled Santas and they were just cookies. "Good."

"Thanks." She sat back in the chair. "That wasn't so hard, was it?"

"What?"

"Talking to me." She folded her legs up beneath her, took another sip of her wine and continued. "We've been sitting in this room together for five nights now and usually, the only voice I hear is my own."

He frowned, took the wine and drank. Gave him an excuse for not addressing that remark. Of course, it was true, but that wasn't the point. He hadn't asked her to join him every night, had he? When she only looked at him, waiting, he finally said, "Didn't seem to bother you any."

"Oh, I don't mind talking to myself—"

"No kidding."

She grinned. "But it's more fun talking to other people."

Sam told himself not to notice how her hair shined golden in the firelight. How her eyes gleamed and her mouth curved as if she were always caught on the verge of a smile. His gaze dropped to the plain blue shirt she wore and how the buttons pulled across her chest. Her jeans were faded and soft, clinging to her legs as she curled up and got comfortable. Red polish decorated her toes. Why that gave him a quick, hot jolt, he couldn't have said.

Everything in him wanted to pull her out of that chair, wrap his arms around her and take her tantalizing mouth in a kiss that would sear both of them. And *why*, he asked himself, did he suddenly feel like a cheating husband? Because since Dani, no other woman had pulled at him like this. And even as he wanted Joy, he hated that he wanted her. The cookie turned to chalk in his mouth and he took a sip of wine to wash it down.

"Okay, someone just had a dark thought," she mused.

"Stay out of my head," Sam said, slanting her a look.

Feeling desire didn't mean that he welcomed it. Life had been—not easier—but more clear before Joy walked into his house. He'd known who he was then. A widower. A father without a child. And he'd wrapped himself up in memories designed to keep him separate from a world he wasn't interested in anyway.

Yet now, after less than a week, he could feel those layers of insulation peeling away and he wasn't sure how to stop it or even if he wanted to. The shredding of his cloak of invisibility was painful and still he couldn't stop it.

Dinner with Joy and Holly had tripped him up, too, and he had a feeling she'd known it would. If he'd been smart, he would have walked out of the room as soon as he'd seen them at the table. But one look into Joy's and Holly's eyes had ended that idea before it could begin. So instead of having his solitary meal, he'd been part of a unit—and for a few minutes, he'd enjoyed it. Listening to Holly's excited chatter, sharing knowing looks with Joy. Then, of course, he remembered that Joy and Holly weren't *his*. And that was what he had to keep in mind.

Taking another drink of the icy wine, he shifted his gaze to the fire. Safer to look into the flames than to stare at the deep blue of her eyes. "Yeah," he said, finally responding to her last statement, "I don't really talk to people anymore."

"No kidding." She threw his earlier words back at him, and Sam nodded at the jab.

"Kaye tends to steer clear of me most of the time."

"Kaye doesn't like talking to people, either," Joy said, laughing. "You two are a match made in heaven."

"There's a thought," he muttered.

She laughed again, and the sound of it filled every empty corner of the room. It was both balm and torture to hear it, to know he *wanted* to hear it. How was it possible that she'd made such an impact on him in such a short time? He hadn't even noticed her worming her way past his defenses until it was impossible to block her.

"So," she asked suddenly, pulling him from his thoughts, "any idea where I can find a puppy?"

"No," he said shortly, then decided there was no reason to bark at her because he was having trouble dealing with her. He looked at her. "I don't know people around here."

"See, you should," she said, tipping her head to one side to look at him. "You've lived here five years, Sam."

"I didn't move here for friends." He came to the mountains to find the peace that still eluded him.

"Doesn't mean you can't make some." Sighing, she turned her head to the flames. "If you did know people, you could help me on the puppy situation." Shaking her head, she added, "I've got her princess dolls and a fairy princess dress and the other small things she asked for. The puppy worries me."

He didn't want to think about children's Christmas dreams. Sam remembered another child dictating letters to Santa and waking to the splendor of Christmas morning. And through the pain he also recalled how he and his wife had worked to make those dreams come true for their little boy. So, though he hated it, he said, "You could get her a stuffed puppy with a note that Santa will bring her the real thing as soon as the puppy's ready for a new home."

She tipped her head to one side and studied him, a wide smile on her face. God, when she smiled, her eyes shone and something inside him fisted into knots.

"A note from Santa himself? That's a good idea. I think Holly would love that he's going to make a special trip just for her." Clearly getting into it, she continued, "I could make up a certificate or something. You know—" she deepened her voice for dramatic effect "—*this is to certify that Holly Curran will be receiving a puppy from Santa as soon as the puppy is ready for a home*." Wrinkling her brow, she added thoughtfully, "Maybe I could draw a Christmas border on the paper and we could frame it for her—you know, with Santa's signature—and hang it in her bedroom. It could become an heirloom, something she passes down to her kids."

He shrugged, as if it meant nothing, but in his head, he could see Holly's excitement at a special visit from Santa *after* Christmas. But once December was done, he wouldn't be seeing Joy or Holly again, so he wouldn't know how the Santa promise went, would he? Frowning to himself, he tried to ignore the ripple of regret that swept through him.

"Okay, I am not responsible for your latest frown."

"What?" He turned his head to look at her again.

She laughed shortly. "Nothing. So, what'd you work on today?"

"Seriously?" Usually she just launched into a monologue.

"Well, you're actually speaking tonight," she said with a shrug, "so I thought I'd ask a question that wasn't rhetorical."

"Right." Shaking his head, he said, "I'm starting a new project."

"Another table?"

"No."

"Talking," she acknowledged, "but still far from chatty."

"Men are not chatty."

"Some men you can't shut up," she argued. "If it's not a table you're working on, what is it?"

"Haven't decided yet."

"You know, in theory, a job like that sounds wonderful." She took a sip of wine. "But I do better with a schedule all laid out in front of me. I like knowing that website updates are due on Monday and newsletters have to go out on Tuesday, like that."

"I don't like schedules."

She watched him carefully, and his internal radar went on alert. When a woman got that particular look in her eye—curiosity—it never ended well for a man.

"Well," she said softly, "if you haven't decided on a project yet, you could give me some help with the Santa certificate."

"What do you mean?" He heard the wariness in his own voice.

"I mean, you could draw Christmassy things around the borders, make it look beautiful." She paused and when she spoke again, the words came so softly they were almost lost in the hiss and snap of the fire in front of them. "You used to paint."

And in spite of those flames less than three feet from him, Sam went cold right down to the bone. "I used to."

She nodded. "I saw some of your paintings online. They were beautiful."

He took a long drink of wine, hoping to ease the hard knot lodged in his throat. It didn't help. She'd looked him up online. Seen his paintings. Had she seen the rest, as well? Newspaper articles on the accident? Pictures of his dead wife and son? Pictures of him at their funeral, desperate, grieving, throwing a punch at a photographer? God he hated that private pain was treated as public entertainment.

"That was a long time ago," he spoke and silently congratulated himself on squeezing the words from a dry, tight throat.

"Almost six years."

He snapped a hard look at her. "Yeah. I *know*. What is it you're looking for here? Digging for information? Pointless. The world already knows the whole story."

"Talking," she told him. "Not digging."

"Well," he said, pushing to his feet, "I'm done talking."

"Big surprise," Joy said, shaking her head slowly.

"What's that supposed to mean?" Damn it, had he really just been thinking that spending time with her was a good thing? He looked down into those summer-blue eyes and saw irritation sparking there. Well, what the hell did *she* have to be mad about? It wasn't *her* life being picked over.

"It means, I knew you wouldn't want to talk about any of this."

"Yet, you brought it up anyway." Hell, Kaye knew the whole story about Sam's life and the tragedy he'd survived, but at least she never threw it at him. "What the hell? Did some reporter call you asking for a behind-the-scenes exclusive? Haven't they done enough articles on me yet? Or maybe you want to write a tell-all book, is that it?"

"Wow." That irritation in her eyes sparked from mild to barely suppressed fury in an instant. "You really think I would do that? To you? I would never sell out a friend."

"Oh," he snapped, refusing to be moved by the statement, "we're friends now?"

"We could be, if you would stop looking at everyone around you like a potential enemy."

"I told you I didn't come here for friends," he reminded her. Damn it, the fire was heating the air. That had to be why breathing was so hard. Why his chest felt tight.

"You've made that clear." Joy took a breath that he couldn't seem to manage, and he watched as the fury in her eyes softened to a glimmer. "Look, I only said something because it seemed ridiculous to pretend I didn't know who you were."

He rubbed the heel of his hand at the center of his chest, trying to ease the ball of ice lodged there. "Fine. Don't pretend. Just ignore it."

"What good will that do?" She set her wine down on the table and stood up to face him. "I'm sorry but—"

"Don't. God, don't say you're sorry. I've had more than enough of that, thanks. I don't want your sympathy." He pushed one hand through his hair and felt the heat of the fire on his back.

This place had been his refuge. He'd buried his past back east and come here to get away from not only the press, but also the constant barrage of memories assaulting him at every familiar scene. He'd left his family because their pity had been thick enough to choke him. He'd left *himself* behind when he came to the mountains. The man he'd once been. The man who'd been so wrapped up in creating beauty that he hadn't noticed the beauty in his own life until it had been snatched away.

"Well, you've got it anyway," Joy told him and reached out to lay one hand on his forearm.

Her touch fired everything in him, heat erupting with a rush that jolted his body to life in a way he hadn't experienced in too many long, empty years. And he resented the hell out of it.

He pulled away from her, and his voice dripped ice as he said, "Whatever it is you're after, you should know I don't want another woman in my life. Another child. Another loss."

Her gaze never left his, and those big blue pools of sympathy and irritation threatened to drown him.

"Everybody loses, Sam," she said quietly. "Houses, jobs, people they love. You can't insulate yourself from that. Protect yourself from pain. It's how you respond to the losses you experience that defines who you are."

He sneered at her. She had no idea. "And you don't like how I responded? Is that it? Well, get in line."

"Loss doesn't go away just because you're hiding from it."

Darkness beyond the windows seemed to creep closer, as if it were finding a way to slip right inside him. This room with its bright wood and soft lights and fire-lit shadows felt as if it were the last stand against the dark, and the light was losing.

Sam took a deep breath, looked down at her and said tightly, "You don't know what you're talking about."

Her head tipped to one side and blond curls fell against her neck. "You think you're the only one with pain?"

Of course not. But his own was too deep, too ingrained to allow him to give a flying damn what someone else might be suffering. "Just drop it. I'm done with this."

"Oh no. This you don't get to ignore. You think I don't know loss?" She moved in closer, tipped her head back and sent a steely-blue stare into his eyes. "My parents died when I was eight. I grew up in foster homes because I wasn't young enough or cute enough to be adopted."

"Damn it, Joy——" He'd seen pain reflected in his own eyes often enough to recognize the ghosts of it in hers. And he felt like the bastard he was for practically insisting that she dredge up her own past to do battle with his.

"As a foster kid I was never 'real' in any of the families I lived with. Always the outsider. Never fitting in. I didn't have friends, either, so I went out and made some."

"Good for you."

"Not finished. I had to build everything I have for myself *by* myself. I wanted to belong. I wanted family, you know?"

He started to speak, but she held up one hand for silence, and damned if it didn't work on him. He couldn't take his eyes off her as he watched her dip into the past to defend her present.

"I met Holly's father when I was designing his website. He was exciting and he loved me, and I thought it was forever—it lasted until I told him about Holly."

And though Sam felt bad, hearing it, watching it, knowing she'd had a tough time of it, he couldn't help but ask, "Yeah? Did he die? Did he take Holly away from you, so that you knew you'd never see her again?"

She huffed out a breath. "No, but——"

"Then you don't know," Sam interrupted, not caring now if he sounded like an unfeeling jerk. He wouldn't feel bad for the child she'd once been. *She* was the one who had dragged the ugly past into the present. "You can't possibly *know*, and I'm not going to stand here defending myself and my choices to you."

"Great," she said, nodding sharply as her temper once again rose to meet his. "So you'll just keep hiding yourself away until the rest of your life slides past?"

Sam snapped, throwing both hands high. "Why the hell do you care if I do?"

"Because I *saw* you with Holly," Joy said, moving in on him again, flavoring every breath he took with the scent of summer flowers that clung to her. "I saw your kindness. She needed that. Needs a male role model in her life and—"

"Oh, stop. Role models. For God's sake, I'm no one's father figure."

"Really?" She jammed both hands on her hips. "Better to shut yourself down? Pretend you're alone on a rock somewhere?"

"For me, yeah."

"You're lying."

"You don't know me."

"You'd like to think so," Joy said. "But you're not that hard to read, Sam."

Sam shook his head. "You're here to run the house, not psychoanalyze me."

"Multitasker, remember?" She smiled and he resented her for it. Resented knowing that he wanted her in spite of the tempers spiking between them. Hell, maybe *because* of it. He hated knowing that maybe she had a point. He really hated realizing that whatever secrets he thought he'd been keeping were no more private than the closest computer with an internet connection.

And man, it bugged him that she could go from anger to smiles in a blink.

"This isn't analysis, Sam." She met his gaze coolly, steadily, firelight dancing in her eyes. "It's called conversation."

"It's called my *family*," he said tightly, watching the reflection of flame and shadow in the blue of her eyes.

"I know. And—"

"Don't say you're sorry."

"I have to," she said simply. "And I am."

"Great. Thanks." God he wanted to get out of there. She was too close to him. He could smell her shampoo and the scent of flowers—Jasmine? Lilies?—fired a bolt of desire through him.

"But that's not all I am," she continued. "I'm also a little furious at you."

"Yeah? Right back at you."

"Good," she said, surprising him. "If you're angry at least you're *feeling* something." She moved in closer, kept her gaze locked with his and said, "If you love making furniture and working with wood, great. You're really good at it."

He nodded, hardly listening, his gaze shifting to the open doorway across the room. It—and the chance of escape—seemed miles away.

"But you shouldn't stop painting," she added fiercely. "The worlds you created were beautiful. Magical."

That magic was gone now, and it was better that way, he assured himself. But Sam couldn't remember a time when anyone had talked to him like this. Forcing him to remember. To face the darkness. To face himself. One reason he'd moved so far from his parents, his sister, was that they had been so careful. So cautious in everything they'd said as if they were all walking a tightrope, afraid to make the wrong move, say the wrong thing.

Their...*caution* had been like knives, jabbing at him constantly. Creating tiny nicks that festered and ached with every passing minute. So he'd moved here, where no one knew him. Where no one would offer sympathy he didn't want or advice he wouldn't take. He'd never counted on Joy.

"Why?" she asked. "Why would you give that up?"

It had been personal. So deeply personal he'd never talked about it with anyone, and he wasn't about to start now. Chest tight, mouth dry, he looked at her and said, "I'm not talking about this with you."

With anyone.

He took a step or two away from her, then spun back and around to glare down at her. In spite of the quick burst of fury inside him, sizzling around and between them, she didn't seem the least bit intimidated. Another thing to admire about her, damn it. She was sure of herself even when she was wrong.

"I already told you, Sam. You don't scare me."

"That's a damn shame," he muttered, trying not to remember that his mother had warned him about lonely old recluses muttering to themselves. He turned from her again, and this time she reached out and grabbed his arm as he moved away from her.

"Just stop," she demanded. "Stop and talk to me."

He glanced down at her hand on his arm and tried not to relish the heat sliding from her body into his. Tried not to notice that every cell inside him was waking up with a jolt. "Already told you I'm not talking about this."

"Then don't. Just stay. Talk to me." She took a deep breath, gave his arm a squeeze, then let him go. "Look, I didn't mean to bring any of this up tonight."

"Then why the hell did you?" He felt the loss of her touch and wanted it back.

"I don't like lying."

Scowling now, he asked, "What's that got to do with anything?"

Joy folded both arms in front of her and unconsciously lifted them until his gaze couldn't keep from admiring the pull of her shirt and the curve of those breasts. He shook his head and attempted to focus when she started talking again.

"I found out today about your family and not saying something would have felt like I was lying to you."

Convoluted, but in a weird way, she made sense. He wasn't much for lies, either, except for the ones he told his mother every time he assured her that he was fine. And truth be told, he would have been fine with Joy pretending she knew nothing about his past. But it was too late now for pretense.

"Okay, great. Conscience clear. Now let's move on." He started walking again and this time, when Joy tugged on his arm to get him to stop, he whirled around to face her.

Her blue eyes went wide, her mouth opened and he pulled her into him. It was instinct, pure, raw instinct, that had him grabbing her close. He speared his fingers through those blond curls, pulled her head back and kissed her with all the pent-up frustration, desire and, yeah, even temper that was clawing at him.

Surprised, it took her only a second or two to react. Joy wrapped her arms around his waist and moved in even closer. Sam's head exploded at the first, incredible taste of her. And then he wanted more. A groan slid from her throat, and that sound fed the flames enveloping him. God, he'd had no idea what kissing her would do to him. He'd been thinking about this for days, and having her in his arms made him want the feel of her skin beneath his hands. The heat of her body surrounding his.

All he could think was to get her clothes off her. To cup her breasts, to take each of her nipples into his mouth and listen to the whimpering sounds of pleasure she would make as he took her. He wanted to look down into blue eyes and watch them go blind with passion. He wanted to feel her hands sliding across his skin, holding him tightly to her.

His kiss deepened farther, his tongue tangling with hers in a frenzied dance of desire that pumped through him with the force and rush of a wildfire screaming across the hillsides.

Joy clung to him, letting him know in the most primal way that she felt the same. That her own needs and desires were pushing at her. He took her deeper, held her tighter and spun her around toward the closest couch. Heart pounding, breath slamming in and out of his lungs, he kept his mouth fused to hers as he laid her down on the wide, soft cushions and followed after, keeping her close to his side. She arched up, back bowing as he ran one hand up and down the length of her. All he could think about was touching her skin, feeling the heat of her. He flipped the button of her jeans open, pulled down the zipper, then slid his hand down, across her abdomen, feeling her shiver with every inch of flesh he claimed. His fingers slipped beneath the band of her panties and she lifted her hips as he moved to cup her heat.

She gasped, tore her mouth from his and clutched at

his shoulders when he stroked her for the first time. He loved the feel of her—slick, wet, hot. His body tightened painfully as he stared into her eyes. His mind fuzzed out and his body ached. He touched her, again and again, stroking, pushing into her heat, caressing her inside and out, driving them both to the edge of insanity.

"Sam—" She breathed his name and that soft, whispered sound rattled him.

When had she become so important? When had touching her become imperative? He took her mouth, tangling his tongue with hers, taking the taste of her deep inside him as he felt her body coil tighter with the need swamping her. She rocked into his hand, her hips pumping as he pushed her higher, faster. He pulled his head back, wanting, needing to see her eyes glaze with passion when the orgasm hit her.

He wasn't disappointed. She jolted in his arms when his thumb stroked across that one small nub of sensation at the heart of her. Everything she was feeling flashed through her eyes, across her features. He was caught up, unable to tear his gaze from hers. Joy Curran was a surprise to him on so many levels, he felt as though he'd never really learn them all. And at the moment, he didn't have to. Right now, he wanted only to hold her as she shattered.

She called his name again and he clutched her to him as her body trembled and shivered in his grasp. Her climax rolled on and on, leaving her breathless and Sam more needy than ever.

His body ached to join hers. His heart pounded in a fast gallop that left him damn near shaking with the want clawing at him.

"Sam," she whispered, reaching up to cup his face with her palms. "Sam, I need—"

He knew just what she needed because he needed it too. He shifted, pulled his hand free of her body and thought only about stripping them both out of their clothes.

In one small, rational corner of his mind, Sam admitted to himself that he'd never known anything like this before. This pulsing, blinding, overpowering sense of need and pleasure and craving to be part of a woman. To be locked inside her body and lose himself in her. Never.

Not even with Dani.

That thought broke him. He pulled back abruptly and stared down at Joy like a blind man seeing the light for the first time. Both exhilarated and terrified. A bucket full of ice water dumped on his head wouldn't have shocked him more.

He fought for breath, for balance, but there wasn't any to be had. His own mind was shouting at him, telling him he was a bastard for feeling more for Joy than he had for his wife. Telling him to deny it, even to himself. To bury these new emotions and go back to feeling nothing. It was safer.

"That's it," he said, shaking his head, rolling off the couch, then taking a step, then another, away from her. "I can't do this."

"Sure you can," Joy assured him, a confused half smile on her face as her breath came in short, hard gasps. She pushed herself up to her elbows on the couch. Her hair was a wild tumble of curls and her jeans still lay open, invitingly. "You were doing great."

"I *won't* do this." His eyes narrowed on her. "Not again."

"Sam, we should talk—"

He actually laughed, though to him it sounded harsh, strained as it scraped against his throat. "Talking doesn't solve everything and it won't solve this. I'm going out to the workshop."

Joy watched him go, her lips still buzzing from that kiss. Her heart still pounding like a bass drum. She might even have gone after him if her legs weren't trembling so badly she was forced to drop into the closest chair.

What the hell had just happened?

And how could she make it happen again?

Seven

Joy didn't see Sam at all the next morning, and maybe that was just as well.

She'd lain awake most of the night, reliving the whole scene, though she could admit to herself she spent more time reliving the kiss and the feel of his amazingly talented fingers on her body than the argument that had prompted it. Even now, though, she cringed a little remembering how she'd thrown the truth of his past at him out of nowhere. Honestly, what had she been thinking, just blurting out the fact that she knew about his family? She hadn't been thinking at all—that was the problem.

She'd stared into those amazing eyes of his and had seen him shuttered away, closing himself off, and it had just made her so angry, she'd confronted him without considering what it might do to the tenuous relationship they already had.

In Kaye's two-bedroom suite off the kitchen, there had been quiet in Joy's room and innocent dreams in Holly's. The house seemed to sigh with a cold wind that whipped through the pines and rattled glass panes. And Joy hadn't been able to shut off her brain. Or her body. But once she'd gotten past the buzz running rampant through her veins, all she'd been able to think about was the look in his eyes when she'd brought up his lost family.

Lying there in the dark, she'd assured herself that once she'd said the words, opened a door into his past, there'd been no going back. She could still see the shock in his eyes when she'd brought it up, and a twinge of guilt wrapped itself around her heart. But it was no match for the ribbon of anger that was there as well.

Not only had he walked away from his talent, but he'd shut himself off from life. From any kind of future or happiness. Why? His suffering wouldn't bring them back. Wouldn't restore the family he'd lost.

"Mommy, are you all done now?"

Joy came out of her thoughts and looked at her daughter, beside her at the kitchen table. Behind them, the outside world was gray and the pines bent nearly in half from that wind sweeping in off the lake. Still no snow and Joy was beginning to think they wouldn't have a white Christmas after all.

But for now, in the golden lamplight, she looked at Holly, doing her alphabet and numbers on her electronic tablet. The little girl was squirming in her seat, clearly ready to be done with the whole sit-down-and-work thing.

"Not yet, baby," Joy said, and knew that if her brain hadn't been filled with images of Sam, she'd have been finished with the website update a half hour ago. But no, all she could think of was the firelight in his eyes. The taste of his mouth. The feel of his hard body pressed to hers. And the slick glide of his fingers.

Oh, boy.

"Almost, honey," she said, clearing her throat and focusing again on the comments section of her client's website. For some reason people who read books felt it was okay to go on the author's website and list the many ways the author could have made the book better. Even when they loved it, they managed to sneak in a couple of jabs. It was part of Joy's job to remove the comments that went above and beyond a review and deep into the realm of harsh criticism.

"Mommy," Holly said, her heels kicking against the rungs of the kitchen chair, "when can we gooooooo?"

A one-syllable word now six syllables.

"As soon as I'm finished, sweetie," Joy promised, focusing on her laptop screen rather than the never-ending loop of her time with Sam. Once the comment section was cleaned up, Joy posted her client's holiday letter to her fans, then closed up the site and opened the next one.

Another holiday letter to post and a few pictures the author had taken at the latest writers' conference she'd attended.

"How much longer, though?" Holly asked, just a touch of a wheedling whine in her voice. "If we don't go soon all the Christmas trees will be *gone*."

Drama, thy name is Holly, Joy thought with a smile. Reaching out, she gave one of the girl's pigtails a tug. "Promise, there will be lots of trees when we get into town. But remember, we're getting a little one this year, okay?" Because of the Grinch and his aversion to all things festive.

"I know! It's like a fairy tree cuz it's tiny and can go on a table to put in our room cuz Sam doesn't like Christmas." Her head tipped to one side. "How come he doesn't, Mommy? Everybody likes presents."

"I don't know, baby." She wasn't about to try to explain Sam's penchant for burying himself in a loveless, emotionless well. "You should ask him sometime."

"I'll ask him now!" She scrambled off her chair and Joy thought about calling her back as she raced to get her jacket. But why should she? Joy had already seen Sam with Holly. He was kind. Patient. And she knew darn well that even if the man was furious with *her*, he wouldn't take it out on Holly.

And maybe it would be good for him to be faced with all that cheerful optimism. All that innocence shining around her girl.

In seconds, Holly was back, dancing in place on the toes of her pink princess sneakers. Joy zipped up the jacket, pulled up Holly's hood and tied it at the neck. Then she took a moment to just look at the little girl who was really the light of her life. Love welled up inside her, thick and rich, and she heard Sam's voice in her mind again.

Did he take Holly away from you, so that you knew you'd never see her again?

That thought had Joy grabbing her daughter and pulling her in close for a tight hug that had Holly wriggling for freedom. He was right, she couldn't really *know* what he'd survived. She didn't even want to imagine it.

"You're squishing me, Mommy!"

"Sorry, baby." She swallowed the knot in her throat

and gave her girl a smile. "You go ahead and play with Sam. I'll come get you when it's time to go. As soon as I finish doing the updates on this website. Promise."

"Okay!" Holly turned to go and stopped when Joy spoke up again.

"No wandering off, Holly. Right to the workshop."

"Can't I look at my fairy house Sam helped me make? There might be fairies there now."

Boy, she was really going to miss this imaginative age when Holly grew out of it. But, though the fairy house wasn't exactly *inside* the woods, it was close enough that a little girl might be tempted to walk in more deeply and then end up getting lost. So, no. "We'll look later."

"Okay, 'bye!" And she was gone like a tiny pink hurricane.

Joy glanced out the window and watched her daughter bullet across the lawn to the workshop and then slip inside the doors. Smiling to herself, she thought she'd give a lot to see Sam's reaction to his visitor.

"Hi, Sam! Mommy said I could come play with you!"

She didn't catch him completely by surprise. Thankfully, Sam had spotted the girl running across the yard and had had time to toss a heavy beige tarp over his latest project. Although why he'd started on it was beyond him. A whim that had come on him two days ago, he'd thrown himself into it late last night when he'd left Joy in the great room.

Guilt had pushed him away from her, and it was guilt that had kept him working half the night. Memories crowded his brain, but it was thoughts of Joy herself that kept him on edge. That kiss. The heavy sigh of her breath as she molded herself to him. The eager response and matching need that had thrown him harder than he'd expected.

Shaking his head, he grumbled, "Don't have time to play." He turned to his workbench to find *something* to do.

"I can help you like I did with the fairy house. I want to see if there are fairies there but Mommy said I couldn't go by myself. Do you want to go with me? Cuz we can be busy outside, too, can't we?" She walked farther into the room and, as if she had radar, moved straight to the tarp draped across his project. "What's this?"

"Mine," he said and winced at the sharpness of his tone. But the girl, just like her mother, was impossible to deflate. She simply turned that bright smile of hers on him and said, "It's a secret, right? I like secrets. I can tell you one. It's about Lizzie's mommy going to have another baby. She thinks Lizzie doesn't know but Lizzie heard her mommy tell her daddy that she passed the test."

Too much information coming too quickly. He'd already learned about the wonderful Lizzie and her puppy. And this latest news blast might come under the heading of TMI.

"I wanted a sister, too," Holly said and walked right up to his workbench, climbing onto the stool she'd used the last time she was there. "But Mommy says I have to have a puppy instead and that's all right cuz babies cry a lot and a puppy doesn't…"

"Why don't we go check the fairy house?" Sam said, interrupting the flow before his head exploded. Getting her out of the shop seemed the best way to keep her from asking about the tarp again. It wasn't as if he *wanted* to go look for fairies in the freezing-cold woods.

"Oh, boy!" She squirmed off the stool, then grabbed his hand with her much smaller one.

Just for a second, Sam felt a sharp tug at the edges of his heart, and it was painful. Holly was older than Eli had been, he told himself, and she was a girl—so completely different children. But he couldn't help wondering what Eli would have been like at Holly's age. Or as he would be now at almost nine. But Eli would always be three years old. Just finding himself. Just becoming more of a boy than a baby and never a chance to be more.

"Let's go, Sam!" Holly pulled on his hand and leaned forward as if she could drag him behind her if she just tried hard enough.

He folded his fingers around hers and let her lead him from the shop into the cold. And he listened to her talk, heard again about puppies and fairies and princesses, and told himself that maybe this was his punishment. Being lulled into affection for a child who wasn't his. A child who would disappear from his life in a few short weeks.

And he wasn't completely stupid, he told himself. He could see through Joy's machinations. She wanted to wake him up, she'd said. To drag him back into the land of the living, and clearly, she was allowing her daughter to be part of that program.

"There it is!" Holly's excitement ratcheted up another level, and Sam thought the girl's voice hit a pitch that only dogs should have been able to hear. But her absolute pleasure in the smallest things was hard to ignore, damn it.

She let go of his hand and ran the last few steps to the fairy house on her own. Bending down, she inspected every window and even opened the tiny door to look inside. And Sam was drawn to the girl's absolute faith that she would see *something*. Even disappointment didn't jar the thrill in her eyes. "I don't see them," she said, turning her head to look at him.

"Maybe they're out having a picnic," he said, surprising himself by playing into the game. "Or shopping."

"Like Mommy and me are gonna do," Holly said, jumping up and down as if she simply couldn't hold back the excitement any more. "We're gonna get a Christmas tree today."

He felt a hitch in the center of his chest, but he didn't say anything.

"We're getting a little one this time to put in our room cuz you don't like Christmas. How come you don't like Christmas, Sam?"

"I…it's complicated." He hunched deeper into his black leather jacket and stuffed both hands into the pockets.

"Compulcated?"

"Complicated," he corrected, wondering how the hell he'd gotten into this conversation with a five-year-old.

"Why?"

"Because it's about a lot of things all at once," he said, hoping to God she'd leave it there. He should have known better.

Her tiny brow furrowed as she thought about it. Finally, though, she shrugged and said, "Okay. Do you think fairies go buy Christmas trees? Will there be lights in their little house? Can I see 'em?"

So grateful to have left the Christmas thing behind,

he said, "Maybe if you look really hard one night you'll see some."

"I can look *really* hard, see?" Her eyes squinted and her mouth puckered up, showing him just how strong her looking power was.

"That's pretty hard." The wind gave a great gust and about knocked Holly right off her feet. He reached out, steadied her, then said, "You should go on back to the house with your mom."

"But we're not done looking." She grabbed his hand again, and this time, it was more comforting than unsettling. Pulling on him, she wandered over to one side of the fairy house, where the pine needles lay thick as carpet on the ground. "Could we make another fairy house and put it right here, by this big tree? That's like a Christmas tree, right? Maybe the fairies would put lights on it, too."

He was scrambling now. He'd never meant to get so involved. Not with the child. Not with her mother. But Holly's sweetness and Joy's...*everything*...kept sucking him in. Now he was making fairy houses and secret projects and freezing his ass off looking for invisible creatures.

"Sure," he said, in an attempt to get the girl moving toward the house. "We can build another one. In a day or two. Maybe."

"Okay, tomorrow we can do it and put it by the tree and the fairies will have a Christmas house to be all nice and warm. Can we put blankets and stuff in there, too?"

Tomorrow. Just like her mother, Holly heard only what she wanted to hear and completely disregarded everything else. He glanced at the house and somehow wasn't surprised to see Joy in the kitchen window, watching them. Across the yard, their gazes met and heat lit up the line of tension linking them.

All he could think of was the taste of her. The feel of her. The gnawing realization that he was going to have her. There was no mistaking the pulse-pounding sensations linking them. No pretending that it wasn't there. Guilt still chewing at him, he knew that even that wouldn't be enough to keep him from her.

And when she lifted one hand and laid it palm flat on the window glass, it was as if she was touching him. Feeling what he was feeling and acknowledging that she, too, knew the inevitable was headed right at them.

The trunk was filled with grocery bags, the backseat held a Charlie Brown Christmas tree on one side and Holly on the other, and now, Joy was at her house for the boxes of decorations they would need.

"Our house is tiny, huh, Mommy?"

After Sam's house, *anything* would look tiny, but in this case especially. "Sure is, baby," she said, "but it's ours."

She noted Buddy Hall's shop van in the driveway and hurriedly got Holly out of the car and hustling toward the house. Funny, she'd never really noticed before that they didn't have many trees on their street, Joy thought. But spending the last week or so at Sam's house—surrounded by the woods and a view of the lake—she couldn't help thinking that her street looked a little bare. But it wasn't Sam's house that intrigued her. It was the man himself. Instantly, she thought of the look he'd given her just that morning. Even from across the wide yard, she'd felt the power of that stare, and her blood had buzzed in reaction. Even now, her stomach jumped with nerves and expectation. She and Sam weren't finished. Not by a long shot. There was more coming. She just wasn't sure what or when. But she couldn't wait.

"Stay with me, sweetie," Joy said as they walked into the house together.

"Okay. Can I have a baby sister?"

Joy stopped dead on the threshold and looked down at her. "What? Where did that come from?"

"Lizzie's getting a new sister. It's a secret but she is and I want one, too."

Deb was pregnant? Why hadn't she told? And how the heck did Holly know before Joy did? Shaking her head, she told herself they were all excellent questions that would have to be answered later. For now, she wanted to check on the progress of the house repairs.

"Buddy?" she called out.

"Back here." The deep voice came from the kitchen, so Joy kept a grip on Holly and headed that way.

Along the way, her mind kept up a constant comparison between her own tiny rental and the splendor of Sam's place. The hallway alone was a fraction of the length of his. The living room was so small that if four people were in there at the same time, they'd be in sin. The kitchen, she thought sadly, walking into the room, looked about as big as the island in Sam's kitchen. Its sad cabinets needed paint and really just needed to be torn down and replaced, but since she was just a renter, it wasn't up to her. And the house might be small and a little on the shabby side, but it was her home. The one she'd made for her and Holly, so there was affection along with the exasperation.

"How's it going, Buddy?" she asked.

"Not bad." He stood up, all five feet four inches of him, with his barrel chest and broader stomach. A gray fringe of hair haloed his head, and his bright blue eyes sparkled with good humor. "Just sent Buddy Junior down to the hardware store. Thought while I was here we could fix the hinges on some of these cabinets. Some of 'em hang so crooked they're making me dizzy."

Delighted, Joy said, "Thank you, Buddy. That's going the extra mile."

"Not a problem." He pushed up the sleeves of his flannel shirt, took a step back and looked at the gaping hole where a light switch used to be. "Got the wiring all replaced and brought up to code out in the living room, but I'm checking the rest, as well. You've got some fraying in here and a hot wire somebody left uncapped in the smaller bedroom—"

Holly's bedroom, Joy thought and felt a pang of worry. God, if the fire had started in her daughter's room in the middle of the night, maybe they wouldn't have noticed in time. Maybe smoke inhalation would have knocked them out and kept them out until—

"No worries," Buddy said, looking right at her. "No point in thinking about what-ifs, either," he added as if he could look at her and read her thoughts. And he probably could. "By the time this job's done I guarantee all the wiring. You and the little one there will be safe as houses."

"What's a safe house?" Holly asked.

Buddy winked at her. "This one, soon's I'm done."

"Thank you, Buddy. I really appreciate it." But maybe, Joy told herself, it was time to find a new house for her and her daughter. Something newer. Safer. Still, that was a thought for later on, so she put it aside for now.

"I know you do and we're getting it done as fast as we can." He gave his own work a long look. "The way it's looking, you could be back home before Christmas."

Back home. Away from Sam. Away from what she was beginning to feel for him. Probably best, she told herself, though right at the moment, she didn't quite believe it. As irritating as the man could be, he was so much more. And that more was drawing her in.

"Appreciate that, too," Joy said. "We're just here to pick up some Christmas decorations, then we'll get out of your hair."

He grinned and scrubbed one hand across the top of his bald head. "You'd have quite the time getting *in* my hair. You two doing all right up the mountain?"

"Yes." Everyone in town was curious about Sam, she thought. Didn't he see that if he spent more time talking to people they'd be less inclined to talk about him and wonder? "It's been great. Sam helped Holly build a fairy house."

"Is that right?"

"It's pretty and in the woods and I'm going to bring some of my dolls to put in it to keep the fairies company and Sam's gonna help me make another one, too. He's really nice. Just crabby sometimes."

"Out of the mouths of babes," Joy murmured with a smile. "Well, we've got to run. Trees to decorate, cookies to bake."

"You go ahead then," Buddy said, already turning back to his task. Then over his shoulder he called out, "You be sure to tell Sam Henry my wife, Cora, loves that rocking chair he made. She bought it at Crafty and now I can't hardly get her out of it."

Joy smiled. "I'll tell him."

Then with Holly rummaging through her toys, Joy bundled up everything Christmas. A few minutes later, they were back in the car, and she was thinking about the crabby man who made her want things she shouldn't.

Of course, she had to stop by Deb's first, because hello, *news*. "Why didn't you tell me you're pregnant?"

Deb's eyes went wide and when her jaw dropped she popped a mini apple pie into it. "How did you know?"

"Lizzie told Holly, Holly told me."

"Lizzie—" Deb sighed and shook her head. "You think your kids don't notice what's going on. Boy, I'm going to have to get better at the secret thing."

"Why a secret?" Joy picked up a tiny brownie and told herself the calories didn't count since it was so small. Drawing it out into two bites, she waited.

"You know we lost one a couple of years ago," Deb said, keeping her voice low as there were customers in the main room, separated from them only by the swinging door between the kitchen and the store's front.

"Yeah." Joy reached out and gave her friend a sympathetic pat on the arm.

"Well, this time we didn't want to tell anyone until we're at least three months. You know?" She sighed again and gave a rueful smile. "But now that Lizzie's spreading the word…"

"Bag open, cat out," Joy said, grinning. "This is fabulous. I'm happy for you."

"Thanks. Me, too."

"Of course, now Holly wants a baby, too."

Deb gave her a sly look. "You could do something about that, you know."

"Right. Because I'm such a great single mom I should do it again."

"You are and it wouldn't kill you," Deb told her, "but I was thinking more along the lines of gorgeous hermit slash painter slash craftsman."

"Yeah, I don't think so." Of course, she immediately thought of that kiss and the tension that had been coiled in her middle all day. Briefly, her brain skipped to hazy images of her and Sam and Holly living in that big beautiful house together. With a couple more babies running around and a life filled with hot kisses, warm laughter and lots of love.

But fantasies weren't real life, and she'd learned long ago to concentrate on what was real. Otherwise, building dreams on boggy ground could crush your heart. Yes, she cared about Sam. But he'd made it clear he wasn't interested beyond stoking whatever blaze was burning between them. And yet, she thought, brain still racing, he was so good with Holly. And Joy's little girl was blossoming, having a man like Sam pay attention to her. Spend time with her.

Okay, her mind warned sternly, *dial it back now, Joy. No point in setting yourself up for that crush.*

"You say no, but your eyes are saying yum." Deb filled a tray with apple pies no bigger than silver dollars, laying them all out on paper doilies that made them look like loosely wrapped presents.

"Yum is easy—it's what comes after that's hard."

"Since when are you afraid of hard work?"

"I'm not, but—" Not the same thing, she told herself, as working to make a living, to build a life. This was bringing a man out of the shadows, and what if once he was out he didn't want her anyway? No, that way lay pain and misery, and why should she set herself up for that?

"You're alone, he's alone, match made in heaven."

"Alone isn't a good enough reason for anyone, Deb." She stopped, snatched another brownie and asked, "When did this get to be about me instead of you?"

"Since I hate seeing my best friend—a completely wonderful human being—all by herself."

"I'm not alone. I have Holly."

"And I love her, too, but it's not the same and you know it."

Slumping, Joy leaned one hip against the counter and nibbled at her second brownie. "No, it's not. And okay, fine—I'm…intrigued by Sam."

"Intrigued is good. Sex is better."

Sadly, she admitted, "I wouldn't know."

"Yeah, that would be my point."

"It's not that easy," Joy said wistfully. Then she glanced out the window at the house across the yard where Holly and Lizzie were probably driving Sean Casey insane about now. "I mean, he's—and I'm—"

"Something happened."

Her gaze snapped to Deb's. "Just a kiss."

"Yay. And?"

"And," Joy admitted, "then he got a little more involved and completely melted my underwear."

"Wow." Deb gave a sigh and fluttered one hand over her heart.

"Yeah. We were arguing and we were both furious

and he kissed me and—" she slapped her hands together "—boom."

"Oh, boom is good."

"It's great, but it doesn't solve anything."

"Honey," Deb asked with a shake of her head, "who cares?"

Joy laughed. Honestly, Deb was really good for her. "Okay, I'm heading back to the house. Even when it's this cold outside, I shouldn't be leaving the groceries in the car this long."

"Fine, but I'm going to want to hear more about this 'boom.'"

"Yeah," Joy said, "me, too. So are the girls still on for the sleepover?"

"Are you kidding? Lizzie's been planning this for days. Popcorn, princess movies and s'mores cooked over the fireplace."

Ordinarily, Holly would be too young for a sleepover, but Joy knew Deb was as crazy protective as she was. "Okay, then I'll bring her to your house Saturday afternoon."

"Don't forget to pray for me," Deb said with a smile. "Two five-year-olds for a night filled with squeals…"

"You bet."

"And take that box of brownies with you. Sweeten up your hermit and maybe there'll be more 'boom.'"

"I don't know about that, but I will definitely take the brownies." When she left the warm kitchen, she paused on the back porch and tipped her face up to the gray sky. As she stood there, snow drifted lazily down and kissed her heated cheeks with ice.

Maybe it would be enough to cool her off, she told herself, crossing the yard to Deb's house to collect Holly and head home. But even as she thought it, Joy realized that nothing was going to cool her off as long as her mind was filled with thoughts of Sam.

Eight

Once it started snowing, it just kept coming. As if an invisible hand had pulled a zipper on the gray, threatening clouds, they spilled down heavy white flakes for days. The woods looked magical, and every day, Holly insisted on checking the fairy houses—there were now two—to see if she could catch a glimpse of the tiny people living in them. Every day there was disappointment, but her faith never wavered.

Sam had to admire that even as his once-cold heart warmed with affection for the girl. She was getting to him every bit as much as her mother was. In different ways, of course, but the result was the same. He was opening up, and damned if it wasn't painful as all hell. Every time that ice around his heart cracked a little more, and with it came the pain that reminded him why the ice had been there in the first place.

He was on dangerous ground, and there didn't seem to be a way to back off. Coming out of the shadows could blind a man if he wasn't careful. And that was one thing Sam definitely was.

Once upon a time, things had been different. *He* had been different. He'd gone through life thinking nothing could go wrong. Though at the time, everywhere he turned, things went his way so he couldn't really be blamed for figuring it would always be like that.

His talent had pushed him higher in the art world than he'd ever believed possible, but it was his own ego that had convinced him to believe every accolade given. He'd thought of himself as blessed. As *chosen* for greatness. And looking back now, he could almost laugh at the deluded man he'd been.

Almost. Because when he'd finally had his ass handed to him, it had knocked the world out from under his feet. Feeling bulletproof only made recovering from a crash that much harder. And he couldn't even really say he'd recovered. He'd just marched on, getting by, getting through. What happened to his family wasn't something you ever got *over*. The most you could do was keep putting one foot in front of the other and hope that eventually you got somewhere.

Of course, he'd gotten *here*. To this mountain with the beautiful home he shared with a housekeeper he paid to be there. To solitude that sometimes felt like a noose around his neck. To cutting ties to his family because he couldn't bear their grief as well as his own.

He gulped down a swallow of hot coffee and relished the burn. He stared out the shop window at the relentless snow and listened to the otherworldly quiet that those millions of falling flakes brought. In the quiet, his mind turned to the last few days. To Joy. The tension between them was strung as tight as barbed wire and felt just as lethal. Every night at dinner, he sat at the table with her and her daughter and pretended his insides weren't churning. Every night, he avoided meeting up with Joy in the great room by locking himself in the shop to work on what was under that tarp. And finally, he lay awake in his bed wishing to hell she was lying next to him.

He was a man torn by too many things. Too twisted around on the road he'd been walking for so long to know which way to head next. So he stayed put. In the shop. Alone.

Across the yard the kitchen light sliced into the dimness of the gray morning when Holly jerked the door open and stepped outside. He watched her and wasn't disappointed by her shriek of excitement. The little girl turned back to the house, shouted something to her mother and waited, bouncing on her toes until Joy joined her at the door. Holly pointed across the yard toward the trees and, with a wide grin on her face, raced down the steps and across the snow-covered ground.

Her pink jacket and pink boots were like hope in the gray, and Sam smiled to himself, wondering when he'd fallen for the kid. When putting up with her had become caring for her. When he'd loosened up enough to make a tiny dream come true.

Sam was already outside when Holly raced toward him in a wild flurry of exhilaration. He smiled at the shine in her eyes, at the grin that lit up her little face like a sunbeam. Then she threw herself at him, hugging his legs, throwing her head back to look up at him.

"Sam! Sam! Did you see?" Her words tumbled over

each other in the rush to share her news. She grabbed his hand and tugged, her pink gloves warm against his fingers. "Come on! Come on! You have to see! They came! They came! I knew they would. I knew it and now they're here!"

Snow fell all around them, dusting Holly's jacket hood and swirling around Joy as she waited, her gaze fixed on his. And suddenly, all he could see were those blue eyes of hers, filled with emotion. A long, fraught moment passed between them before Holly's insistence shattered it. "Look, Sam. Look!"

She tugged him down on the ground beside her, then threw her arms around his neck and held on tight. Practically vibrating with excitement, Holly gave him a loud, smacking kiss on the cheek, then pulled back and looked at him with wonder in her eyes. "They came, Sam. They're living in our houses!"

Still reeling from that freely given hug and burst of affection, Sam stood up on unsteady legs. Smiling down at the little girl as she crawled around the front of the houses, peering into windows that shone with tiny Christmas lights, he felt another chunk of ice drop away from his heart. In the gray of the day, those bright specks of blue, green, red and yellow glittered like magic. Which was, he told himself, what Holly saw as she searched in vain to catch a glimpse of the fairies themselves.

He glanced at Joy again and she was smiling, a soft, knowing curve of her mouth that gleamed in her eyes, as well. There was something else in her gaze, too—beyond warmth, even beyond heat, and he wondered about it while Holly spun long, intricate stories about the fairies who lived in the tiny houses in the woods.

* * *

"You didn't have to do this," Joy said for the tenth time in a half hour.

"I'm gonna have popcorn with Lizzie and watch the princess movie," Holly called out from the backseat.

"Good for you," Sam said with a quick glance into the rearview mirror. Holly was looking out the side window, watching the snow and making her plans. He looked briefly to Joy. "How else were you going to get into town?"

"I could have called Deb, asked her or Sean to come and pick up Holly."

"Right, or we could do it the easy way and have me drive you both in." Sam kept his gaze on the road. The snow was falling, not really heavy yet, but determined. It was already piling up on the side of the road, and he didn't even want to think about Joy and Holly, alone in a car, maneuvering through the storm that would probably get worse. A few minutes later, he pulled up outside the Casey house and was completely stunned when, sprung from her car seat, Holly leaned over and kissed his cheek. "'Bye, Sam!"

It was the second time he'd been on the receiving end of a simple, cheerfully given slice of affection that day, and again, Sam was touched more deeply than he wanted to admit. Shaken, he watched Joy walk Holly to her friend's house and waited until she came back, alone, and slid into the car beside him.

"She hardly paused long enough to say goodbye to me." Joy laughed a little. "She's been excited by the sleepover for days, but now the fairy houses are the big story." She clicked her seat belt into place, then turned to face him. "She was telling Lizzie all about the lights in the woods and promising that you and she will make Lizzie a fairy house, too."

"Great," he said, shaking his head as he backed out of the driveway. He wasn't sure how he'd been sucked into the middle of Joy's and Holly's lives, but here he was, and he had to admit—though he didn't like to—that he was *enjoying* it. Honestly, it worried him a little just how much he enjoyed it.

He liked hearing them in his house. Liked Holly popping in and out of the workshop, sharing dinner with them at the big dining room table. He even actually liked building magical houses for invisible beings. "More fairies."

"It's your own fault," she said, reaching out to lay one hand on his arm. "What you did was—it meant a lot. To Holly. To *me*."

The warmth of her touch seeped down into his bones and quickly spread throughout his body. Something else he liked. That jolt of heat when Joy was near. The constant ache of need that seemed to always be with him these days. He hadn't wanted a woman like this in years. He swallowed hard against the demand clawing at him and turned for the center of town and the road back to the house.

"We're not in a hurry, are we?" she asked.

Sam stopped at a red light and looked at her warily. "Why?"

"Because, it's early, but we could stay in town for a while. Have dinner at the steak house…"

She gave him a smile designed to bring a man to his knees. And it was working.

"You want to go out to dinner?" he asked.

"Well," she said, shrugging. "It's early, but that won't kill us."

He frowned and threw a glance out the windshield at the swirls of white drifting down from a leaden sky. "Still snowing. We should get up the mountain while we still can."

She laughed and God, he loved the sound of it—even if it was directed at him and his lame attempt to get out of town.

"It's not a blizzard, Sam. An hour won't hurt either of us."

"Easy for you to say," Sam muttered darkly. "You *like* talking to people." The sound of her laughter filled the truck and eased his irritation as he headed toward the restaurant.

Everybody in town had to be in the steak house, and Joy thought it was a good thing. She knew a lot of people in Franklin and she made sure to introduce Sam to most of them. Sure, it didn't make for a relaxing dinner—she could actually *see* him tightening up—but it felt good to watch people greet him. To tell him how much they loved the woodworking he did. And the more uncomfortable he got with the praise, the more Joy relished it.

He'd been too long in his comfort zone of solitude. He'd made himself an island, and swimming to the mainland would be exhausting. But it would so be worth the trip.

"I've never owned anything as beautiful as that bowl you made," Elinor Cummings gushed, laying one hand on Sam's shoulder in benediction. She was in her fifties, with graying black hair that had been ruthlessly sprayed into submission.

"Thanks." He shot Joy a look that promised payback in the very near future. She wasn't worried. Like an injured animal, Sam would snarl and growl at anyone who came too close. But he wouldn't bite.

"I love what you did with the bowl. The rough outside, looks as though you just picked it up off the forest floor—" Elinor continued.

"I did," Sam said, clearly hoping to cut her off, but pasting a polite, if strained, smile on his face.

"—and the inside looks like a jewel," she continued, undeterred from lavishing him with praise. "All of those lovely colors in the grain of that wood, all so polished, and it just gleams in the light." She planted one hand against her chest and gave a sigh. "It's simply lovely. Two sides of life," she mused, "that's what it says to me, two sides, the hard and the good, the sad and the glad. It's lovely. Just lovely."

"All right now, Ellie," her husband said, with an understanding wink for Sam and Joy, "let's let the man eat. Good to meet you, Sam."

Sam nodded, then reached for the beer in front of him and took a long pull. The Cummingses had been just the last in a long stream of people who'd stopped by their table to greet Joy and meet Sam. Every damn one of them had given him a look that said *Ah, the hermit. That's what he looks like!*

And then had come the speculative glances, as they wondered whether Sam and Joy were a couple, and that irritated him, as well. This was what happened when you met people. They started poking their noses into your life and pretty soon, that life was open season to anyone with a sense of curiosity. As the last of the strangers went back to their own tables, he glared at Joy.

"You're enjoying this, aren't you?"

In the light of the candle at their table, her eyes sparkled as she grinned. "I could try to deny it, but why bother? Yes, I am. It's good to see you actually forced to talk to people. And Elinor clearly loves your work. Isn't it nice to hear compliments?"

"It's a bowl." He sighed. "Nothing deep or meaningful to the design. Just a bowl. People always want to analyze, interpret what the artist meant. Sometimes a bowl is just a bowl."

She laughed and shook her head. "You can't fool me. I've seen your stuff in Crafty. Nothing about what you make is 'just' anything. People love your work, and if you gave them half a chance, they'd like you, too."

"And I want that because…"

"Because it's better than being a recluse." Joy leaned forward, bracing her elbows on the table. "Honestly, Sam, you can't stay on the mountain by yourself forever."

He hated admitting even to himself that she was right. Hell, he'd talked more, listened more, in the last couple of weeks than he had in years. His house wasn't empty. Wasn't filled with the careful quiet he normally knew. Kaye generally left him to his own devices, so he was essentially alone, even when his housekeeper was there. Joy and Holly had pushed their way into the center of his life and had shown him just how barren it had been.

But when they left, his life would slide back onto its original course and the silence would seem even deeper. And God, he didn't like the thought of that.

* * *

Sam frowned. "Why are we really here?"

"To eat that amazing steak, for one," Joy said, sipping at her wine. Interesting, she thought, how his facial expressions gave hints to what he was thinking. And even more interesting how fast a smile from him could dissolve into the more familiar scowl. She'd have given a lot in that moment to know exactly what was running through his mind.

"And for another?"

"To show you how nice the people of Franklin are. To prove to you that you can meet people without turning into a pillar of salt…" She sat back, sipped at her wine again and kept her voice lighter than she felt. "Admit it. You had a good time."

"The steak was good," he said grudgingly, but she saw a flash of a smile that appeared and disappeared in a heartbeat.

"And the company."

His gaze fixed on hers. "You already know I like the company."

"I do," she said and felt a swirl of nerves flutter into life in the pit of her belly. Why was it this man who could make her feel things she'd never felt before? Life would have been so much easier if she'd found some nice, uncomplicated guy to fall for. But then she wouldn't be able to look into those golden-brown eyes of his, would she? "But you had a good time talking to other people, too. It just makes you uncomfortable hearing compliments."

"Think you know me, don't you?"

"Yep," she said, smiling at him in spite of the spark of irritation in his eyes. Just as Holly had once said, *he's not mean, he's just crabby.* He didn't fool her anymore. Even when he was angry, it didn't last. Even when she ambushed him with knowledge of his past, he didn't cling to the fury that had erupted inside him. Even when he didn't want to spend time with a child, he went out of his way to make her dreams come true.

Joy's heart ached with all she was feeling, and she wondered if he could see it in her eyes.

The room was crowded. The log walls were smoke-stained from years of exposure to the wood fireplace that even now boasted a roaring blaze. People sat at round tables and a few leather booths along one wall while the wall facing Main Street was floor-to-ceiling windows, displaying the winter scene unfolding outside. Tonight, the music pumping through the speakers overhead was classical, something weepy with strings and piano. And sitting across the table from her, looking like he'd rather be anywhere else but there, was the man who held her heart.

Stupid? Maybe. But there was no going back for Joy now. She'd been stumbling over him a little every day, of course. His kindness to Holly. His company in the dead of night when the house sat quiet around them. His kiss. The way his eyes flared with heat and more whenever he looked at her. His reluctant participation in the "family" dinners in the dining room. All of those things had been drawing her in, making her fall.

But today, she'd simply taken the final plunge.

He must have gone into town on his own and bought those silly little fairy lights. Then he'd sneaked out into the freezing cold late at night when he wouldn't be seen. And he'd decorated those tiny houses because her little girl had believed. He'd given Holly that. Magic.

Sam had sparked her imagination, protected her dreams and her fantasies. Joy had watched her baby girl throw herself into the arms of the man she trusted, loved, and through a sheen of tears had seen Sam hold Holly as tenderly as if she'd been made of glass. And in that one incredible moment, Joy told herself, he'd completely won her heart. Whether he wanted it or not was a different question.

She, Joy thought, was toast.

He could pretend to be aloof, crabby, disinterested all he wanted now, and she wouldn't believe it. He'd given her daughter a gift beyond price and she would always love him for that.

"What?" he asked, frowning a little harder. "What is it?"

She shook her head. "Nothing."

The frown came back instantly. "Makes a man nervous when a woman gets that thoughtful look in her eyes."

"Nervous is good, though I doubt," she said quietly, "that you ever have to worry about nerves."

"You might be surprised," he murmured, then said more firmly, "Let's go before the storm settles in and we're stuck down here."

Right then, Joy couldn't think of anywhere she'd rather be than back in that amazing house, alone with Sam. She looked him dead in the eye and said softly, "Good idea."

The ride up the mountain seemed to take forever, or maybe it was simply because Joy felt so on edge it was as if her skin was one size too tight. Every inch of her buzzed with anticipation because she knew what she wanted and knew she was done waiting. The tension between them had been building for days now, and to-night, she wanted to finally release it. To revel in being with a man she loved—even if she couldn't tell him how she felt.

At the house, they left the car in the garage and walked through the connecting door into the mudroom, where they hung their jackets on hooks before heading into the kitchen. Joy hit a switch on the wall, and the soft lights above the table blinked into life. Most of the room was still dark, and that was just as she wanted it. When she turned to Sam, she went up on her toes, cupped his face in her palms and kissed him, putting everything she was feeling into it.

Her heartbeat jumped into a frantic rhythm, her stomach swirled with excitement and the ache that had been building inside her for days began to pulse. It took only a second for Sam to react. To have his arms come around her. He lifted her off her feet, and she wrapped herself around him like a ribbon around a present.

As if he'd only been awaiting her signal, he took her with a desperation that told Joy he wanted her as much as she wanted him. She *felt* the hunger pumping off him in thick waves and gave herself up to it, letting it feed her own until a raging storm overtook them both. His mouth covered hers, his tongue demanding entry. She gave way and sighed in growing need as he groaned and kissed her harder, deeper.

His hands, those talented, strong hands, dropped to her bottom. He turned her around so fast her stomach did a wild spin, then he slammed her up against the back door. Joy hardly felt it. She'd never experienced anything like what swept over her in those few frantic moments. Every inch of her body was alive with sensations. Her skin was buzzing, her blood boiling, and her mind was a tangled, hazy mass of thoughts that pretty much went, *yes, harder, now, be inside me.*

Her fingers scraped through his hair, held his head to hers. Every breath came strangled, harsh, and she didn't care. All she wanted, all she needed, was the taste of him filling her. The feel of his hands holding her. Then, when she became light-headed, she thought, okay, maybe air, too.

She broke the kiss, letting her head drop back as she gasped for breath. Staring up at the dimly lit ceiling, she concentrated solely on the feel of Sam's mouth at her throat, latching on to the pulse point at the base of her neck. He tasted, he nibbled, he licked, and she sighed heavily.

"Oh, boy. That feels really…" She gasped again. *"Good."*

With his mouth against her throat, he smiled. "You taste good, too."

"Thanks." She chuckled and the sound bubbled up into the room. "Always good to hear."

"I've wanted my hands on you for days." He lifted his head and waited for her to look at him. His eyes were alight with a fire that seemed to be sweeping both of them along in an inferno. "I tried to keep my distance, but it's been killing me."

"Me, too," she said, holding him a little tighter. "I've been dreaming about you."

One corner of his mouth lifted. "Yeah? Well, time to wake up." He let her slide down the length of his body until she was on her feet again. "Let's go."

"Where?"

"Upstairs, where the beds are." He started pulling

her. "After waiting this long, we're not doing this on the kitchen floor."

Right about then, Joy thought, the floor looked pretty good. Or the granite island. Or just the stupid wall she'd been up against a second ago. Especially since her knees felt like rubber and she wasn't sure she'd make it all the way up those stairs. Then she realized they didn't have to.

"Yeah, but my bed's quicker." She gave a tug, too, then grinned when he looked at her in admiration.

"Good thinking. I do like a smart woman." He scooped her up again, this time cradling her in his arms, and headed for Kaye's suite.

"Well, I always wanted to be swept off my feet." Really, her poor, foolish heart was stuttering at being carried off to bed. The romance of it tugged at everything inside her. He stepped into the darkened suite, and she hit the light switch for the living area as he passed it.

Instantly, the tiny, misshapen Christmas tree burst into electric life. Softly glowing lights burned steadily all around the room, but it was the silly tree that had center stage.

"What the—" He stopped, his grip on her tightening, and let his gaze sweep around the room. So Joy looked, too, admiring all she and Holly had done to their temporary home. Sam hadn't wanted the holidays leaking out into the main house, so they'd gone overboard here, in their corner of it. Christmas lights lined the doorways and were draped across the walls like garland. The tiny tree stood on a table and was practically bowed under the weight of the ornaments, popped corn and strings of lights adorning it.

After a long minute or two, he shook his head. "That tree is sad."

"It is not," she argued, spearing it with a critical eye. "It's loved." She looked past the tree in the window to the night outside and the fairy lights just visible through the swirls of snow, and her heart dissolved all over again. Cupping his cheek in her palm, she turned his face to hers. "You lit up Holly's world today with those strings of lights."

He scowled but there wasn't much punch to it. "I hated seeing her check for signs every day and not getting any. But she never stopped believing."

Her heart actually filled up and spilled over into her chest. How could she *not* love a man who'd given life to her baby's imagination?

"I put 'em on a timer," Sam said, "so they'll go off and on at different times and Holly will have something to watch for."

Shaking her head, she looked into his eyes and whispered, "I don't have the words for what I'm feeling right now."

"Then we're lucky. No words required."

He kissed her again and Joy surrendered to the fire. She forgot about everything else but the taste of him, the feel of him. She wanted to stroke her hands all over his leanly muscled body, feel the warm slide of flesh to flesh. Lifting her face, she nibbled at his throat and smiled when she heard him groan tightly.

She hardly noticed when he carried her through the main room and dropped her onto her bed. *Wild*, was all she could think. Wild for him, for his touch, for his taste. She'd been alone for so long, having this man, *the* man with her, was almost more than she could stand.

He felt the same, because in a few short seconds, they were both naked, clothes flying around the room as they tore at them until there was nothing separating them. The quilt on the bed felt cool beneath her, but he was there, sliding on top of her, to bring the heat.

"Been wanting to peel you out of those sweaters you wear for days now," he murmured, trailing kisses up from her belly to just below her breasts.

"Been wanting you to do it," she assured him and ran the flat of her hands over his shoulders in long, sensuous strokes.

His hands moved over her, following every line, every curve. She gasped when he dipped his head to take first one hard nipple then the other into his mouth. Damp heat fractured something inside her as his teeth, tongue, lips teased at her sensitive skin. She was writhing mindlessly, chasing the need, when he dipped one hand to her center and cupped her heat completely.

Joy's mind simply splintered from the myriad sensations slamming into her system all at once. She hadn't felt this way in…ever. He shifted, kissing her mouth, tangling his tongue with hers as those oh-so-talented fingers dipped inside her heat. She lifted her hips into his touch and held his head to hers as they kissed, as they took and gave and then did it all again. Their breath mingled, their hearts pounded in a wild tandem that raced faster and faster as they tasted, explored, discovered.

It was like being caught in a hurricane. There was no safe place to hide, even if she'd wanted to. And she didn't. She wanted the storm, more than she'd ever wanted anything in her life. Demand, need, hands reaching, mouths seeking. Hushed words flew back and forth between them, whispers, breathless sighs. Heat ratcheted up in the tiny bedroom as outside, the snow fell, draping the world in icy white.

Sam's hand at her core drove her higher, faster. A small ripple of release caught her and had Joy calling his name as she shivered, shuddered in response. But she'd barely recovered from that tiny explosion before he pushed her again. His fingers danced over her body, inside and out, caressing, stroking until she thought she'd lose what was left of her mind if he didn't get inside her. Now.

Whimpering, Joy didn't care. All she could think of was the release she wanted more than her next breath. "Be inside me," she told him, voice breaking on every word as air struggled in and out of her lungs.

"Now," he agreed in a strained whisper.

Shadows filled the room, light from the snow, reflections of the lights in the living area. He took her mouth again in a frenzied kiss that stole her breath and gave her his. She arched into him as he moved over her, parting her thighs and sliding into her with one long thrust.

Joy gasped, her head tipping back into the pillow, her hips lifting to welcome him, to take him deeper. His hands held her hips, his fingers digging into her skin as he drove into her again and again. She locked her legs around his hips, pulling him tighter to her, rocking with him, following the frenzied rhythm he set.

The storm claimed them. Hunger roared up into the room and overtook them both. There was nothing in the world but that need and the race to completion. Their bodies moved together, skin to skin, breath to breath. They raced to the edge of the cliff together, and together they took the leap, locked in each other's arms.

* * *

"I think I'm blind."

Sam pushed off her and rolled to one side. "Open your eyes."

"Oh. Right." She looked at him and Sam felt the solid punch of her gaze slam into him. His body was still humming, his blood still pounding in his ears. He'd just had the most intense experience of his life and he wanted her again. Now.

He stroked one hand down her body, following the curve of breast to belly to hip. She shivered and he smiled. He couldn't touch her enough. The feel of her was addictive. How could his craving for her be as sharp now as it had been before? He should be relaxed. Instead, he felt more fired up. The need building inside him was sharper now because he *knew* what he'd been missing. Knew what it was to be inside her, to feel her wrapped around him, holding him tight. To look into her eyes and watch passion burst like fireworks on the Fourth.

It felt as if cold, iron bands were tightening around his chest. Danger. He knew it. He knew that feeling anything for Joy was a one-way trip to disaster, pain and misery. Yet it seemed that he didn't have any choice about that.

"Well." She blew out a breath and gave him a smile that had his body going rock hard again. "That was amazing. But I'm suddenly so thirsty I could drink a gallon of water."

"I'll get some," he told her, "as soon as I'm sure my legs will hold me."

"Isn't that a nice thing to say? There's no hurry," she said, turning into him, snuggling close. She buried her face in the curve of his neck and gave a sigh. "Here's good."

"Here's great." He rolled onto his back, pulling her over with him until she lay sprawled across his chest. Her blond curls tumbled around her face and her eyes sparkled in the dim light. "You caught me by surprise with that kiss."

She folded her arms on his chest and grinned down at him. "Well, then, you have an excellent reaction time."

"Not complaining." He hadn't been prepared for that kiss, and it had pushed him right over the edge of the control he'd been clinging to for days. Wincing a little, he thought he should have taken his time with her. To slowly drive them both to the breaking point. Instead, he'd been hit by an unstoppable force and hadn't been able to withstand it. They'd rushed together so quickly he hadn't—Sam went completely still as reality came crashing down on him, obliterating the buzz of satisfaction as if it had never been.

"What is it? Sam?"

He looked up into her eyes and called himself every kind of name he could think of. How could he have been so stupid? So careless? It was too late now, he told himself grimly. Too late to do anything but worry. "Joy, the downside to things happening by surprise is you're not prepared for it."

She smiled. "I'd say you were plenty prepared."

He rolled again, flopping her over onto the mattress and leaning over her, staring her in the eyes. "I'm trying to tell you that I hope to hell you're on birth control because I wasn't suited up."

Nine

Sam watched her as, for a second or two, she just stared at him as if she were trying to make sense of a foreign language. And since he was staring into those clear blue eyes of hers, he *saw* the shift of emotions when what he'd said finally sunk in.

And even then, the uppermost thought in his mind was her scent and how it clung to her skin and seeped into his bones. Every breath he drew pulled her inside him, until summer flowers filled every corner of his heart, his soul.

What the hell was wrong with him? *Focus.* He'd led them both into a risky situation, and he had to keep his mind on what could, potentially, be facing them. It had been a long time since he'd been with anyone, sure. But it was Joy herself who had blown all thought, all reason, right out of his head with that one surprise kiss in the kitchen. After that, all he'd been able to think about was getting her naked. To finally have her under him, over him. He'd lost control for the first time in his life, and even though the consequences could be steep, he couldn't really regret any of it.

"Oh. Well." Joy lifted one hand and pushed his hair back from his face. Her touch sent a fresh new jolt of need blasting through him, and he had to grit his teeth in the effort to hold on to what was left of the tattered threads of his control.

"Are you," he asked, voice tight, "on birth control?"

"No."

One word. One simple word that hit the pit of his stomach like a ball of ice. "Okay. Look. This is my fault, Joy. I shouldn't have…"

"Fault? If you're looking to place blame here, you're on your own," she said, sliding her fingers through his hair. "This isn't on you alone, so don't look like you're about to be blindfolded and stood up against a wall in front of a firing squad."

He frowned and wondered when he'd become so easy to read.

"You weren't alone in this room, Sam," she said. "This is on me as much as you. We got…carried away—"

He snorted. "Yeah, you could say that."

"—and we didn't think. We weren't prepared," she finished as if he hadn't interrupted her.

He laughed shortly but there was no humor behind it. This had to be the damnedest after-sex conversation he'd ever had. He should have known that Joy wouldn't react as he would have expected her to. No recriminations, no gnashing of teeth, just simple acceptance for what couldn't be changed.

Still. "That's the thing," he said with a shake of his

head. "I thought I was. Prepared, I mean. When I went into town to get those damn fairy lights, I also bought condoms."

She drew her head back and grinned down at him. "You're kidding. Really?"

"Yes, really. They're upstairs. In my room."

She laughed and shook her head. "That's perfect. Well, in your defense, you did try to get me upstairs…"

"True." But they probably wouldn't have made it, as hot as they'd both been. Most likely, they'd have stopped and had at each other right there on the stairs anyway.

"And I love that you bought condoms," she said, planting a soft kiss on his mouth. "I love that you wanted me as much as I wanted you."

"No question about that," he admitted, though the rest of this situation was settling in like rain clouds over an outdoor party.

"But you realize that now everyone in Franklin knows you bought them."

"What?"

"Oh, yes," she said, nodding sagely. "By now, word has spread all over town and everyone is speculating about just what's going on up here."

"Perfect." Small-town life, he told himself, knowing she was right. He hadn't thought about it. Hadn't considered that by buying condoms at the local pharmacy he was also feeding fuel to the gossip. It had been so long since he'd been part of a community that he hadn't given it a thought, but now he remembered the speculative gleam in the cashier's eye. The smile on the face of the customer behind him in line. "Damn."

"We're the talk of the town," Joy assured him, still smiling. "I've always wanted to be gossiped about."

All of that aside for the moment, Sam couldn't understand how she could be so damned amused by any of this. All he could feel was the bright flash of panic hovering on the edges of his mind. By being careless, he might have created a child. He'd lost a child already. Lost his son. How could he make another and not have his heart ripped out of his chest?

"Forget what people are saying, Joy," he said, and his tone, if nothing else, erased her smile. "Look, whatever happens—"

"You can get that unnerved look off your face," she said softly. "I'm a big girl, Sam. I can take care of myself. You don't owe me anything, and I don't need you to worry about me or what might happen."

"I'll decide what I owe, Joy," he told her. It didn't matter what she said, Sam told himself. He would worry anyway. He laid one hand on her belly and let it lay there, imagining what might already be happening deep within her.

"Sam." She cupped his face in her hands and waited until he looked into her eyes. "Stop thinking. Can we just enjoy what we shared? Leave it at that?"

His heartbeat thundered in his chest. Just her touch was enough to push him into forgetting everything but her. Everything but this moment. He wanted her even more than he had before and didn't know how that was possible. She was staring up at him with those wide blue eyes of hers, and Sam thought he could lose himself in those depths. Maybe she was right. At least for now, for this moment, maybe it was better if they stopped thinking, worrying, wondering. Because these moments were all they had. All they would ever have.

He wasn't going to risk loss again. He wouldn't put

his soul up as a hostage to fate, by falling in love, having another family that the gods could snatch from him. A future for them was out of the question. But they had tonight, didn't they?

"Come with me," he said, rolling off the bed and taking her hand to pull her up with him.

"What? Why? Where?"

"My room. Where the condoms live." He kept pulling her after him and she half ran to keep up. "We can stop and get water—or wine—on the way up."

"Wine. Condoms." She tugged him to a stop, then plastered herself against him until he felt every single inch of her body pressed along his. Then she stepped back. "Now, that kind of thinking is a good thing. I like your plan. Just let me get my robe."

Amazing woman. She could be wild and uninhibited in bed but quailed about walking naked through an empty house.

"You don't need a robe. We're the only ones here. There are no neighbors for five miles in any direction, so no one can look in the windows."

"It's cold so I still want it," she said, lifting one hand to cup his cheek.

For a second, everything stopped for Sam. He just stared at her. In the soft light, her skin looked like fine porcelain. Her hair was a tumbled mass of gold and her eyes were as clear and blue as the lake. Her seductively sly smile curved a mouth that was made to be kissed. If he were still an artist, Sam thought, he'd want to paint her like this. Just as she was now.

That knowing half smile on her face, one arm lifted toward him, with the soft glow of Christmas lights behind her. She looked, he thought, like a pagan goddess,

a woman born to be touched, adored, and that's how
he would paint her. If he still painted, which he didn't.
And why didn't he?

Because he'd lost the woman he'd once loved.
A woman who had looked at him as Joy did now. A
woman who had given him a son and then taken him
with her when she left.

Pain grabbed his heart and squeezed.

Instantly, she reacted. "Sam? What is it?"

"I want you," he said, moving in on her, backing her
into the wall, looking down into her eyes.

"I know, I feel the same way."

He nodded, swallowed hard, then forced the words
out because they had to be said. Even if she pulled away
from him right now, they had to be said. "But if you're
thinking there's a future here for us, don't. I'm not that
guy. Not anymore."

"Sam—" Her hands slid up and down his arms, and
he was grateful for the heat she kindled inside him. "I
didn't ask you for anything."

"I don't want to hurt you, Joy." Yet he knew he
would. She was the kind of woman who would spin
dreams for herself, her daughter. She would think about
futures. As a mother, she had to. As a former father, he
couldn't. Not again. Just the thought of it sharpened the
pain in his heart. If he was smart, he'd end this with
Joy right now.

But apparently, he had no sense at all.

She gave him another smile and went up on her toes
to kiss him gently. "I told you. You don't have to worry
about me, Sam. I know what I'm doing."

He wished that were true. But there would be time

enough later for regrets, for second-guessing decisions made in the night. For now, there was Joy.

A few days later, Joy was upstairs, looking out Sam's bedroom window at the workshop below. Holly was out there with Sam right now, probably working on more fairy houses. Since the first two were now filled with fairy families, Holly was determined to put up a housing development at the foot of the woods.

Her smile was wistful as she turned away and looked at the big bed with the forest green comforter and mountain of pillows. She hadn't been with Sam up here since that first night. He came to her now, in Kaye's room, where they made love with quiet sighs and soft whispers so they wouldn't wake Holly in the next room. And after hours wrapped together, Sam left her bed early in the morning so the little girl wouldn't guess what was happening.

It felt secret and sad and wonderful all at the same time. Joy was in love and couldn't tell him because she knew he didn't want to hear it. She might be pregnant and knew he wouldn't want to hear that, either. Every morning when he left her, she felt him go just a bit further away. And one day soon, she knew, he wouldn't come back. He was distancing himself from her, holding back emotionally so that when she left at the end of the month he wouldn't miss her.

Why couldn't he see that he didn't *have* to miss her? It was almost impossible to believe she'd known Sam for less than three weeks. He was so embedded in her heart, in her life, she felt as if she'd known him forever. As if they'd been meant to meet, to find each other. To be together. If only Sam could see that as clearly as Joy did.

The house phone rang and she answered without looking at the caller ID. "Henry residence."

"Joy? Oh, it's so nice to finally talk to you!" A female voice, happy.

"Thanks," she said, carrying the phone back to the window so she could look outside. "Who is this?"

"God, how stupid of me," the woman said with a delighted laugh. "I'm Catherine Henry, Sam's mother."

Whoa. A wave of embarrassment swept over her. Joy was standing in Sam's bedroom, beside the bed where they'd had sex, and talking to his mother. Could this be any more awkward? "Hello. Um, Sam's out in the workshop."

"Oh, I know," she said and Joy could almost see her waving one hand to dismiss that information. "I just talked to him and your adorable daughter, Holly."

"You did?" Confused, she stared down at the workshop and watched as Sam and Holly walked out through the snow covering the ground. Sam was carrying the latest fairy house and Holly, no surprise, was chattering a mile a minute. Joy's heart ached with pleasure and sorrow.

"Holly tells me that she and Sam are making houses for fairies and that my son isn't as crabby as he used to be."

"Oh, for—" Joy closed her eyes briefly. "I'm so sorry—"

"Don't be silly. He *is* crabby," Catherine told her. "But he certainly seemed less so around your little girl."

"He's wonderful with her."

There was a pause and then a sniffle as if the woman was fighting tears. "I'm so glad. I've hoped for a long time to see my son wake up again. Find happiness again. It sounds to me like he is."

"Oh," Joy spoke up quickly, shaking her head as if Sam's mother could see her denial, "Mrs. Henry—"

"Catherine."

"Fine. Catherine, please don't make more of this than there is. Sam doesn't want—"

"Maybe not," she interrupted. "But he needs. So much. He's a good man, Joy. He's just been lost."

"I know," Joy answered on a sigh, resting her hand on the ice-cold windowpane as she watched the man she loved and her daughter kneeling together in the snow. "But what if he doesn't want to be found?"

Another long pause and Catherine said, "Kaye's told me so much about you, Joy. She thinks very highly of you, and just speaking to your daughter tells me that you're a wonderful mother."

"I hope so," she said, her gaze fixed on Sam.

"Look, I don't know how you feel, but if you don't mind my saying, I can hear a lot in your voice when you speak of Sam."

"Catherine—" If she couldn't tell Sam how she felt she certainly couldn't tell his *mother*.

"You don't have to say anything, dear. Just please. Do me a favor and don't give up on him."

"I don't want to." Joy could admit that much. "I… care about him."

"I'm so glad." The next pause was a short one. "After the holidays I'm going to come and visit Sam. I hope we can meet then."

"I'd like that," Joy said and meant it. She just hoped that she would still be seeing Sam by then.

When the phone call ended a moment later, she hung

up the phone and walked back to the window to watch the two people in the world she loved most.

"Will more fairies move in and put up some more lights like the other ones did?" Holly asked, kneeling in the snow to peek through the windows of the tiny houses.

"We'll have to wait and see, I guess," Sam told her, setting the new house down on a flat rock slightly above the others.

"I bet they do because now they have friends here and—"

Sam smiled to himself as the little girl took off on another long, rambling monologue. He was going to miss spending time with Holly. As much as he'd fought against it in the beginning, the little girl had wormed her way into his heart—just like her mother had. In his own defense, Sam figured there weren't many people who could have ignored a five-year-old with as much charm as this one. Even the cold didn't diminish her energy level. If anything, he thought, it pumped her up. Her little cheeks were rosy, her eyes, so much like her mother's, sparkled.

"Do fairies have Christmas trees?"

"What?"

"Like Mommy and me got a tiny little tree because you don't like Christmas, but maybe if you had a great big tree you'd like Christmas more, Sam."

He slid a glance at her. He'd caught on to Holly's maneuvers. She was giving him that sly smile that he guessed females were born knowing how to deliver.

"You want a big Christmas tree," he said.

"I like our little one, but I like big ones, too, and

we could make it really pretty with candy canes and we could make popcorn and put it on, too, and I think you'd like it."

"I probably would," he admitted. Hell, just because he was against Christmas didn't mean a five-year-old had to put up with a sad little tree tucked away in her room. "Why don't you go get your mom and we'll cut down a tree."

Her eyes went wide. "Cut it down ourselves? In the woods?"

"You bet. You can help." As long as he had his hands over hers on the hatchet, showing her how to do it without risking her safety. Around them, the pines rustled in the wind and sounded like sighs. The sky was heavy and gray and looked ready to spill another foot or two of snow any minute. "You can pick out the tree—as long as it's not a giant," he added with a smile.

She studied him thoughtfully for so long, he had to wonder what she was thinking. Nothing could have prepared him, though, for what she finally said. "You're a good daddy."

He sat back on his heels to look at her, stunned into silence. Snow was seeping into the legs of his jeans, but he paid no attention. "What?"

"You're a good daddy," she said again and moved up to lay one hand on his cheek. "You help me with stuff and you show me things and I know you used to have a little boy but he had to go to heaven with his mommy and that's what makes you crabby."

Air caught in his chest. Couldn't exhale or inhale. All he could do was watch the child watching him.

How did she know about Eli? Had her mother told her? Or had she simply overheard other adults talking about him? Kids, he knew, picked up on more than the grown-ups around them ever noticed. As Holly watched him, she looked so serious. So solemn, his heart broke a little.

"But if you want," she went on, her perpetually high-pitched, fast-paced voice softening, "I could be your little girl and you could be *my* daddy and then you wouldn't be crabby or lonely anymore."

His heart stopped. He felt it take one hard beat and then clutch. Her eyes were filled with a mixture of sadness and hope, and that steady gaze scorched him. This little girl was offering all the love a five-year-old held and hoping he'd take it. But how could he? How could he love a child again and risk losing that child? But wasn't he going to lose her anyway? Because of his own fears and the nightmares that had never really left him?

Sam had been so careful, for years, to stay isolated, to protect his heart, to keep his distance from the world at large. And now there was a tiny girl who had pierced through his defenses, showing him just how vulnerable he really was.

She was still looking at him, still waiting, trusting that he would want her. Love her.

He did. He already loved her, and that wasn't something he could admit. Not to himself. Not to the child who needed him. Sam had never thought of himself as a coward, but damned if he didn't feel like one now. How could he give her what she needed when the very thought of loving and losing could bring him to his knees?

He stood up, grabbed her and pulled her in for a tight hug, and her little arms went around his neck and clung as if her life depended on it. There at the edge of the woods with fairy magic shining in the gray, he was humbled by a little girl, shattered by the love freely offered.

"Do you want to be my daddy, Sam?" she whispered.

How to get out of this without hurting her? Without ripping his own heart out of his chest? Setting her down again, he crouched in front of her and met those serious blue eyes. "I'm proud you would ask me, Holly," he said, knowing just how special that request had been. "But this is pretty important, so I think you should talk to your mom about this first, okay?"

Not a no, not a yes. He didn't want to hurt her, but he couldn't give her what she wanted, either. Joy knew her daughter best. She would know how to let her down without crushing that very tender heart. And Joy knew—because he'd told her—that there was no future for them. What surprised him, though, was how much he wished things were different—that he could have told that little girl he would be her daddy and take care of her and love her. But he couldn't do it. Wouldn't do it.

"Okay, Sam." Holly grinned and her eyes lit up. "I'll go ask her right now, okay? And then we can show her the new fairy house and then we can get our big tree and maybe have hot chocolate and—" She took off at a dead run, still talking, still planning.

He turned to look at the house and saw Joy in the bedroom window, watching them. Would he always see her there, he wondered? Would he walk through his empty house and catch the faint scent of summer flowers? Would he sit in the great room at night and wait for her to come in and sit beside him? Smile at him? Would he spend the rest of his life reaching across the bed for her?

A few weeks ago, his life was insular, quiet, filled with the shadows of memories and the ghosts he carried with him everywhere. Now there would be *more* ghosts. The only difference being, he would have *chosen* to lose Joy and Holly.

That thought settled in, and he didn't like it. Still looking up at Joy, Sam asked himself if maybe he was wrong to pass up this opportunity. Maybe it was time to step out of the shadows. To take a chance. To risk it all.

A scream ripped his thoughts apart and in an instant, everything changed. Again.

Five stitches, three hot chocolates and one Christmas tree later, they were in the great room, watching the lights on the big pine in the front window shine. They'd used the strings of lights Joy had hung on the walls in their room, and now the beautiful pine was dazzling. There were popcorn chains and candy canes they'd bought in town as decorations. And there was an exhausted but happy little girl, asleep on the couch, a smile still curving her lips.

Joy brushed Holly's hair back from her forehead and kissed the neat row of stitches. It had been a harrowing, scary ride down the mountain to the clinic in town. But Sam had been a rock. Steady, confident, he'd already had Holly in his arms heading for his truck by the time Joy had come downstairs at a dead run.

Hearing her baby scream, watching her fall and then seeing the bright splotch of blood on the snow had shaken Joy right down to the bone. But Holly was crying and reaching for her, so she swallowed her own fear to try to ease Holly's. The girl had hit her head on a rock under the snow when she fell. A freak accident, but seeing the neat row of stitches reminded Joy how fragile her child was. How easily hurt. Physically. Emotionally.

Sam stood by the tree. "You want me to carry her to bed?"

"Sure. Thanks."

He nodded and stalked across the room as if every step was vibrating with repressed energy. But when he scooped Holly into his arms, he was gentle. Careful. She followed after him and neither of them spoke again until Holly was tucked in with her favorite stuffed dog and they were safely out in the great room again.

Sam walked to the fireplace, stared down into the flames as if looking for answers to questions he hadn't asked, and shoved both hands into his pockets. Joy walked over to join him, hooked her arm through his and wasn't really surprised when he moved away. Hurt, yes. But not surprised.

She'd known this was coming. Maybe Holly being hurt had sped up the process, but Joy had been expecting him to pull away. To push her aside. He had been honest from the beginning, telling her that they had no future. That he didn't want forever because, she knew, he didn't trust in promises.

He cared for her. He cared for Holly, but she knew he didn't want to and wouldn't want to hear how much she loved him, so she kept it to herself. Private pain she could live with. She didn't think she could bear him throwing her love back in her face and dismissing it.

"Sam…"

"Scared me," he admitted in a voice so low she almost missed the words beneath the hiss and snap of the fire.

"I know," Joy said softly. "Me, too. But Holly's fine, Sam. The doctor said she wouldn't even have a scar."

"Yeah, and I'm glad of that." He shook his head and looked at her, firelight and shadow dancing over his features, glittering in his eyes. "But I can't do this again, Joy."

"Do what?" Heart aching, she took a step toward him, then stopped when he took one back.

"You know damn what," he ground out. Then he took a deep breath and blew it out. "The thing is, just before Holly got hurt, I was thinking that maybe I could. Maybe it was time to try again." He looked at her. "With you."

Hope rose inside her and then crashed again when he continued.

"Then that little girl screamed, and I knew I was kidding myself." Shaking his head slowly, he took another deep breath. "I lost my family once, Joy. I won't risk that kind of pain again. You and Holly have to go."

"If we go," she reminded him, "you *still* lose us."

He just stared at her. He didn't have an answer to that, and they both knew it.

"Yeah, I know. But you'll be safe out there and I won't have to wonder and worry every time you leave the damn house."

"So you'll never think of us," she mused aloud. "Never wonder what we're doing, if we're safe, if we're happy."

"I didn't say that," he pointed out. "But I can block that out."

"Yeah, you're good at blocking out."

"It's a gift." The smile that touched his mouth was wry, unhappy and gone in an instant.

"So just like that?" she asked, her voice low, throbbing with banked emotions that were nearly choking her. "We leave and what? You go back to being alone in this spectacular cage?" She lifted both hands to encompass the lovely room and said, "Because no matter how beautiful it is, it's still a *cage*, Sam."

"And it's my business." His voice was clipped, cold, as if he'd already detached from the situation. From *her*.

Well, she wasn't going to make it that easy on him.

"It's not just your business, Sam. It's mine. It's Holly's. She told me she asked you to be her daddy. Did that mean nothing to you?"

"It meant *everything*," he said, his voice a growl of pain and anger. "It's not easy to turn away from you. From her."

"Then don't do it."

"I have to."

Fury churned in the pit of her stomach and slid together with a layer of misery that made Joy feel sick to her soul. "How could I be in love with a man so stubborn he refuses to see what's right in front of him?"

He jolted. "Who said anything about love?"

"I did," she snapped. She wasn't going to walk away from him never saying how she felt. If he was going to throw her away like Mike had, like every foster parent she'd ever known had, then he would do it knowing the full truth. "I love you."

"Well," he advised, "*stop*."

She choked out a laugh that actually scraped at her throat. Amazing. As hurt as she was, she could still be amused by the idiot man who was willing to toss aside what most people never found. "Great. Good idea. I'll get right on that."

He grabbed her upper arms and drew her up until

they were eye to eye. "Damn it, Joy, I told you up front that I'm not that guy. That there was no future for us."

"Yes, I guess I'm a lousy listener." She pulled away from him, cleared her throat and blinked back a sheen of tears because she *refused* to cry in front of him. "It must be your immense load of charm that dragged me in. That warm, welcoming smile."

He scowled at her.

"No, it was the way that you grudgingly bent to having us here. It was your gentleness with Holly, your sense of humor, your kiss, your touch, the way you look at me sometimes as if you don't know quite what to do with me." She smiled sadly. "I fell in love and there's no way out for me now. You're it, Sam."

He scrubbed one hand across his face as if he could wipe away her words, her feelings.

"You don't have to love me, Sam." That about killed her to say, but it was truth.

"I didn't want to hurt you, Joy."

"I believe you. But when you *care*, you hurt. That's life. But if you don't love me, try to love someone else." Oh God, the thought of that tore what was left of her heart into tiny, confetti-sized pieces. "But stop hiding out here in this palace of shadows and live your life."

"I like my life."

"No you don't," she countered, voice thick with those unshed tears. "Because you don't have one. What you have is sacrifice."

He pushed both hands through his hair then let them fall to his sides. "What the hell are you talking about?"

She took a breath, steadying herself, lowering her voice, *willing* him to hear her. "You've locked yourself away, Sam. All to punish yourself for surviving. What happened to your family was terrible, I can't even imagine the pain you lived through. But you're still alive, Sam. Staying closed down and shut off won't alter what happened. It won't bring them back."

His features went tight, cold, his eyes shuttered as they had been so often when she first met him.

"You think I don't know that?" He paced off a few steps, then whirled around and came right back. His eyes glittered with banked fury and pain. "Nothing will bring them back. Nothing can change why they died, either."

"What?" Confused, worried, she waited.

"You know why I had to drive you into town for Holly's sleepover?"

"Of course I do." She shook her head, frowning. "My car wouldn't start."

"Because I took the damn distributor cap off."

That made no sense at all. "What? Why?"

Now he scrubbed his hands over his face and gave a bitter sigh. "Because, I couldn't let you drive down the mountain in the snow."

"Sam…"

Firelight danced around the room but looked haunting as it shadowed his face, highlighting the grief carved into his features, like a mask in stone. As she watched him, she saw his eyes blur, focus on images in his mind rather than the woman who stood just opposite him.

"I was caught up in a painting," he said. "It was a commission. A big one and I wanted to keep at it while I was on a roll." He turned from her, set both hands on the fireplace mantel and stared down into the crackling flames. "There was a family reunion that weekend and Dani was furious that I didn't want to go. So I told her to take Eli and go ahead. That I'd meet her at the re-union as soon as I was finished." He swiveled his head to look at Joy. "She was on the interstate and a front tire blew. Dani lost control of the car and slammed into an oncoming semi. Both she and Eli died instantly."

Joy's heart ripped open, and the pain she felt for him nearly brought her to her knees. But she kept quiet, wanting him to finish and knowing he needed to get it all said.

"If I'd been driving it might have been different, but I'll never know, will I?" He pushed away from the mantel and glared at her, daring her to argue with him. "I chose my work over my family and I lost them. You once asked me why I don't paint anymore, and there's your reason. I chose my work over what should have been more im-portant. So I don't paint. I don't go out. I don't—"

"Live," she finished for him. "You don't *live*, Sam. Do you really think that's what Dani would want for you? To spend the next fifty years locked away from ev-erything and everyone? Is that how she wanted to live?"

"Of course not," he snapped.

"Then what's the point of the self-flagellation?" Joy demanded, walking toward him, ignoring the instinc-tive step back he took. "If you'd been in that car, you might have died, too."

"You don't know that."

"You don't, either. That's the point."

Outside, the wind moaned as it slid beneath the eaves. But tonight, it sounded louder, like a desperate keening, as if even the house was weeping for what was ending.

Trying again, Joy said, "My little girl loves you. I love you. Can you really let that go so easily?"

His gaze snapped to hers. "I told you that earlier today, I actually thought that maybe I could risk it. Maybe there was a chance. And then Holly was hurt and my heart stopped."

"Kids get hurt, Sam," she said, still trying, though she could see in his eyes that the fight was over. His decision was made whether she agreed or not. "We lose people we shouldn't. But life keeps going. *We* keep going. The world doesn't stop, Sam, and it shouldn't."

"Maybe not," he said softly. "But it's going to keep going without me."

Ten

Joy spent the next few days taking care of business. She buried the pain beneath layers of carefully constructed indifference and focused on what she had to do. In between taking care of her clients, she made meals for Sam and froze them. Whatever else happened after she left this house, he wouldn't starve.

If she had her way, she wouldn't leave. She'd stay right here and keep hammering at his hard head until she got through. And maybe, one day, she'd succeed. But then again, maybe not. So she couldn't take the chance. It was one thing to risk her own heart, but she wouldn't risk Holly's. Her daughter was already crazy about Sam. The longer they stayed here in this house, the deeper those feelings would go. And before long, Sam would break her baby's heart. He might not mean to, but it was inevitable.

Because he refused to love them back. Sooner or

later, Holly would feel that and it would crush her. Joy wouldn't let that happen.

She would miss this place, though, she told herself as she packed up Holly's things. Glancing out the bedroom window, she watched her little girl and Sam placing yet another fairy house in the woods. And she had to give the man points for kindness.

She and Sam hadn't really spoken since that last night when everything had been laid out between them. They'd sidestepped each other when they could, and when they couldn't they'd both pretended that everything was fine. No point in upsetting Holly, after all. And despite—or maybe because of how strained things were between her and Sam—he hadn't changed toward Holly. That alone made her love him more and made it harder to leave. But tomorrow morning, she and Holly would wake up back in their own house in Franklin.

"Thank God Buddy finished the work early," she muttered, folding up the last of Holly's shirts and laying them in the suitcase.

Walking into the kitchen of her dreams, Joy sighed a little, then took out a pad of paper and a pen. Her heart felt heavy, the knot of emotion still stuck at the base of her throat, and every breath seemed like an event. She hated leaving. Hated walking away from Sam. But she didn't have a choice any longer. Sitting on a stool at the granite counter, she made a list for Sam of the food she had stocked for him. There was enough food in the freezer now to see him through to when Kaye returned.

Would he miss her? she wondered. Would he sit in that dining room alone and remember being there with her and Holly? Would he sit in the great room at night and wish Joy was there beside him? Or would he wipe it all out of his mind? Would she become a story never talked about like his late wife? Was Joy now just another reason to block out life and build the barricades around his heart that much higher?

She'd hoped to pull Sam out of the shadows—now she might have had a hand in pushing him deeper into the darkness. Sighing a little, she got up, stirred the pot of beef stew, then checked the bread in the oven.

When she looked out the window again, she saw the fairy lights had blinked on and Holly was kneeling beside Sam in the snow. She couldn't hear what was being said, but her heart broke a little anyway when her daughter laid her little hand on Sam's shoulder. Leaving was going to be hard. Tearing Holly away was going to be a nightmare. But she had to do it. For everyone's sake.

Two hours later, Holly put on her stubborn face.

"But I don't wanna go," Holly shouted and pulled away from her mother to run down the hall to the great room. "Sam! Sam! Mommy says we're leaving and I don't want to go cuz we're building a fairy house and I have to help you put it in the woods so the fairies can come and—"

Joy walked into the main room behind her daughter and watched as Holly threw herself into Sam's lap. He looked at Joy over the child's head even as he gave the little girl a hug.

"Tell her we have to stay, Sam, cuz I'm your helper now and you need me."

"I do," he said, and his voice sounded rough, scratchy. "But your mom needs you, too, so if she says it's time to go, you're going to have to."

She tipped her head back, looking at him with rivers of tears in her eyes. "But I don't want to."

"I know. I don't want you to, either." He gave her what looked to Joy like a wistful smile, then tugged on one of her pigtails. "Why don't I finish up the fairy house and then bring it to you so you can give it to Lizzie."

She shook her head so hard, her pigtails whipped back and forth across her eyes. "It's not the same, Sam. Can't I stay?"

"Come on, Holly," Joy spoke up quickly because her own emotions were taking over. Tears were close, and watching her daughter's heart break was breaking her own. "We really have to go."

Holly threw her a furious look, brows locked down, eyes narrowed. "You're being mean."

"I'm your mom," Joy said tightly, keeping her own tears at bay. "That's my job. Now come on."

"I love you, Sam," Holly whispered loud enough for her voice to carry. Then she gave him a smacking kiss on the cheek and crawled off his lap. Chin on her chest, she walked toward Joy with slow, dragging steps, as if she was pulling each foot out of mud along the way.

Joy saw the stricken look on Sam's face and thought, *Good. Now you know what you've given up. What you're allowing yourself to lose.*

Head bowed, shoulders slumped, Holly couldn't have been more clear in her desolation. Well, Joy knew just how she felt. Taking the little girl's hand, she gave it a squeeze and said, "Let's go home, sweetie."

They headed out the front door, and Joy didn't look back. She couldn't. For the first time in days, the sun was out, and the only clouds in the sky were big and

white and looked as soft and fluffy as Santa's beard.
The pines were covered in snow, and the bare branches
of the aspens and birches looked like they'd been decorated with lace as the snow lay on every tiny twig. It
was magical. Beautiful.

And Joy took no pleasure in any of it.

Holly hopped into her car seat and buckled herself in
while Joy did a quick check of everything stuffed into
the car. Their tiny tree was in the backseat and their
suitcases in the trunk. Holly sat there glowering at the
world in general, and Joy sighed because she knew her
darling daughter was going to make her life a living
hell for the next few days at least.

"That's it then," Joy said, forcing a smile as she
turned to look at Sam. He wore that black leather jacket,
and his jeans were faded and stacked on the toes of his
battered work boots. His hair was too long, his white
long-sleeved shirt was open at the neck, and his brown
eyes pinned her with an intensity that stole her breath.

"Drive safely."

"That's all you've got?" she asked, tipping her head
to one side to study him.

"What is there left to say?" he countered. "Didn't
we get it all said a few days ago?"

"Not nearly, but you still don't understand that, do
you?" He stood on his drive with the well-lit splendor of
his house behind him. In the front window, the Christmas tree they'd decorated together shone in a fiery blaze
of color, and behind her, she knew, there were fairy
lights shining at the edge of the woods.

She looked up at him, then moved in closer. He didn't
move, just locked his gaze with hers as she approached.
When she was close enough, she cupped his cheeks in

her palms and said softly, "We would have been good for you, Sam. I would have been. You and I could have been happy together. We could have built something that most people only dream about." She went up on her toes, kissed his grim, unyielding mouth, then looked at him again. "I want you to remember something. When you lost your family there was nothing you could do about it. *This* time, it's your choice. You're losing and you're letting it happen."

His mouth tightened, his eyes flashed, but he didn't speak, and Joy knew it was over.

"I'm sorry for you," she said, "that you're allowing your own pain to swallow your life."

Before he could tell her to mind her own business, she turned and walked to the car. With Holly loudly complaining, she fired up the engine, put it in gear and drove away from Sam Henry and all the might-have-beens that would drive her crazy for the rest of her life.

For the next few days, Sam settled back into what his life was like pre-Joy and Holly. He worked on his secret project—that didn't really need to be a secret anymore, because he always finished what he started. He called his mother to check in because he should— but when she asked about Joy and Holly, he evaded, not wanting to talk about them any more than he wanted to think about them.

He tried to put the two females out of his mind, but how could he when he sensed Joy in every damn corner of his house?

In Kaye's suite, Joy's scent still lingered in the air. But the rooms were empty now. No toys, no stuffed dog. Joy's silky red robe wasn't hanging on the back of the door, and that pitiful excuse for a Christmas tree was gone as if it had never been there at all.

Every night, he sat in the great room in front of the fire and looked at the tree in the window. That it was there amazed him. Thinking about the night he and Joy and Holly had decorated it depressed him. For so many years, he'd avoided all mention of Christmas because he hadn't wanted to remember.

Now, though, he *did* want to. He relived every moment of the time Joy and Holly had been a part of his life. But mostly, he recalled the afternoon they had *left* him. He remembered Holly waving goodbye out the rear window of her mother's car. He remembered the look in Joy's eyes when she kissed him and told him that he was making a mistake by letting her go. And he particularly remembered Joy's laugh, her smile, the taste of her mouth and the feel of her arms around him when he was inside her.

Her image remained uppermost in his mind as if she'd been carved there. He couldn't shake it and didn't really want to. Remembering was all he had. The house was too damn quiet. Hell, he spent every day and most of the night out in the workshop just to avoid the suffocating silence. But it was no better out there because a part of him kept waiting for Holly to rush in, do one of her amazing monologues and climb up on the stool beside him.

When he was working, he found himself looking at the house, half expecting to see Joy in one of the windows, smiling at him. And every time he didn't, another piece of him died. He'd thought that he could go back to his old life once they were gone. Slide back into the shadows, become again the man fate had made him. But that hadn't happened and now, he realized, it never could.

He wasn't the same man because of Joy. Because she had brought him back to life. Awakened him after too many years spent in a self-made prison.

"So what the hell are you going to do about it?" he muttered, hating the way his voice echoed in the vast room. He picked up his beer, took a long drink and glared at the glittering Christmas tree. The night they'd decorated it flooded his mind.

Holly laughing, a fresh row of stitches on her forehead to remind him just how fear for her had brought him to his knees. Joy standing back and telling him where lights were missing. The three of them eating more candy canes than they hung and finally, Holly falling asleep, not knowing that he was going to screw everything up.

He pushed up out of the chair, walked to the tree and looked beyond it, to the lights in the fairy houses outside. There were pieces of both of them all over this place, he thought. There was no escaping the memories this time, even if he wanted to.

Turning, he looked around the room and felt the solitude press in on him. The immense room felt claustrophobic. Joy should be here with him, drinking wine and eating "winter" cookies. Holly should be calling for a drink of water and trying to stay up a little later.

"Instead," he muttered, like the hermit he was, "you're alone with your memories."

Joy was right, he told himself. Fate had cheated him once, stealing away those he loved best. But he'd done it to himself this time. He'd taken his second chance and thrown it away because he was too afraid to grab on and never let go. He thought about all he'd lost—all he was about to lose—and had to ask himself if pain was really all he had. Was that what he'd become? A man devoted to keeping his misery alive and well no matter the cost?

He put his beer down, stalked out of the room and headed for the workshop. "Damned if it is."

Christmas morning dawned with a soft snow falling, turning the world outside the tiny house in Franklin into a postcard.

The small, bent-over tree stood on a table in the living room, and even the multiple strings of lights it boasted couldn't make it a quarter as majestic as the tree they'd left behind in Sam's great room. But this one, Joy assured herself, was *theirs*. Hers and Holly's. And that made it perfect. They didn't need the big tree. Or the lovely house. Or Sam. They had each other and that was enough.

It just didn't *feel* like enough anymore. Giving herself a mental kick for even thinking those words, Joy pushed thoughts of Sam out of her mind. No small task since the last four or five days had been a study in loneliness. Holly was sad, Joy was miserable, and even the approach of Christmas hadn't been enough to lift the pall that hung over them both.

Deb had tried to cheer her, telling her that everything happened for a reason, but really? When the reason was a stubborn, foolish man too blind to see what he was giving up, what comfort was there?

Ignoring the cold hard stone settled around her heart, Joy forced a smile and asked, "Do you want to go outside, sweetie? Try out your new sled?"

Holly sat amid a sea of torn wrapping paper, its festive colors and bold ribbons making it look as though the presents had exploded rather than been opened. Her blond hair was loose, and her pink princess nightgown was tucked up around her knees as she sat cross-legged in the middle of the rubble.

She turned big blue eyes on Joy and said, "No, Mommy, I don't want to right now."

"Really?" Joy was trying to make Christmas good for her daughter, but the little girl missed Sam as much as Joy did, so it was an uphill battle. But they had to get used to being without him, didn't they? He'd made his choice. He'd let them go, and she hadn't heard a word from him since.

Apparently Sam Henry had found a way to go on, and so would she and Holly. "Well, how about we watch your favorite princess movie and drink some hot chocolate?"

"Okay..." The lack of enthusiasm in that word told Joy that Holly was only agreeing to please her mother.

God, she was a terrible person. *She's* the one who had allowed Holly to get too close to Sam in the hopes of reaching him. She had seen her daughter falling in love and hadn't done enough to stop it. She'd been too caught up in the sweetness of Holly choosing her own father to prepare either of them for the time when it all came crashing down on them.

Still, she had to try to reach her baby girl. Ease the pain, help her to enjoy Christmas morning.

"Are you upset because Santa couldn't bring you the puppy you wanted? Santa left you the note," Joy said, mentally thanking Sam for at least coming up with that brilliant idea. "He'll bring you a puppy as soon as he's old enough."

"It's okay. I can play with Lizzie's puppy." Holly got up, walked to her mother and crawled into her lap. Leaning her head against Joy's chest, she sighed heavily. "I want to go see Sam."

Joy's heart gave one hard lurch as everything in her yearned for the same thing. "Oh, honey, I don't think that's a good idea."

"Sure it is." Holly turned in her lap, looked up into her eyes and said softly, "He misses me, Mommy. It's Christmas and he's all by himself and lonely and probably crabby some more cuz we're not there to make him smile and help him with the fairy houses. He *needs* us. And we belong with Sam. It's Christmas and we should be there."

Her baby girl looked so calm, so serious, so *sure* of everything. The last few days hadn't been easy. They'd slipped back into their old life, but it wasn't the same. Nothing was the same anymore. They were a family as they'd always been, but now it felt as if someone was missing.

She'd left Sam to protect Holly. But keeping her away from the man she considered her father wasn't helping her either. It was a fine line to walk, Joy knew. She smoothed Holly's hair back from her face and realized her baby girl was right.

Sam had let them leave, but it was Joy who had packed up and walked out. Neither of them had fought for what they wanted, so maybe it was time to make a stand. Time to let him know that he could try to toss them aside all he wanted—but they weren't going to go.

"You're right, baby, he *does* need us. And we need him." Giving Holly a quick, hard kiss, she grinned and said, "Let's get dressed."

* * *

Sam heard the car pull into the drive, looked out the window and felt his heart jump to life. How was *that* for timing? He'd just been getting into his coat to drive into Franklin and bring his girls home. He felt like Ebenezer Scrooge when he woke up on Christmas morning and realized he hadn't missed it. Hadn't lost his last chance at happiness.

He hit the front door at a dead run and made it to the car before Joy had turned off the engine. Snow was falling, he was freezing, but he didn't give a good damn. Suddenly everything in his world had righted itself. And this time, he was going to grab hold of what was most important and never let it go again.

"Sam! Sam! Hi, Sam!" Holly's voice, hitting that high note, sounded like the sweetest song to him.

"Hi, Holly!" he called back, and while the little girl got herself out of her seat belt, he threw open the driver's door and pulled Joy out. "Hi," he said, letting his gaze sweep over her features before focusing back on the eyes that had haunted him from the first moment they met.

"Hi, Sam. Merry Christmas." She cupped his cheek in her palm, and her touch melted away the last of the ice encasing his heart.

"I missed you, damn it," he muttered and bent to kiss her. That first taste of her settled everything inside him, brought the world back into focus and let him know that he was alive. And grateful.

"We're back!" Holly raced around the car, threw herself at Sam's legs and held on.

Breaking the kiss, he grinned down at the little girl and then reached down to pick her up. Holding her tight, he looked into bright eyes and then spun her in circles until she squealed in delight. "You're back. Merry Christmas, Holly."

She hugged his neck tightly and kissed his cheek with all the ferocity of a five-year-old's love. "Merry Christmas!"

"Come on, you two. It's cold out here." He carried Holly and followed behind Joy as she walked into the house and then turned for the great room. "I've got a couple surprises for you two."

"For Christmas?" Holly gave him a squeeze, then as she saw what was waiting for her, breathed, "Oh my goodness!" That quick gasp was followed by another squeal, this one higher than the one before. She squirmed to get out of Sam's arms, then raced across the room to the oversize fairy castle dollhouse sitting in front of the tree.

Beside him, Sam heard Joy give a soft sigh. When he looked at her, there were tears in her eyes and a beautiful smile on her amazing mouth. His heart gave another hard lurch, and he welcomed it. For the last few days, he'd felt dead inside. Coming back to life was much better.

"You made that for her."

He looked to where the girl he already considered his daughter was exploring the castle he'd built for her. It was red, with turrets and towers, tiny flags flying from the points of those towers. Glass windows opened and closed, and wide double doors swung open. The back of the castle was open for small fingers to explore and redecorate and dream.

"Yeah," he said. "Holly needed a fairy house she could actually play with. I'm thinking this summer we might need to build a tree house, too."

"This summer?" Joy's words were soft, the question hanging in the air between them.

"I've got plans," he said. "And so much to tell you. Ask you."

Her eyes went soft and dreamy and as he watched, they filled with a sheen of tears he really hoped she wouldn't let fall.

"I can't believe you made that for Holly," Joy said, smiling at her daughter's excitement. "She loves it."

"I can't believe you're here," Sam confessed, turning her in his arms so he could hold her, touch her, look into her eyes. Sliding his hands up her arms, over her shoulders to her face, his palms cradled her as his thumbs stroked gently over her soft, smooth skin. "I was coming to you."

"You were?" Wonder, hope lit her eyes, and Sam knew he hadn't blown it entirely. He hadn't let this last best chance at love slip past him.

"You arrived just as I was headed to the garage. I was going to bring you back here to give you your presents. Here. In our home."

Her breath caught and she lifted one hand to her mouth. "*Our* home?"

"If you'll stay," he said. "Stay with me. Love me. Marry me."

"Oh, Sam…"

"Don't answer yet," he said, grinning now as he took her hand and pulled her over to the brightly lit Christmas tree. "Just wait. There's more." Then to the little girl, he said, "There's another present for you, Holly. I think Santa stopped off here last night."

"He *did*?" Holly's eyes went wide as saucers as her smile danced in her eyes. "What did he bring?"

"Open it and find out," he said and pointed to a big white box with a red ribbon.

"How come it has holes in the top?" Holly asked.

"You'll see."

Joy already guessed it. She squeezed Sam's hand as they watched Holly carefully lift off the lid of the box and peer inside. "Oh my goodness!"

The little girl looked up at Sam. "He's for me?"

"She is. It's a girl."

Holly laughed in delight then reached into the box and lifted out a golden retriever puppy. Its fur was white and soft, and Holly buried her face against that softness, whispering and laughing as the puppy eagerly licked her face. "Elsa. I'm gonna name her Elsa," Holly proclaimed and laid out on the floor so her new best friend could jump all over her in wild abandon.

"I can't believe you did that," Joy said, shaking her head and smiling through her tears. "Where did you find a white puppy? I looked everywhere."

Sam shrugged and gave her a half smile. "My sister knew a breeder and, well… I chartered a jet and flew out to Boston to pick her up two days ago."

"Boston." Joy blinked at him. "You flew to Boston to pick up a Christmas puppy so my little girl wouldn't be disappointed."

"*Our* little girl," he corrected. "I love her, Joy. Like she's my own. And if you'll let me, I'll adopt her."

"Oh my God…" Joy bit down hard on her bottom lip and gave up the battle to stem her tears. They coursed down her cheeks in silvery rivers that only made her smile shine more brightly.

"Is that a yes?"

"Yes, of course it's a yes," Joy managed to say when

she threw her arms around him and held on. "She already considers you her father. So do I."

Sam held Joy tight, buried his face in the curve of her neck and said, "I love you. Both of you. So much. I won't ever let you go, Joy. I want you to marry me. Give me Holly. And give us both more children. Help me make a family so strong nothing can ever tear it down."

"You filled my heart, Sam." She pulled back, looked up at him and said, "All of this. What you've done. It's the most amazing moment of my life. My personal crabby hermit has become my hero."

His mouth quirked at the corner. "Still not done," he said and drew her to the other side of the tree.

"You've already given me everything, Sam. What's left?" She was laughing and crying and the combined sounds were like music to him.

The big house felt full of love and promise, and Sam knew that it would never be empty again. There would be so much light and love in the house, shadows would be banished. He had his memories of lost love, and those would never fade, but he wouldn't be ruled by them anymore, either.

When Kaye finally came home from her annual vacation, she was going to find a changed man and a household that was filled with the kind of happiness Sam had thought he'd never find again.

"What is it, Sam?" Joy asked when he pulled her to a stop in front of a draped easel.

"A promise," he said and pulled the sheet from the painting he'd only just finished the night before, to show her what he dreamed. What he wanted. For both of them.

"Oh, Sam." Her heart was in her voice. He heard it and smiled.

* * *

Joy stared at the painting, unable to tear her eyes from it. He'd painted this room, with the giant, lit-up tree, with stacks of presents at its feet, and the hint of fairy lights from the tiny houses in the woods shining through the glass behind it.

On the floor, he'd painted Holly, the puppy climbing all over her as the little girl laughed. He'd painted him and Joy, arms around each other, watching the magic unfold together. And he'd painted Joy pregnant.

There was love and celebration in every stroke of paint. The light was warm and soft and seemed to make the painting glow with everything she was feeling. She took it all in and felt the wonder of it all settle in the center of her heart. He'd painted her a promise.

"I did it all yesterday," he said, snaking both arms around her middle as they stared at his creation. "I've never had a painting come so quickly. And I know it's because this is what's meant to be. You, me, Holly."

"I love it," Joy said softly, turning her face up just enough to meet his kiss. "But we don't know if I'm pregnant."

"If you're not now," he promised, both eyebrows lifting into high arches, "you will be soon. I want lots of kids with you, Joy. I want to live again—risks and all—and I can only do that if you love me."

She turned around in his arms, glanced at her daughter, still giggling with puppy delight, then smiled up at Sam. "I love you so much, Sam. I always will. I want to make that family with you. Have lots of kids. Watch Holly and the others we'll make together grow up with a father who loves them."

"We can do that. Hell," he said, "we can do anything together."

She took a long, deep breath and grinned up at him. "And if you ask me to marry you right this minute, this will be the best Christmas ever."

He dipped into his pocket, pulled out a sapphire and diamond ring and slid it onto her finger while she watched, stunned. Though she'd been hoping for a real proposal, she hadn't expected a ring. Especially one this beautiful.

"It wasn't just a puppy I got in Boston," he said. "Though I will admit my sister helped me pick out this ring."

"Your family knows?"

"Absolutely," he said, bending to kiss her, then kiss the ring on her finger as if sealing it onto her hand. "My mother's thrilled to have a granddaughter and can't wait to meet you both in person. And be prepared, they'll all be descending after the holidays to do just that."

"It'll be fun," she said. "Oh, Sam, I love *you*."

"That's the only present I'm ever going to need," Sam said and kissed her hard and long and deep.

She'd come here this morning believing she would have to fight with Sam to make him admit how much he loved her. The fact that he had been on his way to get her and Holly filled her heart. He wanted her. He loved them both. And he was willing to finally leave the past behind and build a future with her. It really was the best Christmas she'd ever known.

"Hey!" Holly tugged at both of them as the puppy jumped at her feet. "You're kissing! Like mommies and daddies do!"

Joy looked at her little girl as Sam lifted her up to

eye level. "Would you like that, baby girl? Would you like Sam to be your daddy and for all of us to live here forever?"

"For really?"

"For really," Sam said. "I'd like to be your daddy, Holly. And this summer, you and I are going to build you a fairy tree house. How does that sound?"

She gave him a wide, happy grin. "You'll be good at it, Sam. I can tell and I love you lots."

"I love you back, Holly. Always will." He kissed her forehead.

"Can I call you Daddy now?"

"I'd really like that," he said and Joy saw the raw emotion glittering in his eyes.

Their little girl clapped and grinned hugely before throwing her arms around both their necks. "This is the bestest Christmas ever. I got just what I wanted. A puppy. A fairy house. And my own daddy."

Sam looked into Joy's eyes and she felt his love, his pleasure in the moment, and she knew that none of them would ever be lonely again.

"Merry Christmas, Sam."

"Merry Christmas, Joy."

And in the lights of the tree, he sealed their new life with a kiss that had Holly applauding and sent the new puppy barking.

Everything, Joy thought, was *perfect*.

* * * * *

Pick up these other sexy, emotional reads
about wealthy alpha heroes finding family from
USA TODAY *bestselling author Maureen Child!*

THE BABY INHERITANCE
TRIPLE THE FUN
DOUBLE THE TROUBLE
THE COWBOY'S PRIDE AND JOY
HAVE BABY, NEED BILLIONAIRE

Available now from Mills & Boon Desire!

***

MILLS & BOON®

Desire™

PASSIONATE AND DRAMATIC LOVE STORIES

A sneak peek at next month's titles...

In stores from 15th December 2016:

- **One Baby, Two Secrets** – Barbara Dunlop *and*
  The Rancher's Nanny Bargain – Sara Orwig

- **The Tycoon's Secret Child** – Maureen Child *and*
  Single Mum, Billionaire Boss – Sheri WhiteFeather

- **An Heir for the Texan** – Kristi Gold *and*
  The Best Man's Baby – Karen Booth

Just can't wait?
Buy our books online a month before they hit the shops!
www.millsandboon.co.uk

Also available as eBooks.

MILLS & BOON®

EXCLUSIVE EXTRACT

Saoirse Murphy's proposal of a 'convenient' arrangement with paramedic Santiago Valentino soon ignites a very inconvenient passion…

Read on for a sneak preview of
SANTIAGO'S CONVENIENT FIANCÉE
by Annie O'Neil

Saoirse went up on tiptoe and kissed him.

From the moment her lips touched Santiago's she didn't have a single lucid thought. Her brain all but exploded in a vain attempt to unravel the quick-fire sensations. Heat, passion, need, longing, sweet and tangy all jumbled together in one beautiful confirmation that his lips were every bit as kissable as she'd thought they might be.

Snippets of what was actually happening were hitting her in blips of delayed replay.

Her fingers tangled in his silky, soft hair. Santi's wide hands tugged her in tight, right at the small of her back. There was no doubting his body's response to her now. The heated pleasure she felt when one of his hands slipped under her T-shirt elicited an undiluted moan of pleasure. He matched her move for move as if they had been made for one another. Her body's reaction to his felt akin to hitting all hundred watts her body was capable of for the very first time.

She wanted more.

No.

'Oh, I doubt it,' Noah interrupted, but he still didn't sound entirely happy about the idea, which surprised her. Perhaps she'd misread his flirting earlier. Maybe he really was like that with everyone and, now the reality of having to spend time with her had set in, he was less keen on the idea. 'Melissa has quite the packed schedule for the wedding party, you know. She's right—you're going to have to find someone to take over most of your job here.'

Eloise sighed. She *did* know. She'd helped Laurel plan it, after all.

And, now she thought about it, every last bit of the schedule involved the maid of honour and the best man being together.

Noah smiled, a hint of the charm he'd exhibited earlier showing through despite the frown, and Eloise's heart beat twice in one moment as she accepted the inevitable.

She was doomed.

She had the most ridiculous crush on a man who clearly found her a minor inconvenience.

And—even worse—the whole world was going to be watching, laughing at her pretending that she could live in this world of celebrities, mocking her for thinking she could ever be pretty enough, funny enough…just *enough* for Noah Cross.

Don't miss
SLOW DANCE WITH THE BEST MAN
by Sophie Pembroke

Available January 2017
www.millsandboon.co.uk

Copyright © 2016 by Sophie Pembroke

Give a 12 month subscription to a friend today!

Call Customer Services
0844 844 1358[*]

or visit
millsandboon.co.uk/subscriptions

* This call will cost you 7 pence per minute plus your phone company's price per minute access charge.

MILLS & BOON®

Why shop at millsandboon.co.uk?

Each year, thousands of romance readers find their perfect read at millsandboon.co.uk. That's because we're passionate about bringing you the very best romantic fiction. Here are some of the advantages of shopping at www.millsandboon.co.uk:

* **Get new books first**—you'll be able to buy your favourite books one month before they hit the shops

* **Get exclusive discounts**—you'll also be able to buy our specially created monthly collections, with up to 50% off the RRP

* **Find your favourite authors**—latest news, interviews and new releases for all your favourite authors and series on our website, plus ideas for what to try next

* **Join in**—once you've bought your favourite books, don't forget to register with us to rate, review and join in the discussions

Visit **www.millsandboon.co.uk**
for all this and more today!